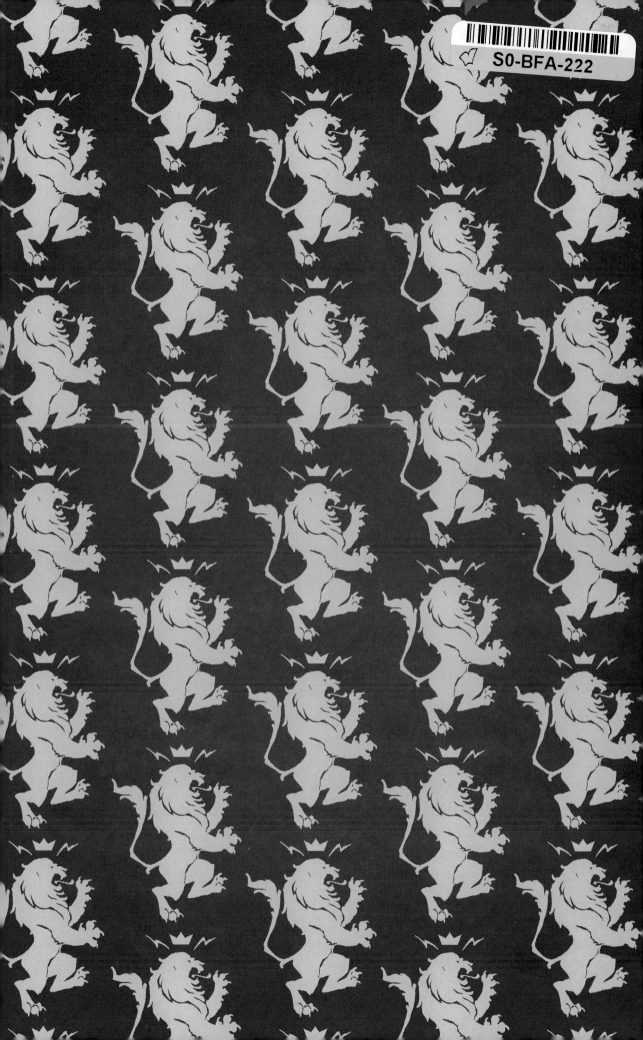

Princeless

Book 2:
GET OVER YOURSELF

DELUXE EDITION

Bryan Seaton: CEO/Publisher
Dave Dwonch: President/Creative Director
Shawn Gabborin: Editor In Chief
Jamal Igle: Director of Marketing
Jim Dietz: Social Media Director
Kevin Freeman: Senior Editor
Jason Martin: Editor
Nicole DAndria: Script Editor
Chad Cicconi: The Patriarchy
Colleen Boyd: Submissions Editor

♔

This book is dedicated to Jeremy Dale
who treated me like I was his brother, talked
about me like I was a genius, and taught me what
kind of comics professional I wanted to be.

-Jeremy Whitley

♔

For the students, friends and family
of Megamoth Studio

-Emily Martin

Princeless Book 2 Issues 1-4
Written by Jeremy Whitley
Illustrated by Emily Martin
Colored by Kelly Lawrence and Brett Grunig
Lettered by Dave Dwonch

The Girl with the Giveaway Ears
Written by Jeremy Whitley
Illustrated by Tara Abbamondi

The Merry Adventures of Prince Ashe: Part 2 – The Girl
Written by Jeremy Whitley
Illustrated by Jessi Sheron

Kira's First Hunt
Written by Jeremy Whitley
Illustrated by Angi Shearstone

Waiting
Written by Jeremy Whitley
Illustrated by Jen Vaughn

The Princess' New Clothes
Written by Jeremy Whitley
Illustrated by Adriana Blake
Colors by Ricardo "DJGomita" Paredes

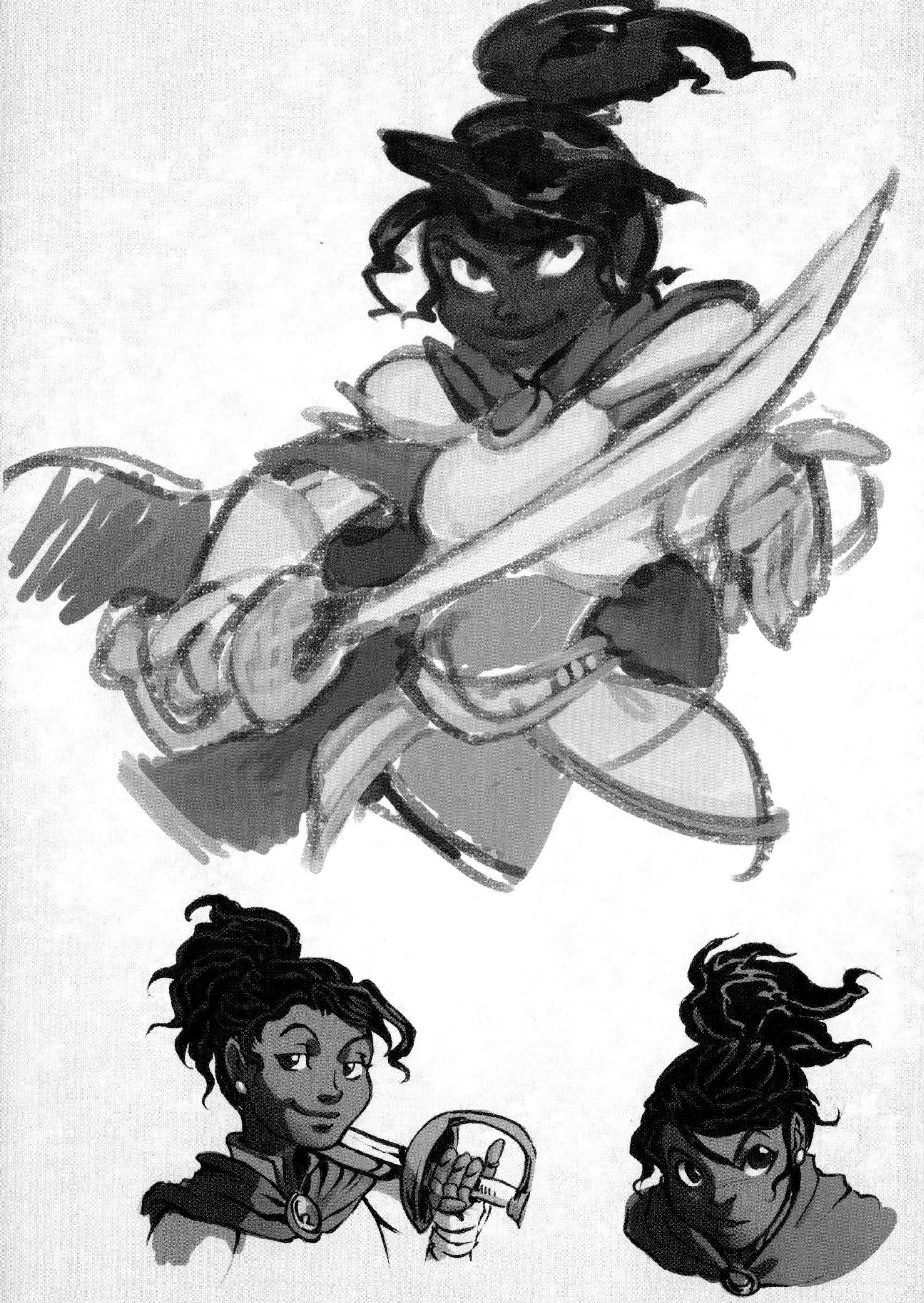

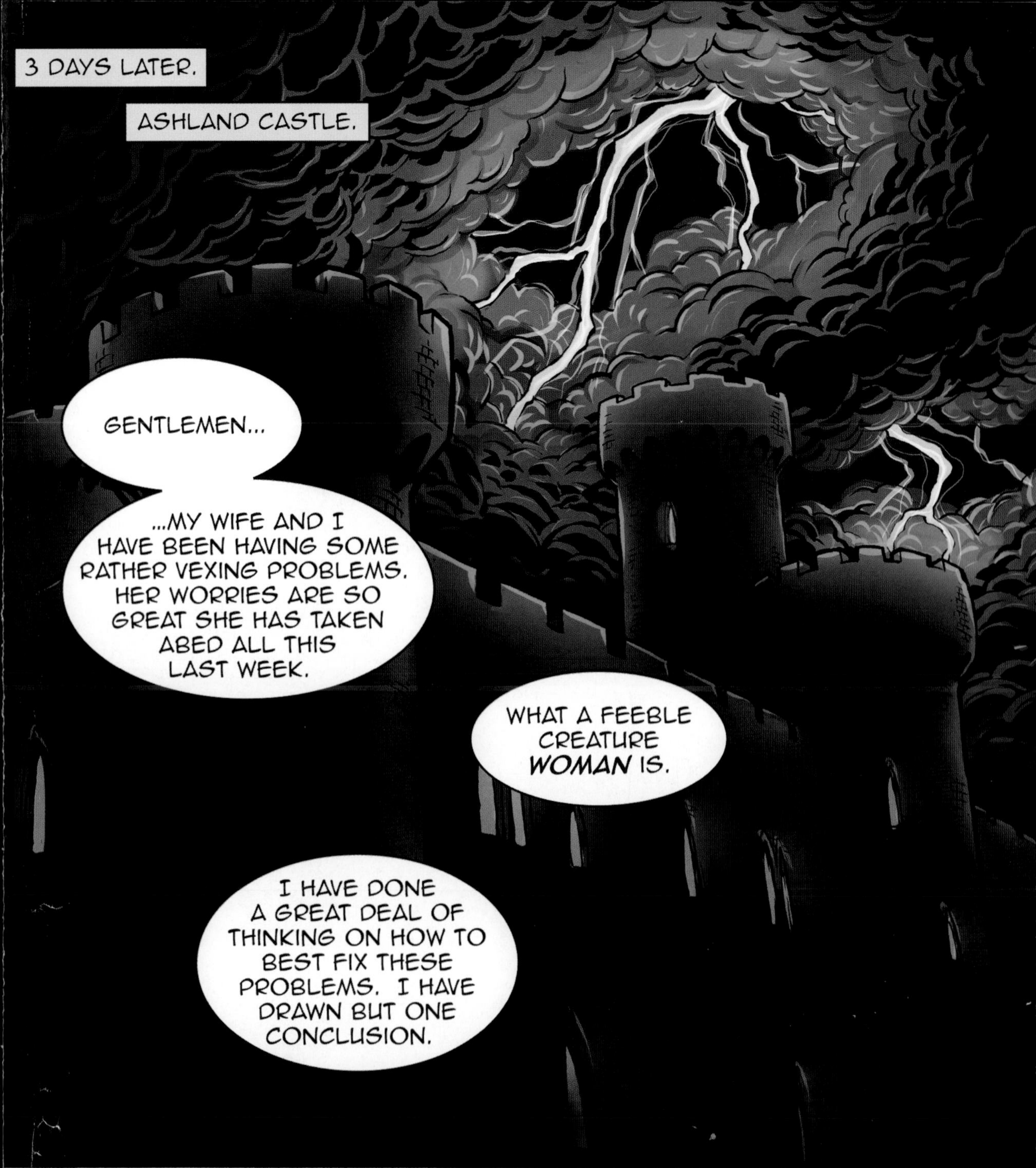
3 DAYS LATER.
ASHLAND CASTLE.
GENTLEMEN...
...MY WIFE AND I HAVE BEEN HAVING SOME RATHER VEXING PROBLEMS. HER WORRIES ARE SO GREAT SHE HAS TAKEN ABED ALL THIS LAST WEEK.
WHAT A FEEBLE CREATURE *WOMAN* IS.
I HAVE DONE A GREAT DEAL OF THINKING ON HOW TO BEST FIX THESE PROBLEMS. I HAVE DRAWN BUT ONE CONCLUSION.

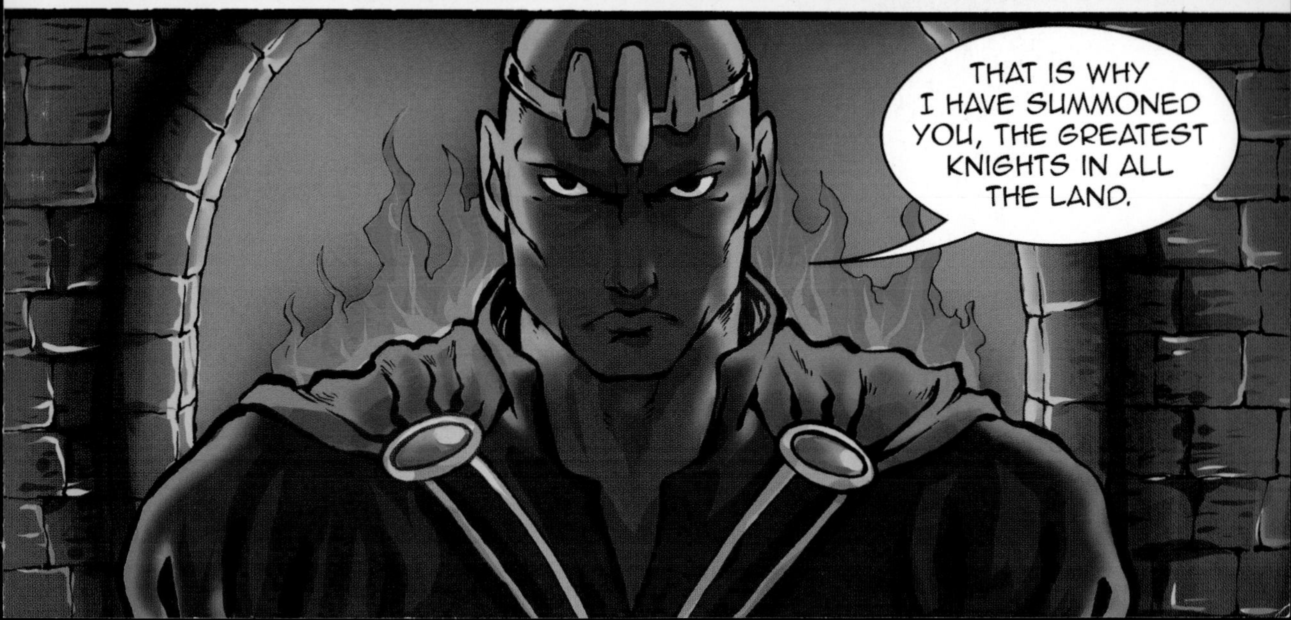
THAT IS WHY I HAVE SUMMONED YOU, THE GREATEST KNIGHTS IN ALL THE LAND.

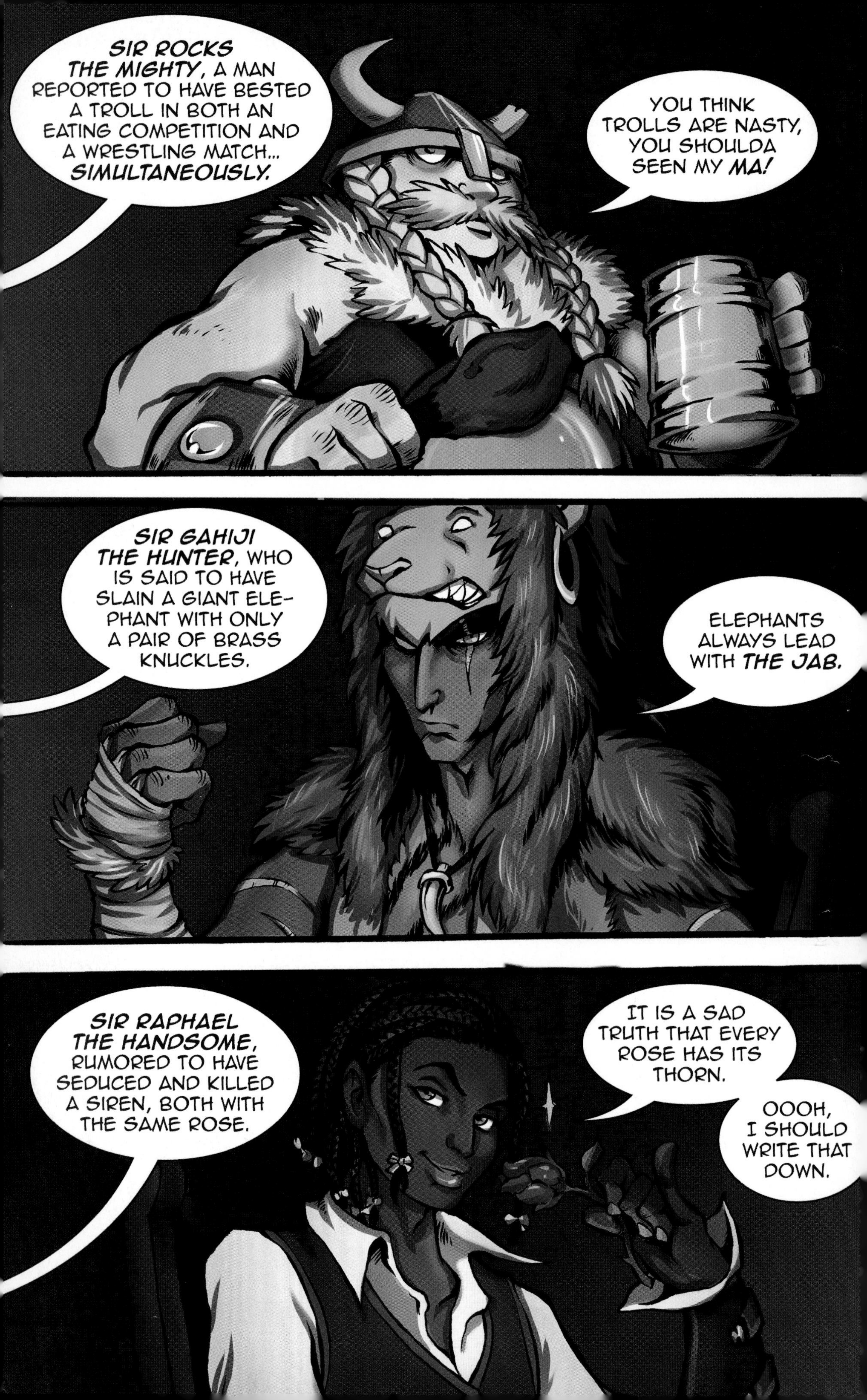
SIR ROCKS THE MIGHTY, A MAN REPORTED TO HAVE BESTED A TROLL IN BOTH AN EATING COMPETITION AND A WRESTLING MATCH... SIMULTANEOUSLY.
YOU THINK TROLLS ARE NASTY, YOU SHOULDA SEEN MY MA!
SIR GAHIJI THE HUNTER, WHO IS SAID TO HAVE SLAIN A GIANT ELE-PHANT WITH ONLY A PAIR OF BRASS KNUCKLES.
ELEPHANTS ALWAYS LEAD WITH THE JAB.
SIR RAPHAEL THE HANDSOME, RUMORED TO HAVE SEDUCED AND KILLED A SIREN, BOTH WITH THE SAME ROSE.
IT IS A SAD TRUTH THAT EVERY ROSE HAS ITS THORN.
OOOH, I SHOULD WRITE THAT DOWN.

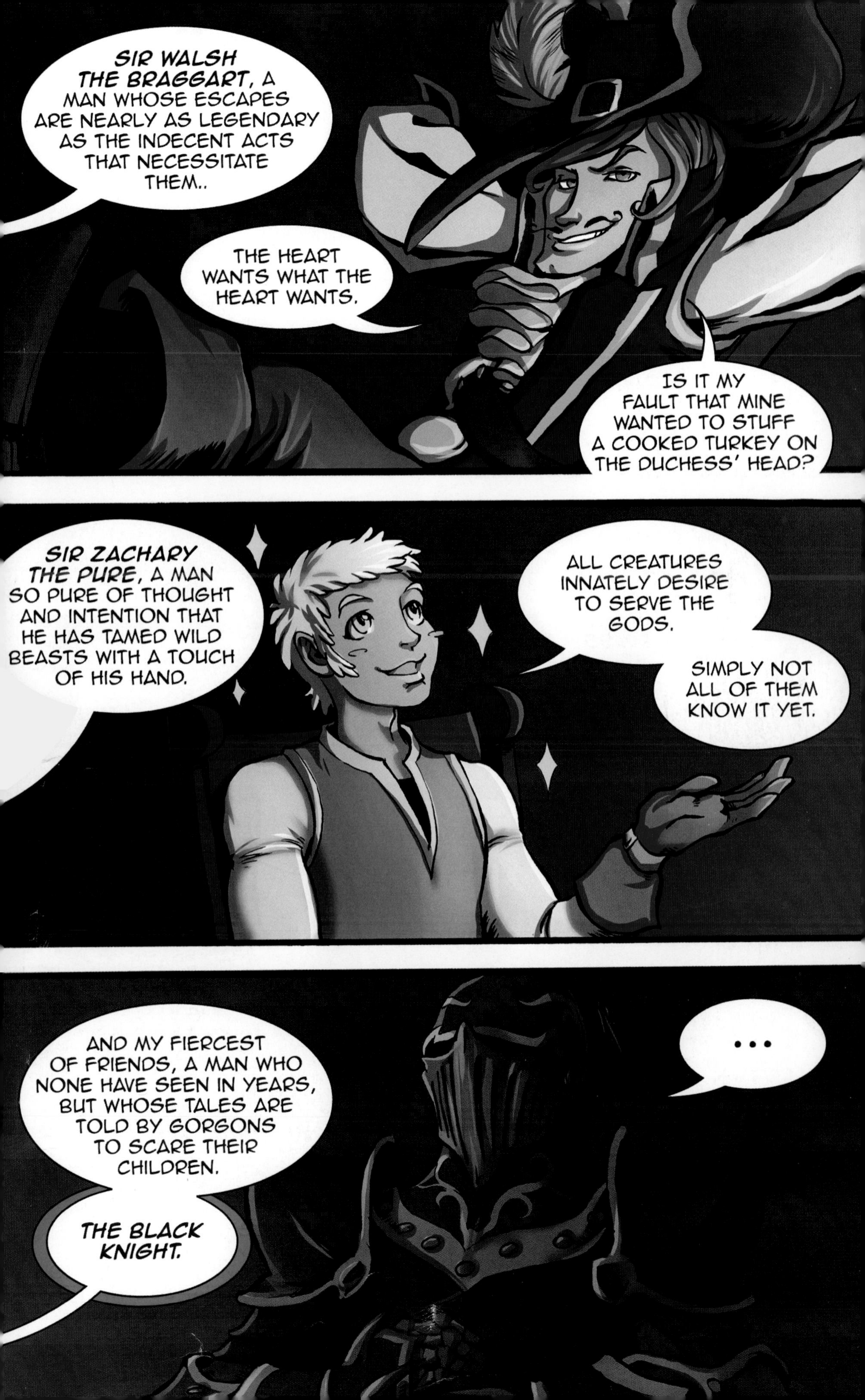
SIR WALSH THE BRAGGART, A MAN WHOSE ESCAPES ARE NEARLY AS LEGENDARY AS THE INDECENT ACTS THAT NECESSITATE THEM..
THE HEART WANTS WHAT THE HEART WANTS.
IS IT MY FAULT THAT MINE WANTED TO STUFF A COOKED TURKEY ON THE DUCHESS' HEAD?
SIR ZACHARY THE PURE, A MAN SO PURE OF THOUGHT AND INTENTION THAT HE HAS TAMED WILD BEASTS WITH A TOUCH OF HIS HAND.
ALL CREATURES INNATELY DESIRE TO SERVE THE GODS.
SIMPLY NOT ALL OF THEM KNOW IT YET.
AND MY FIERCEST OF FRIENDS, A MAN WHO NONE HAVE SEEN IN YEARS, BUT WHOSE TALES ARE TOLD BY GORGONS TO SCARE THEIR CHILDREN.
...
THE BLACK KNIGHT.

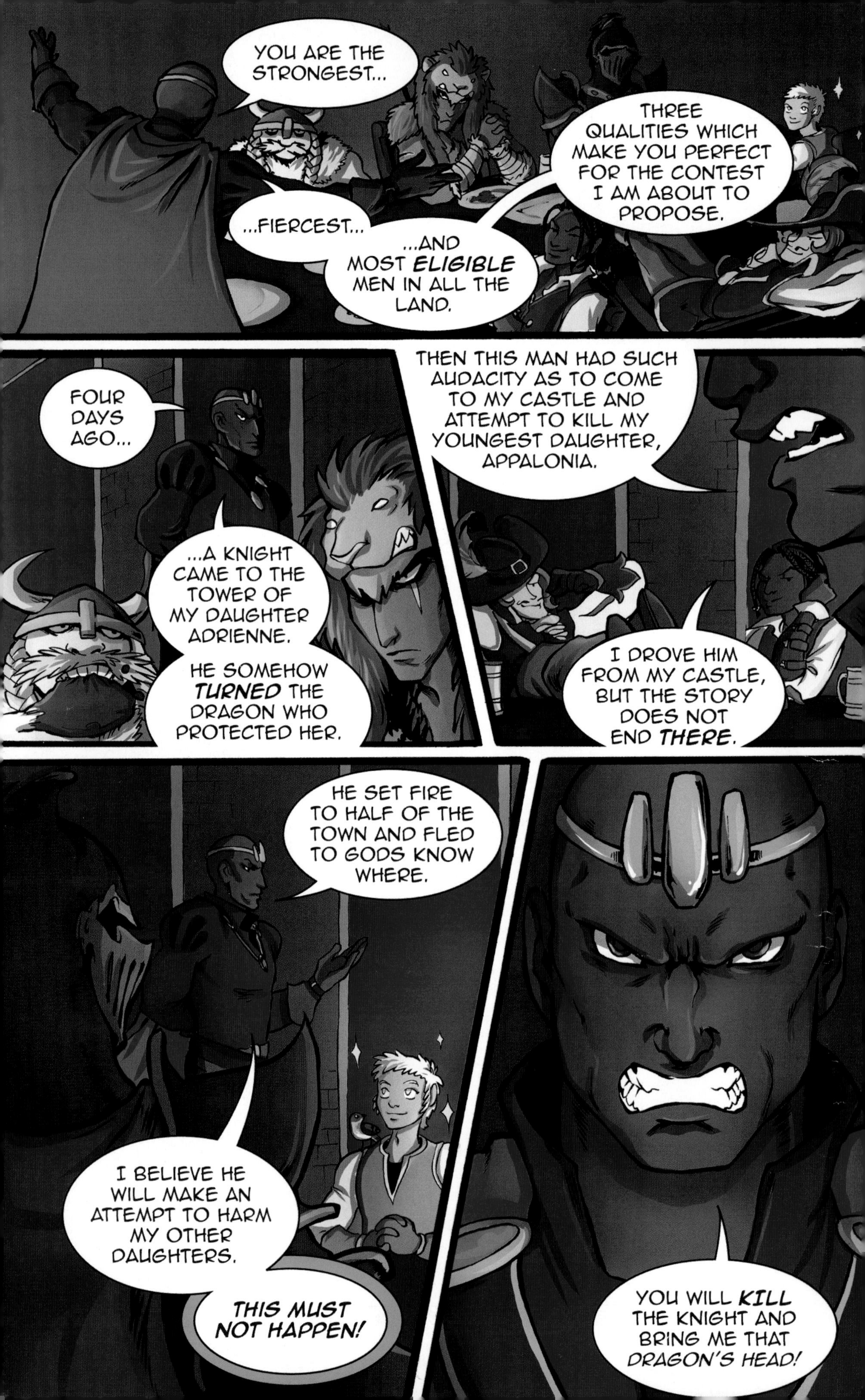
YOU ARE THE STRONGEST...
...FIERCEST...
...AND MOST ELIGIBLE MEN IN ALL THE LAND.
THREE QUALITIES WHICH MAKE YOU PERFECT FOR THE CONTEST I AM ABOUT TO PROPOSE.
FOUR DAYS AGO...
...A KNIGHT CAME TO THE TOWER OF MY DAUGHTER ADRIENNE.
HE SOMEHOW TURNED THE DRAGON WHO PROTECTED HER.
THEN THIS MAN HAD SUCH AUDACITY AS TO COME TO MY CASTLE AND ATTEMPT TO KILL MY YOUNGEST DAUGHTER, APPALONIA.
I DROVE HIM FROM MY CASTLE, BUT THE STORY DOES NOT END THERE.
HE SET FIRE TO HALF OF THE TOWN AND FLED TO GODS KNOW WHERE.
I BELIEVE HE WILL MAKE AN ATTEMPT TO HARM MY OTHER DAUGHTERS.
THIS MUST NOT HAPPEN!
YOU WILL KILL THE KNIGHT AND BRING ME THAT DRAGON'S HEAD!

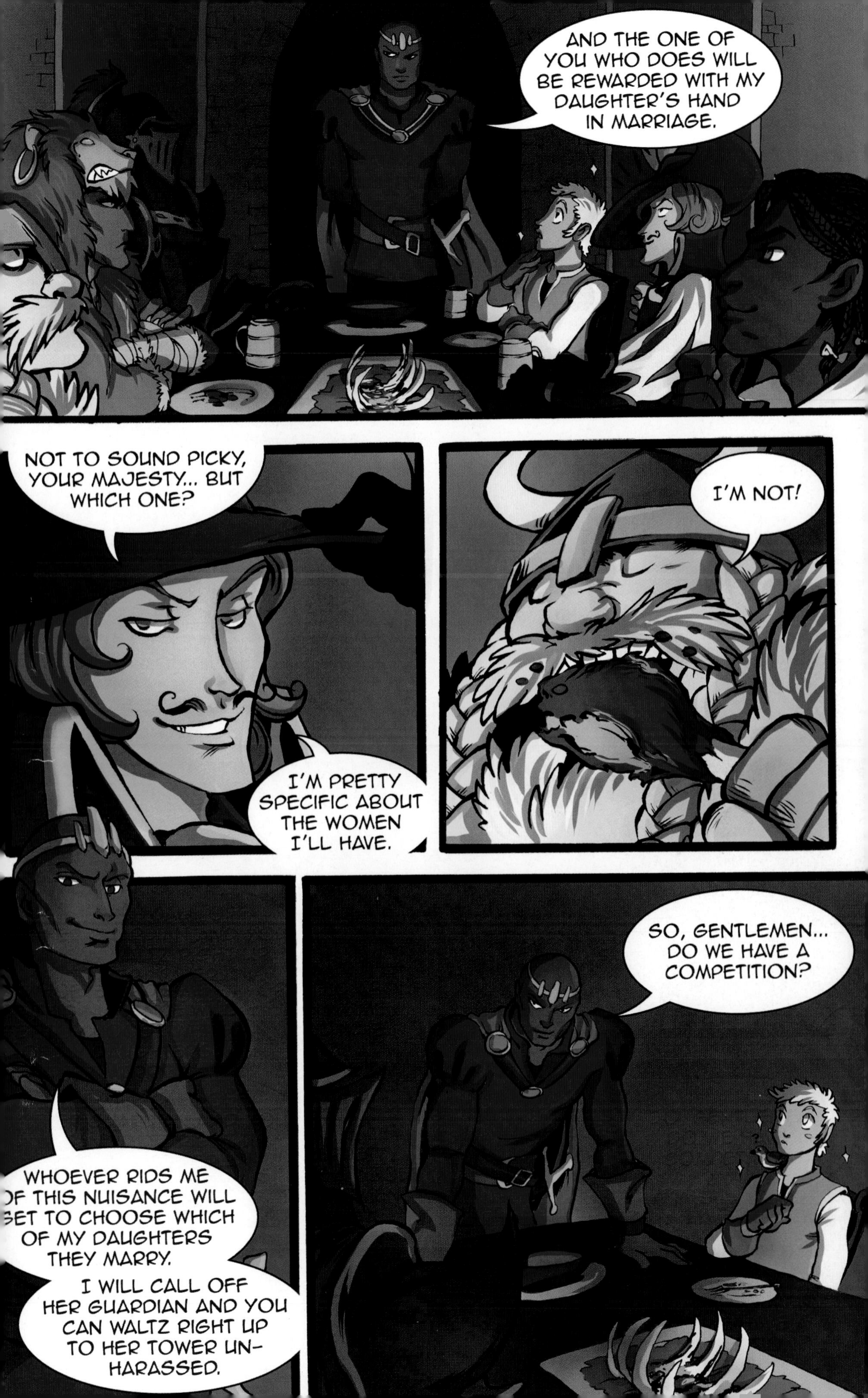
AND THE ONE OF YOU WHO DOES WILL BE REWARDED WITH MY DAUGHTER'S HAND IN MARRIAGE.
NOT TO SOUND PICKY, YOUR MAJESTY... BUT WHICH ONE?
I'M PRETTY SPECIFIC ABOUT THE WOMEN I'LL HAVE.
I'M NOT!
WHOEVER RIDS ME OF THIS NUISANCE WILL GET TO CHOOSE WHICH OF MY DAUGHTERS THEY MARRY.
I WILL CALL OFF HER GUARDIAN AND YOU CAN WALTZ RIGHT UP TO HER TOWER UN-HARASSED.
SO, GENTLEMEN... DO WE HAVE A COMPETITION?

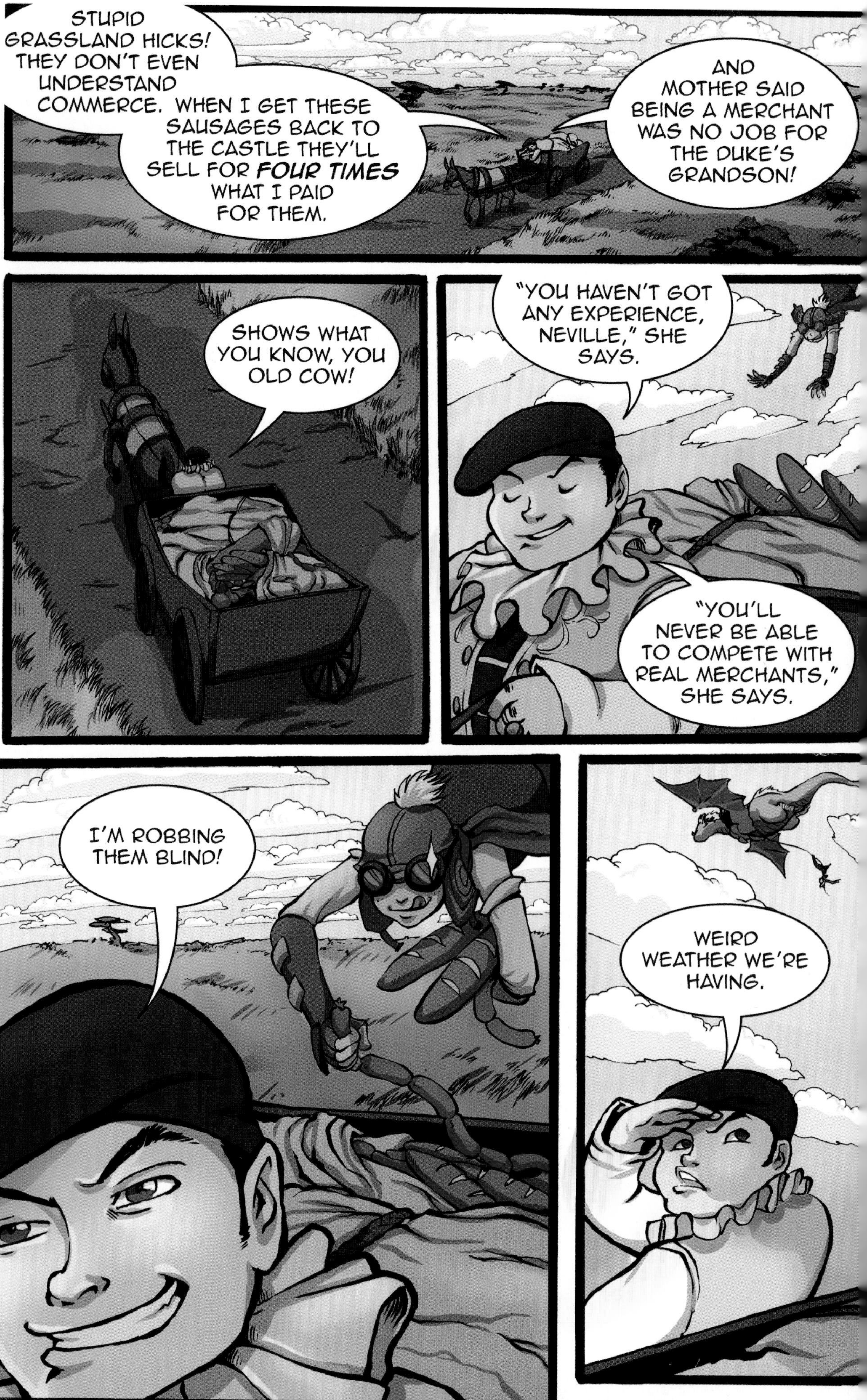
STUPID GRASSLAND HICKS! THEY DON'T EVEN UNDERSTAND COMMERCE. WHEN I GET THESE SAUSAGES BACK TO THE CASTLE THEY'LL SELL FOR *FOUR TIMES* WHAT I PAID FOR THEM.
AND MOTHER SAID BEING A MERCHANT WAS NO JOB FOR THE DUKE'S GRANDSON!
SHOWS WHAT YOU KNOW, YOU OLD COW!
"YOU HAVEN'T GOT ANY EXPERIENCE, NEVILLE," SHE SAYS.
"YOU'LL NEVER BE ABLE TO COMPETE WITH REAL MERCHANTS," SHE SAYS.
I'M ROBBING THEM BLIND!
WEIRD WEATHER WE'RE HAVING.

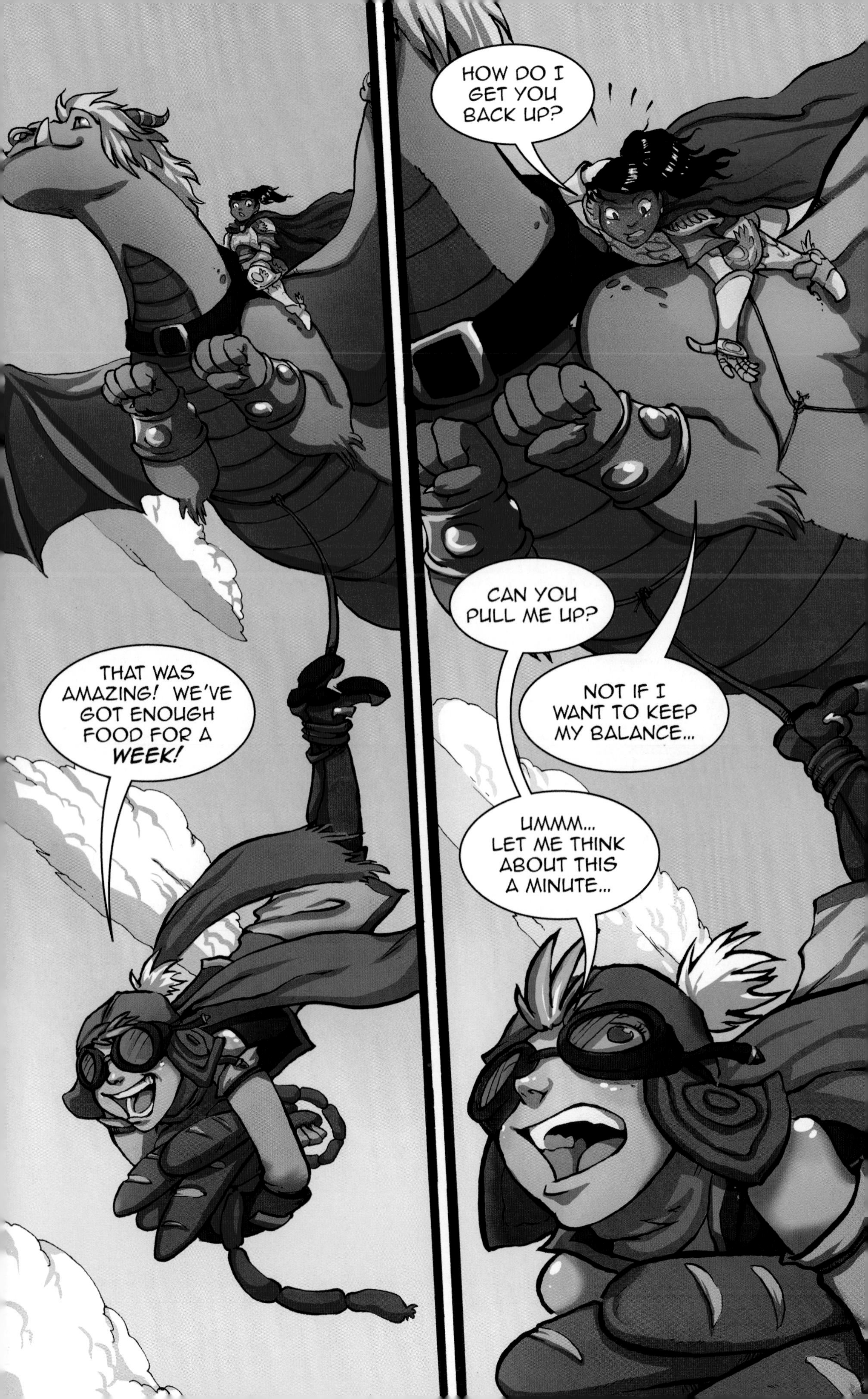
THAT WAS AMAZING! WE'VE GOT ENOUGH FOOD FOR A *WEEK!*
HOW DO I GET YOU BACK UP?
CAN YOU PULL ME UP?
NOT IF I WANT TO KEEP MY BALANCE...
UMMM... LET ME THINK ABOUT THIS A MINUTE...

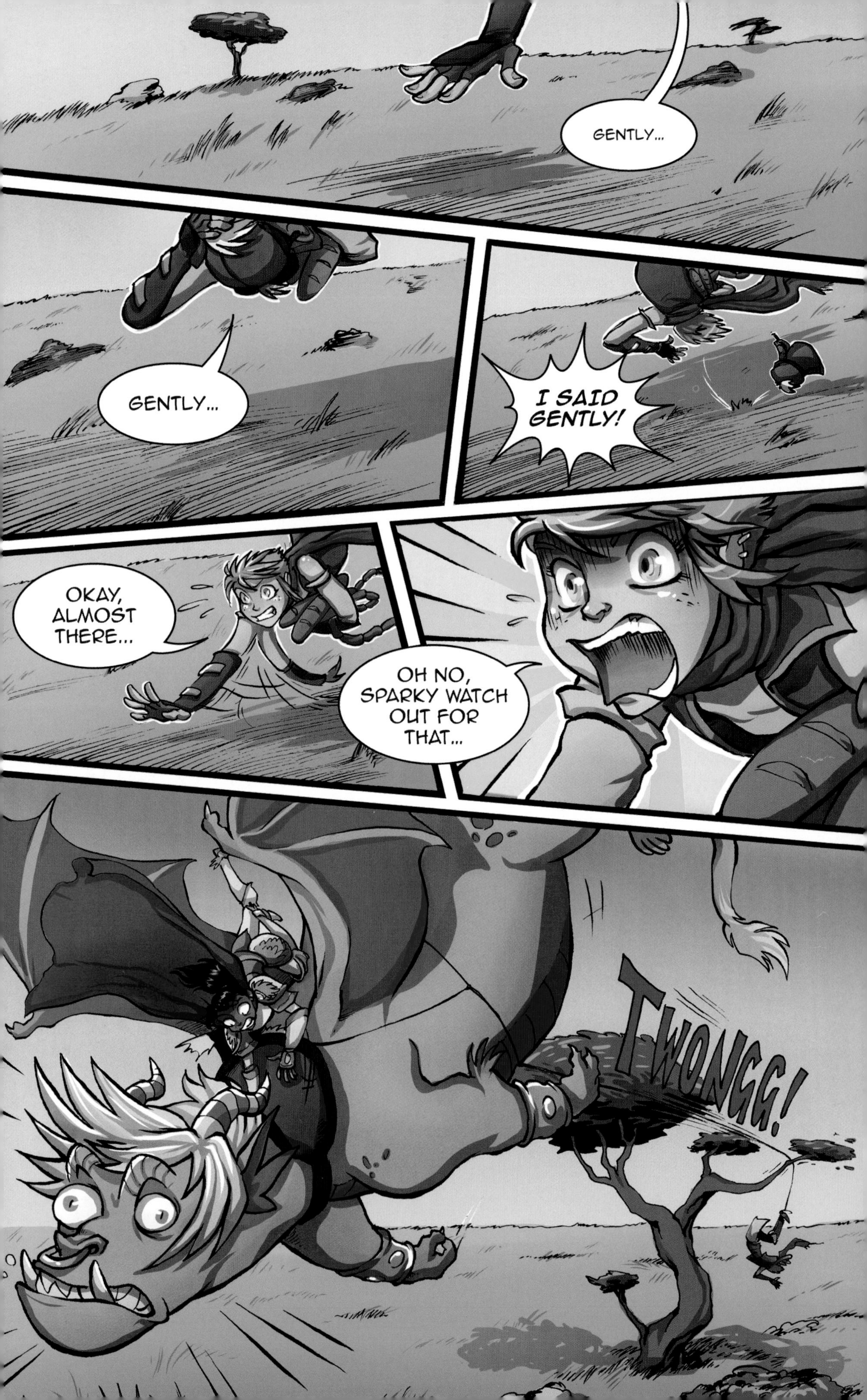
GENTLY...
GENTLY...
I SAID GENTLY!
OKAY, ALMOST THERE...
OH NO, SPARKY WATCH OUT FOR THAT...
TWONGG!

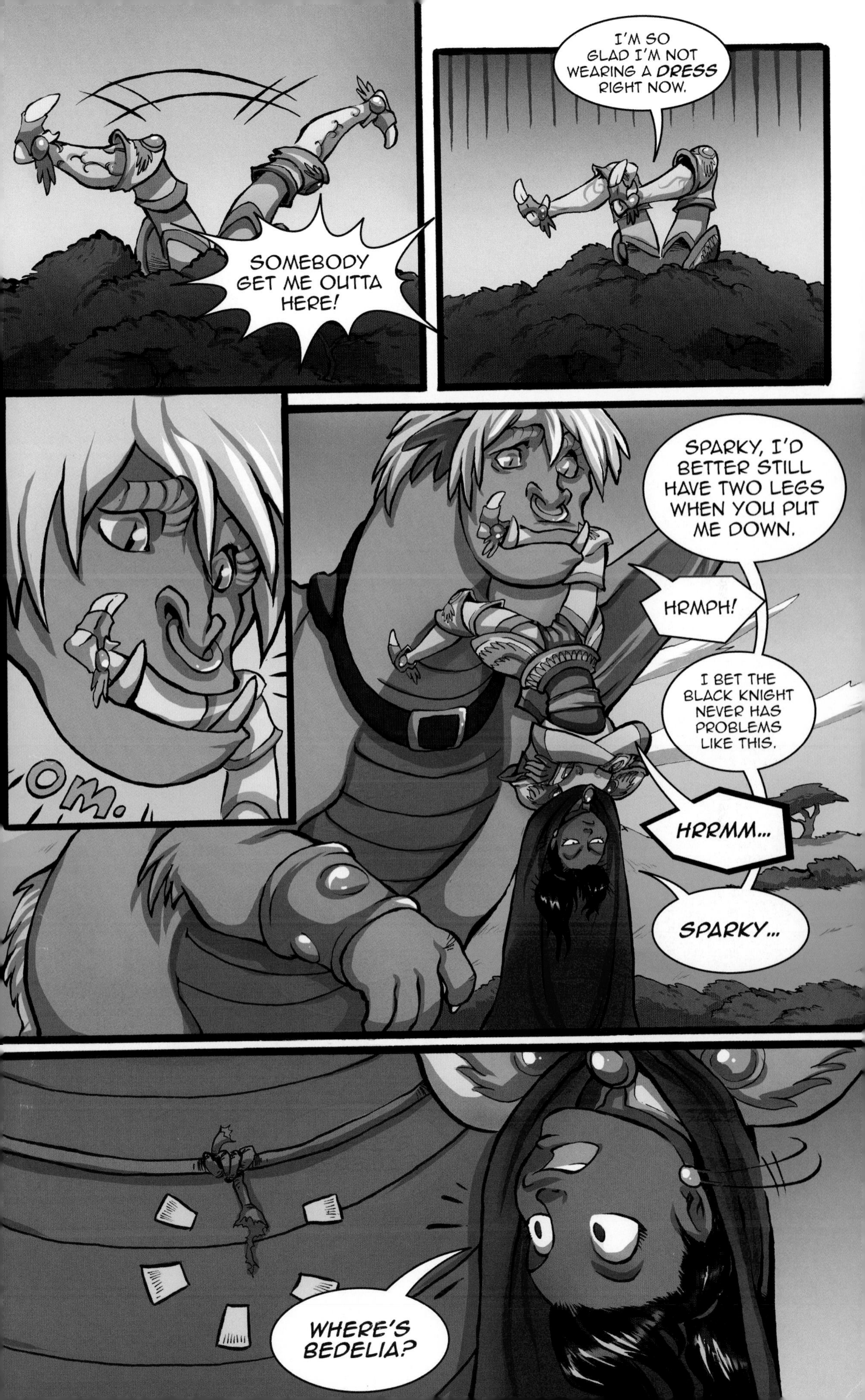

SOMEBODY GET ME OUTTA HERE!
I'M SO GLAD I'M NOT WEARING A *DRESS* RIGHT NOW.
...OM.
SPARKY, I'D BETTER STILL HAVE TWO LEGS WHEN YOU PUT ME DOWN.
HRMPH!
I BET THE BLACK KNIGHT NEVER HAS PROBLEMS LIKE THIS.
HRRMM...
SPARKY...
WHERE'S BEDELIA?

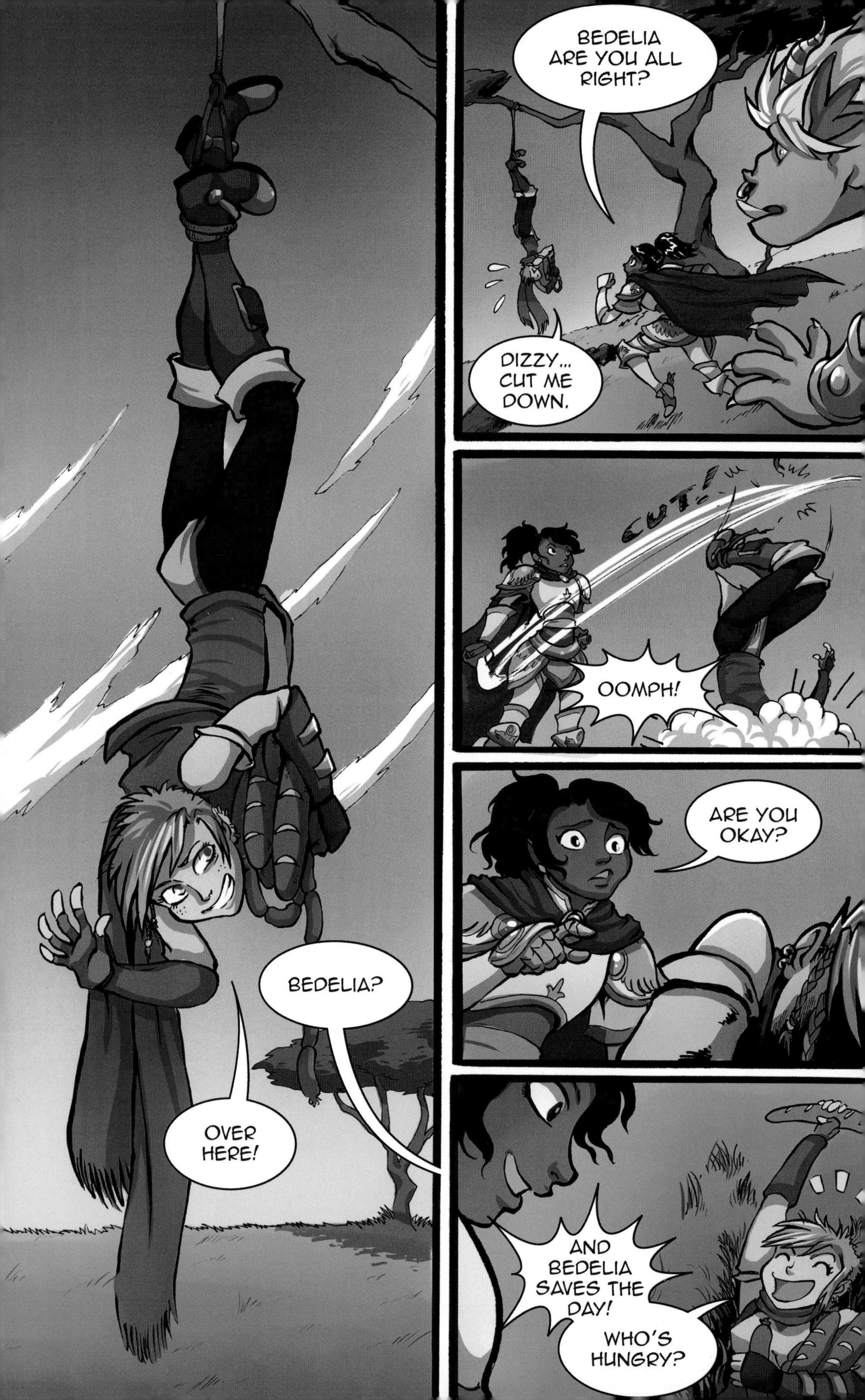
BEDELIA?
OVER HERE!
BEDELIA ARE YOU ALL RIGHT?
DIZZY... CUT ME DOWN.
CUT!
OOMPH!
ARE YOU OKAY?
AND BEDELIA SAVES THE DAY!
WHO'S HUNGRY?

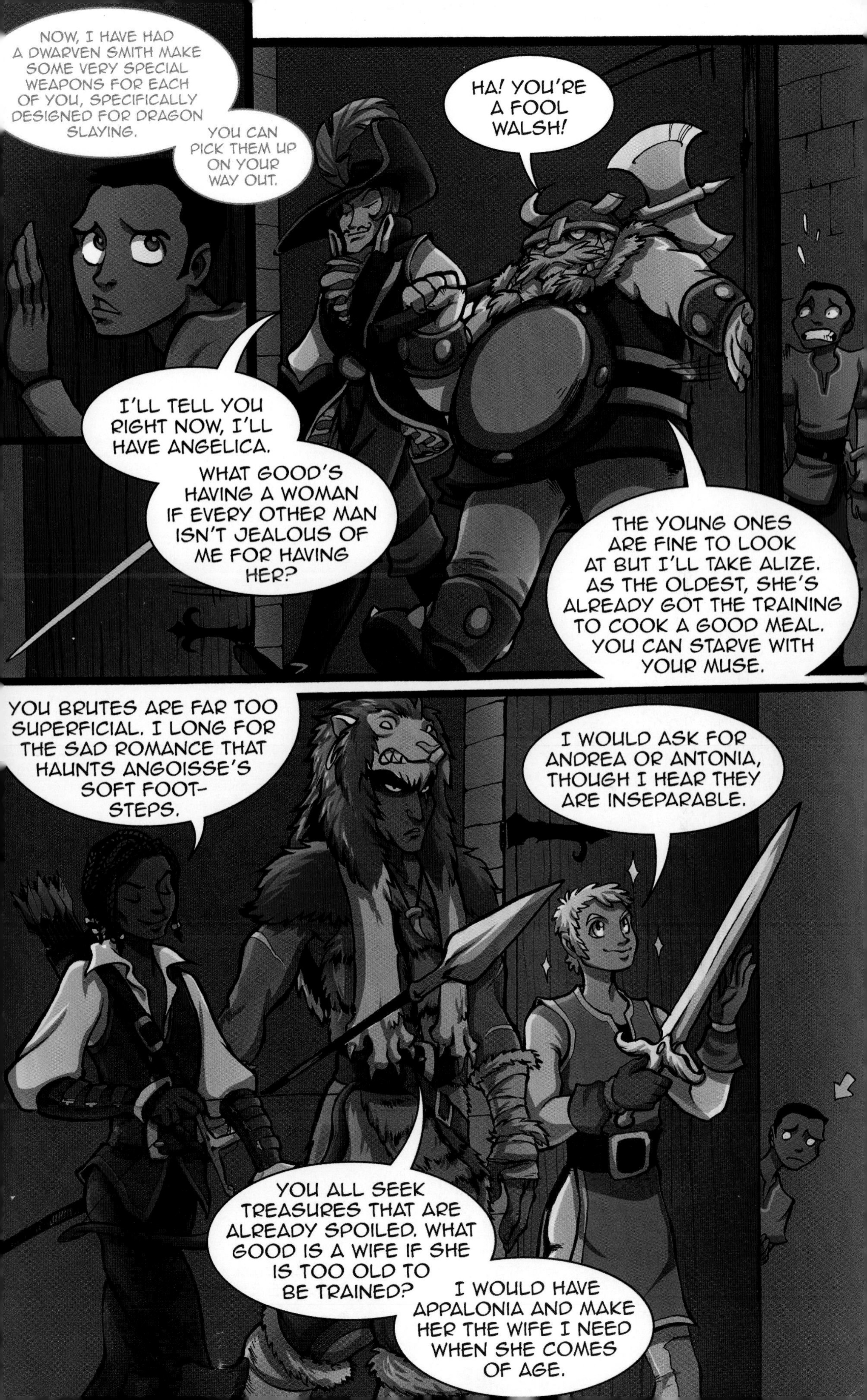
NOW, I HAVE HAD A DWARVEN SMITH MAKE SOME VERY SPECIAL WEAPONS FOR EACH OF YOU, SPECIFICALLY DESIGNED FOR DRAGON SLAYING.
YOU CAN PICK THEM UP ON YOUR WAY OUT.
HA! YOU'RE A FOOL WALSH!
I'LL TELL YOU RIGHT NOW, I'LL HAVE ANGELICA.
WHAT GOOD'S HAVING A WOMAN IF EVERY OTHER MAN ISN'T JEALOUS OF ME FOR HAVING HER?
THE YOUNG ONES ARE FINE TO LOOK AT BUT I'LL TAKE ALIZE. AS THE OLDEST, SHE'S ALREADY GOT THE TRAINING TO COOK A GOOD MEAL. YOU CAN STARVE WITH YOUR MUSE.
YOU BRUTES ARE FAR TOO SUPERFICIAL. I LONG FOR THE SAD ROMANCE THAT HAUNTS ANGOISSE'S SOFT FOOT-STEPS.
I WOULD ASK FOR ANDREA OR ANTONIA, THOUGH I HEAR THEY ARE INSEPARABLE.
YOU ALL SEEK TREASURES THAT ARE ALREADY SPOILED. WHAT GOOD IS A WIFE IF SHE IS TOO OLD TO BE TRAINED?
I WOULD HAVE APPALONIA AND MAKE HER THE WIFE I NEED WHEN SHE COMES OF AGE.

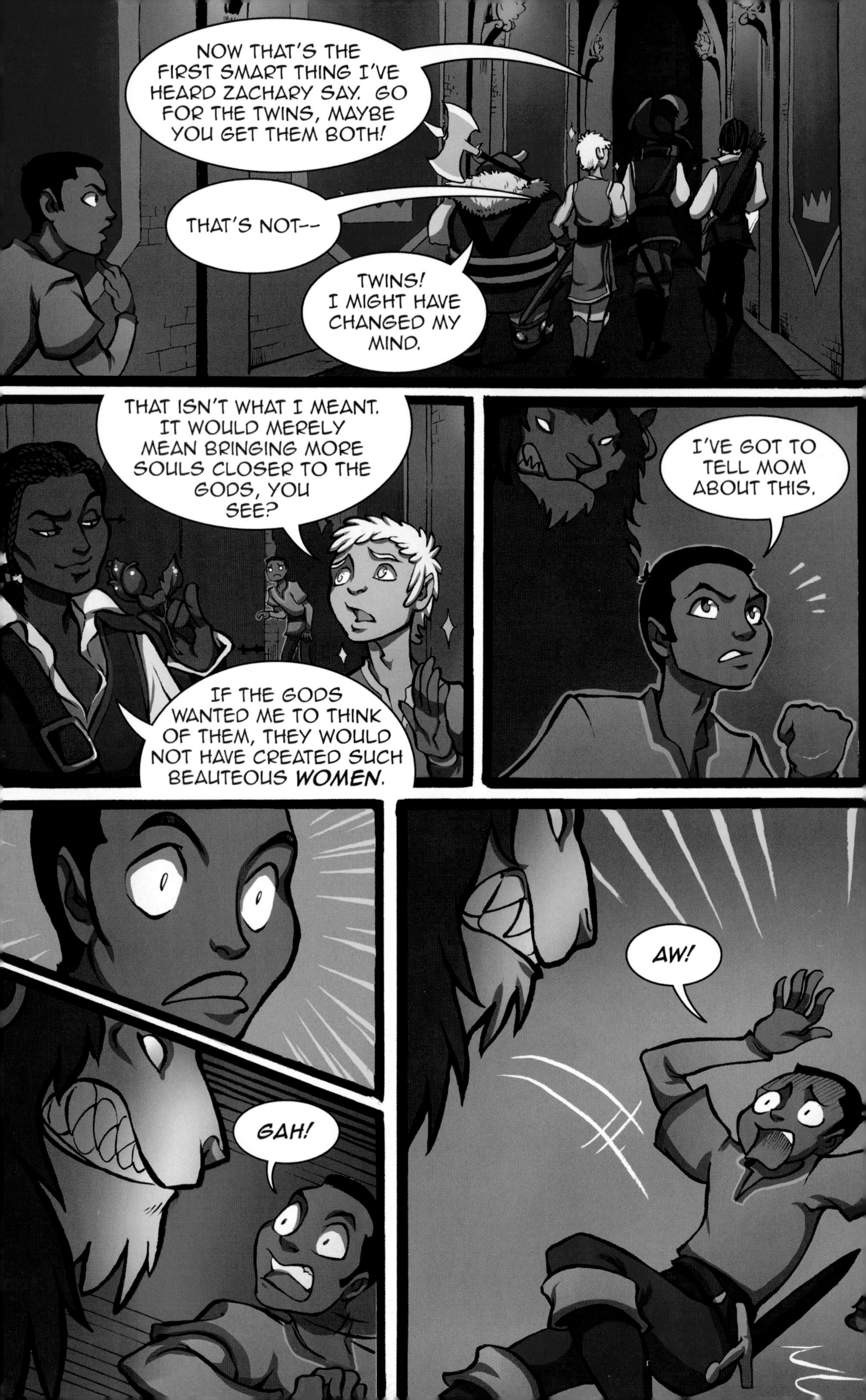

NOW THAT'S THE FIRST SMART THING I'VE HEARD ZACHARY SAY. GO FOR THE TWINS, MAYBE YOU GET THEM BOTH!
THAT'S NOT--
TWINS! I MIGHT HAVE CHANGED MY MIND.
THAT ISN'T WHAT I MEANT. IT WOULD MERELY MEAN BRINGING MORE SOULS CLOSER TO THE GODS, YOU SEE?
IF THE GODS WANTED ME TO THINK OF THEM, THEY WOULD NOT HAVE CREATED SUCH BEAUTEOUS *WOMEN*.
I'VE GOT TO TELL MOM ABOUT THIS.
GAH!
AW!

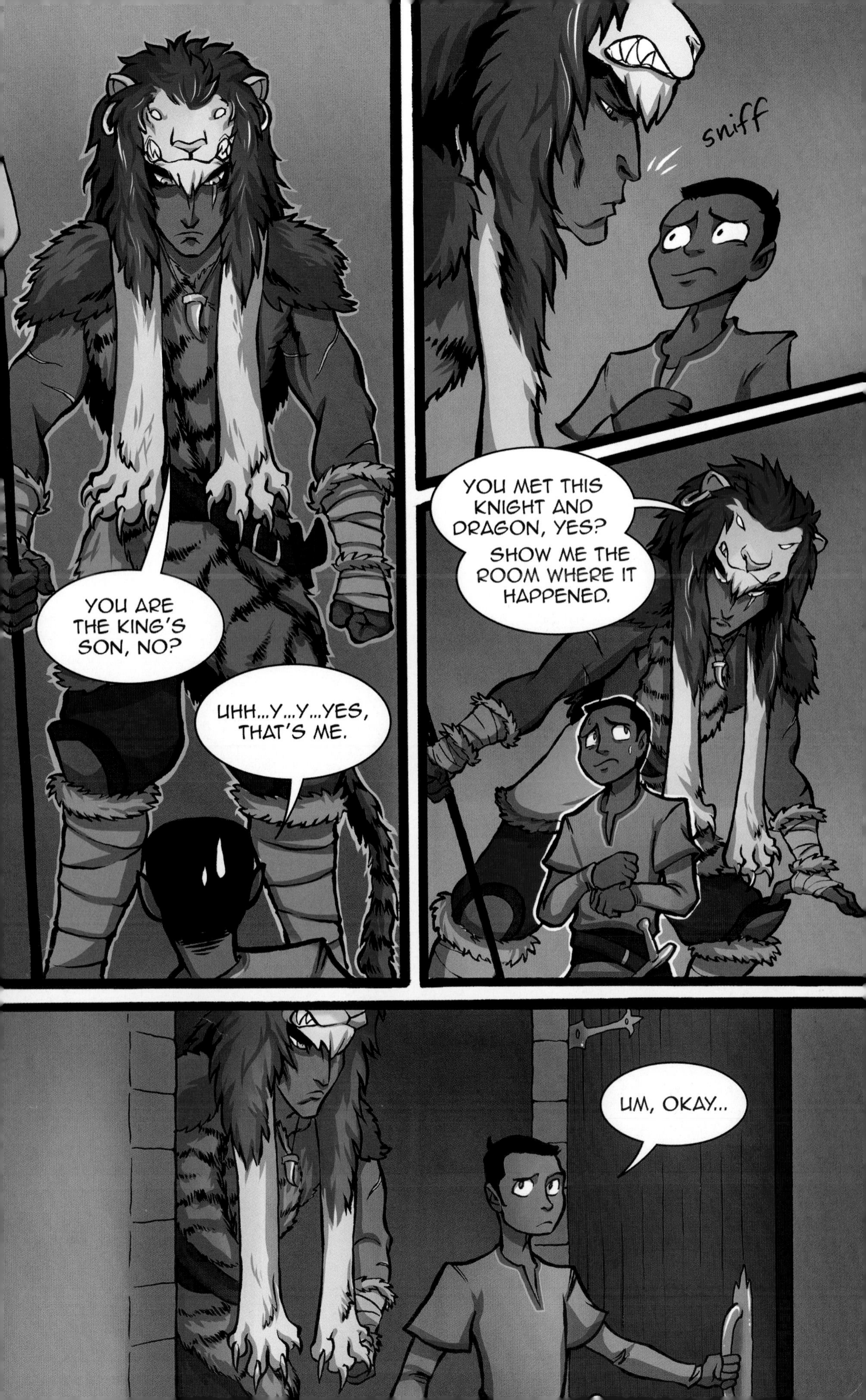
YOU ARE THE KING'S SON, NO?
UHH...Y...Y...YES, THAT'S ME.
sniff
YOU MET THIS KNIGHT AND DRAGON, YES?
SHOW ME THE ROOM WHERE IT HAPPENED.
UM, OKAY...

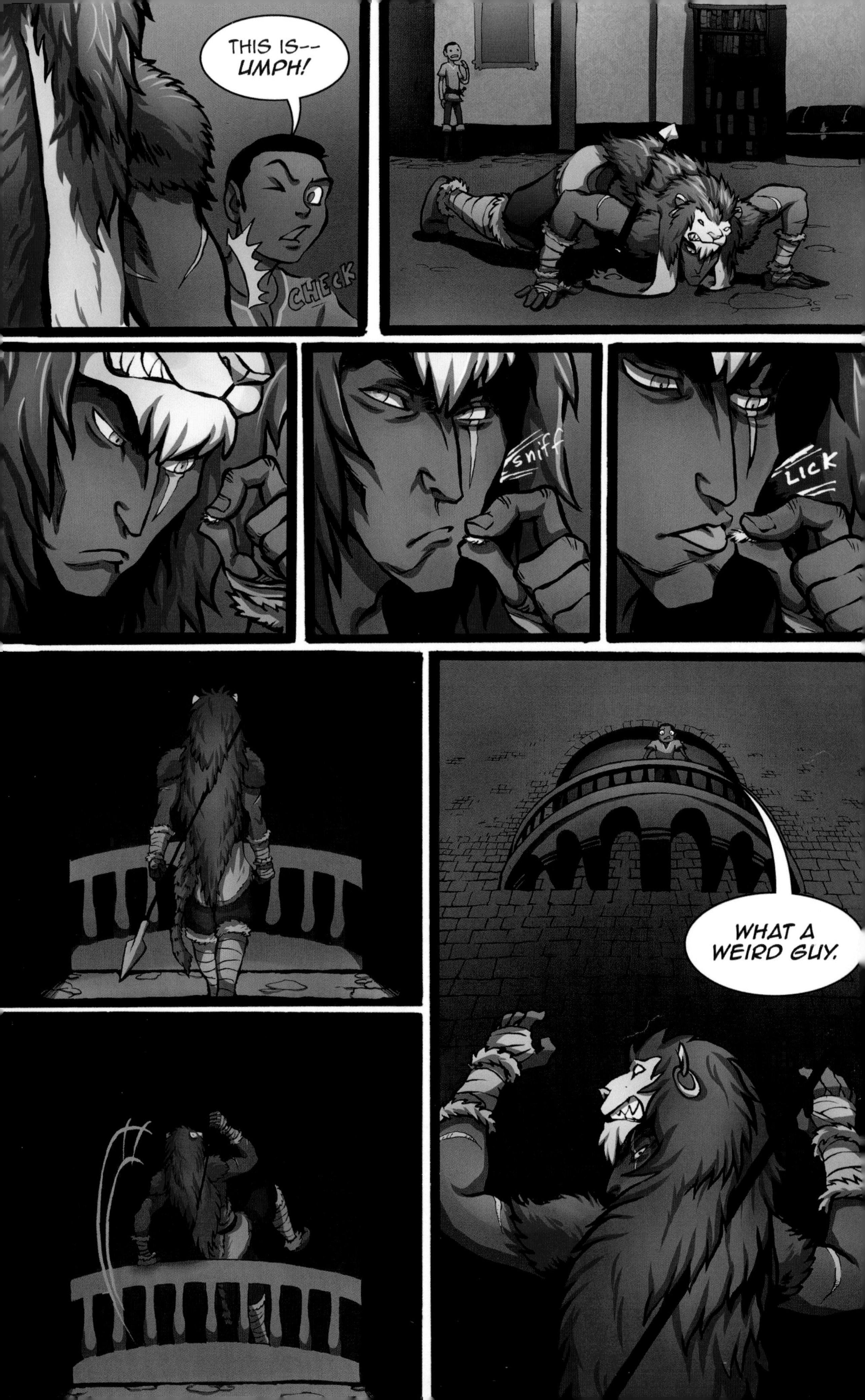
THIS IS--
UMPH!
CHECK
sniff
LICK
WHAT A
WEIRD GUY.

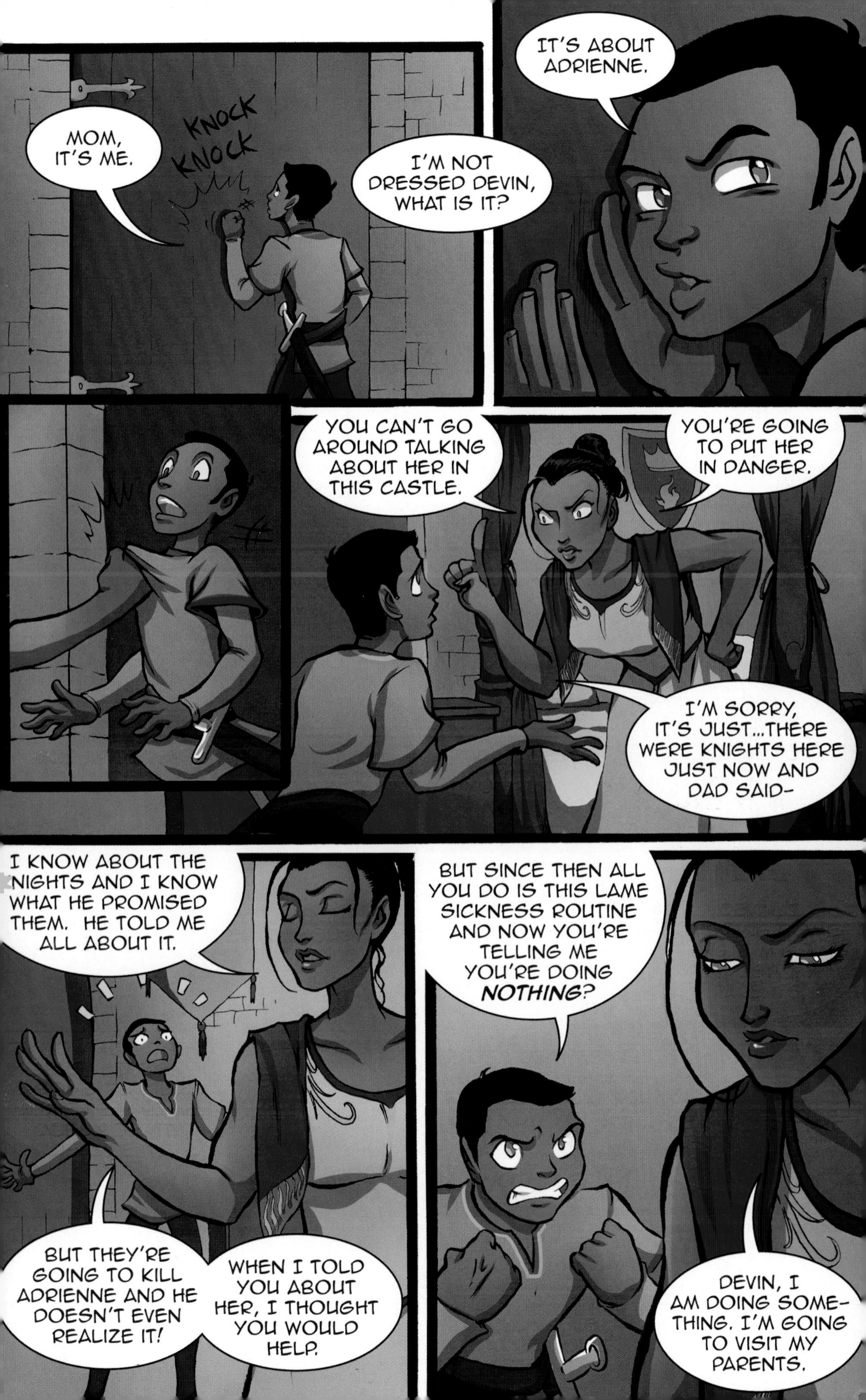
MOM, IT'S ME.
KNOCK KNOCK
I'M NOT DRESSED DEVIN, WHAT IS IT?
IT'S ABOUT ADRIENNE.
YOU CAN'T GO AROUND TALKING ABOUT HER IN THIS CASTLE.
YOU'RE GOING TO PUT HER IN DANGER.
I'M SORRY, IT'S JUST...THERE WERE KNIGHTS HERE JUST NOW AND DAD SAID-
I KNOW ABOUT THE NIGHTS AND I KNOW WHAT HE PROMISED THEM. HE TOLD ME ALL ABOUT IT.
BUT THEY'RE GOING TO KILL ADRIENNE AND HE DOESN'T EVEN REALIZE IT!
WHEN I TOLD YOU ABOUT HER, I THOUGHT YOU WOULD HELP.
BUT SINCE THEN ALL YOU DO IS THIS LAME SICKNESS ROUTINE AND NOW YOU'RE TELLING ME YOU'RE DOING *NOTHING*?
DEVIN, I AM DOING SOMETHING. I'M GOING TO VISIT MY PARENTS.

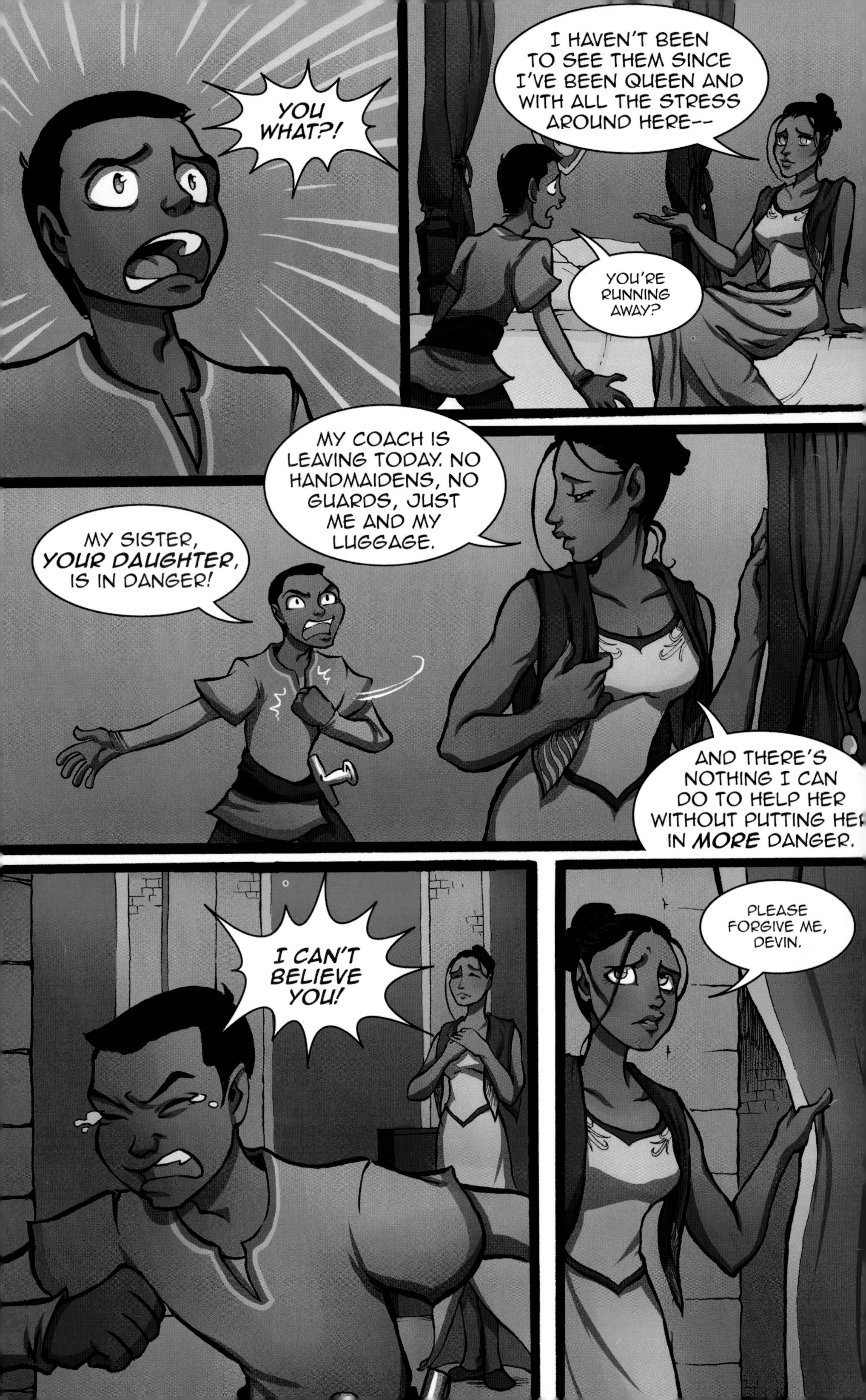

YOU WHAT?!
I HAVEN'T BEEN TO SEE THEM SINCE I'VE BEEN QUEEN AND WITH ALL THE STRESS AROUND HERE--
YOU'RE RUNNING AWAY?
MY COACH IS LEAVING TODAY. NO HANDMAIDENS, NO GUARDS, JUST ME AND MY LUGGAGE.
MY SISTER, *YOUR DAUGHTER*, IS IN DANGER!
AND THERE'S NOTHING I CAN DO TO HELP HER WITHOUT PUTTING HER IN *MORE* DANGER.
I CAN'T BELIEVE YOU!
PLEASE FORGIVE ME, DEVIN.

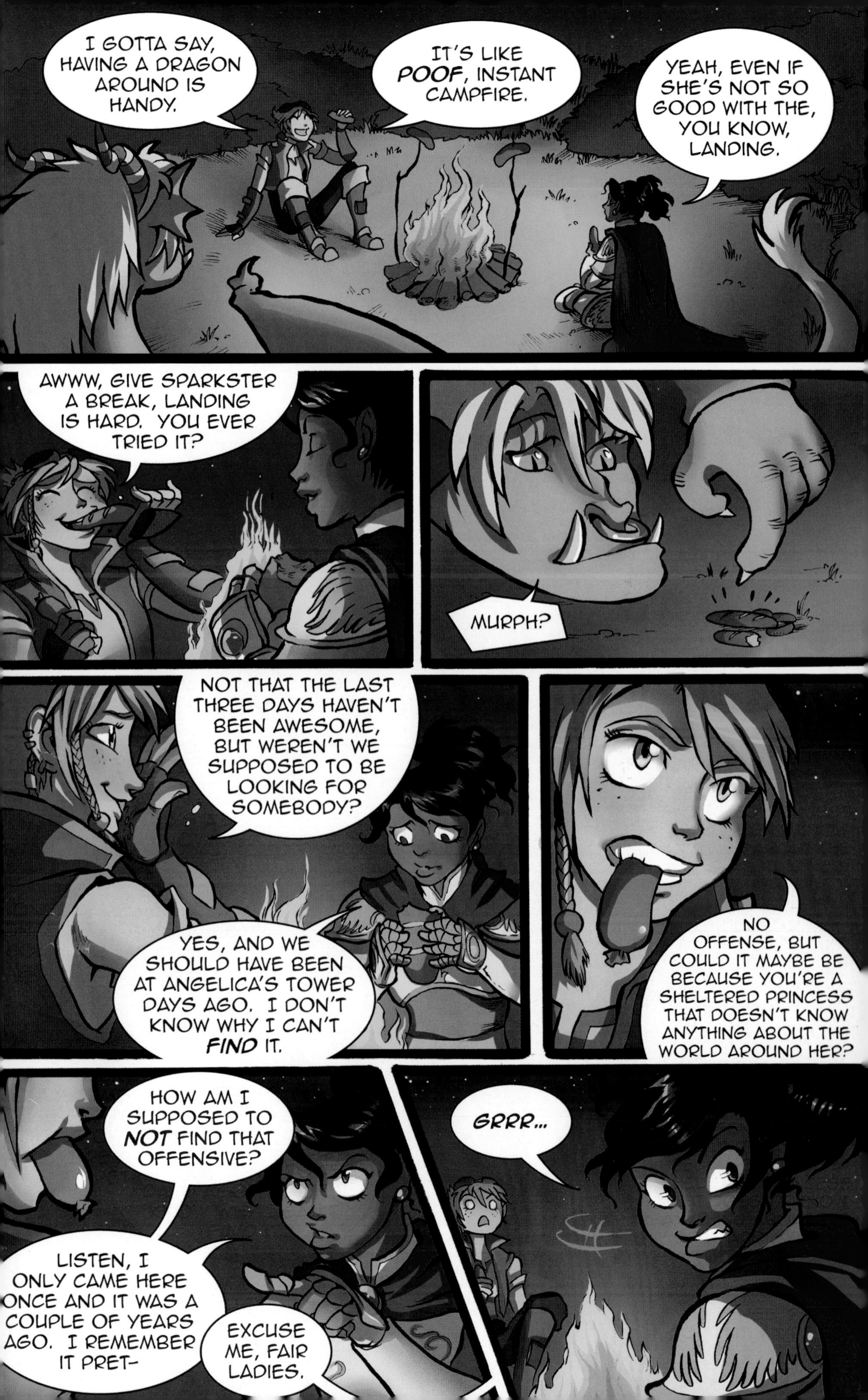
I GOTTA SAY, HAVING A DRAGON AROUND IS HANDY.
IT'S LIKE POOF, INSTANT CAMPFIRE.
YEAH, EVEN IF SHE'S NOT SO GOOD WITH THE, YOU KNOW, LANDING.
AWWW, GIVE SPARKSTER A BREAK, LANDING IS HARD. YOU EVER TRIED IT?
MURPH?
NOT THAT THE LAST THREE DAYS HAVEN'T BEEN AWESOME, BUT WEREN'T WE SUPPOSED TO BE LOOKING FOR SOMEBODY?
YES, AND WE SHOULD HAVE BEEN AT ANGELICA'S TOWER DAYS AGO. I DON'T KNOW WHY I CAN'T FIND IT.
NO OFFENSE, BUT COULD IT MAYBE BE BECAUSE YOU'RE A SHELTERED PRINCESS THAT DOESN'T KNOW ANYTHING ABOUT THE WORLD AROUND HER?
HOW AM I SUPPOSED TO NOT FIND THAT OFFENSIVE?
LISTEN, I ONLY CAME HERE ONCE AND IT WAS A COUPLE OF YEARS AGO. I REMEMBER IT PRET-
EXCUSE ME, FAIR LADIES.
GRRR...

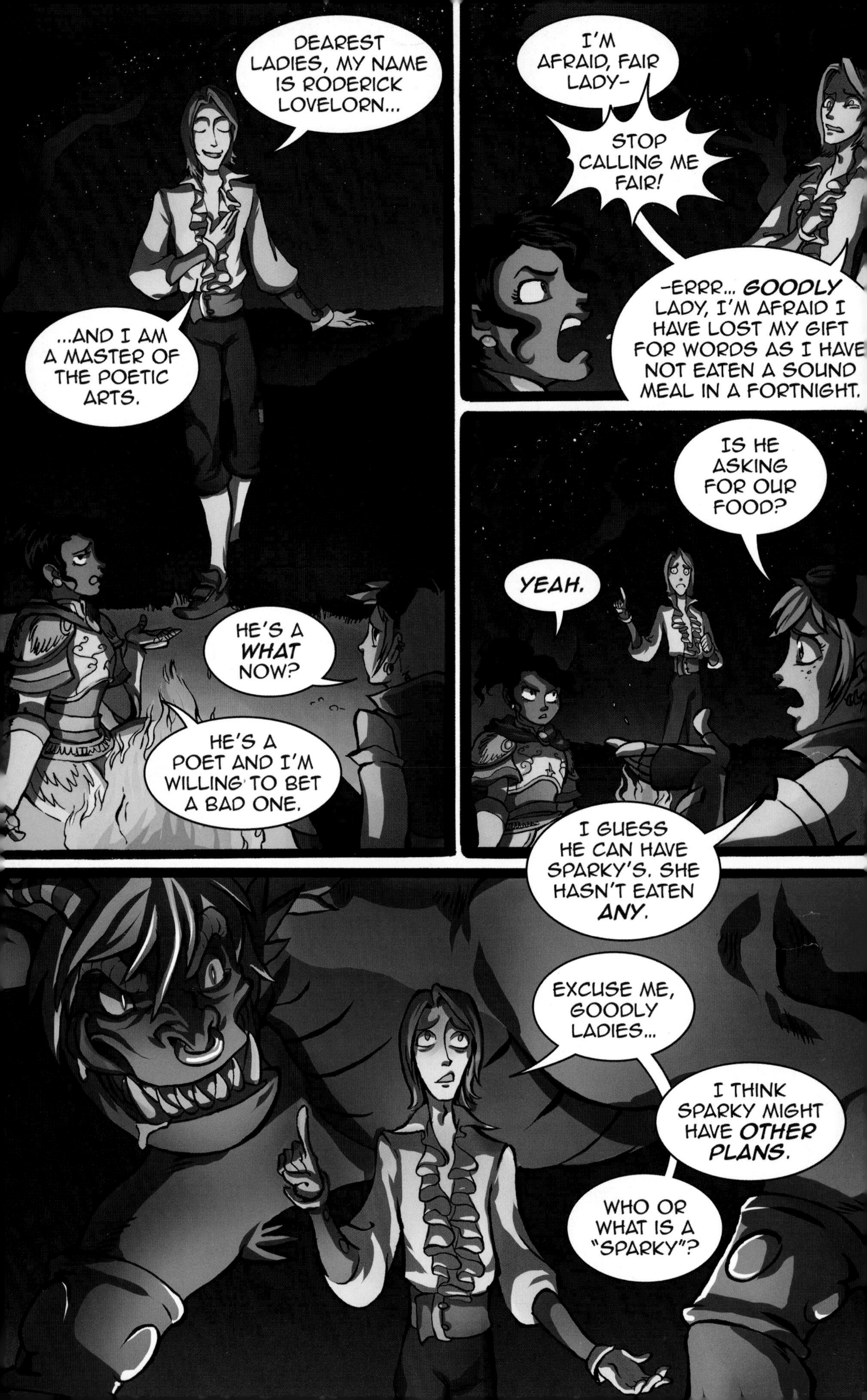
DEAREST LADIES, MY NAME IS RODERICK LOVELORN...
...AND I AM A MASTER OF THE POETIC ARTS.
HE'S A WHAT NOW?
HE'S A POET AND I'M WILLING TO BET A BAD ONE.
I'M AFRAID, FAIR LADY-
STOP CALLING ME FAIR!
-ERRR... GOODLY LADY, I'M AFRAID I HAVE LOST MY GIFT FOR WORDS AS I HAVE NOT EATEN A SOUND MEAL IN A FORTNIGHT.
IS HE ASKING FOR OUR FOOD?
YEAH.
I GUESS HE CAN HAVE SPARKY'S. SHE HASN'T EATEN ANY.
EXCUSE ME, GOODLY LADIES...
I THINK SPARKY MIGHT HAVE OTHER PLANS.
WHO OR WHAT IS A "SPARKY"?

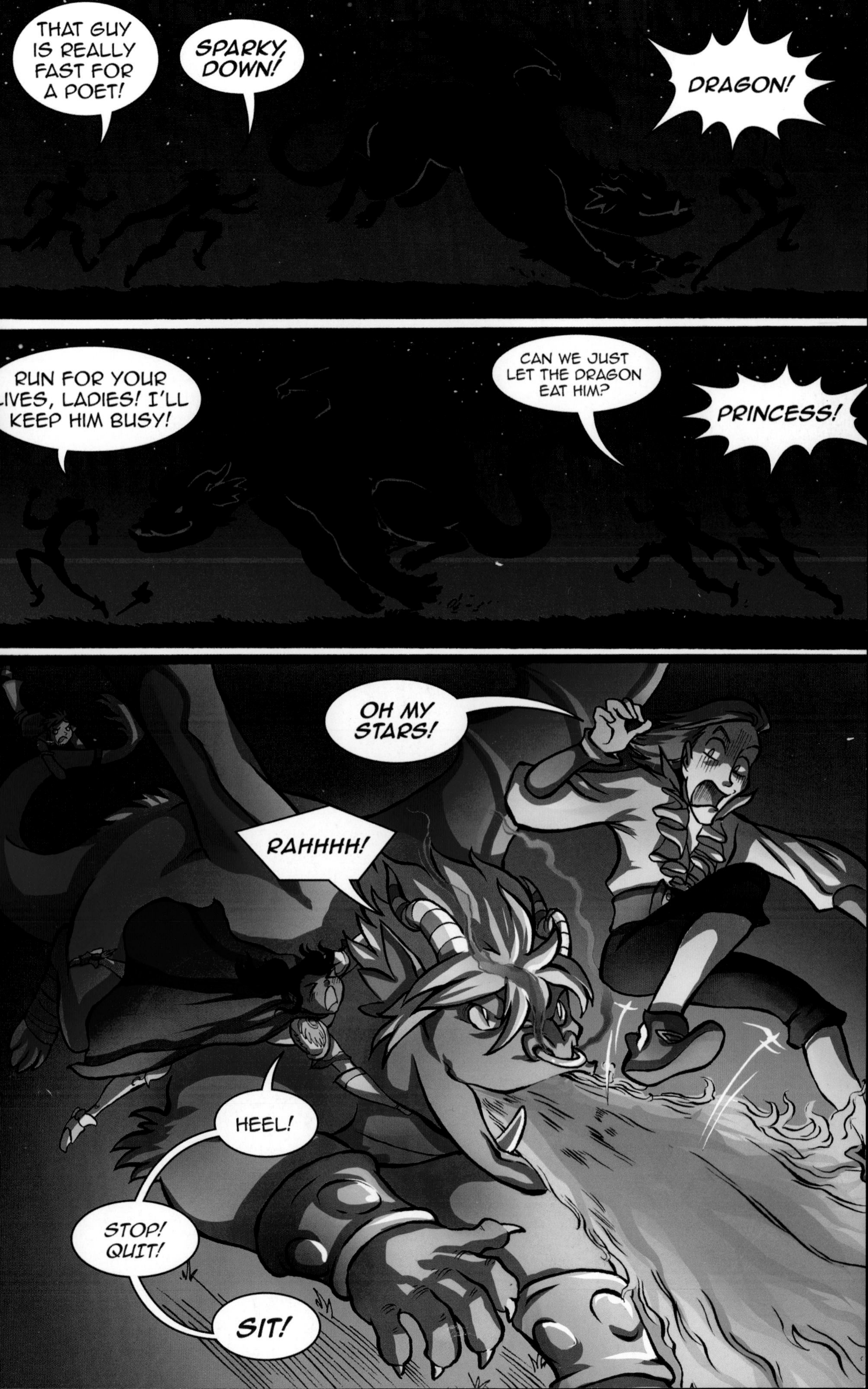

THAT GUY IS REALLY FAST FOR A POET!
SPARKY, DOWN!
DRAGON!
RUN FOR YOUR LIVES, LADIES! I'LL KEEP HIM BUSY!
CAN WE JUST LET THE DRAGON EAT HIM?
PRINCESS!
OH MY STARS!
RAHHHH!
HEEL!
STOP! QUIT!
SIT!

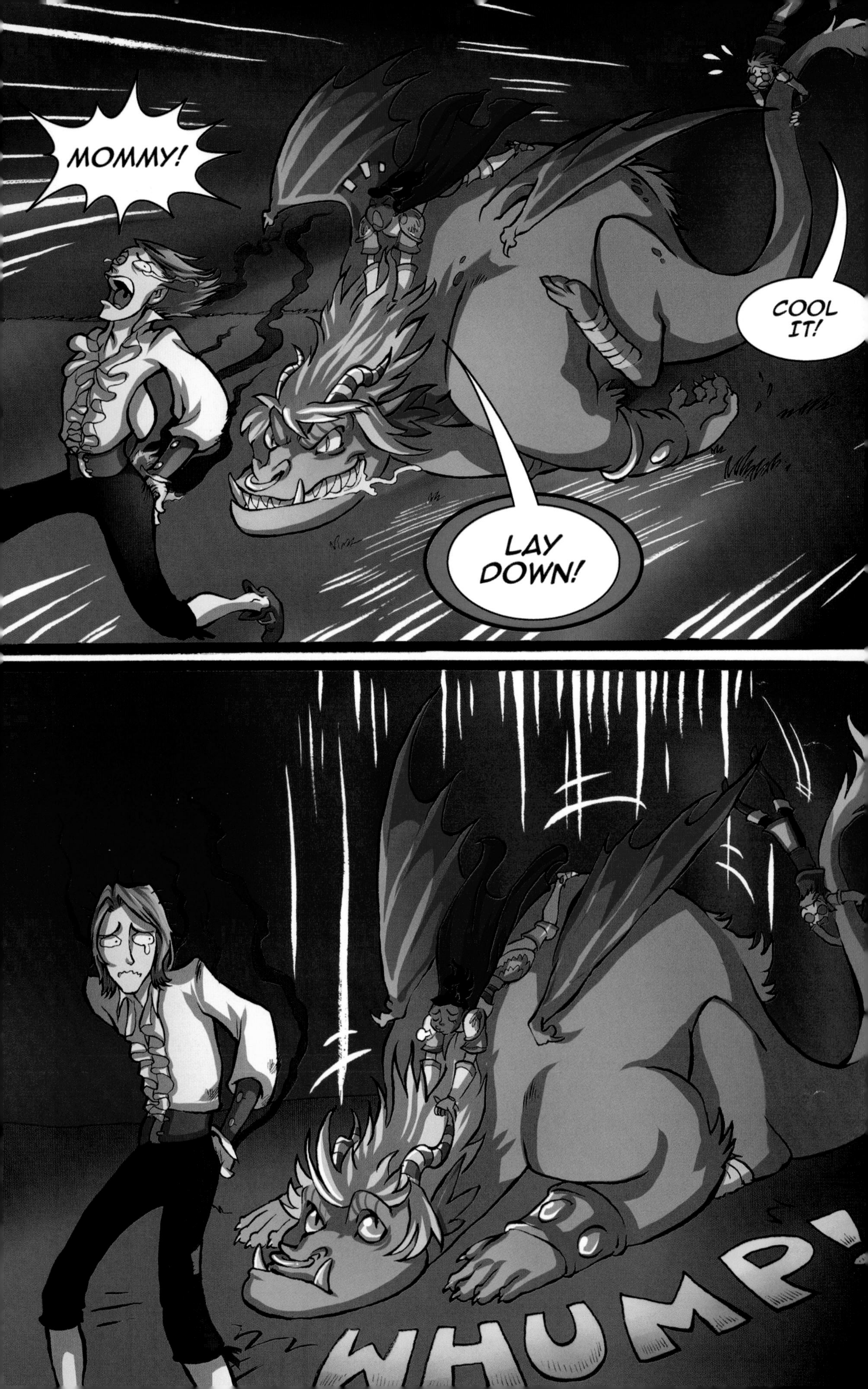

MOMMY!
COOL IT!
LAY DOWN!
WHUMP!

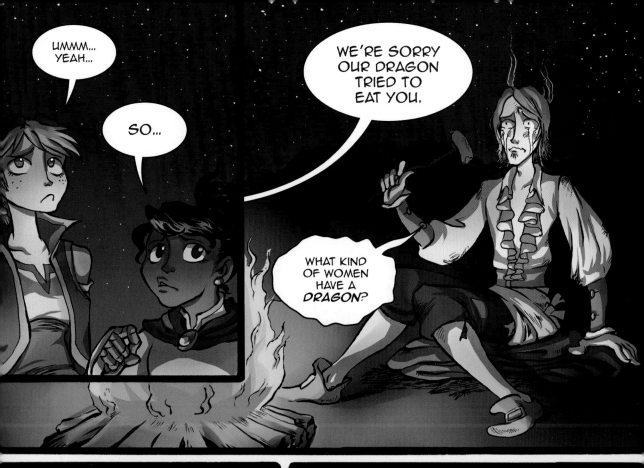

UMMM... YEAH...

SO...

WE'RE SORRY OUR DRAGON TRIED TO EAT YOU.

WHAT KIND OF WOMEN HAVE A *DRAGON*?

SHE'S USUALLY VERY NICE WHEN SHE MEETS PEOPLE.

MAYBE SHE JUST DOESN'T LIKE MEN.

COULD BE. SHE WAS KINDA TRAINED WITH THAT IN MIND.

WHY IS IT EVERY WOMAN I MEET HAS A MAGICAL GUARDIAN.

IT'S JUST NOT FAIR. I'M JUST A *POET*.

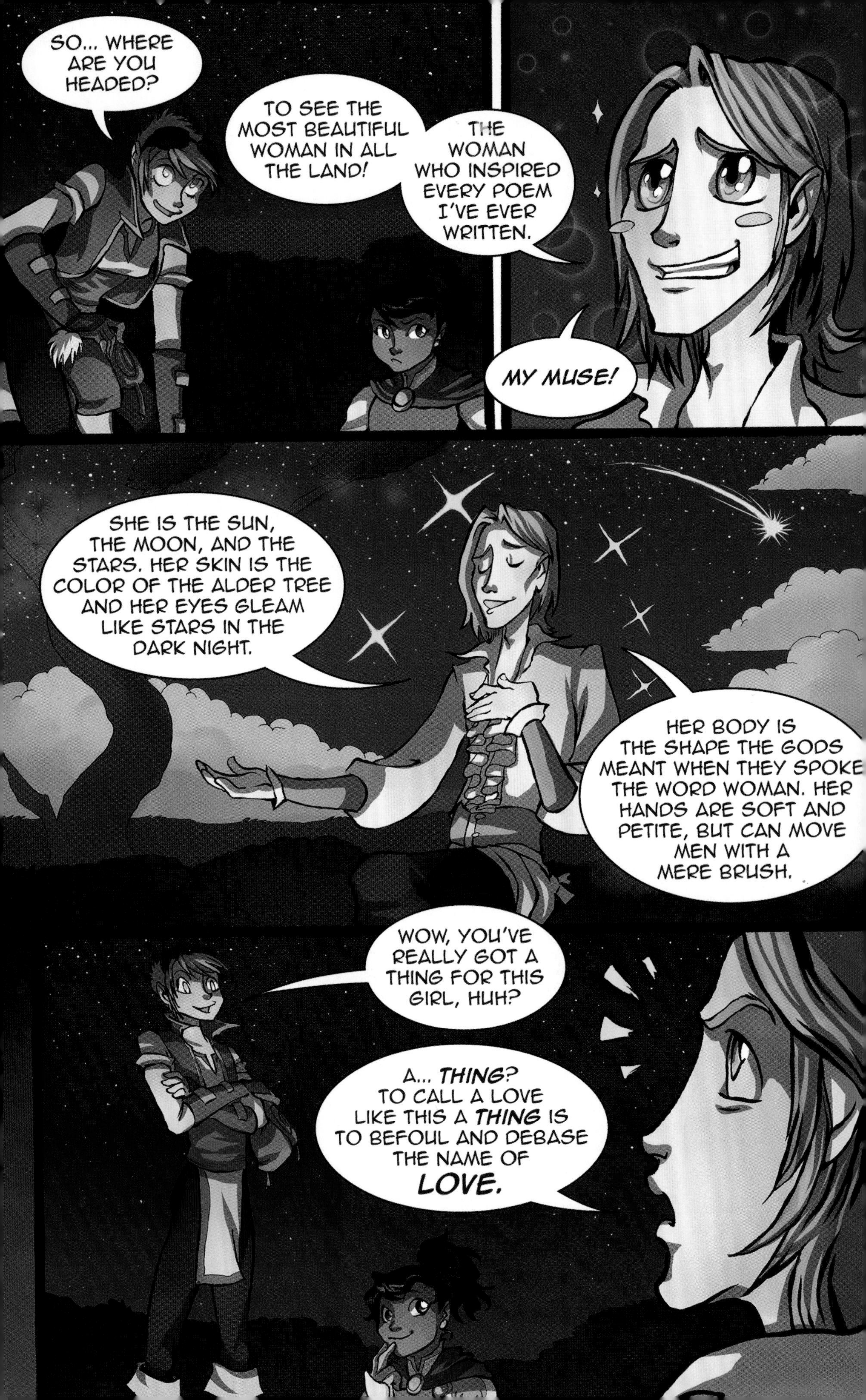
SO... WHERE ARE YOU HEADED?
TO SEE THE MOST BEAUTIFUL WOMAN IN ALL THE LAND!
THE WOMAN WHO INSPIRED EVERY POEM I'VE EVER WRITTEN.
MY MUSE!
SHE IS THE SUN, THE MOON, AND THE STARS. HER SKIN IS THE COLOR OF THE ALDER TREE AND HER EYES GLEAM LIKE STARS IN THE DARK NIGHT.
HER BODY IS THE SHAPE THE GODS MEANT WHEN THEY SPOKE THE WORD WOMAN. HER HANDS ARE SOFT AND PETITE, BUT CAN MOVE MEN WITH A MERE BRUSH.
WOW, YOU'VE REALLY GOT A THING FOR THIS GIRL, HUH?
A... *THING*? TO CALL A LOVE LIKE THIS A *THING* IS TO BEFOUL AND DEBASE THE NAME OF **LOVE.**

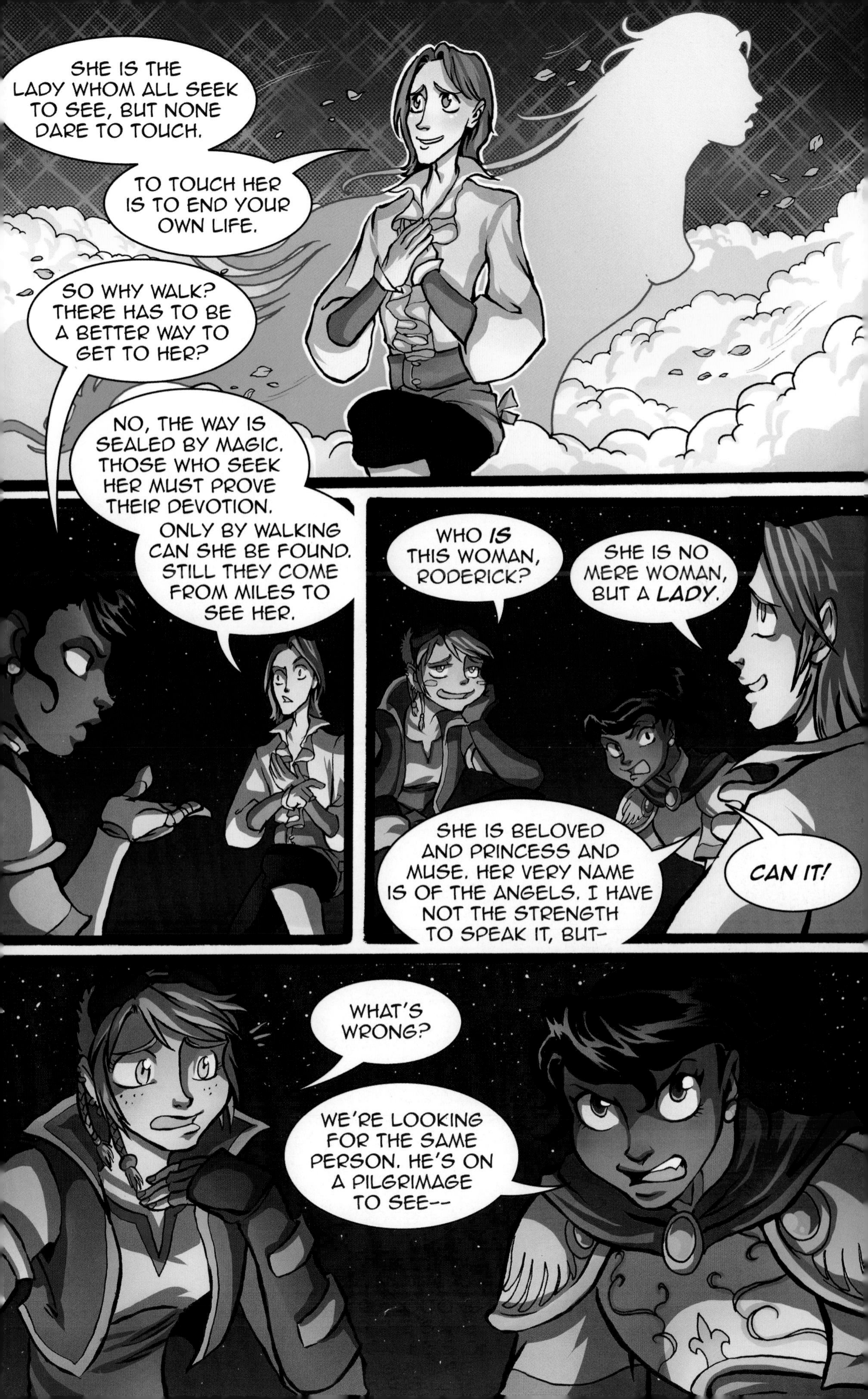
SHE IS THE LADY WHOM ALL SEEK TO SEE, BUT NONE DARE TO TOUCH.
TO TOUCH HER IS TO END YOUR OWN LIFE.
SO WHY WALK? THERE HAS TO BE A BETTER WAY TO GET TO HER?
NO, THE WAY IS SEALED BY MAGIC. THOSE WHO SEEK HER MUST PROVE THEIR DEVOTION.
ONLY BY WALKING CAN SHE BE FOUND. STILL THEY COME FROM MILES TO SEE HER.
WHO *IS* THIS WOMAN, RODERICK?
SHE IS NO MERE WOMAN, BUT A ***LADY***.
SHE IS BELOVED AND PRINCESS AND MUSE. HER VERY NAME IS OF THE ANGELS. I HAVE NOT THE STRENGTH TO SPEAK IT, BUT-
CAN IT!
WHAT'S WRONG?
WE'RE LOOKING FOR THE SAME PERSON. HE'S ON A PILGRIMAGE TO SEE--

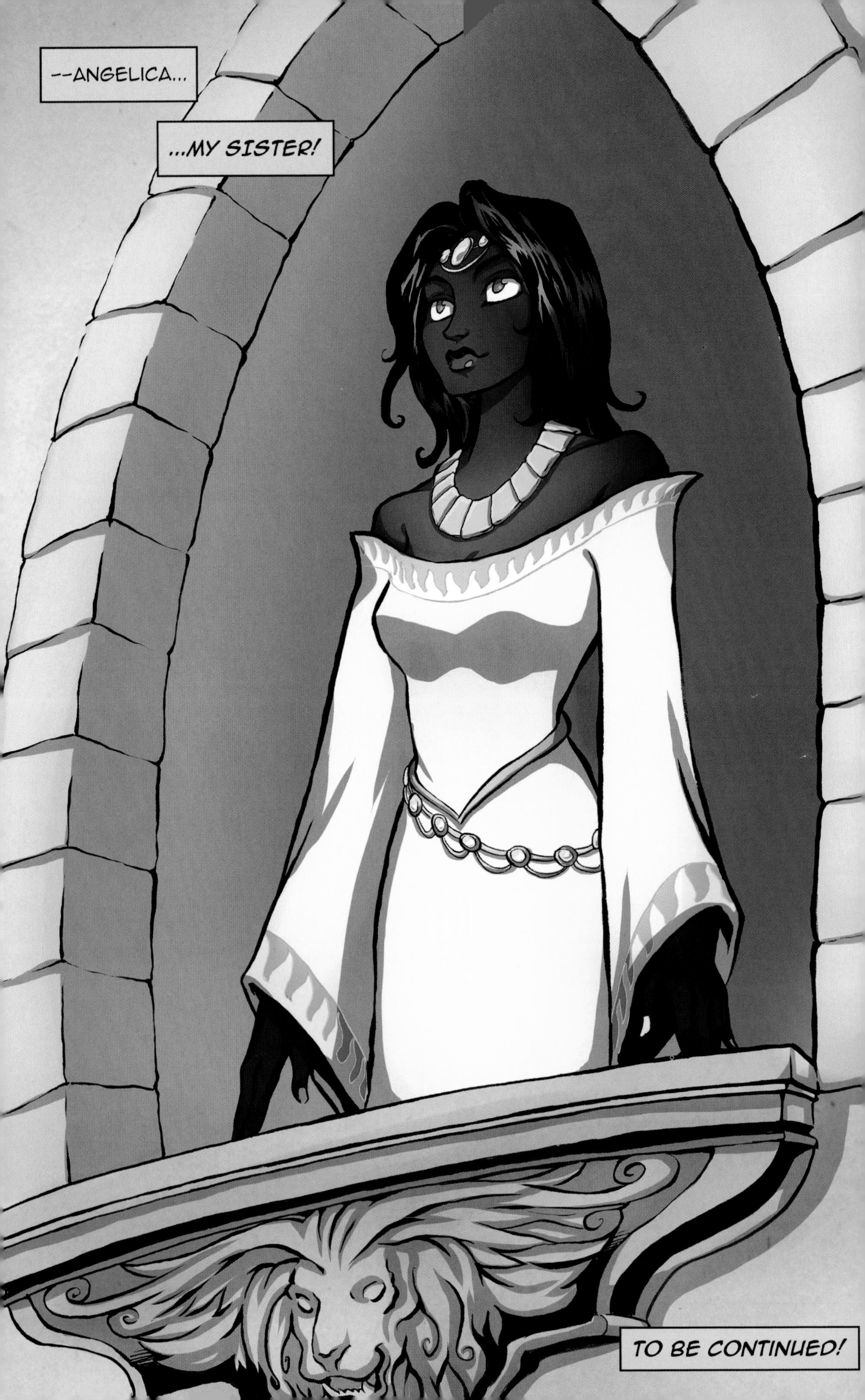
--ANGELICA...
...MY SISTER!
TO BE CONTINUED!

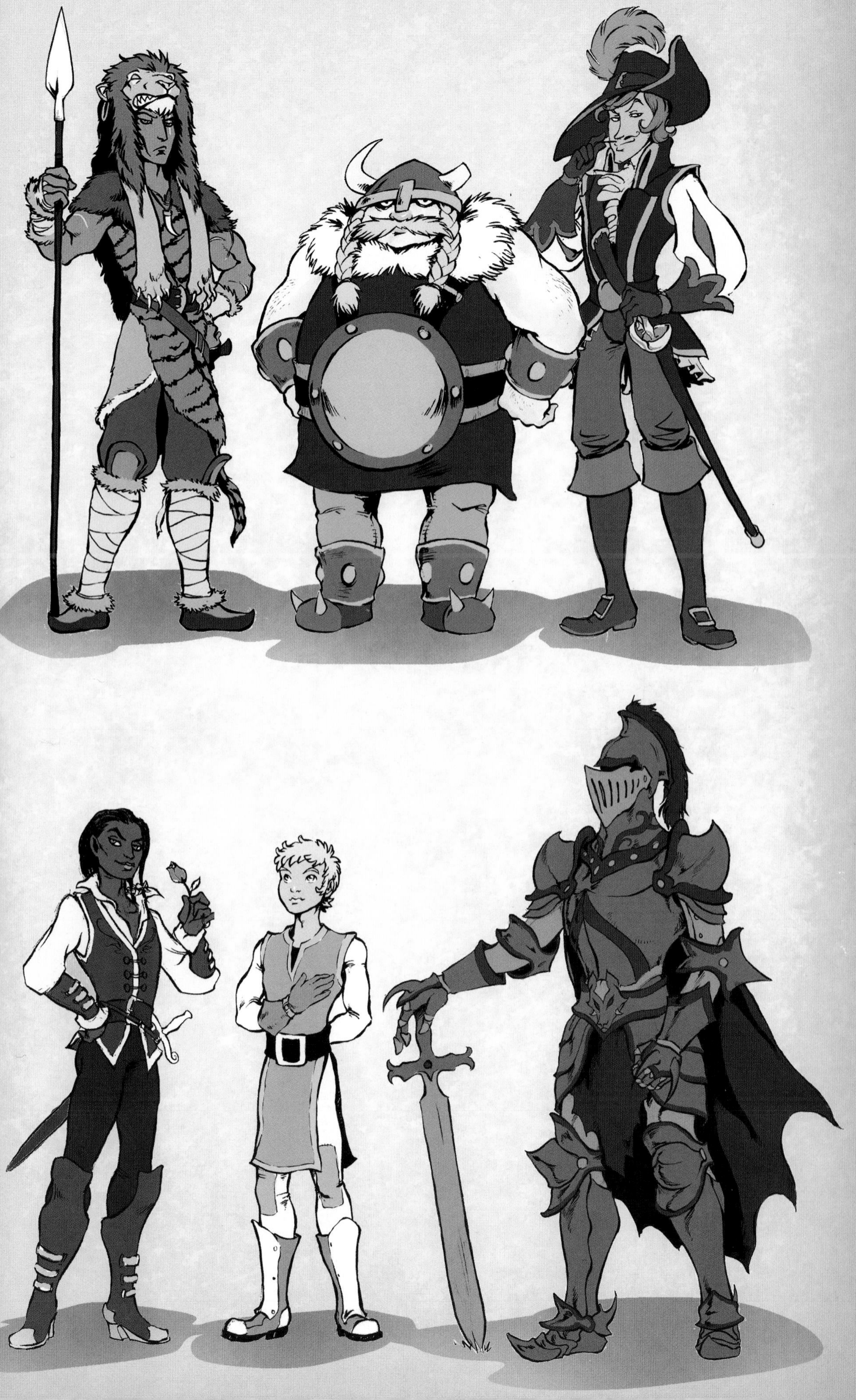

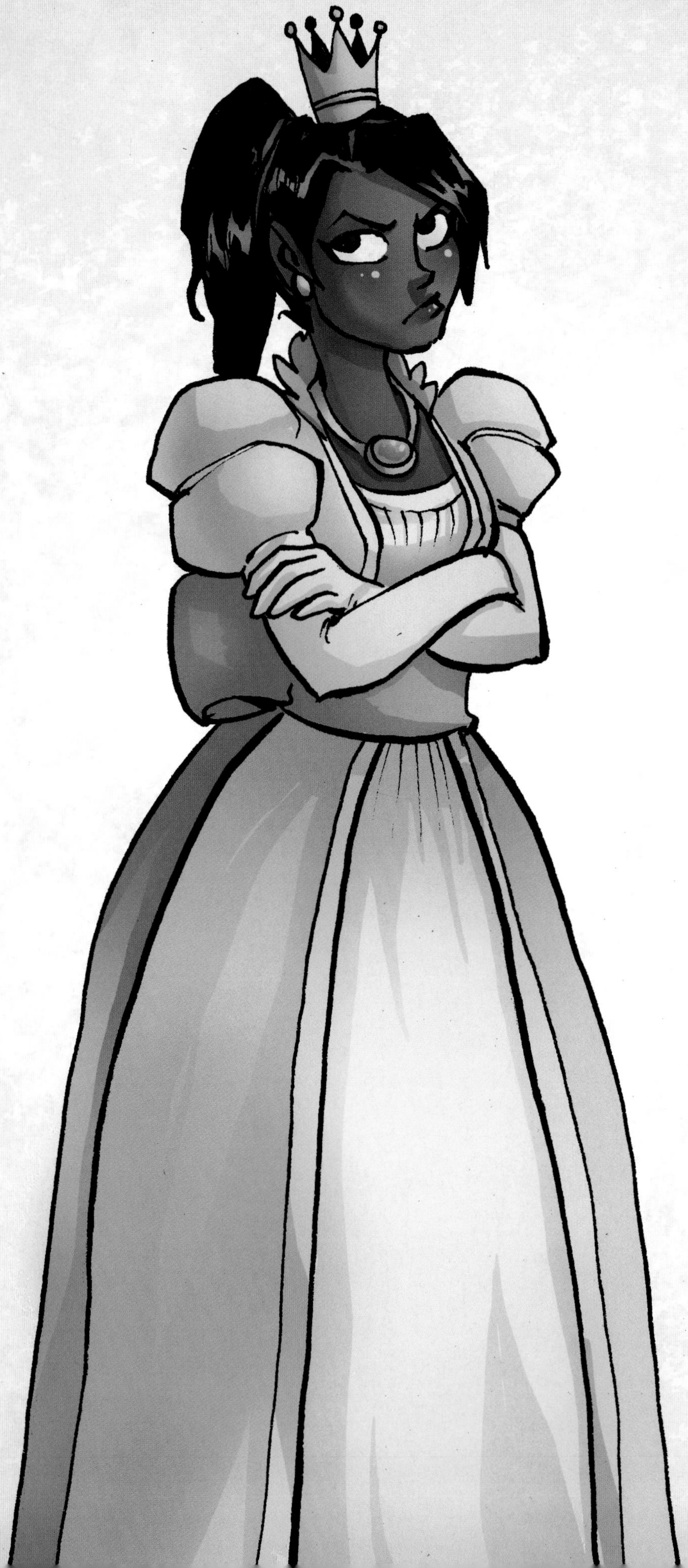

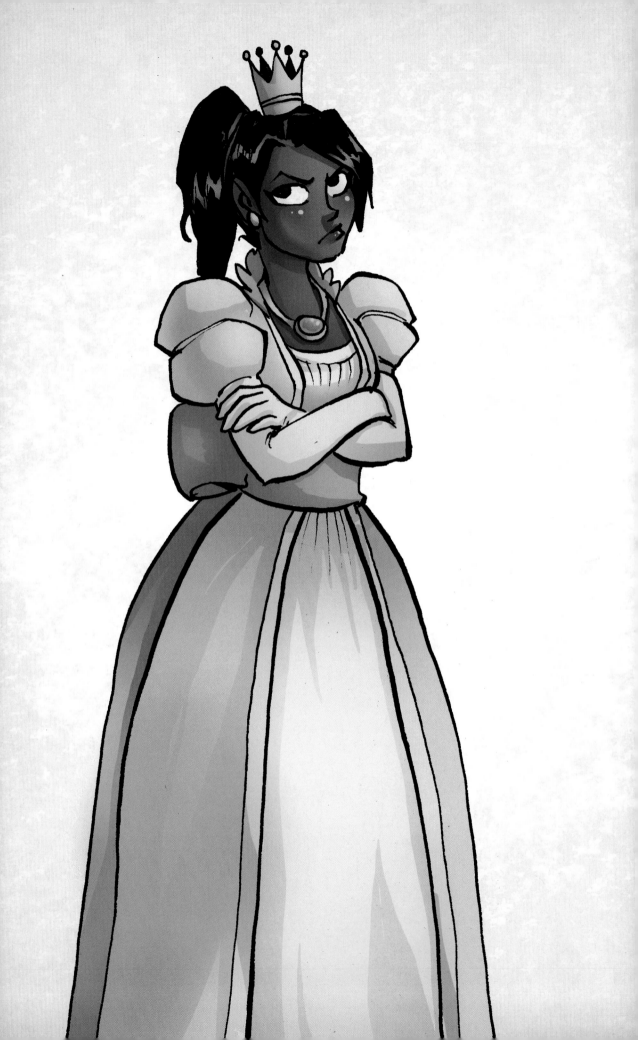

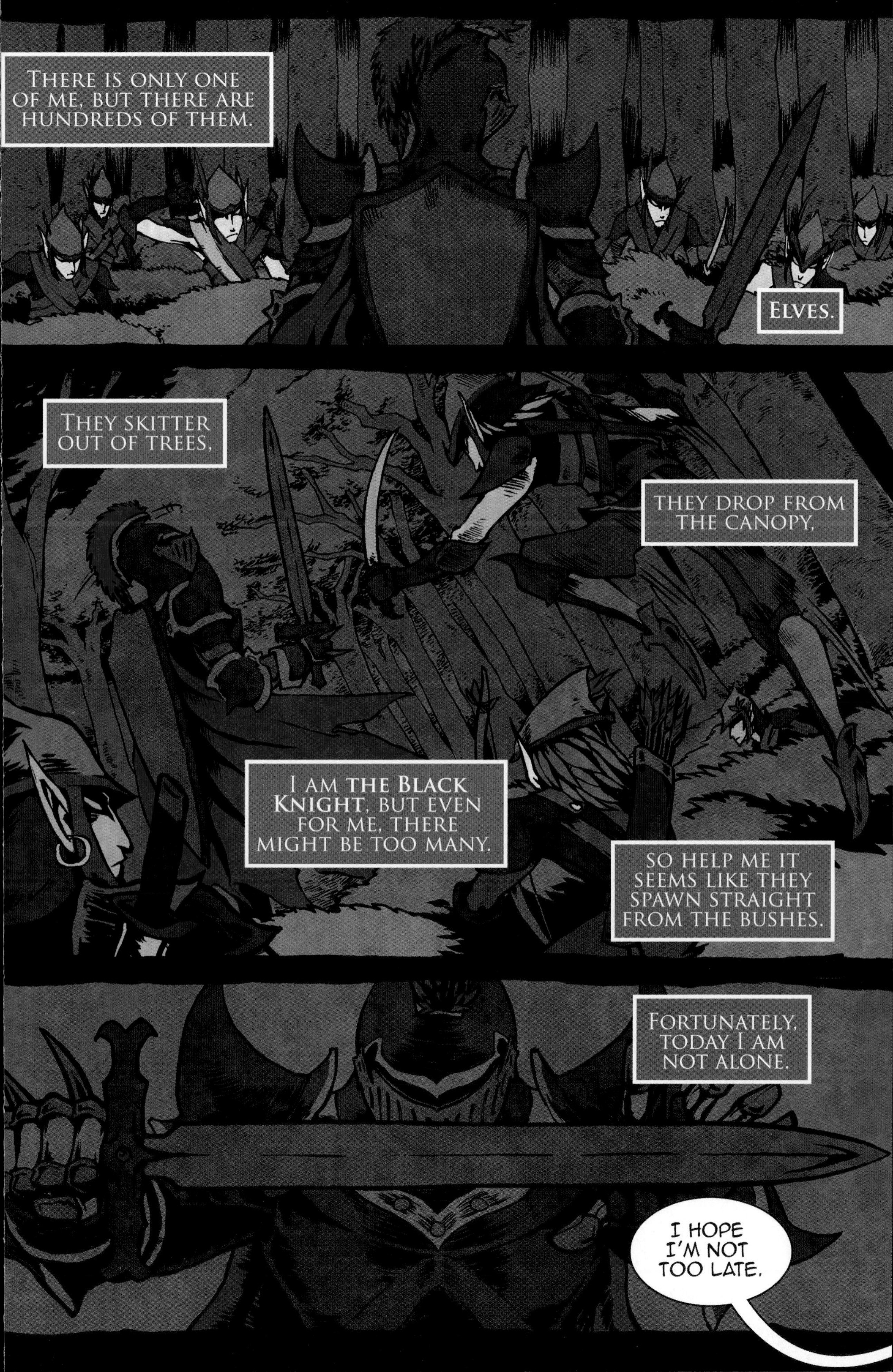
There is only one of me, but there are hundreds of them.
Elves.
They skitter out of trees,
they drop from the canopy,
I am **the Black Knight**, but even for me, there might be too many.
So help me it seems like they spawn straight from the bushes.
Fortunately, today I am not alone.
I hope I'm not too late.

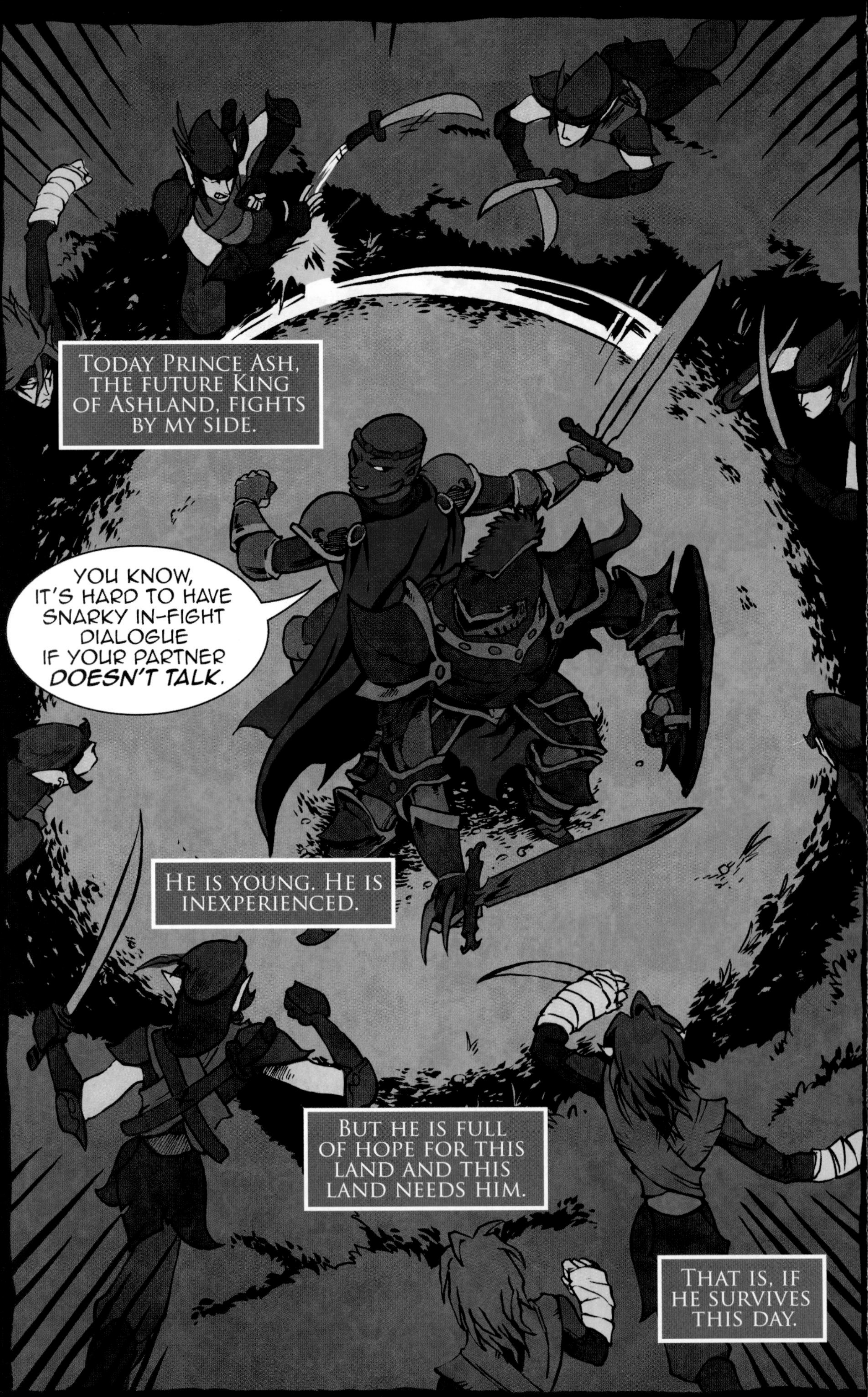
TODAY PRINCE ASH, THE FUTURE KING OF ASHLAND, FIGHTS BY MY SIDE.
YOU KNOW, IT'S HARD TO HAVE SNARKY IN-FIGHT DIALOGUE IF YOUR PARTNER DOESN'T TALK.
HE IS YOUNG. HE IS INEXPERIENCED.
BUT HE IS FULL OF HOPE FOR THIS LAND AND THIS LAND NEEDS HIM.
THAT IS, IF HE SURVIVES THIS DAY.

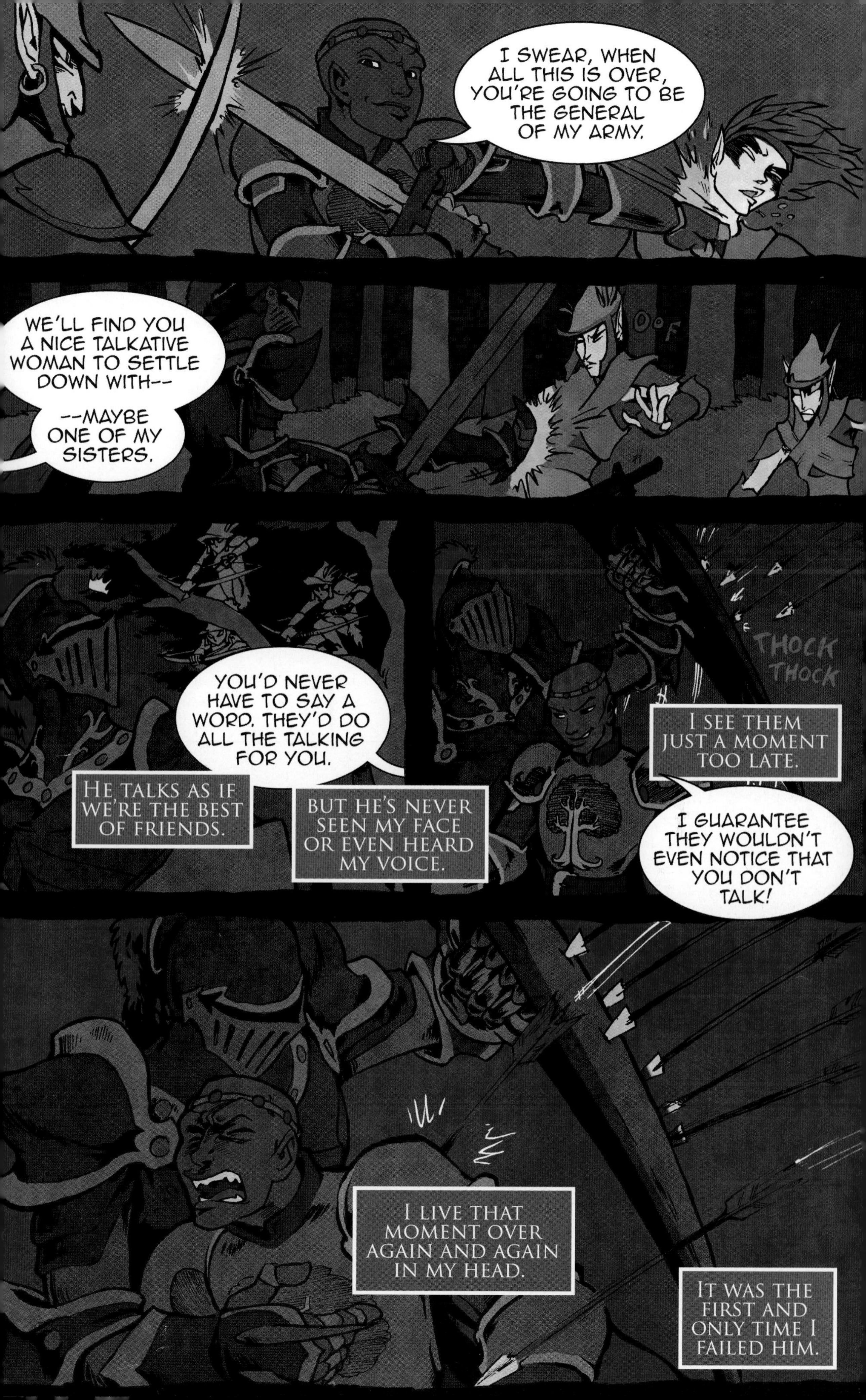
I SWEAR, WHEN ALL THIS IS OVER, YOU'RE GOING TO BE THE GENERAL OF MY ARMY.
WE'LL FIND YOU A NICE TALKATIVE WOMAN TO SETTLE DOWN WITH--
--MAYBE ONE OF MY SISTERS.
OOF
YOU'D NEVER HAVE TO SAY A WORD. THEY'D DO ALL THE TALKING FOR YOU.
HE TALKS AS IF WE'RE THE BEST OF FRIENDS.
BUT HE'S NEVER SEEN MY FACE OR EVEN HEARD MY VOICE.
THOCK THOCK
I SEE THEM JUST A MOMENT TOO LATE.
I GUARANTEE THEY WOULDN'T EVEN NOTICE THAT YOU DON'T TALK!
I LIVE THAT MOMENT OVER AGAIN AND AGAIN IN MY HEAD.
IT WAS THE FIRST AND ONLY TIME I FAILED HIM.

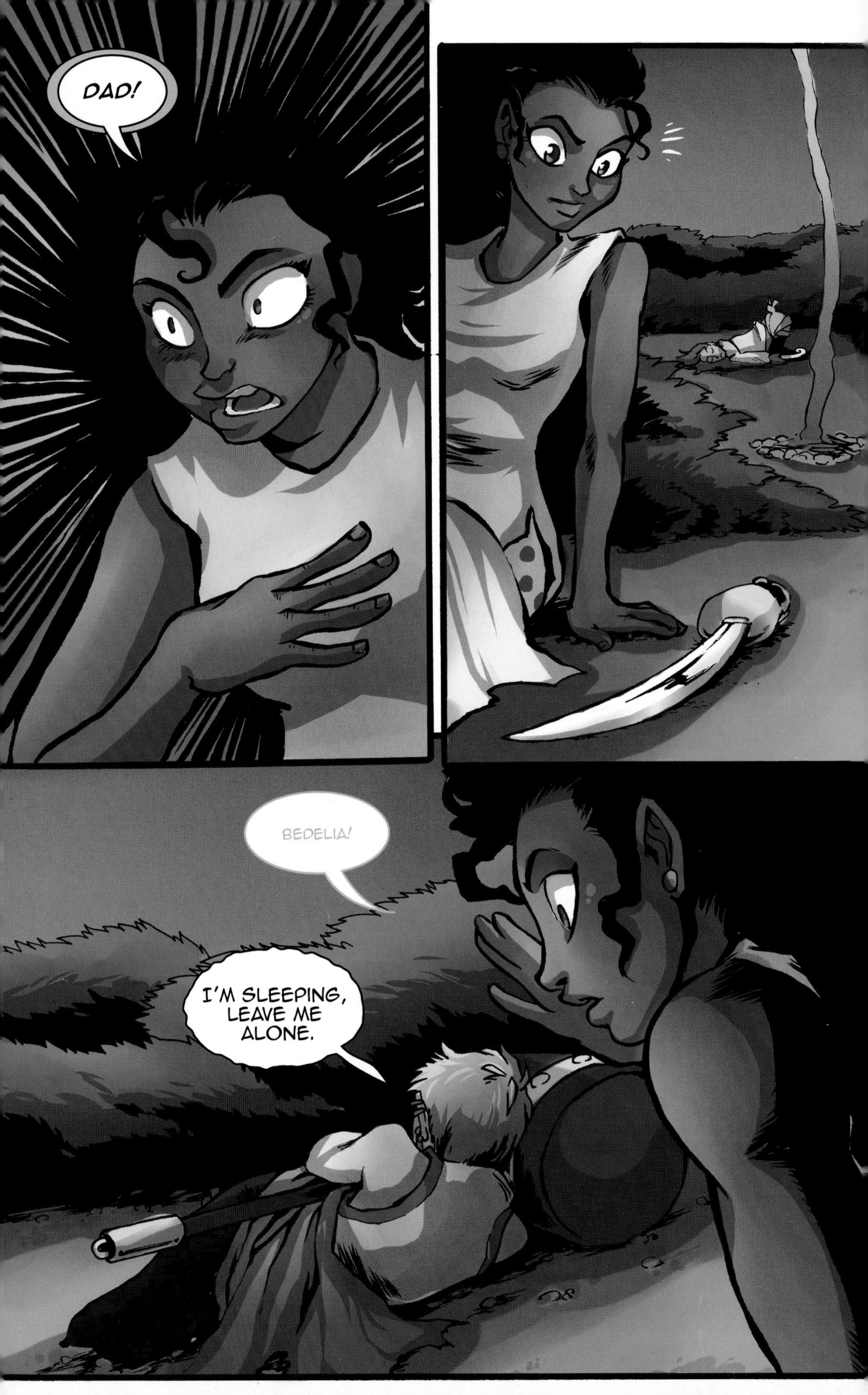
DAD!
BEDELIA!
I'M SLEEPING, LEAVE ME ALONE.

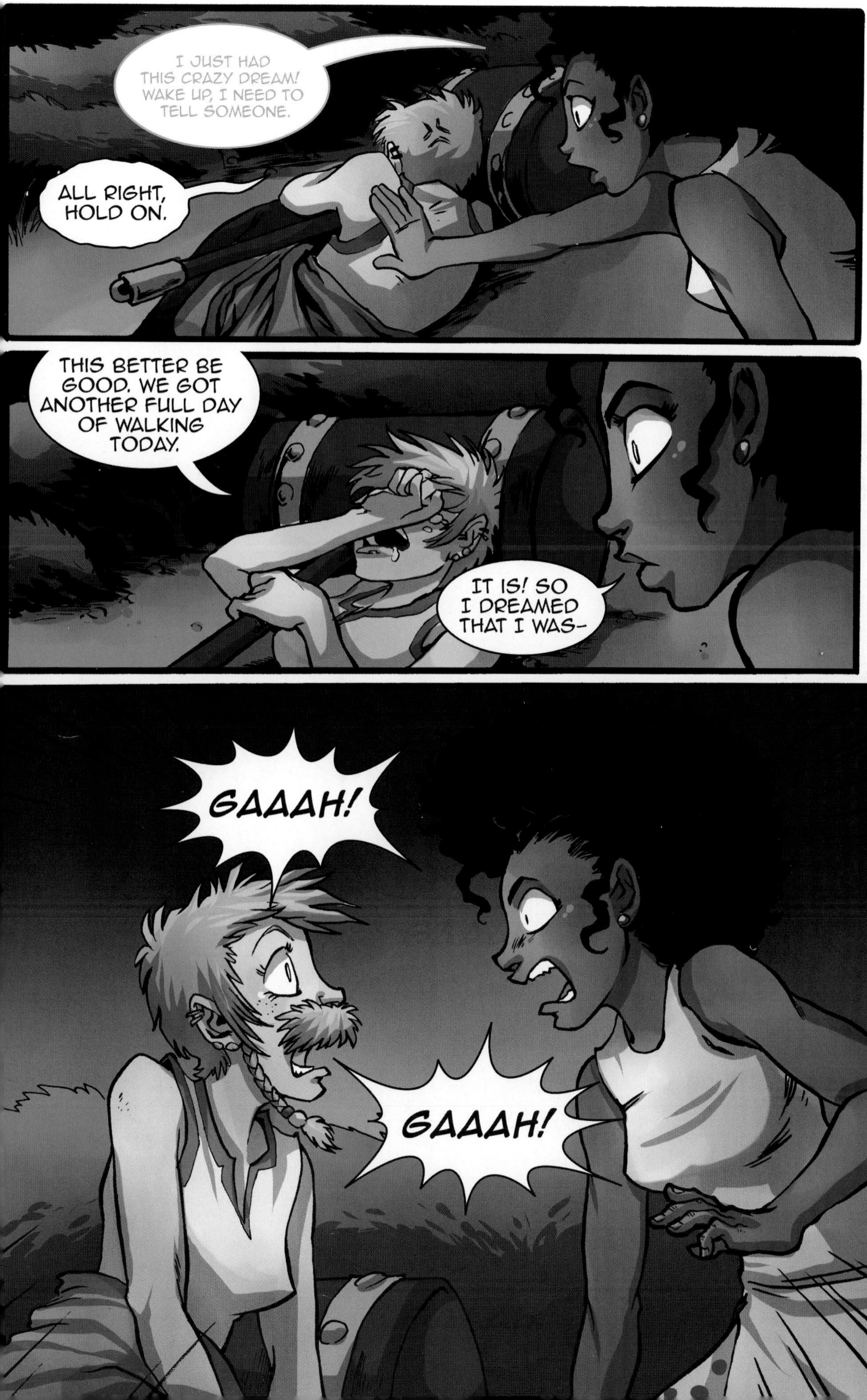
I JUST HAD THIS CRAZY DREAM! WAKE UP, I NEED TO TELL SOMEONE.
ALL RIGHT, HOLD ON.
THIS BETTER BE GOOD. WE GOT ANOTHER FULL DAY OF WALKING TODAY.
IT IS! SO I DREAMED THAT I WAS-
GAAAH!
GAAAH!

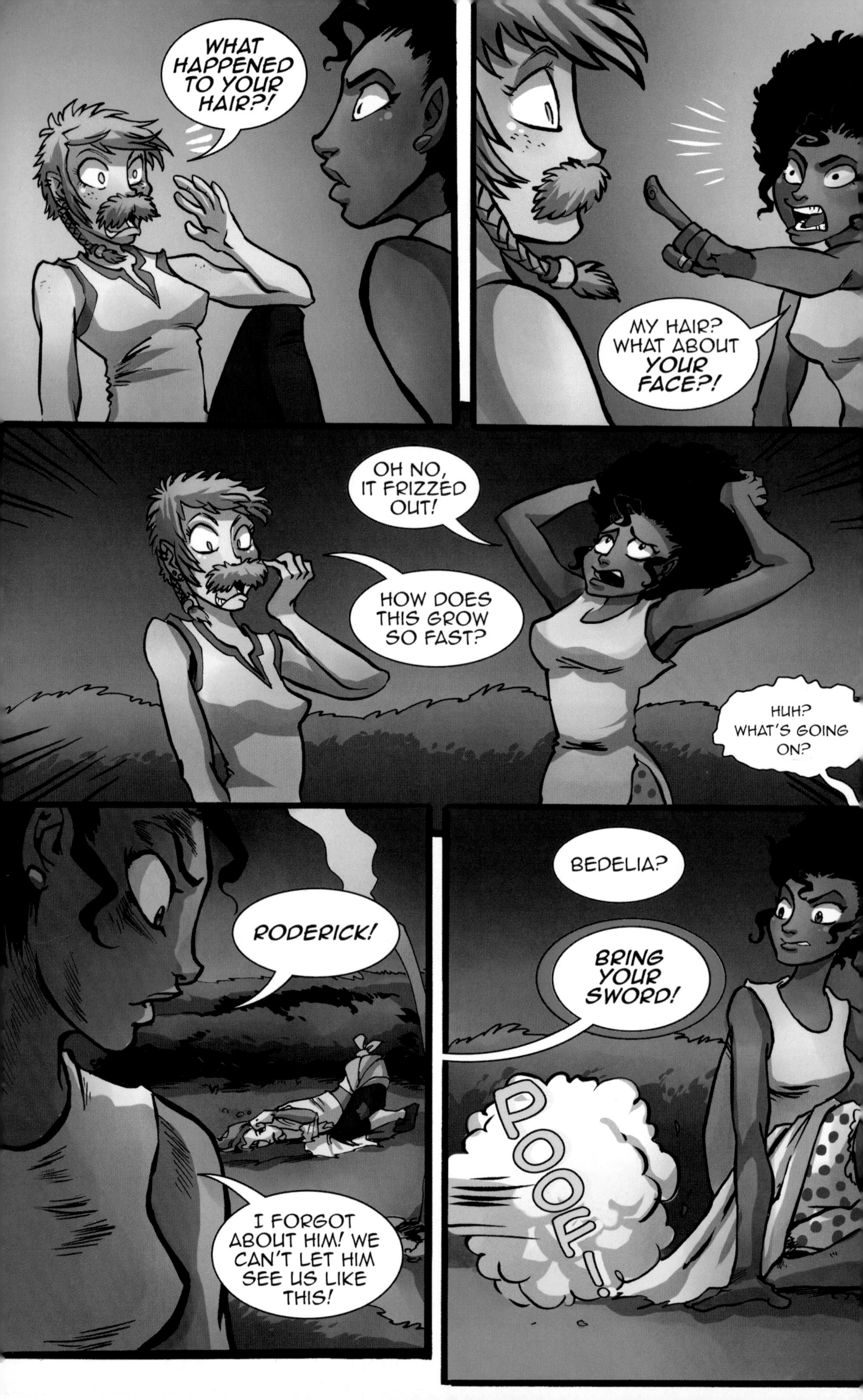
WHAT HAPPENED TO YOUR HAIR?!
MY HAIR? WHAT ABOUT YOUR FACE?!
OH NO, IT FRIZZED OUT!
HOW DOES THIS GROW SO FAST?
HUH? WHAT'S GOING ON?
RODERICK!
I FORGOT ABOUT HIM! WE CAN'T LET HIM SEE US LIKE THIS!
BEDELIA?
BRING YOUR SWORD!
POOF!

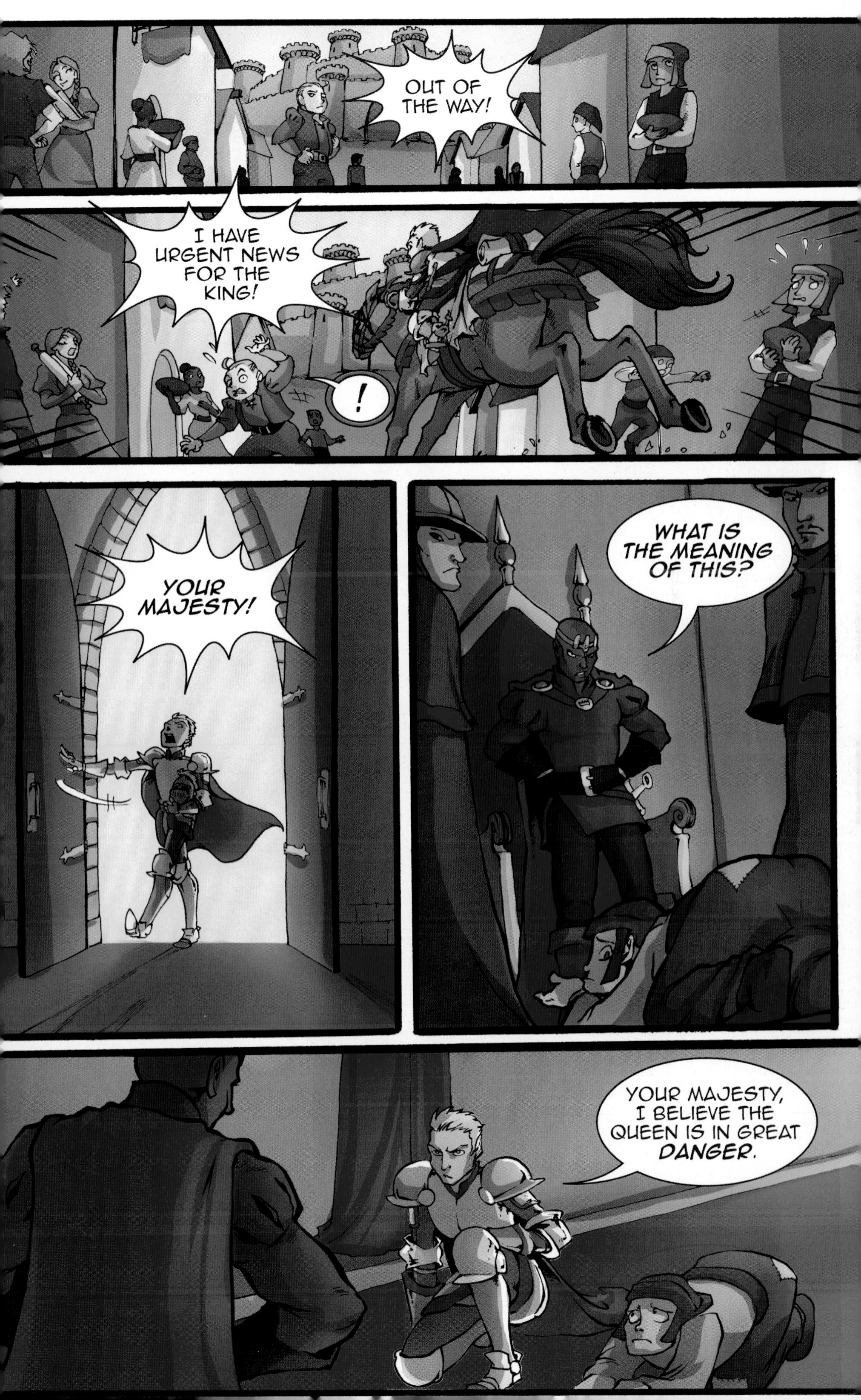
OUT OF THE WAY!
I HAVE URGENT NEWS FOR THE KING!
!
YOUR MAJESTY!
WHAT IS THE MEANING OF THIS?
YOUR MAJESTY, I BELIEVE THE QUEEN IS IN GREAT DANGER.

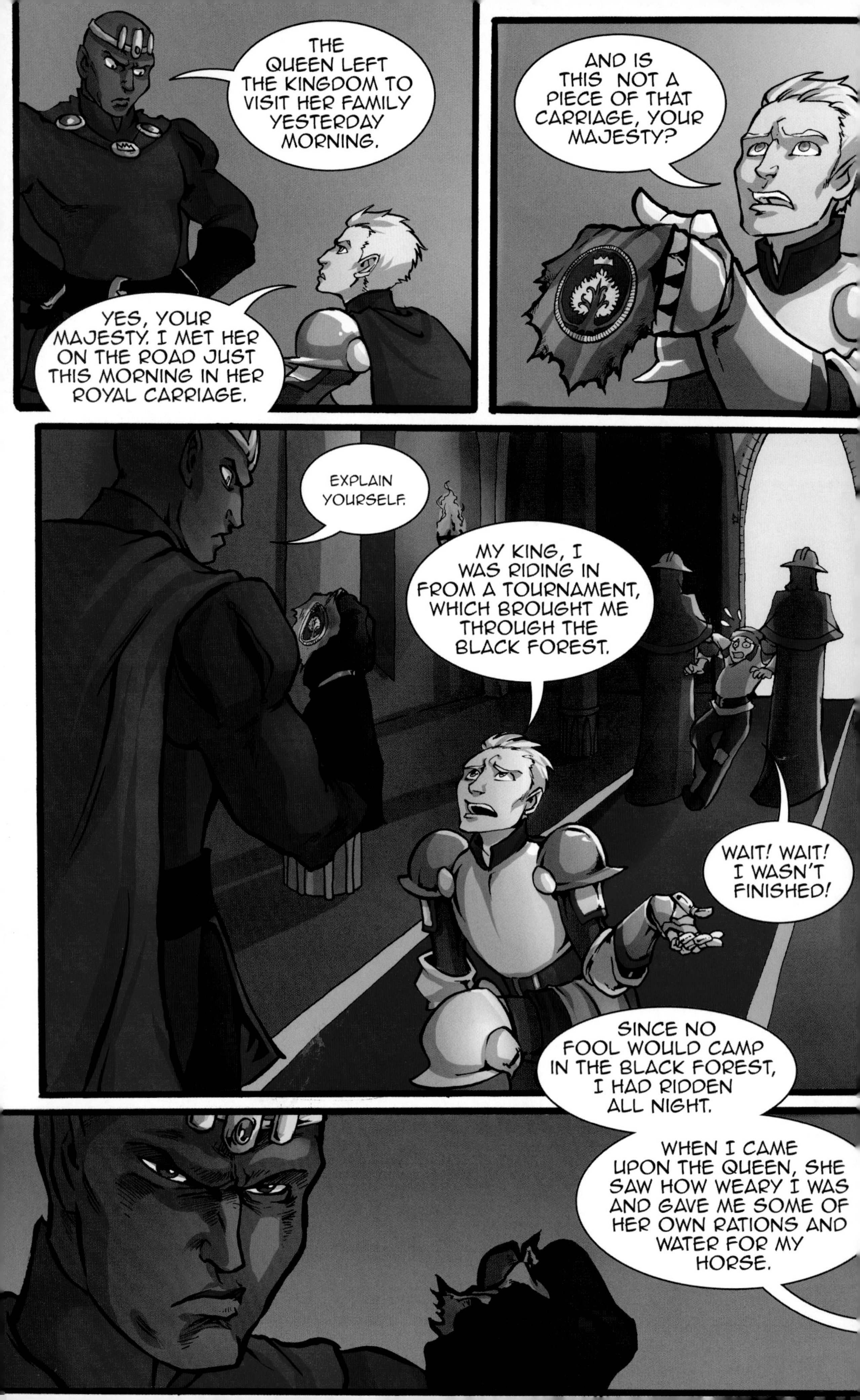
THE QUEEN LEFT THE KINGDOM TO VISIT HER FAMILY YESTERDAY MORNING.
YES, YOUR MAJESTY. I MET HER ON THE ROAD JUST THIS MORNING IN HER ROYAL CARRIAGE.
AND IS THIS NOT A PIECE OF THAT CARRIAGE, YOUR MAJESTY?
EXPLAIN YOURSELF.
MY KING, I WAS RIDING IN FROM A TOURNAMENT, WHICH BROUGHT ME THROUGH THE BLACK FOREST.
WAIT! WAIT! I WASN'T FINISHED!
SINCE NO FOOL WOULD CAMP IN THE BLACK FOREST, I HAD RIDDEN ALL NIGHT.
WHEN I CAME UPON THE QUEEN, SHE SAW HOW WEARY I WAS AND GAVE ME SOME OF HER OWN RATIONS AND WATER FOR MY HORSE.

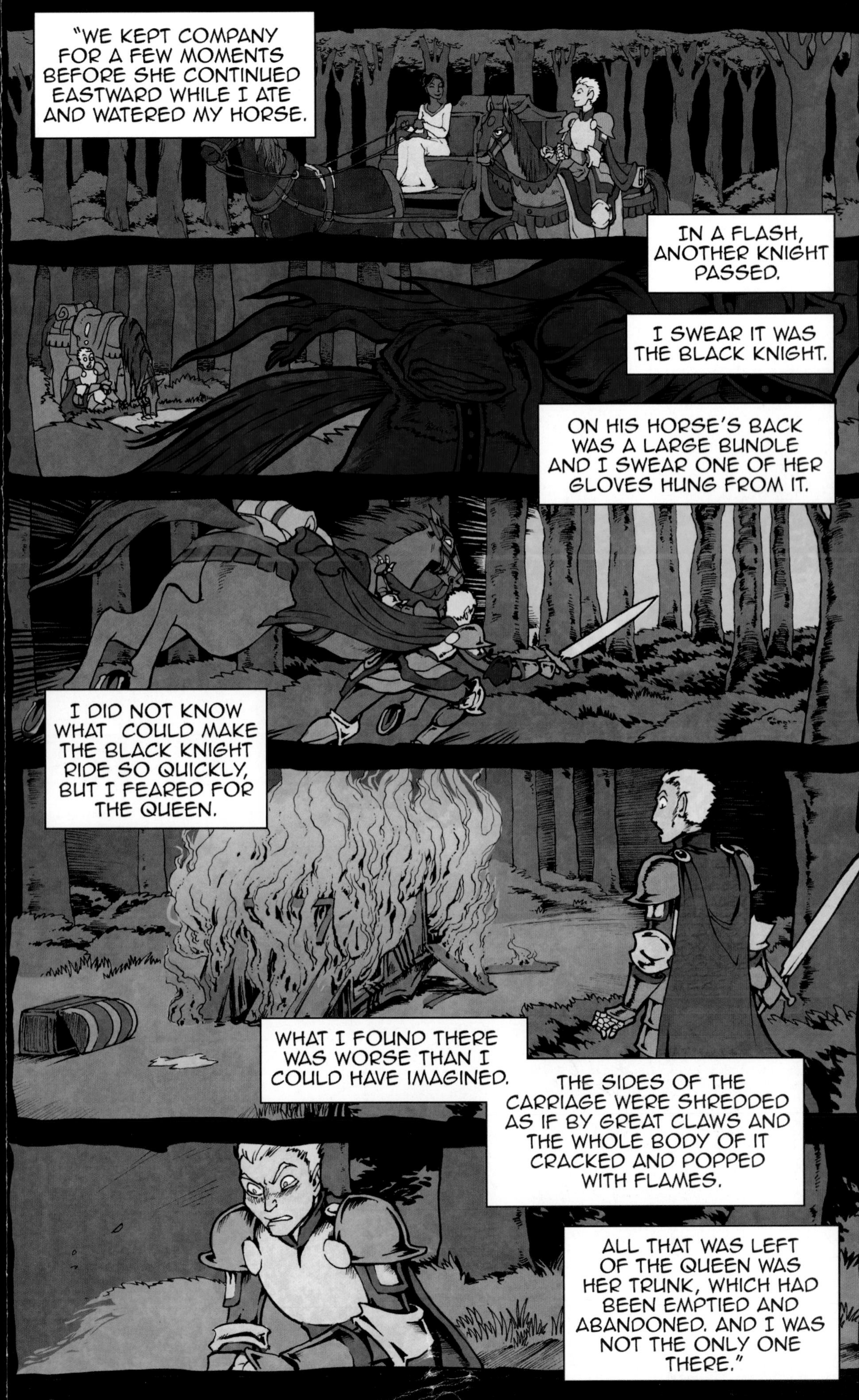
"WE KEPT COMPANY FOR A FEW MOMENTS BEFORE SHE CONTINUED EASTWARD WHILE I ATE AND WATERED MY HORSE.
IN A FLASH, ANOTHER KNIGHT PASSED.
I SWEAR IT WAS THE BLACK KNIGHT.
ON HIS HORSE'S BACK WAS A LARGE BUNDLE AND I SWEAR ONE OF HER GLOVES HUNG FROM IT.
I DID NOT KNOW WHAT COULD MAKE THE BLACK KNIGHT RIDE SO QUICKLY, BUT I FEARED FOR THE QUEEN.
WHAT I FOUND THERE WAS WORSE THAN I COULD HAVE IMAGINED.
THE SIDES OF THE CARRIAGE WERE SHREDDED AS IF BY GREAT CLAWS AND THE WHOLE BODY OF IT CRACKED AND POPPED WITH FLAMES.
ALL THAT WAS LEFT OF THE QUEEN WAS HER TRUNK, WHICH HAD BEEN EMPTIED AND ABANDONED. AND I WAS NOT THE ONLY ONE THERE."

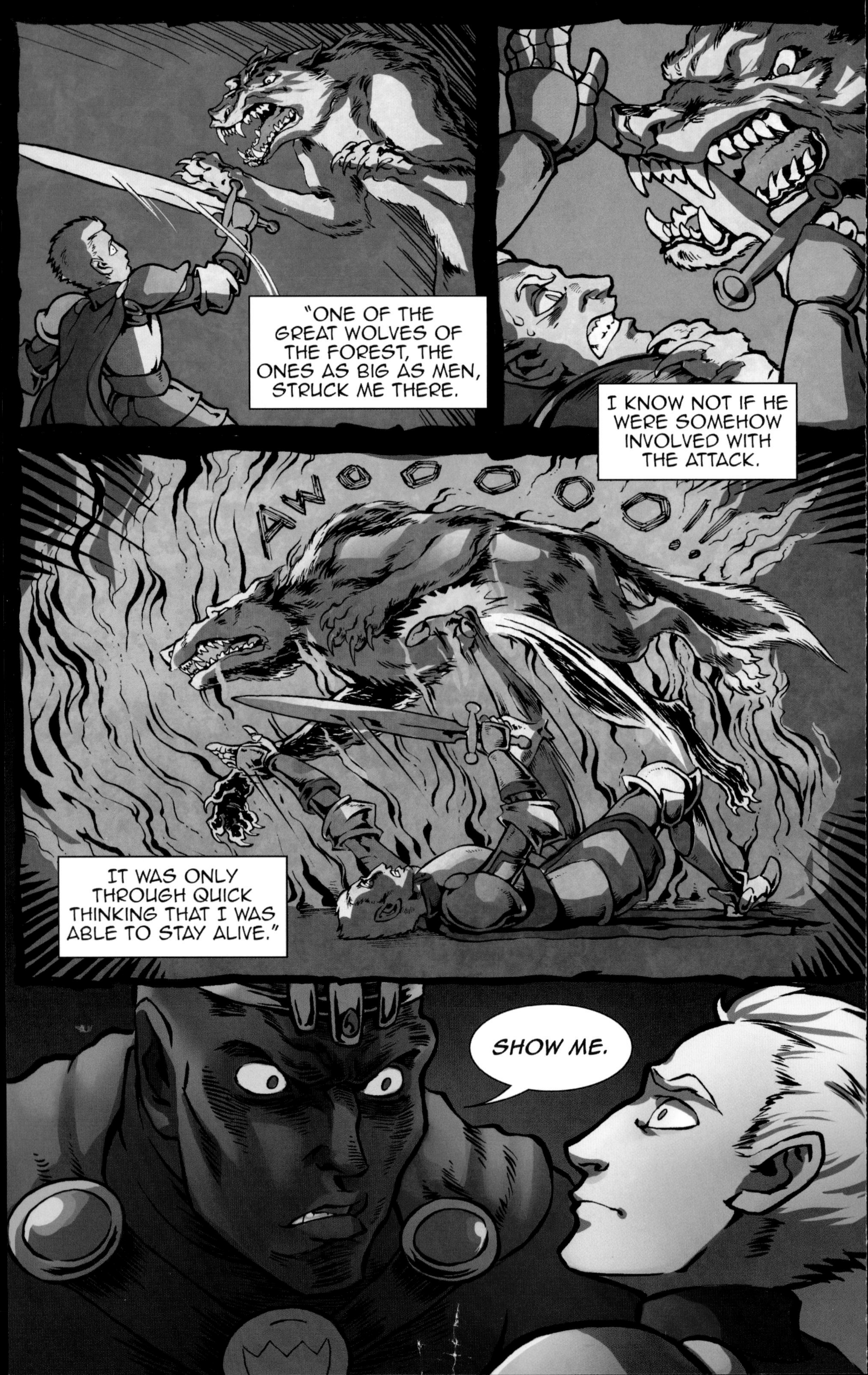
"ONE OF THE GREAT WOLVES OF THE FOREST, THE ONES AS BIG AS MEN, STRUCK ME THERE.
I KNOW NOT IF HE WERE SOMEHOW INVOLVED WITH THE ATTACK.
AWOOOOO!!
IT WAS ONLY THROUGH QUICK THINKING THAT I WAS ABLE TO STAY ALIVE."
SHOW ME.

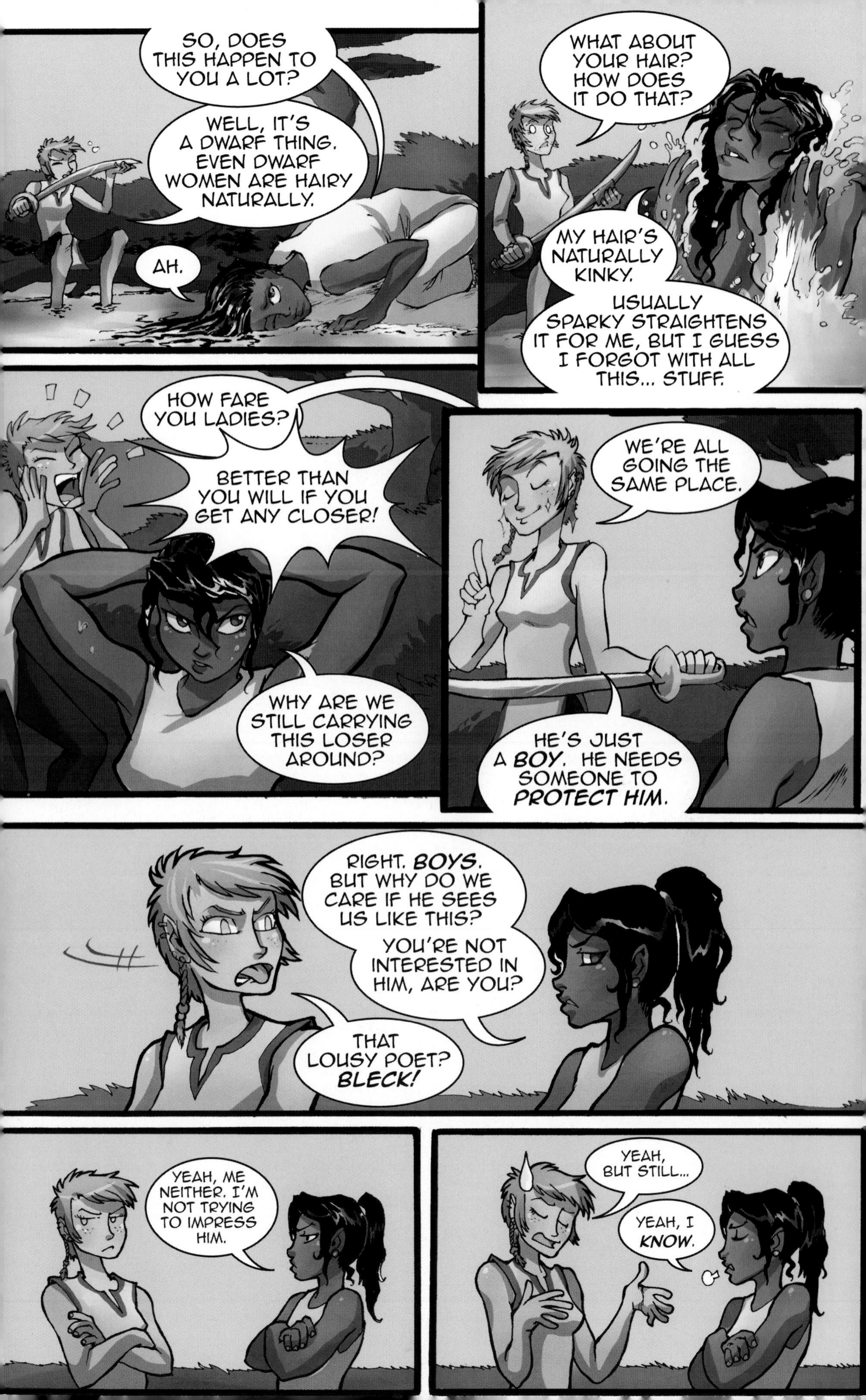
SO, DOES THIS HAPPEN TO YOU A LOT?
WELL, IT'S A DWARF THING. EVEN DWARF WOMEN ARE HAIRY NATURALLY.
AH.
WHAT ABOUT YOUR HAIR? HOW DOES IT DO THAT?
MY HAIR'S NATURALLY KINKY.
USUALLY SPARKY STRAIGHTENS IT FOR ME, BUT I GUESS I FORGOT WITH ALL THIS... STUFF.
HOW FARE YOU LADIES?
BETTER THAN YOU WILL IF YOU GET ANY CLOSER!
WHY ARE WE STILL CARRYING THIS LOSER AROUND?
WE'RE ALL GOING THE SAME PLACE.
HE'S JUST A **BOY**. HE NEEDS SOMEONE TO ***PROTECT HIM***.
RIGHT. ***BOYS***. BUT WHY DO WE CARE IF HE SEES US LIKE THIS?
YOU'RE NOT INTERESTED IN HIM, ARE YOU?
THAT LOUSY POET? ***BLECK!***
YEAH, ME NEITHER. I'M NOT TRYING TO IMPRESS HIM.
YEAH, BUT STILL...
YEAH, I ***KNOW***.

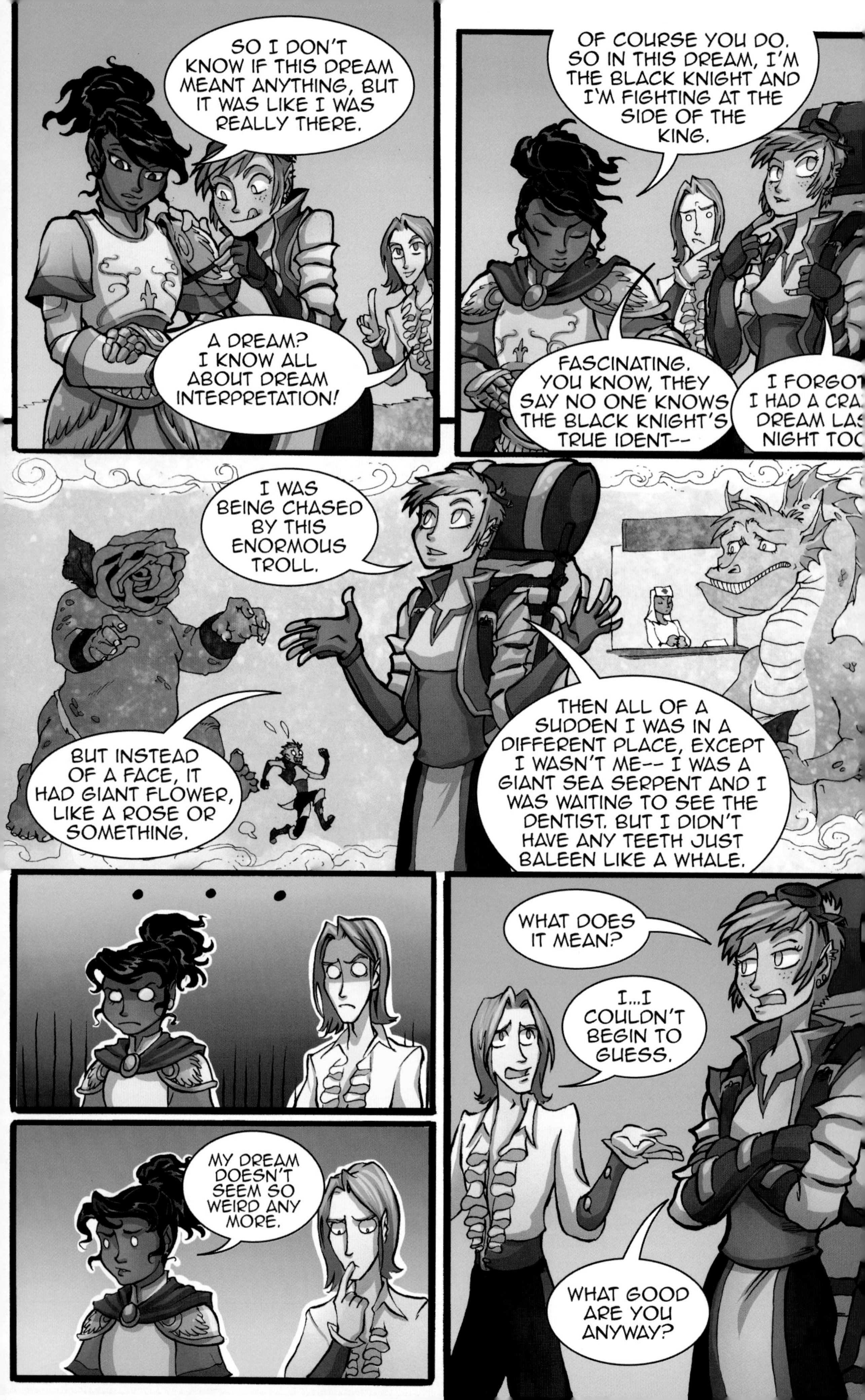
SO I DON'T KNOW IF THIS DREAM MEANT ANYTHING, BUT IT WAS LIKE I WAS REALLY THERE.
A DREAM? I KNOW ALL ABOUT DREAM INTERPRETATION!
OF COURSE YOU DO. SO IN THIS DREAM, I'M THE BLACK KNIGHT AND I'M FIGHTING AT THE SIDE OF THE KING.
FASCINATING. YOU KNOW, THEY SAY NO ONE KNOWS THE BLACK KNIGHT'S TRUE IDENT--
I FORGOT I HAD A CRA DREAM LAS NIGHT TOO
I WAS BEING CHASED BY THIS ENORMOUS TROLL.
BUT INSTEAD OF A FACE, IT HAD GIANT FLOWER, LIKE A ROSE OR SOMETHING.
THEN ALL OF A SUDDEN I WAS IN A DIFFERENT PLACE, EXCEPT I WASN'T ME-- I WAS A GIANT SEA SERPENT AND I WAS WAITING TO SEE THE DENTIST. BUT I DIDN'T HAVE ANY TEETH JUST BALEEN LIKE A WHALE.
• • •
MY DREAM DOESN'T SEEM SO WEIRD ANY MORE.
WHAT DOES IT MEAN?
I...I COULDN'T BEGIN TO GUESS.
WHAT GOOD ARE YOU ANYWAY?

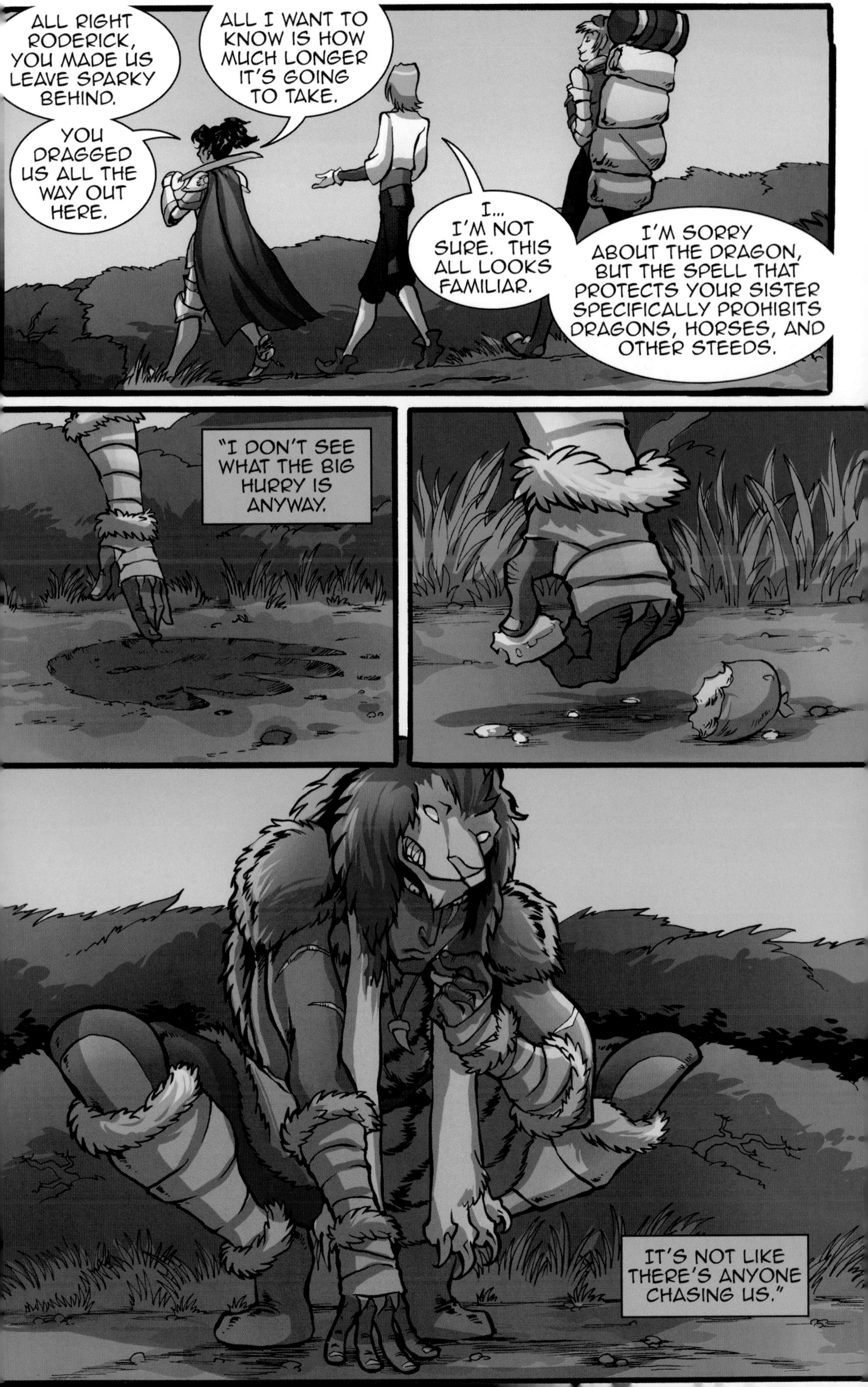
ALL RIGHT RODERICK, YOU MADE US LEAVE SPARKY BEHIND.
YOU DRAGGED US ALL THE WAY OUT HERE.
ALL I WANT TO KNOW IS HOW MUCH LONGER IT'S GOING TO TAKE.
I... I'M NOT SURE. THIS ALL LOOKS FAMILIAR.
I'M SORRY ABOUT THE DRAGON, BUT THE SPELL THAT PROTECTS YOUR SISTER SPECIFICALLY PROHIBITS DRAGONS, HORSES, AND OTHER STEEDS.
"I DON'T SEE WHAT THE BIG HURRY IS ANYWAY.
IT'S NOT LIKE THERE'S ANYONE CHASING US."

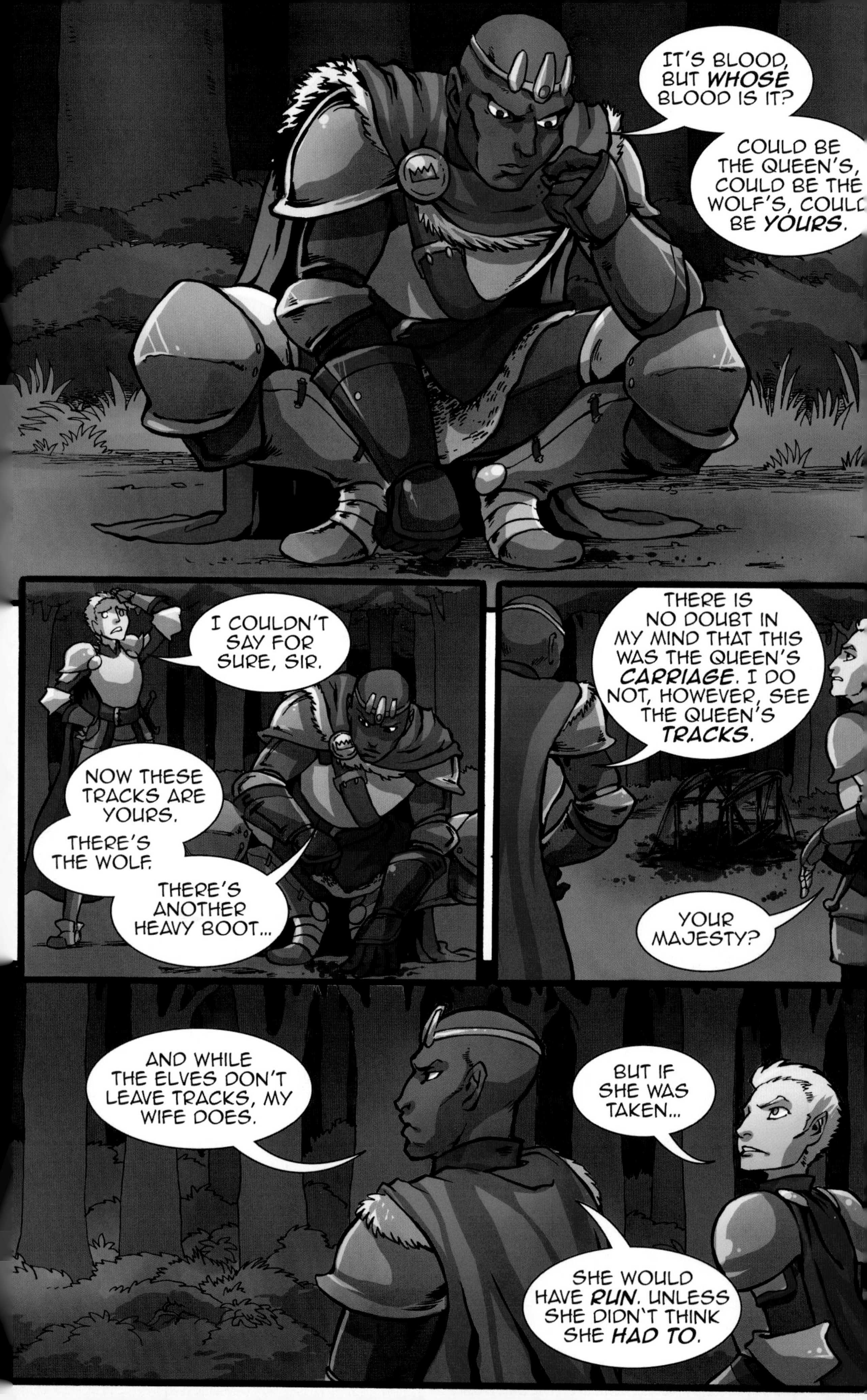
IT'S BLOOD, BUT WHOSE BLOOD IS IT?
COULD BE THE QUEEN'S, COULD BE THE WOLF'S, COULD BE YOURS.
I COULDN'T SAY FOR SURE, SIR.
NOW THESE TRACKS ARE YOURS.
THERE'S THE WOLF.
THERE'S ANOTHER HEAVY BOOT...
THERE IS NO DOUBT IN MY MIND THAT THIS WAS THE QUEEN'S CARRIAGE. I DO NOT, HOWEVER, SEE THE QUEEN'S TRACKS.
YOUR MAJESTY?
AND WHILE THE ELVES DON'T LEAVE TRACKS, MY WIFE DOES.
BUT IF SHE WAS TAKEN...
SHE WOULD HAVE RUN. UNLESS SHE DIDN'T THINK SHE HAD TO.

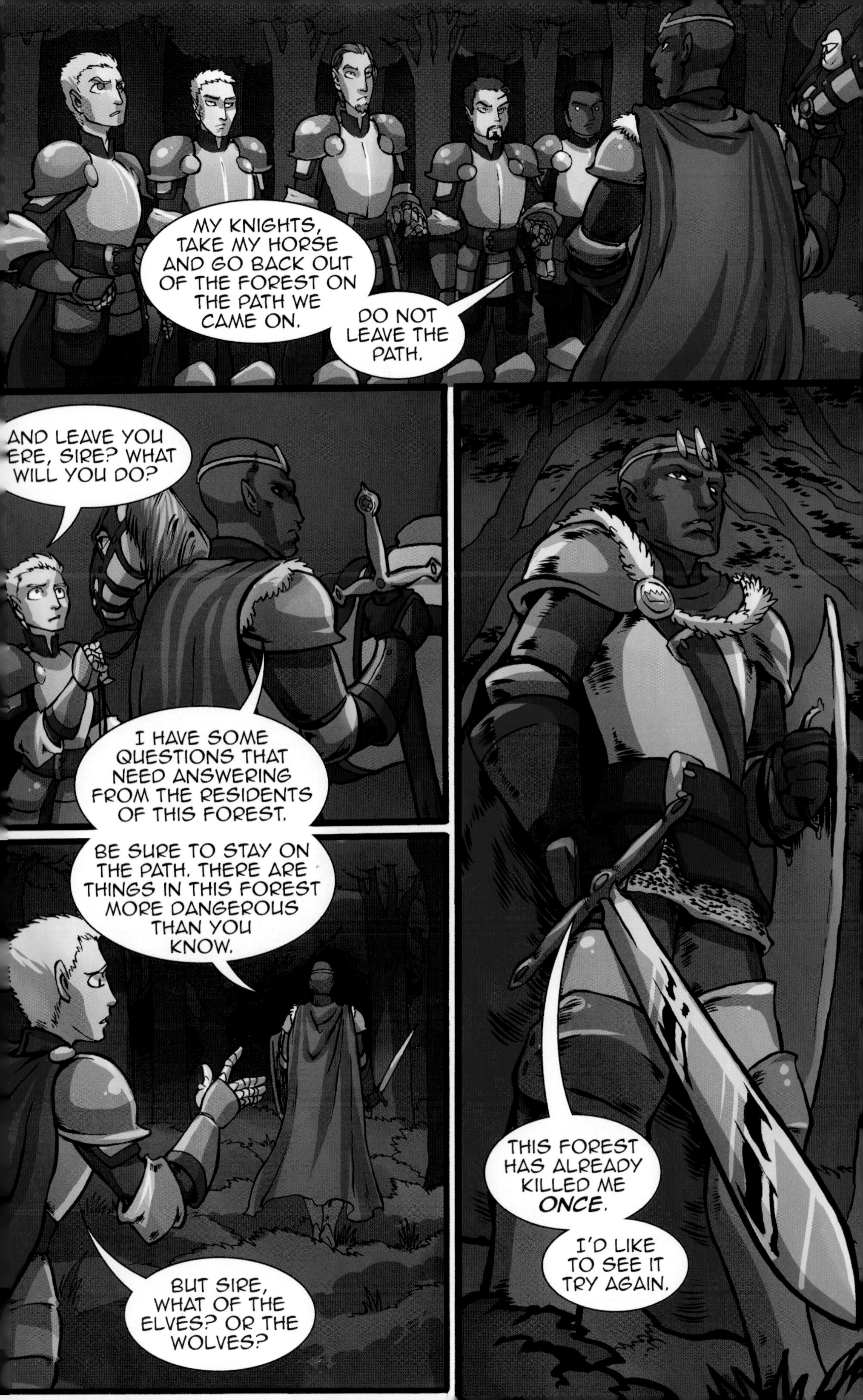
MY KNIGHTS, TAKE MY HORSE AND GO BACK OUT OF THE FOREST ON THE PATH WE CAME ON.
DO NOT LEAVE THE PATH.
AND LEAVE YOU ERE, SIRE? WHAT WILL YOU DO?
I HAVE SOME QUESTIONS THAT NEED ANSWERING FROM THE RESIDENTS OF THIS FOREST.
BE SURE TO STAY ON THE PATH. THERE ARE THINGS IN THIS FOREST MORE DANGEROUS THAN YOU KNOW.
BUT SIRE, WHAT OF THE ELVES? OR THE WOLVES?
THIS FOREST HAS ALREADY KILLED ME *ONCE*.
I'D LIKE TO SEE IT TRY AGAIN.

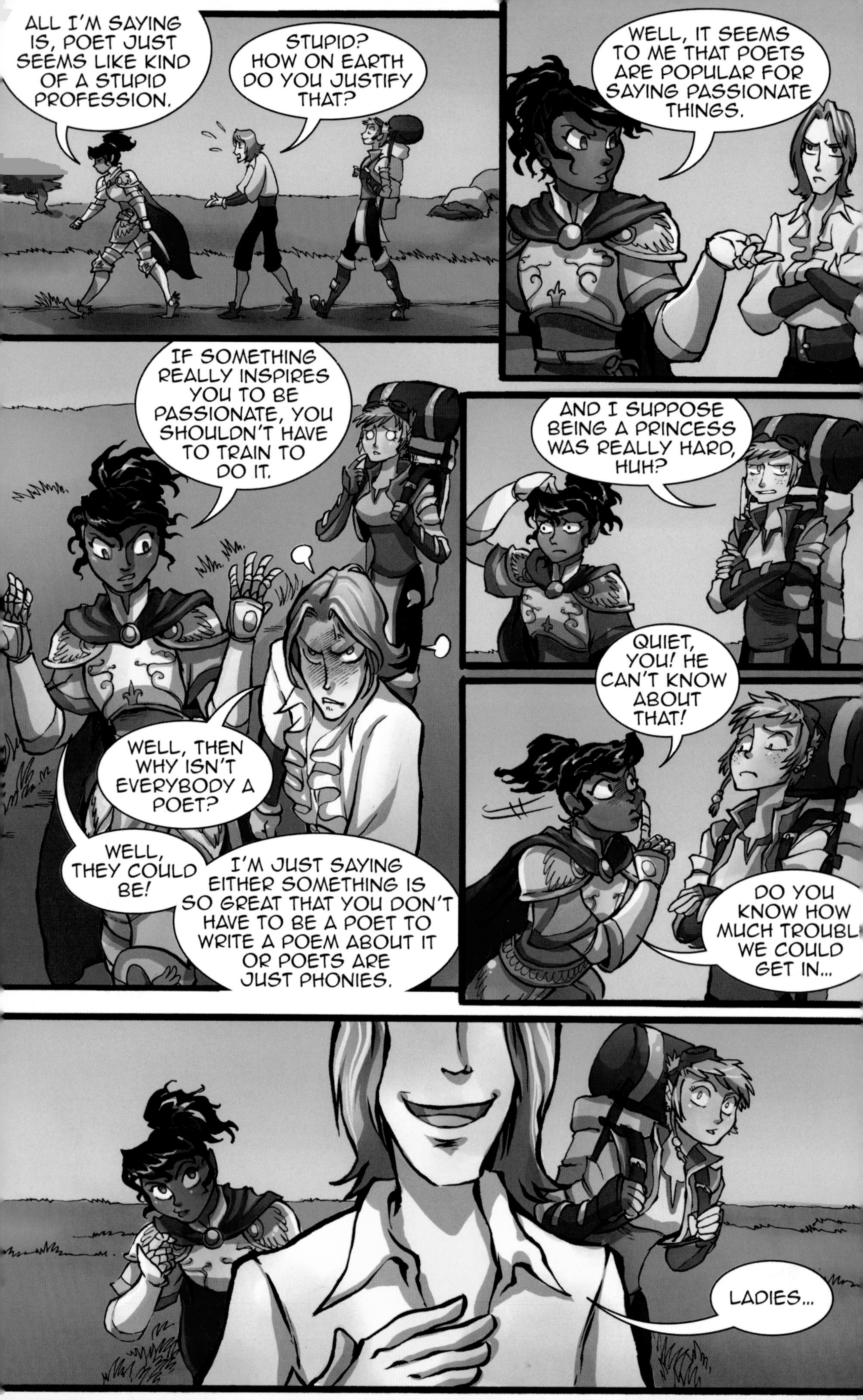
ALL I'M SAYING IS, POET JUST SEEMS LIKE KIND OF A STUPID PROFESSION.
STUPID? HOW ON EARTH DO YOU JUSTIFY THAT?
WELL, IT SEEMS TO ME THAT POETS ARE POPULAR FOR SAYING PASSIONATE THINGS.
IF SOMETHING REALLY INSPIRES YOU TO BE PASSIONATE, YOU SHOULDN'T HAVE TO TRAIN TO DO IT.
WELL, THEN WHY ISN'T EVERYBODY A POET?
WELL, THEY COULD BE!
I'M JUST SAYING EITHER SOMETHING IS SO GREAT THAT YOU DON'T HAVE TO BE A POET TO WRITE A POEM ABOUT IT OR POETS ARE JUST PHONIES.
AND I SUPPOSE BEING A PRINCESS WAS REALLY HARD, HUH?
QUIET, YOU! HE CAN'T KNOW ABOUT THAT!
DO YOU KNOW HOW MUCH TROUBL WE COULD GET IN...
LADIES...

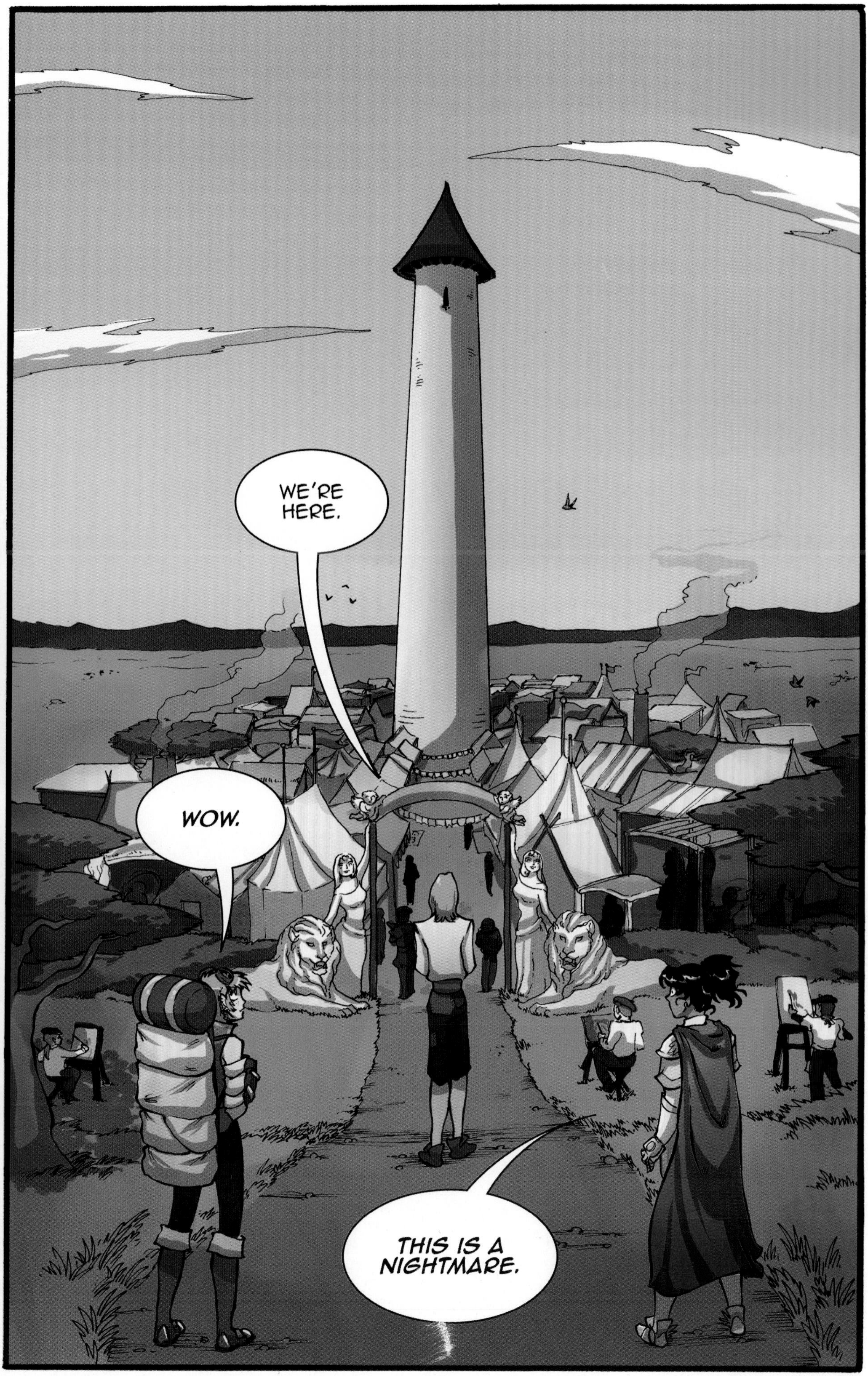
WE'RE HERE.
WOW.
THIS IS A NIGHTMARE.

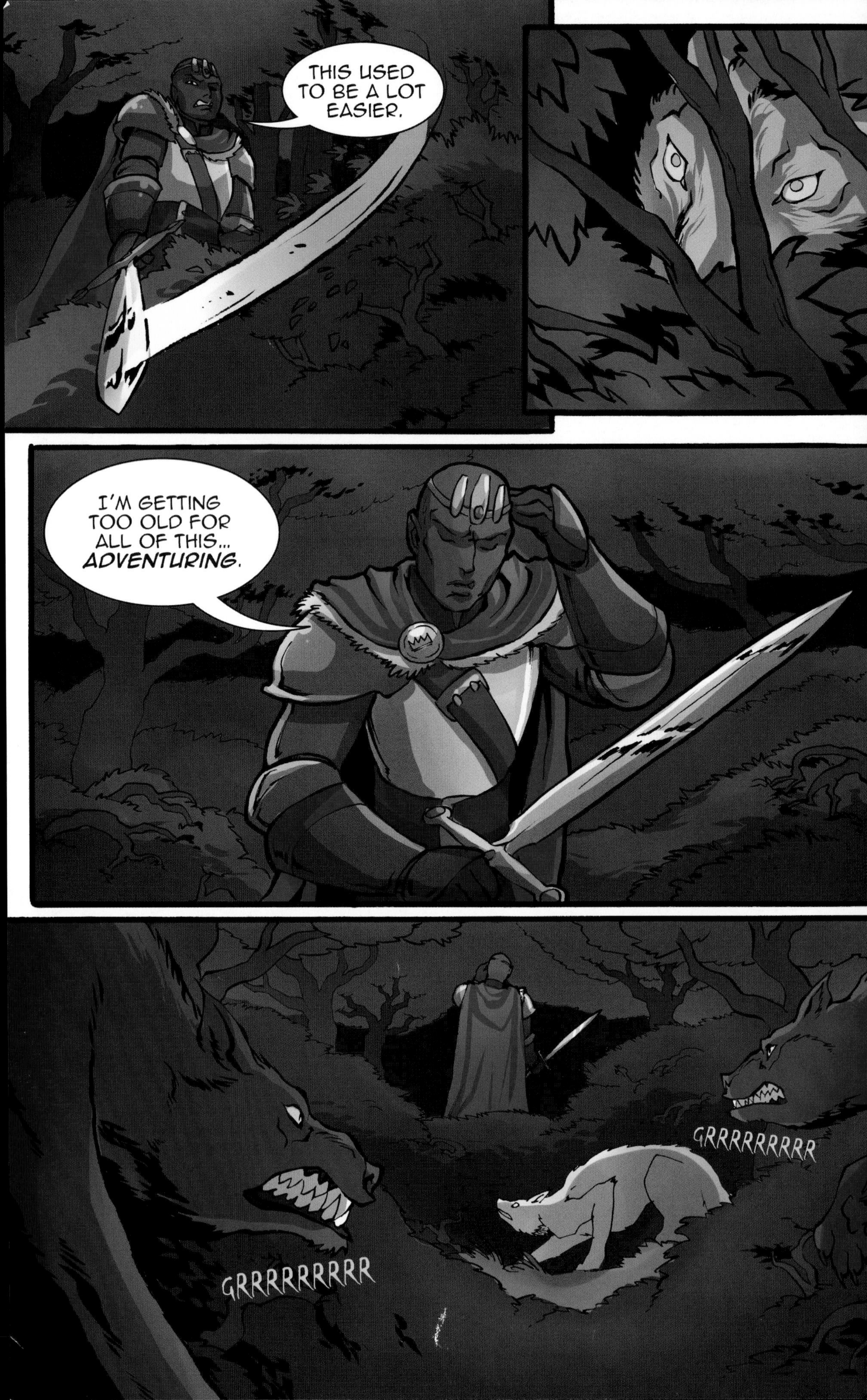
THIS USED TO BE A LOT EASIER.
I'M GETTING TOO OLD FOR ALL OF THIS... ADVENTURING.
GRRRRRRRRR
GRRRRRRRRR

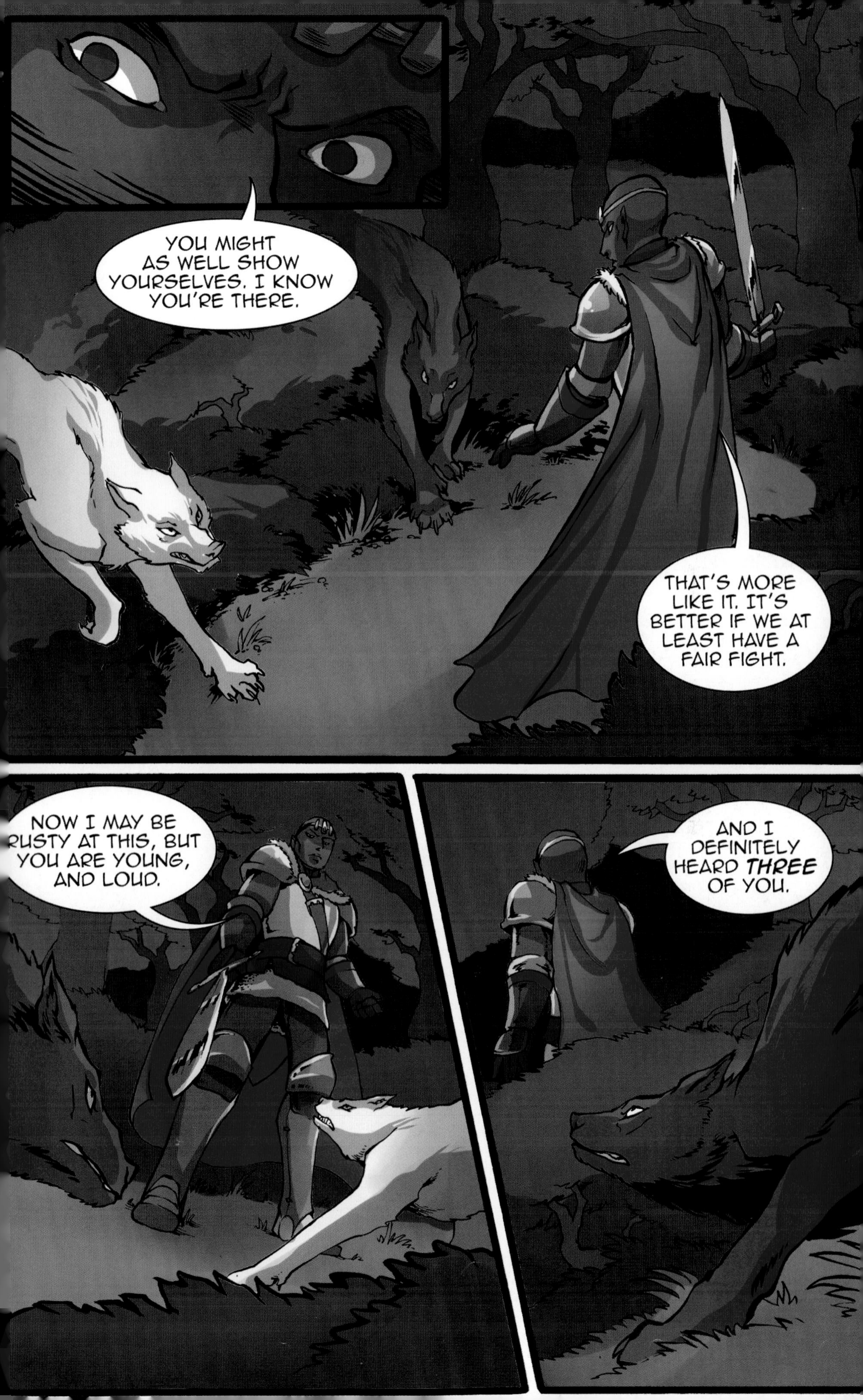
YOU MIGHT AS WELL SHOW YOURSELVES. I KNOW YOU'RE THERE.
THAT'S MORE LIKE IT. IT'S BETTER IF WE AT LEAST HAVE A FAIR FIGHT.
NOW I MAY BE RUSTY AT THIS, BUT YOU ARE YOUNG, AND LOUD.
AND I DEFINITELY HEARD *THREE* OF YOU.

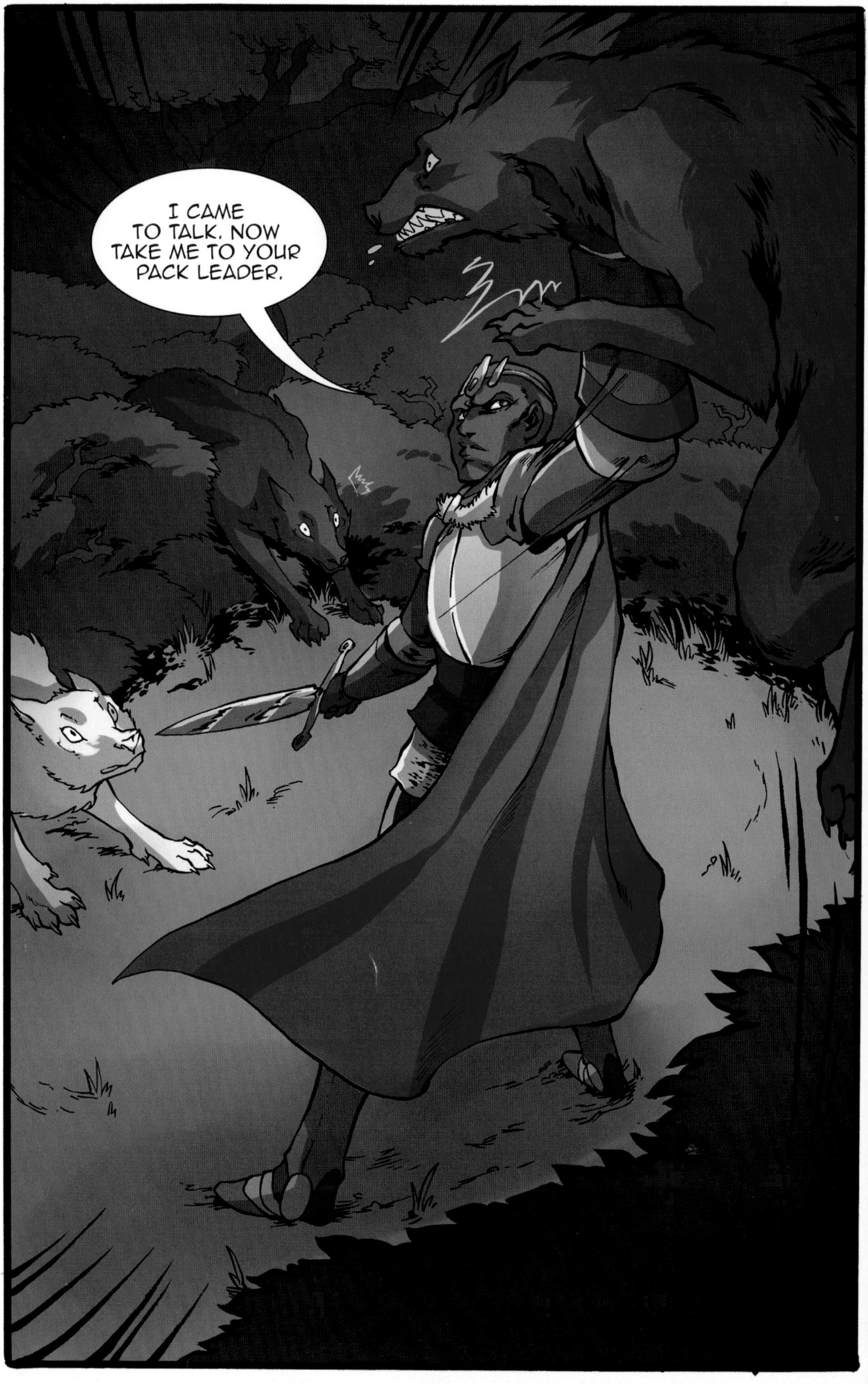
I CAME TO TALK. NOW TAKE ME TO YOUR PACK LEADER.

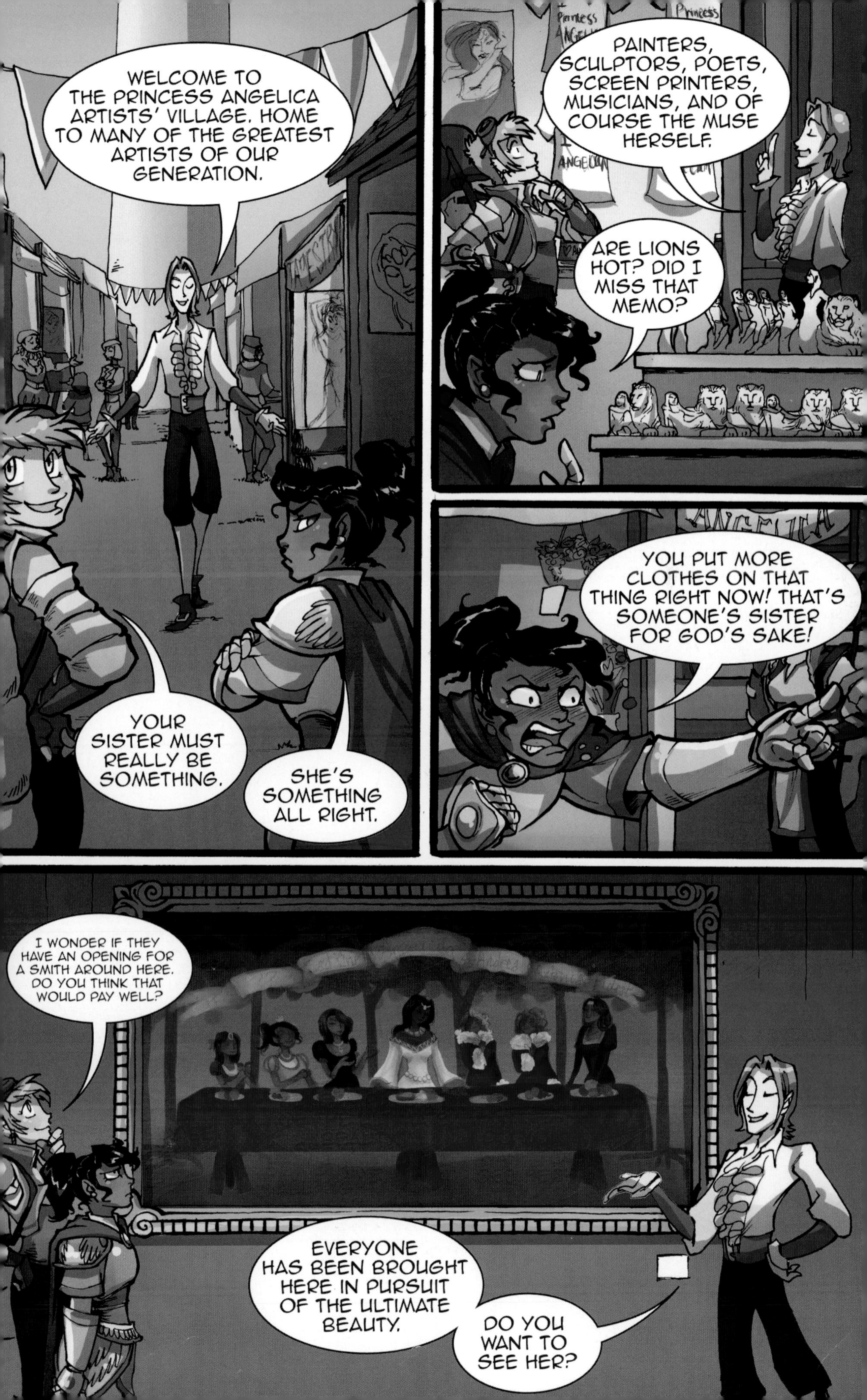
WELCOME TO THE PRINCESS ANGELICA ARTISTS' VILLAGE. HOME TO MANY OF THE GREATEST ARTISTS OF OUR GENERATION.
YOUR SISTER MUST REALLY BE SOMETHING.
SHE'S SOMETHING ALL RIGHT.
PAINTERS, SCULPTORS, POETS, SCREEN PRINTERS, MUSICIANS, AND OF COURSE THE MUSE HERSELF.
ARE LIONS HOT? DID I MISS THAT MEMO?
YOU PUT MORE CLOTHES ON THAT THING RIGHT NOW! THAT'S SOMEONE'S SISTER FOR GOD'S SAKE!
I WONDER IF THEY HAVE AN OPENING FOR A SMITH AROUND HERE. DO YOU THINK THAT WOULD PAY WELL?
EVERYONE HAS BEEN BROUGHT HERE IN PURSUIT OF THE ULTIMATE BEAUTY.
DO YOU WANT TO SEE HER?

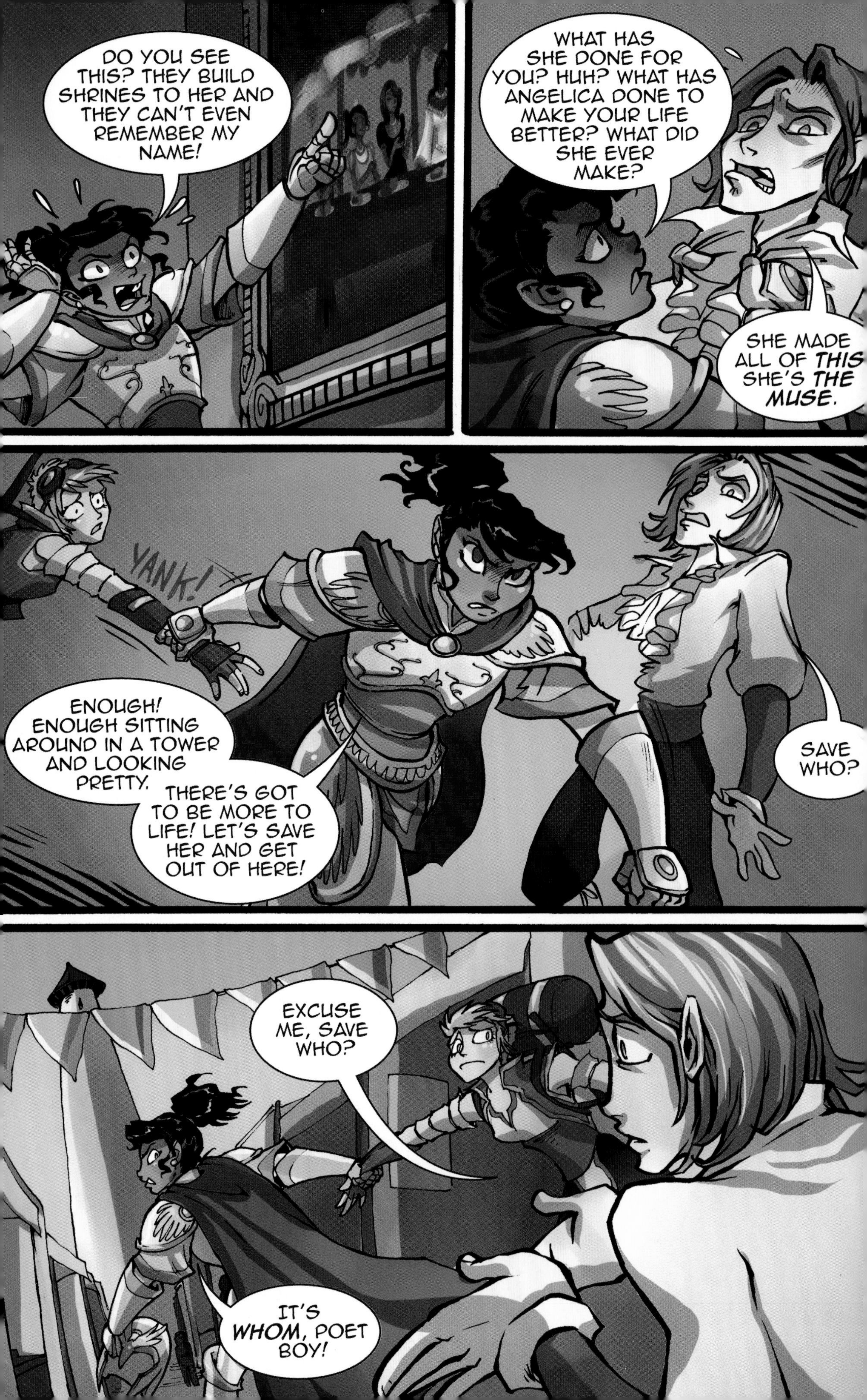
DO YOU SEE THIS? THEY BUILD SHRINES TO HER AND THEY CAN'T EVEN REMEMBER MY NAME!
WHAT HAS SHE DONE FOR YOU? HUH? WHAT HAS ANGELICA DONE TO MAKE YOUR LIFE BETTER? WHAT DID SHE EVER MAKE?
SHE MADE ALL OF *THIS*. SHE'S *THE MUSE*.
YANK!
ENOUGH! ENOUGH SITTING AROUND IN A TOWER AND LOOKING PRETTY.
THERE'S GOT TO BE MORE TO LIFE! LET'S SAVE HER AND GET OUT OF HERE!
SAVE WHO?
EXCUSE ME, SAVE WHO?
IT'S *WHOM*, POET BOY!

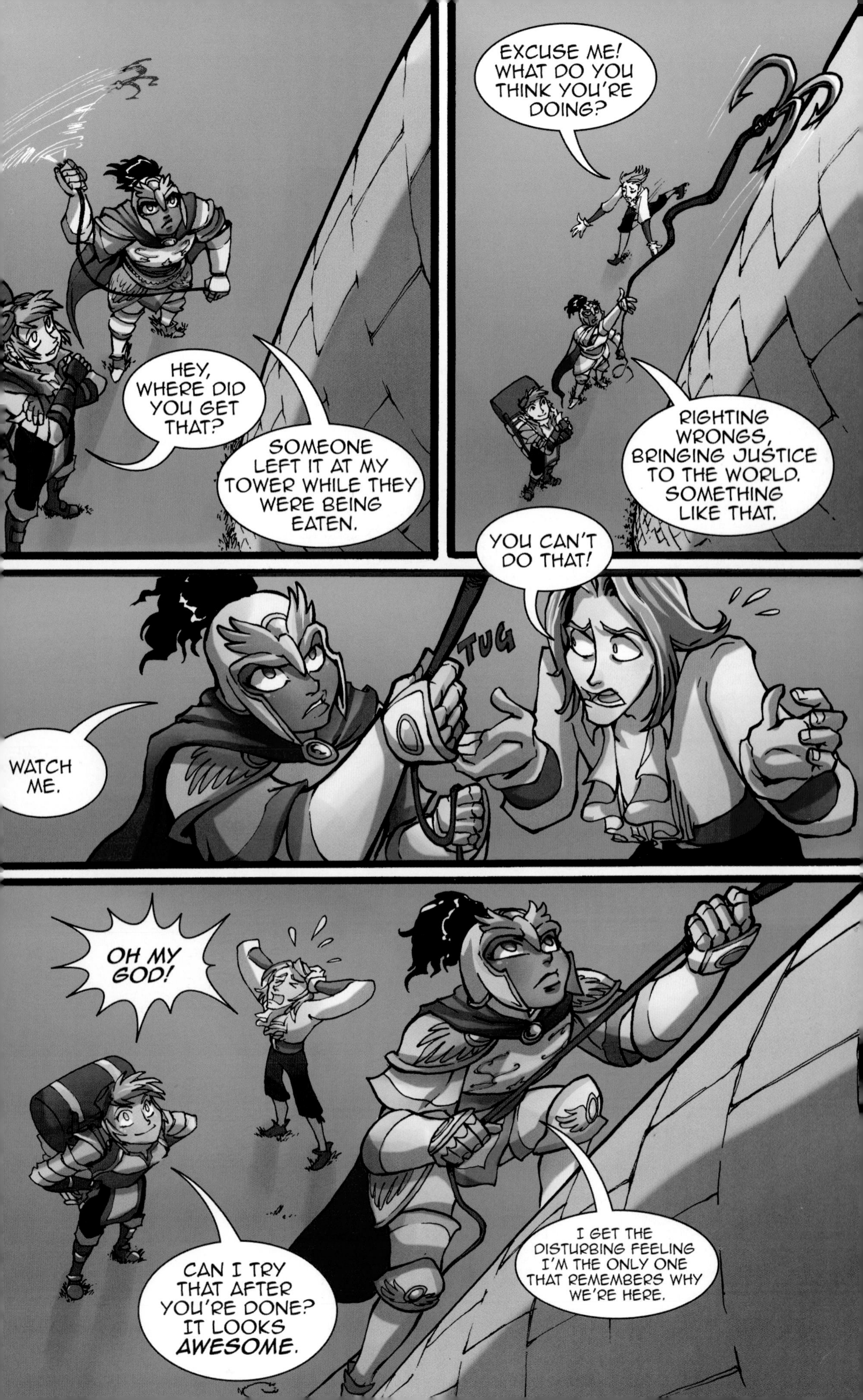
HEY, WHERE DID YOU GET THAT?
SOMEONE LEFT IT AT MY TOWER WHILE THEY WERE BEING EATEN.
EXCUSE ME! WHAT DO YOU THINK YOU'RE DOING?
RIGHTING WRONGS, BRINGING JUSTICE TO THE WORLD. SOMETHING LIKE THAT.
YOU CAN'T DO THAT!
TUG
WATCH ME.
OH MY GOD!
CAN I TRY THAT AFTER YOU'RE DONE? IT LOOKS AWESOME.
I GET THE DISTURBING FEELING I'M THE ONLY ONE THAT REMEMBERS WHY WE'RE HERE.

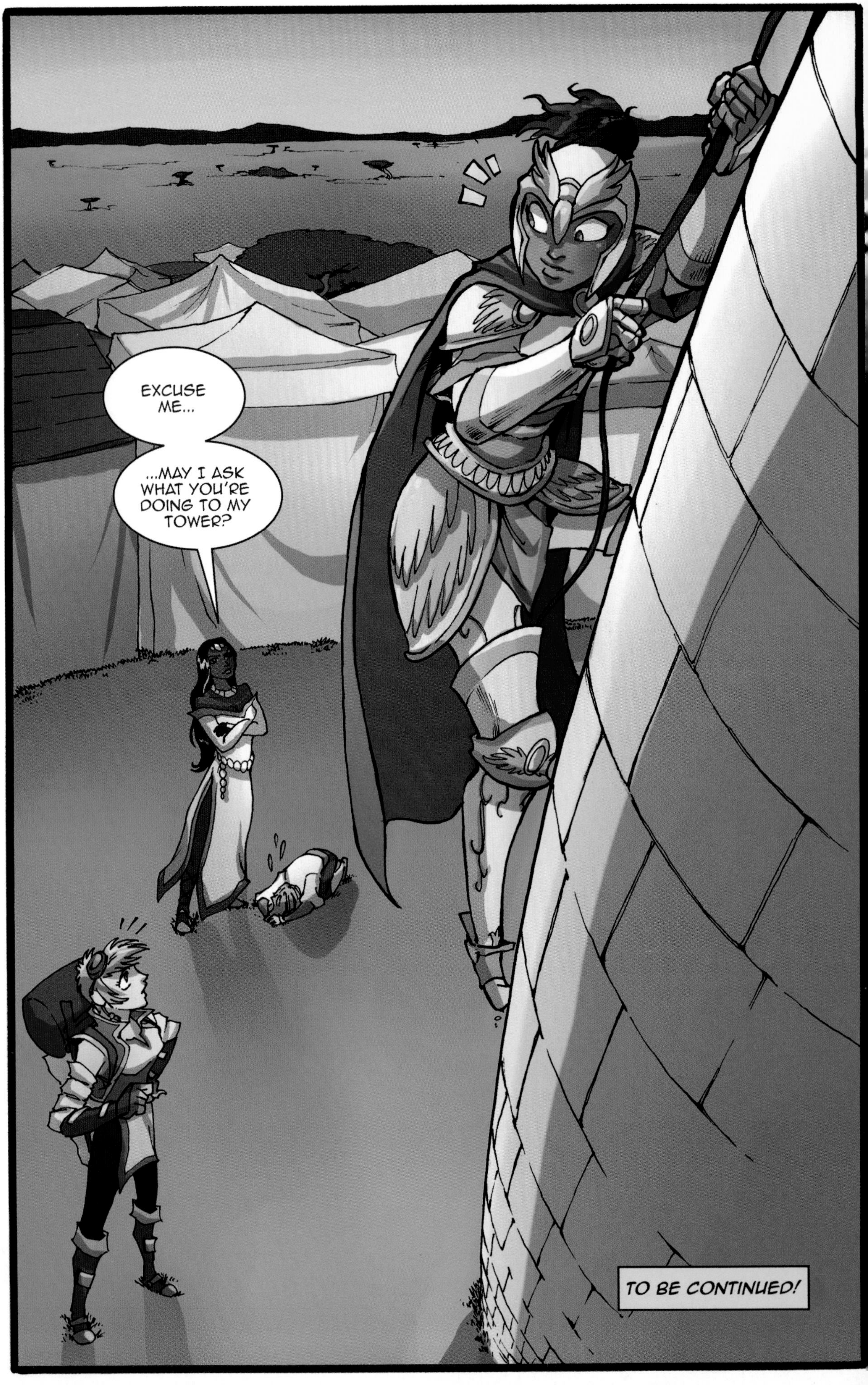
EXCUSE ME...
...MAY I ASK WHAT YOU'RE DOING TO MY TOWER?
TO BE CONTINUED!

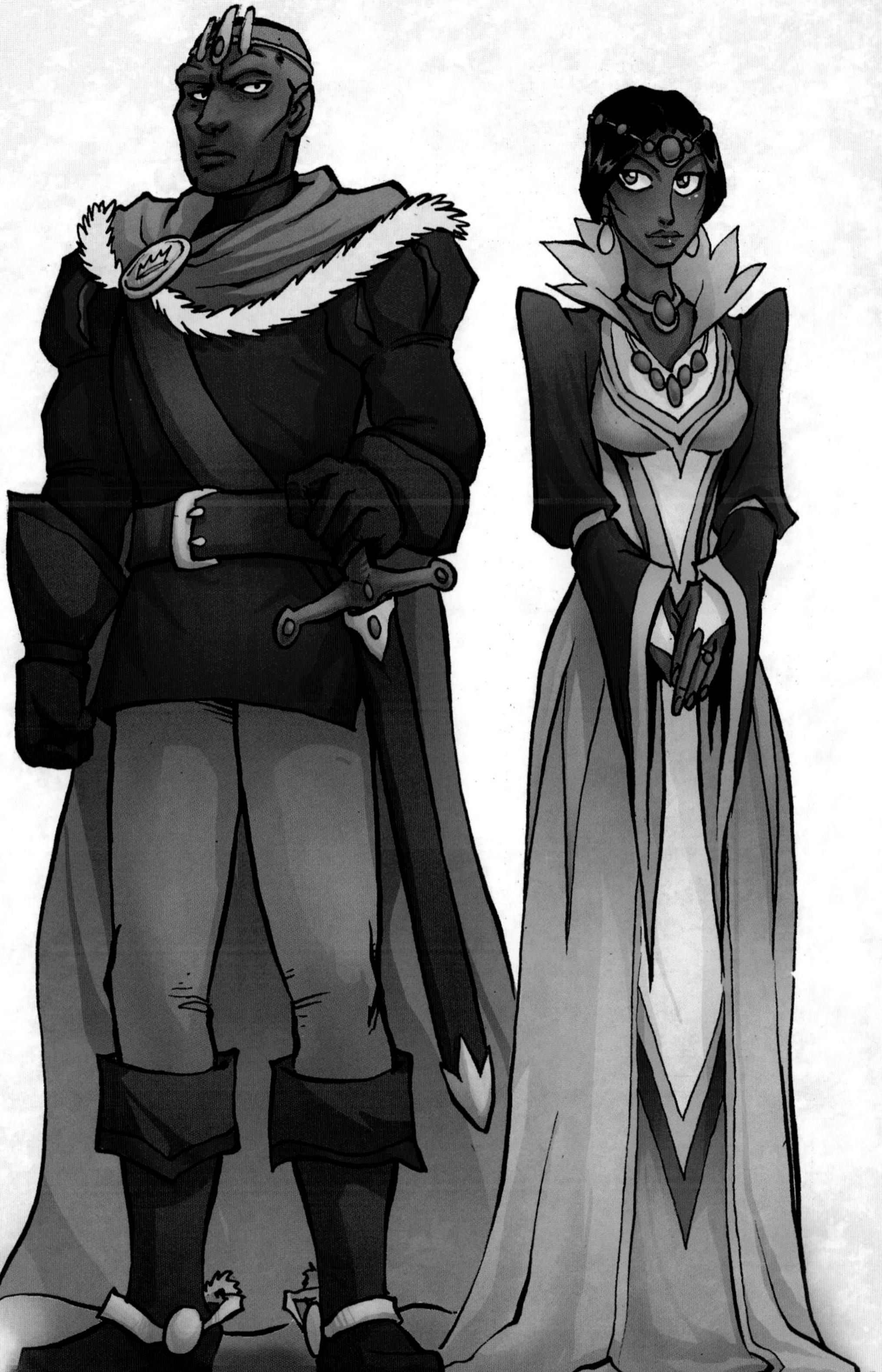

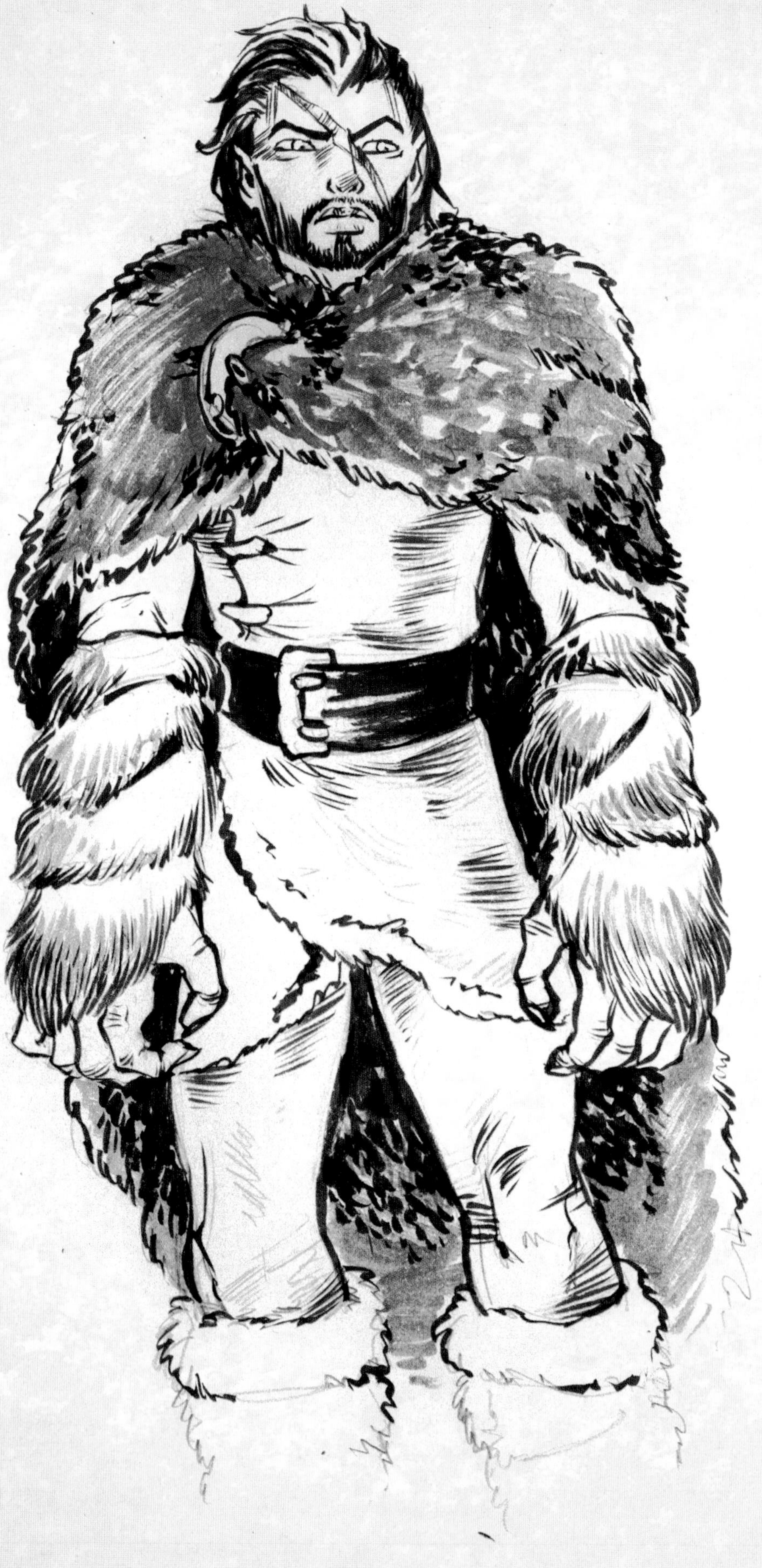

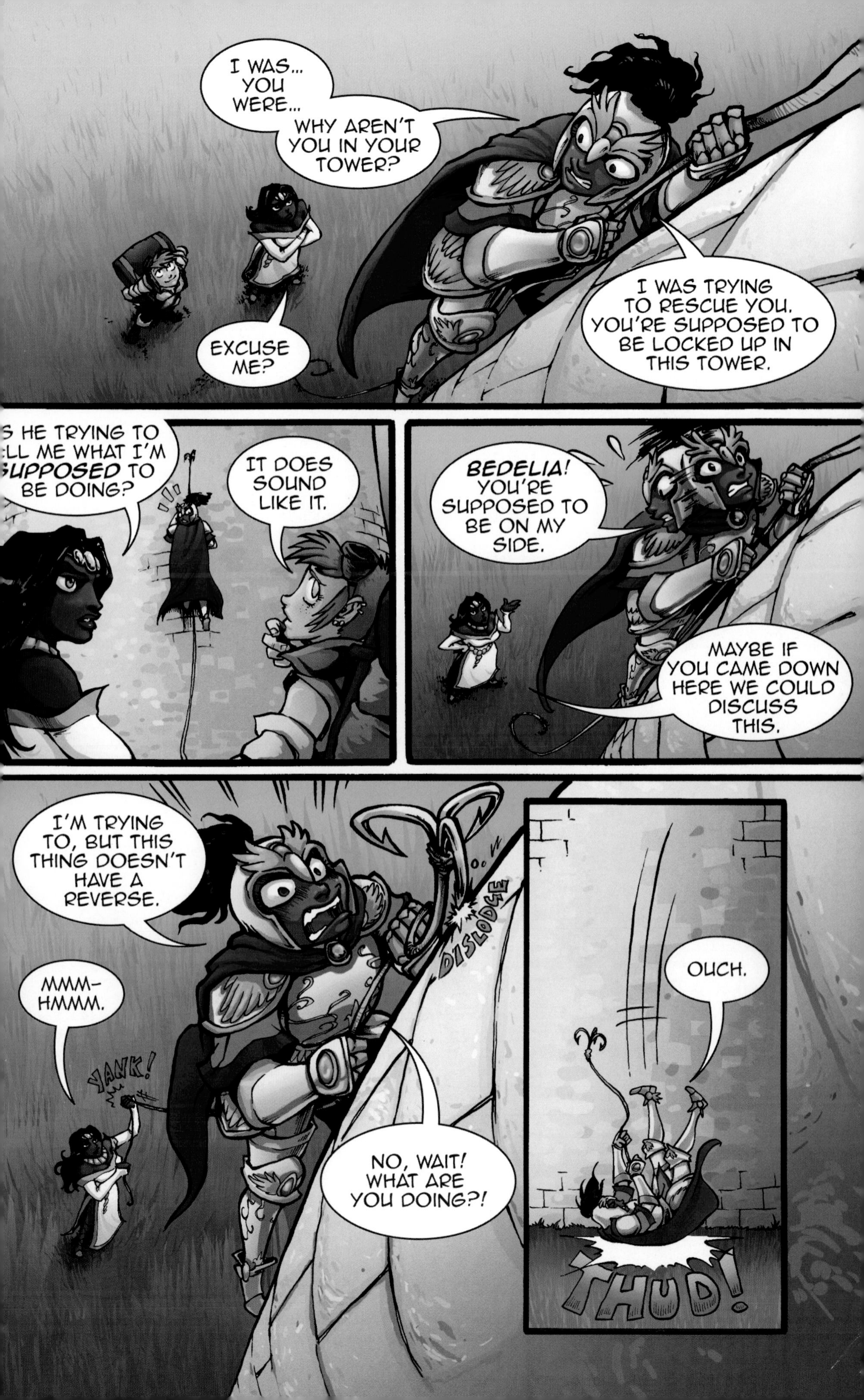
I WAS... YOU WERE... WHY AREN'T YOU IN YOUR TOWER?
EXCUSE ME?
I WAS TRYING TO RESCUE YOU. YOU'RE SUPPOSED TO BE LOCKED UP IN THIS TOWER.
S HE TRYING TO LL ME WHAT I'M SUPPOSED TO BE DOING?
IT DOES SOUND LIKE IT.
BEDELIA! YOU'RE SUPPOSED TO BE ON MY SIDE.
MAYBE IF YOU CAME DOWN HERE WE COULD DISCUSS THIS.
I'M TRYING TO, BUT THIS THING DOESN'T HAVE A REVERSE.
DISLODGE
MMM-HMMM.
YANK!
NO, WAIT! WHAT ARE YOU DOING?!
OUCH.
THUD!

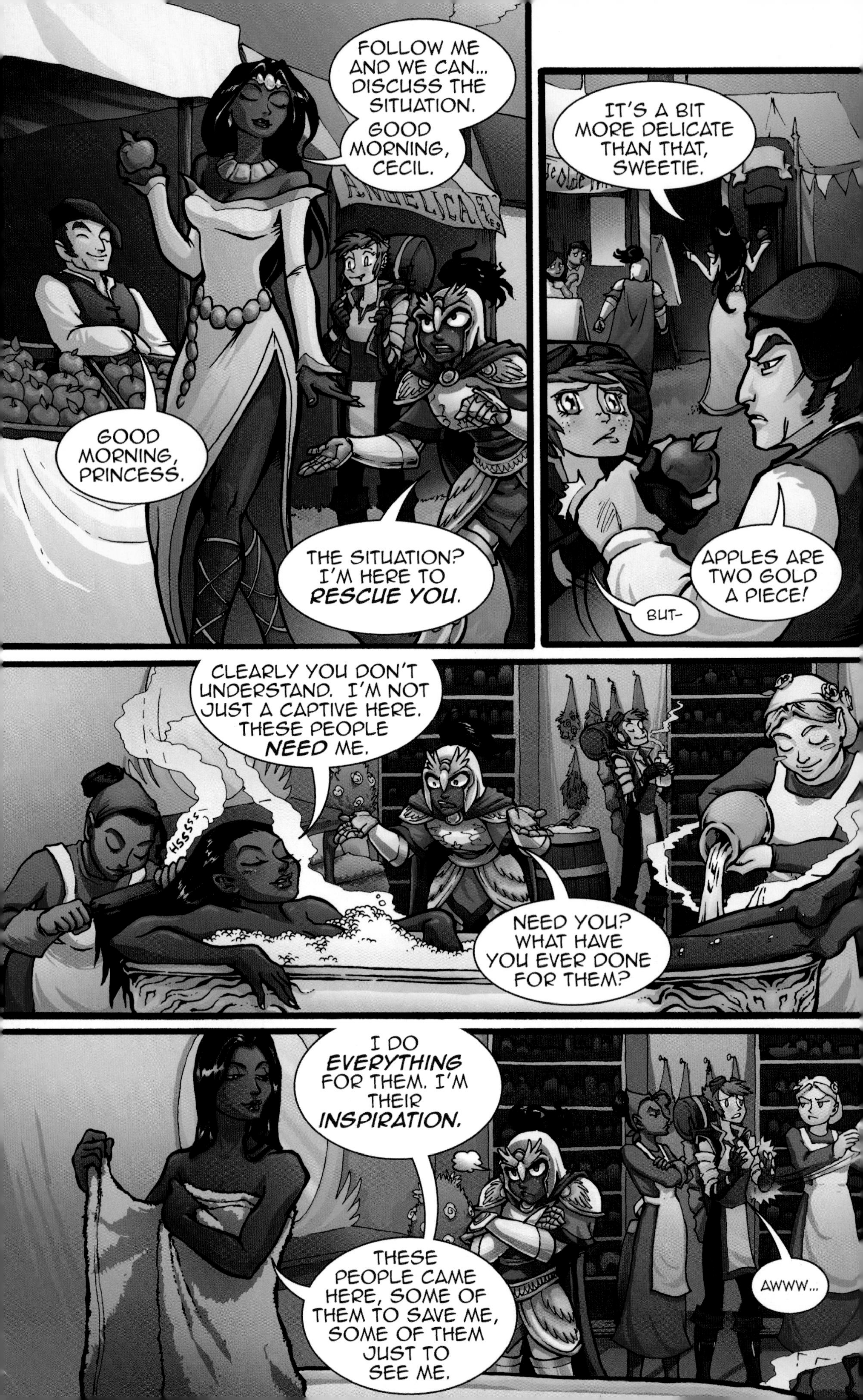
GOOD MORNING, CECIL.
GOOD MORNING, PRINCESS.
FOLLOW ME AND WE CAN... DISCUSS THE SITUATION.
THE SITUATION? I'M HERE TO RESCUE YOU.
ANGELICA'S
IT'S A BIT MORE DELICATE THAN THAT, SWEETIE.
APPLES ARE TWO GOLD A PIECE!
BUT-
CLEARLY YOU DON'T UNDERSTAND. I'M NOT JUST A CAPTIVE HERE. THESE PEOPLE NEED ME.
HSSSS
NEED YOU? WHAT HAVE YOU EVER DONE FOR THEM?
I DO EVERYTHING FOR THEM. I'M THEIR INSPIRATION.
THESE PEOPLE CAME HERE, SOME OF THEM TO SAVE ME, SOME OF THEM JUST TO SEE ME.
AWWW...

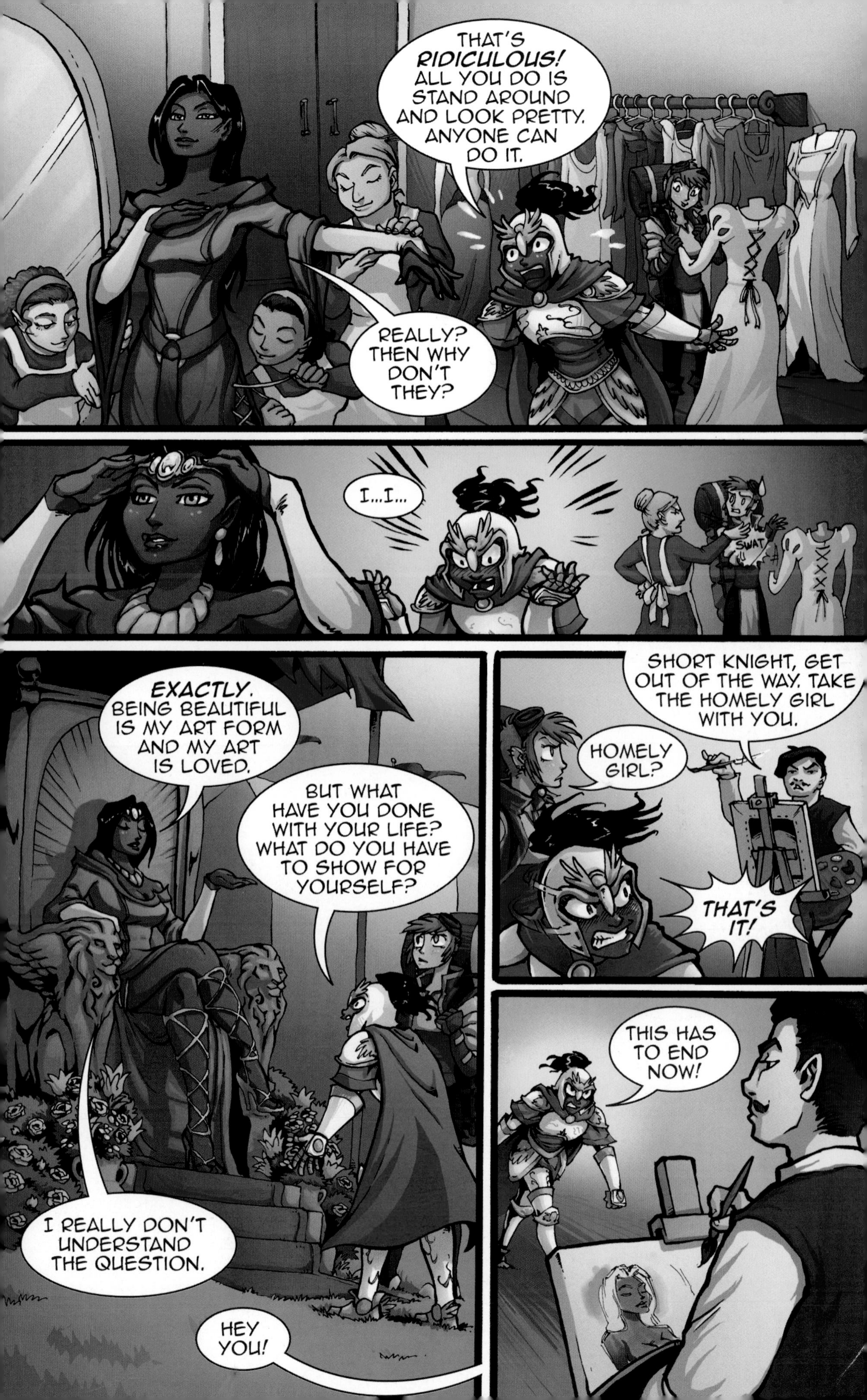
THAT'S *RIDICULOUS!* ALL YOU DO IS STAND AROUND AND LOOK PRETTY. ANYONE CAN DO IT.
REALLY? THEN WHY DON'T THEY?
I...I...
SWAT
EXACTLY. BEING BEAUTIFUL IS MY ART FORM AND MY ART IS LOVED.
BUT WHAT HAVE YOU DONE WITH YOUR LIFE? WHAT DO YOU HAVE TO SHOW FOR YOURSELF?
I REALLY DON'T UNDERSTAND THE QUESTION.
HEY YOU!
SHORT KNIGHT, GET OUT OF THE WAY. TAKE THE HOMELY GIRL WITH YOU.
HOMELY GIRL?
THAT'S IT!
THIS HAS TO END NOW!

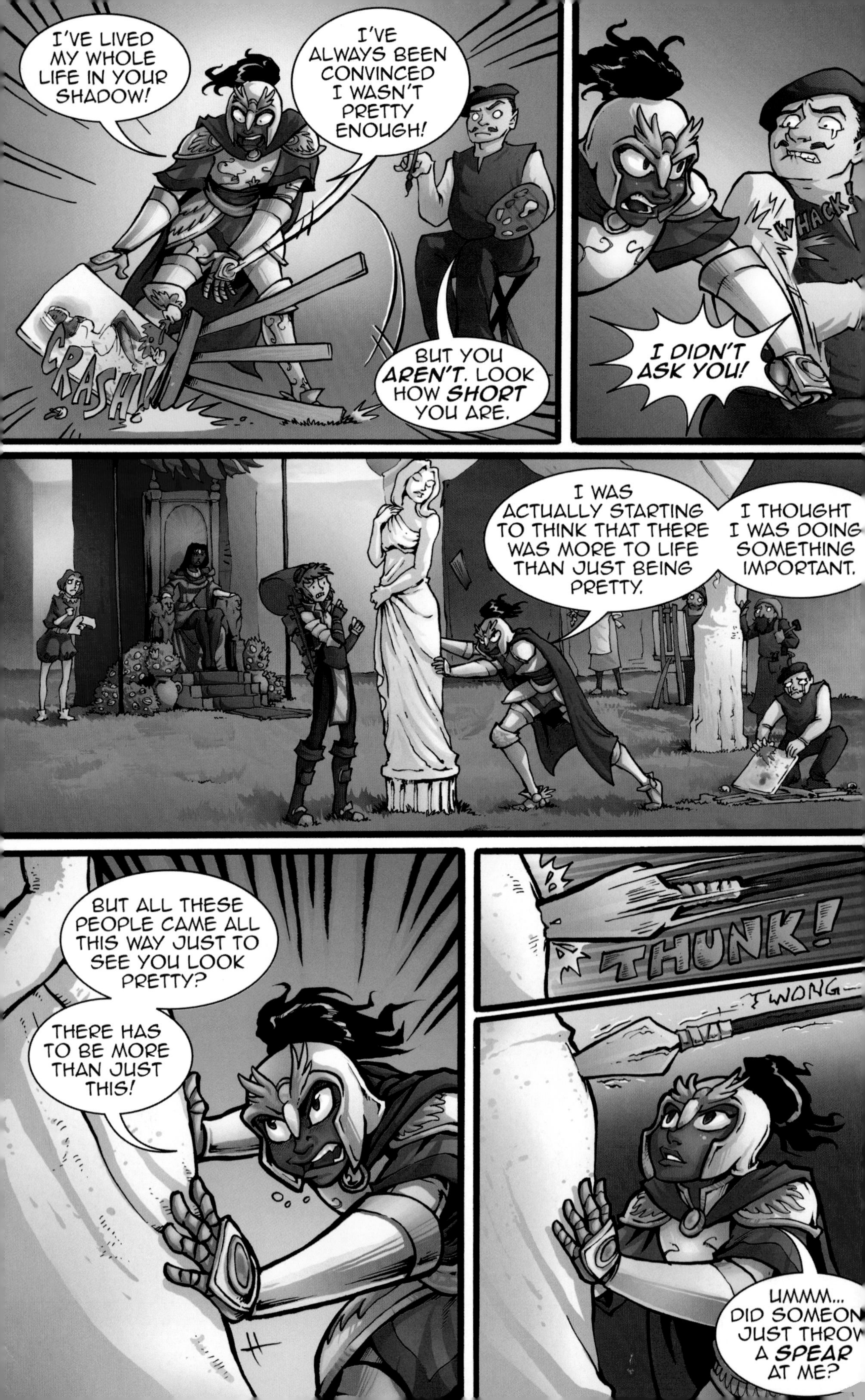
I'VE LIVED MY WHOLE LIFE IN YOUR SHADOW!
I'VE ALWAYS BEEN CONVINCED I WASN'T PRETTY ENOUGH!
CRASH!
BUT YOU AREN'T. LOOK HOW SHORT YOU ARE.
WHACK!
I DIDN'T ASK YOU!
I WAS ACTUALLY STARTING TO THINK THAT THERE WAS MORE TO LIFE THAN JUST BEING PRETTY.
I THOUGHT I WAS DOING SOMETHING IMPORTANT.
BUT ALL THESE PEOPLE CAME ALL THIS WAY JUST TO SEE YOU LOOK PRETTY?
THERE HAS TO BE MORE THAN JUST THIS!
THUNK!
TWONG
UMMM... DID SOMEON JUST THROW A SPEAR AT ME?

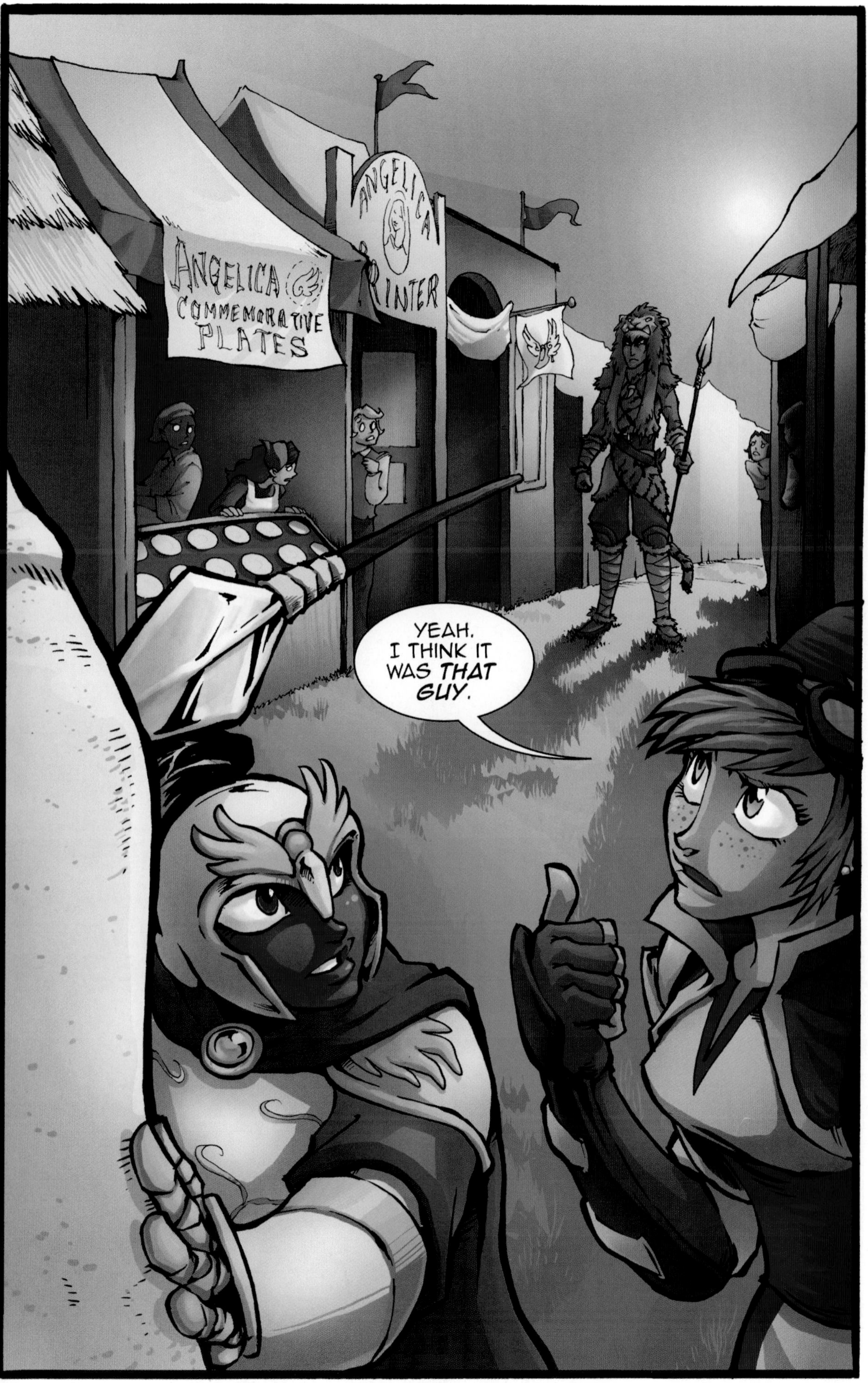
ANGELICA COMMEMORATIVE PLATES
ANGELICA PRINTER
YEAH. I THINK IT WAS *THAT GUY*.

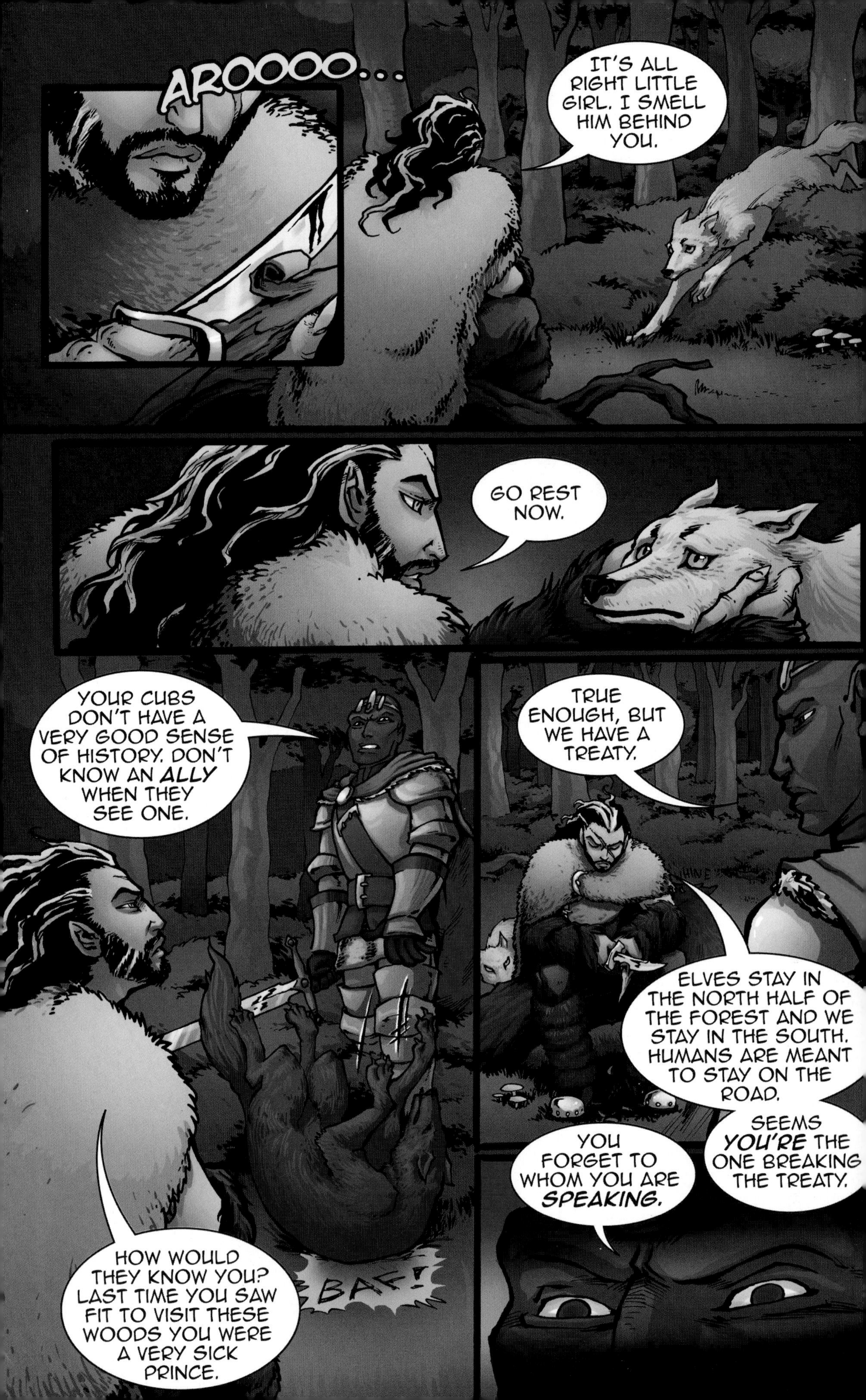
AROOOO...
IT'S ALL RIGHT LITTLE GIRL. I SMELL HIM BEHIND YOU.
GO REST NOW.
YOUR CUBS DON'T HAVE A VERY GOOD SENSE OF HISTORY. DON'T KNOW AN ALLY WHEN THEY SEE ONE.
HOW WOULD THEY KNOW YOU? LAST TIME YOU SAW FIT TO VISIT THESE WOODS YOU WERE A VERY SICK PRINCE.
BAF!
TRUE ENOUGH, BUT WE HAVE A TREATY.
ELVES STAY IN THE NORTH HALF OF THE FOREST AND WE STAY IN THE SOUTH. HUMANS ARE MEANT TO STAY ON THE ROAD.
SEEMS YOU'RE THE ONE BREAKING THE TREATY.
YOU FORGET TO WHOM YOU ARE SPEAKING.

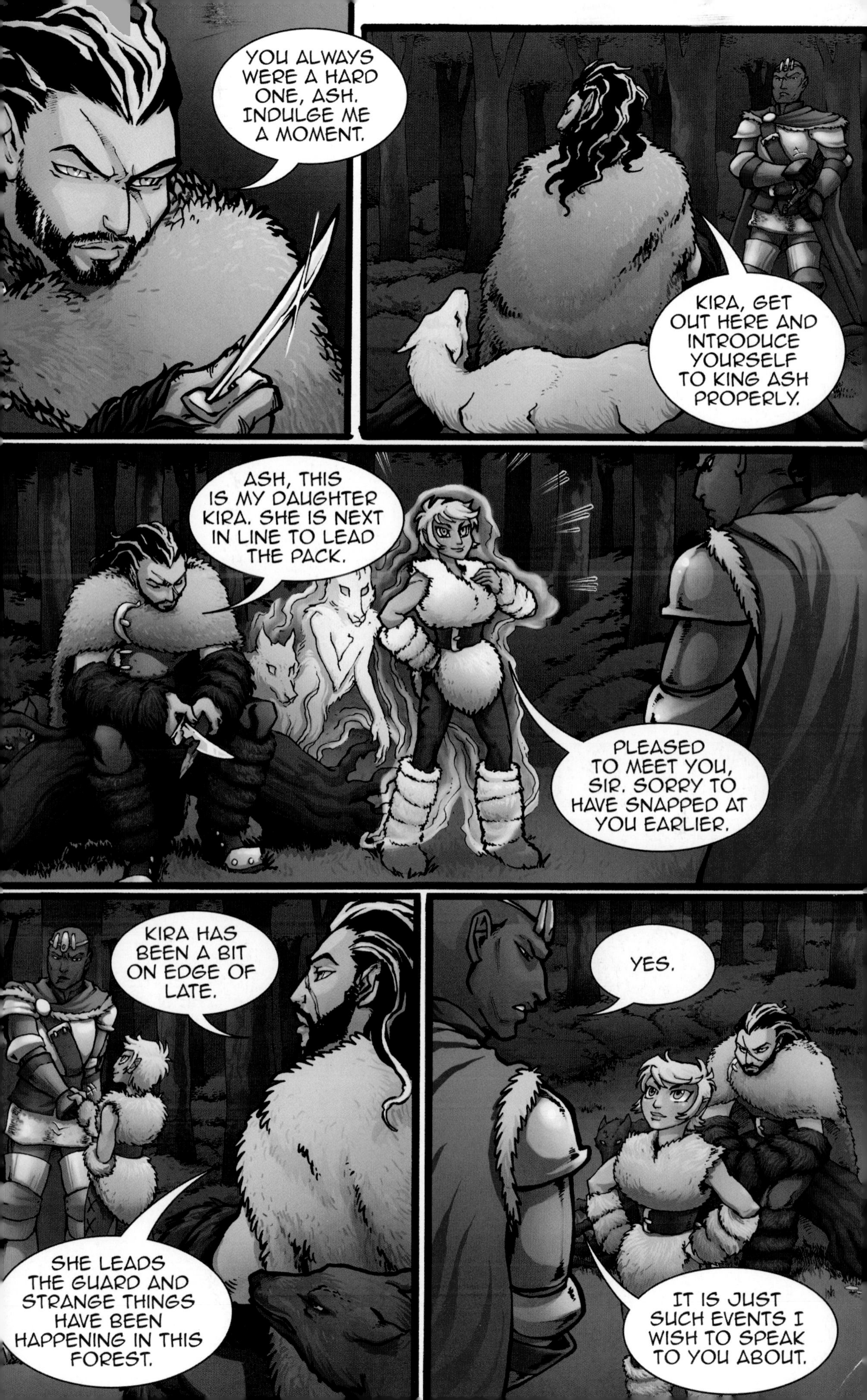
YOU ALWAYS WERE A HARD ONE, ASH. INDULGE ME A MOMENT.
KIRA, GET OUT HERE AND INTRODUCE YOURSELF TO KING ASH PROPERLY.
ASH, THIS IS MY DAUGHTER KIRA. SHE IS NEXT IN LINE TO LEAD THE PACK.
PLEASED TO MEET YOU, SIR. SORRY TO HAVE SNAPPED AT YOU EARLIER.
KIRA HAS BEEN A BIT ON EDGE OF LATE.
SHE LEADS THE GUARD AND STRANGE THINGS HAVE BEEN HAPPENING IN THIS FOREST.
YES.
IT IS JUST SUCH EVENTS I WISH TO SPEAK TO YOU ABOUT.

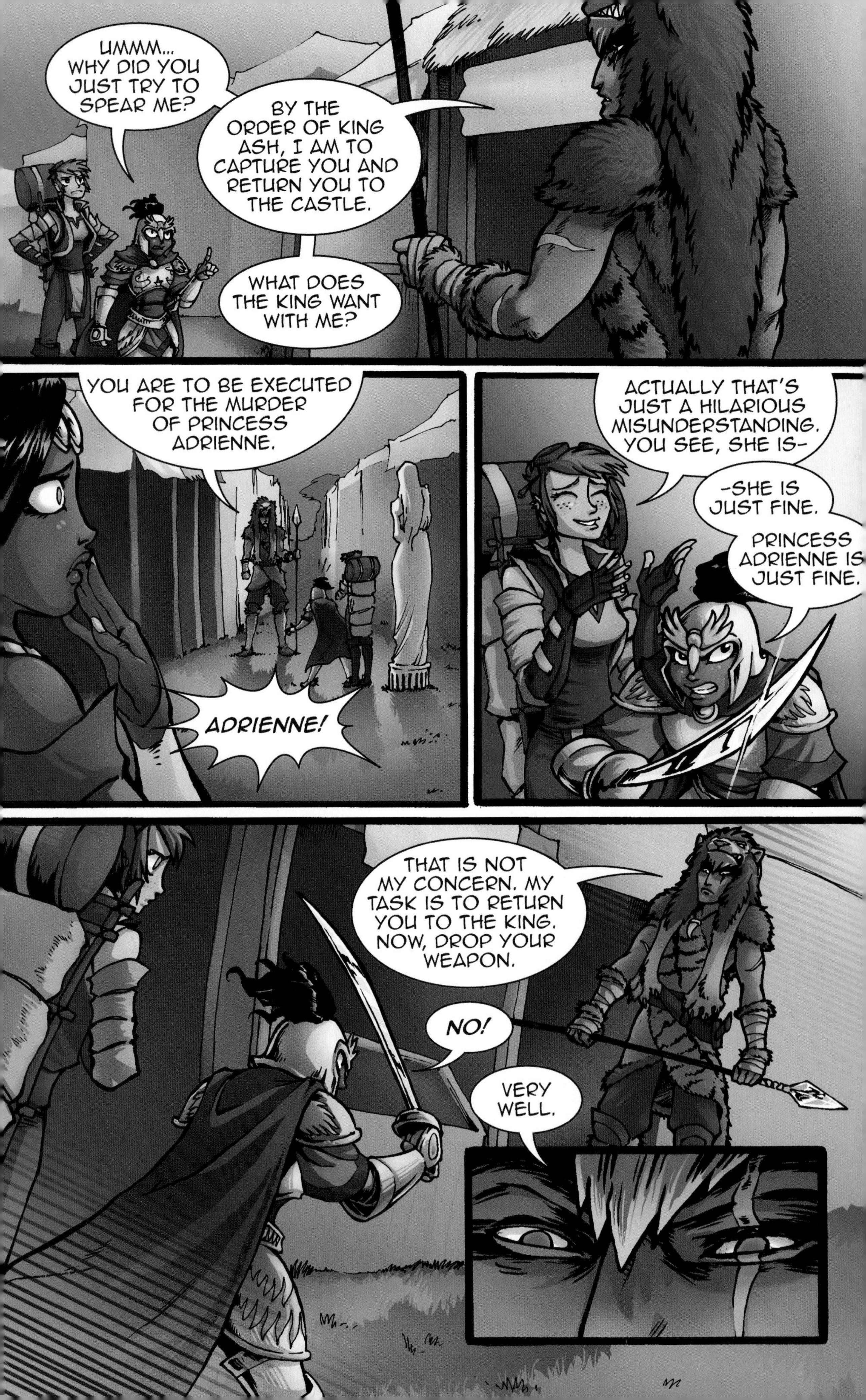
UMMM... WHY DID YOU JUST TRY TO SPEAR ME?
BY THE ORDER OF KING ASH, I AM TO CAPTURE YOU AND RETURN YOU TO THE CASTLE.
WHAT DOES THE KING WANT WITH ME?
YOU ARE TO BE EXECUTED FOR THE MURDER OF PRINCESS ADRIENNE.
ADRIENNE!
ACTUALLY THAT'S JUST A HILARIOUS MISUNDERSTANDING. YOU SEE, SHE IS-
-SHE IS JUST FINE.
PRINCESS ADRIENNE IS JUST FINE.
THAT IS NOT MY CONCERN. MY TASK IS TO RETURN YOU TO THE KING. NOW, DROP YOUR WEAPON.
NO!
VERY WELL.

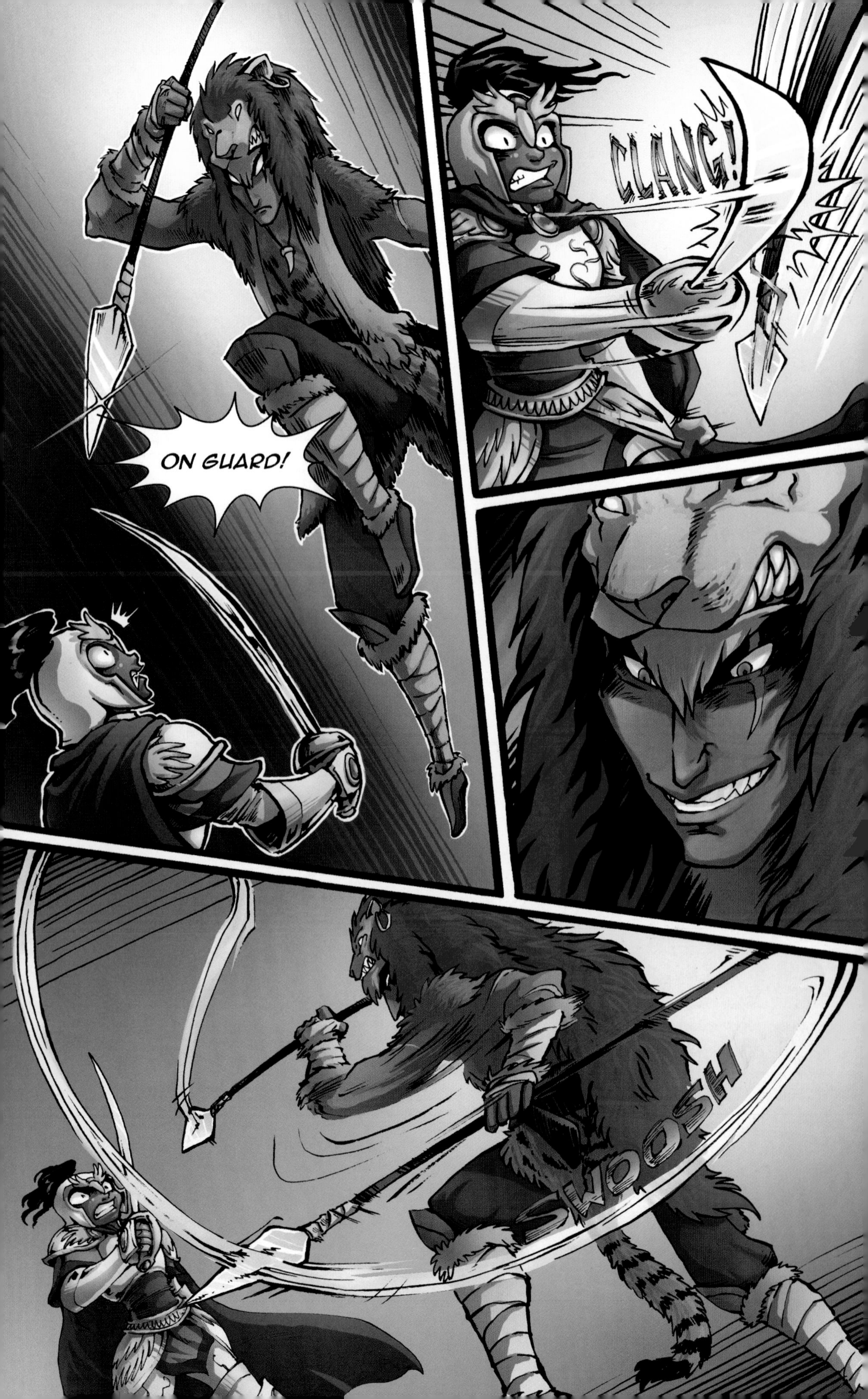
ON GUARD!
CLANG!
WOOSH

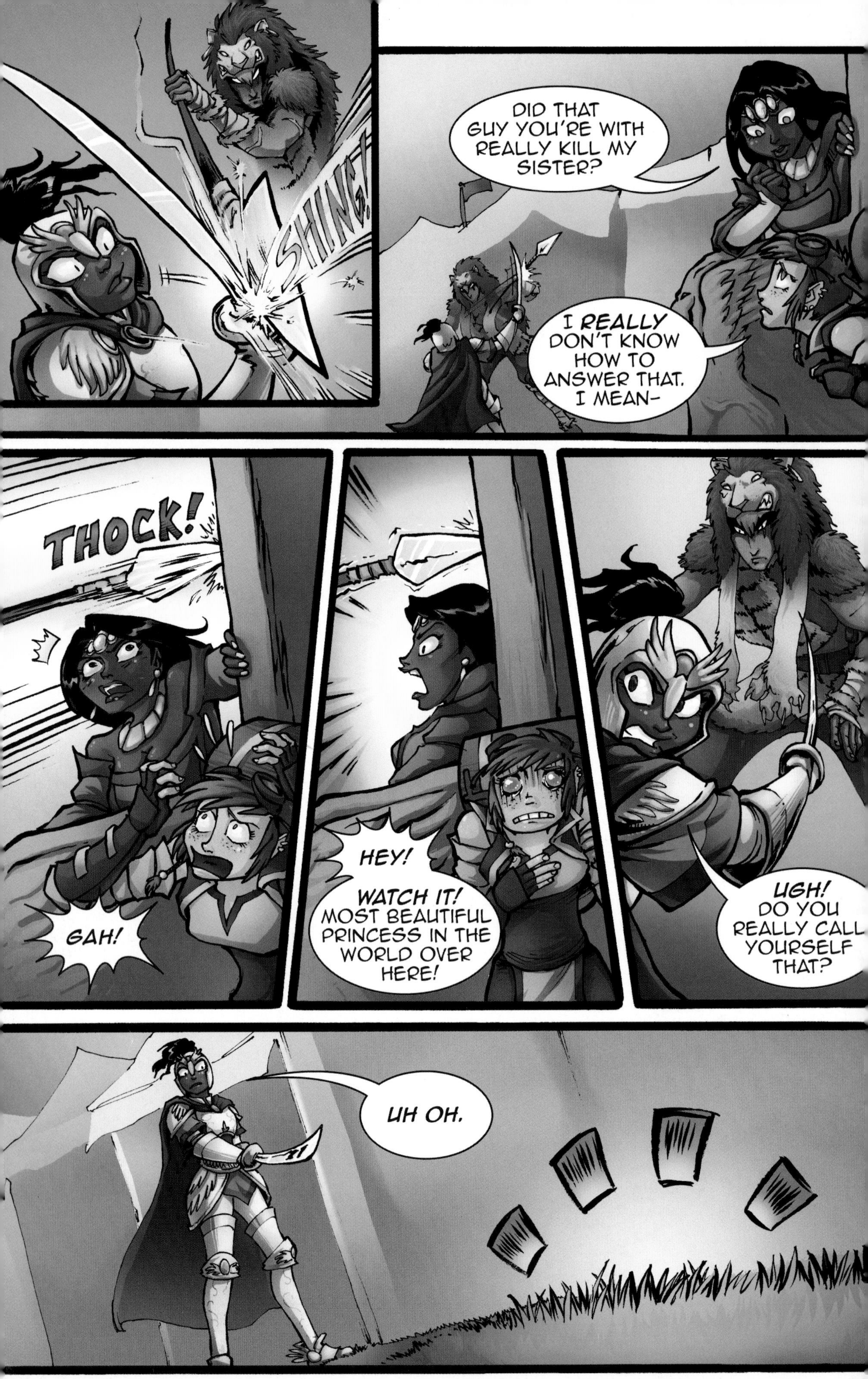
SHING!
DID THAT GUY YOU'RE WITH REALLY KILL MY SISTER?
I REALLY DON'T KNOW HOW TO ANSWER THAT. I MEAN-
THOCK!
GAH!
HEY!
WATCH IT! MOST BEAUTIFUL PRINCESS IN THE WORLD OVER HERE!
UGH! DO YOU REALLY CALL YOURSELF THAT?
UH OH.

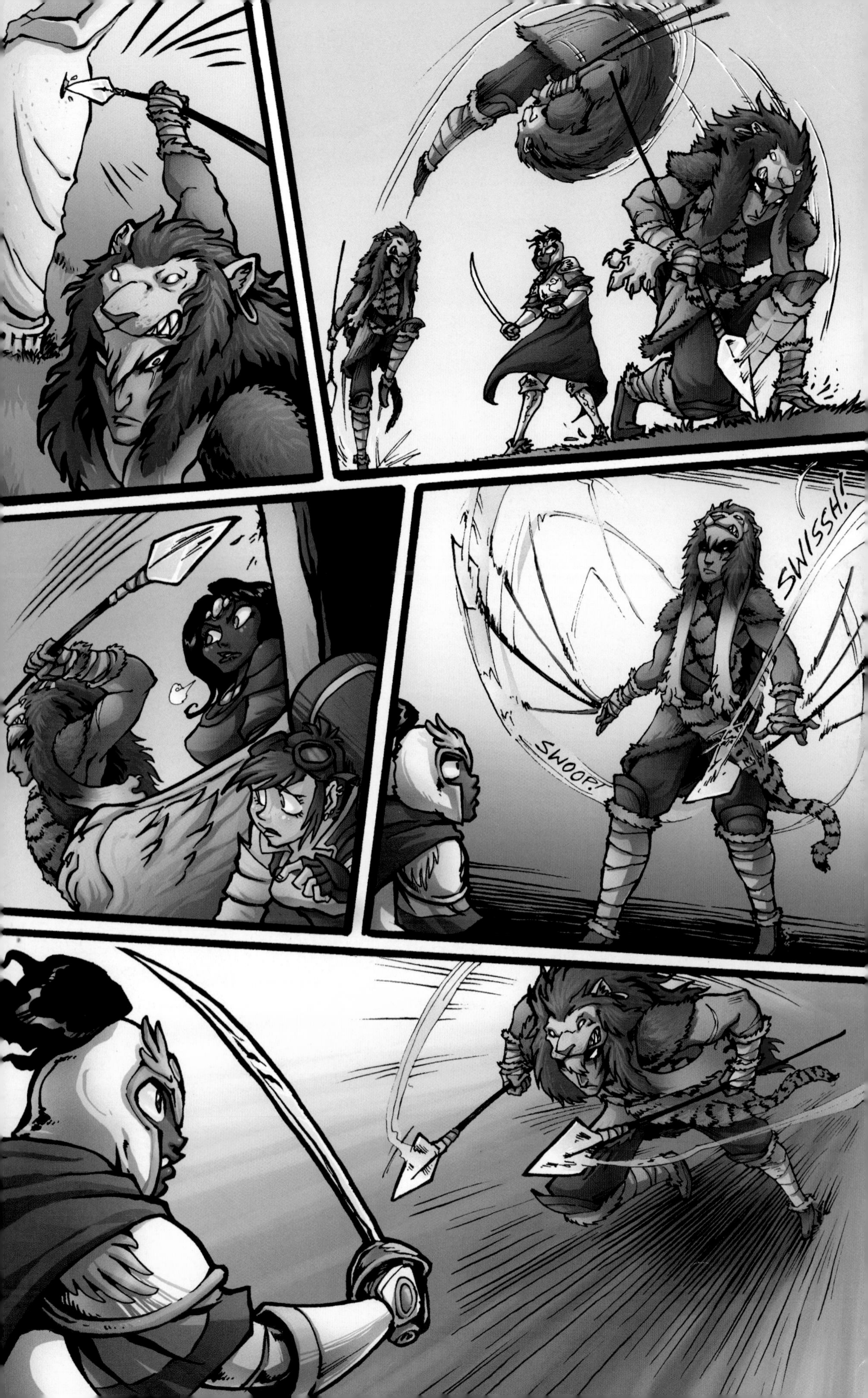
SWISSH!
SWOOP!

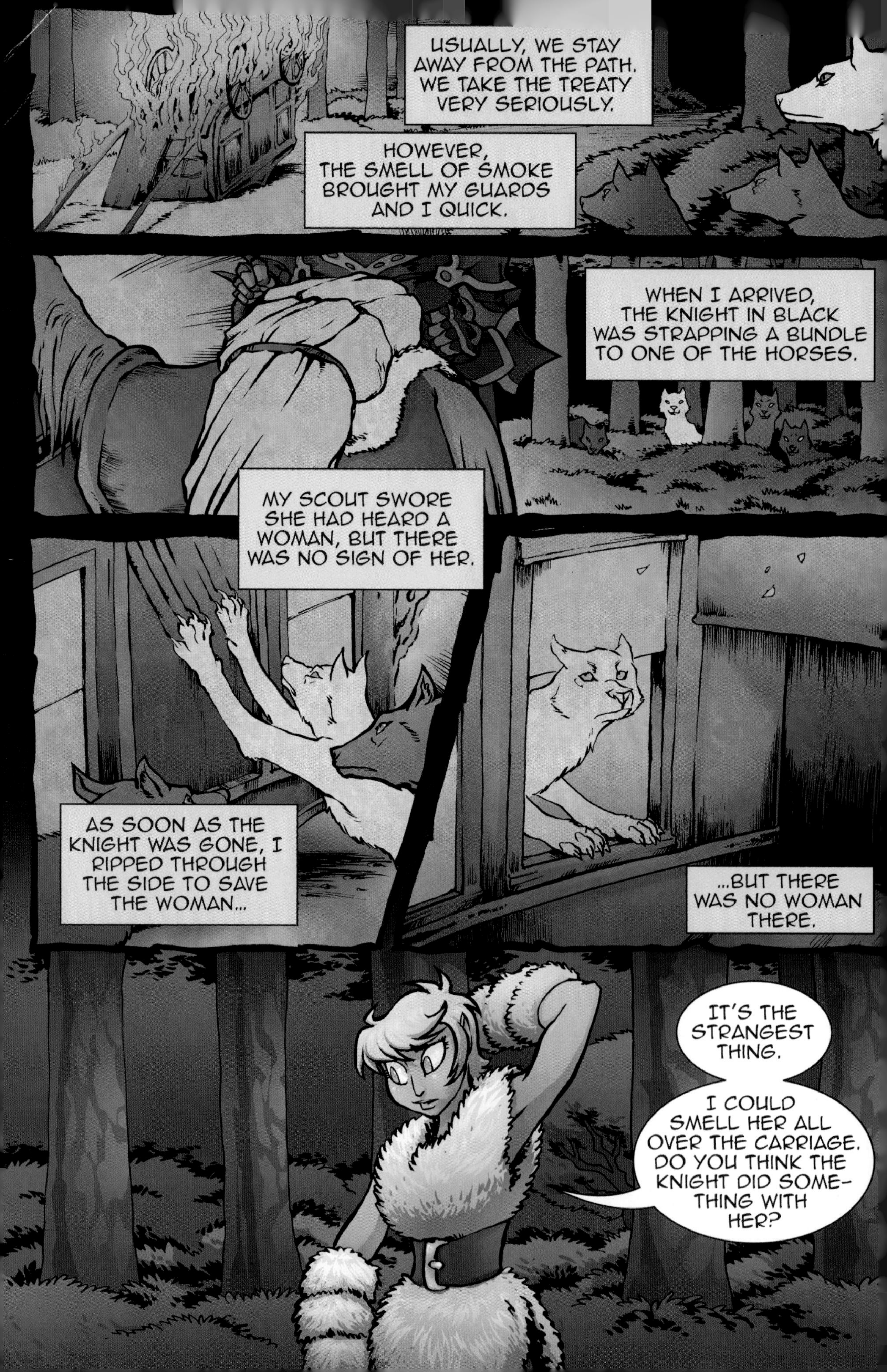
USUALLY, WE STAY AWAY FROM THE PATH. WE TAKE THE TREATY VERY SERIOUSLY.
HOWEVER, THE SMELL OF SMOKE BROUGHT MY GUARDS AND I QUICK.
WHEN I ARRIVED, THE KNIGHT IN BLACK WAS STRAPPING A BUNDLE TO ONE OF THE HORSES.
MY SCOUT SWORE SHE HAD HEARD A WOMAN, BUT THERE WAS NO SIGN OF HER.
AS SOON AS THE KNIGHT WAS GONE, I RIPPED THROUGH THE SIDE TO SAVE THE WOMAN...
...BUT THERE WAS NO WOMAN THERE.
IT'S THE STRANGEST THING.
I COULD SMELL HER ALL OVER THE CARRIAGE. DO YOU THINK THE KNIGHT DID SOME-THING WITH HER?

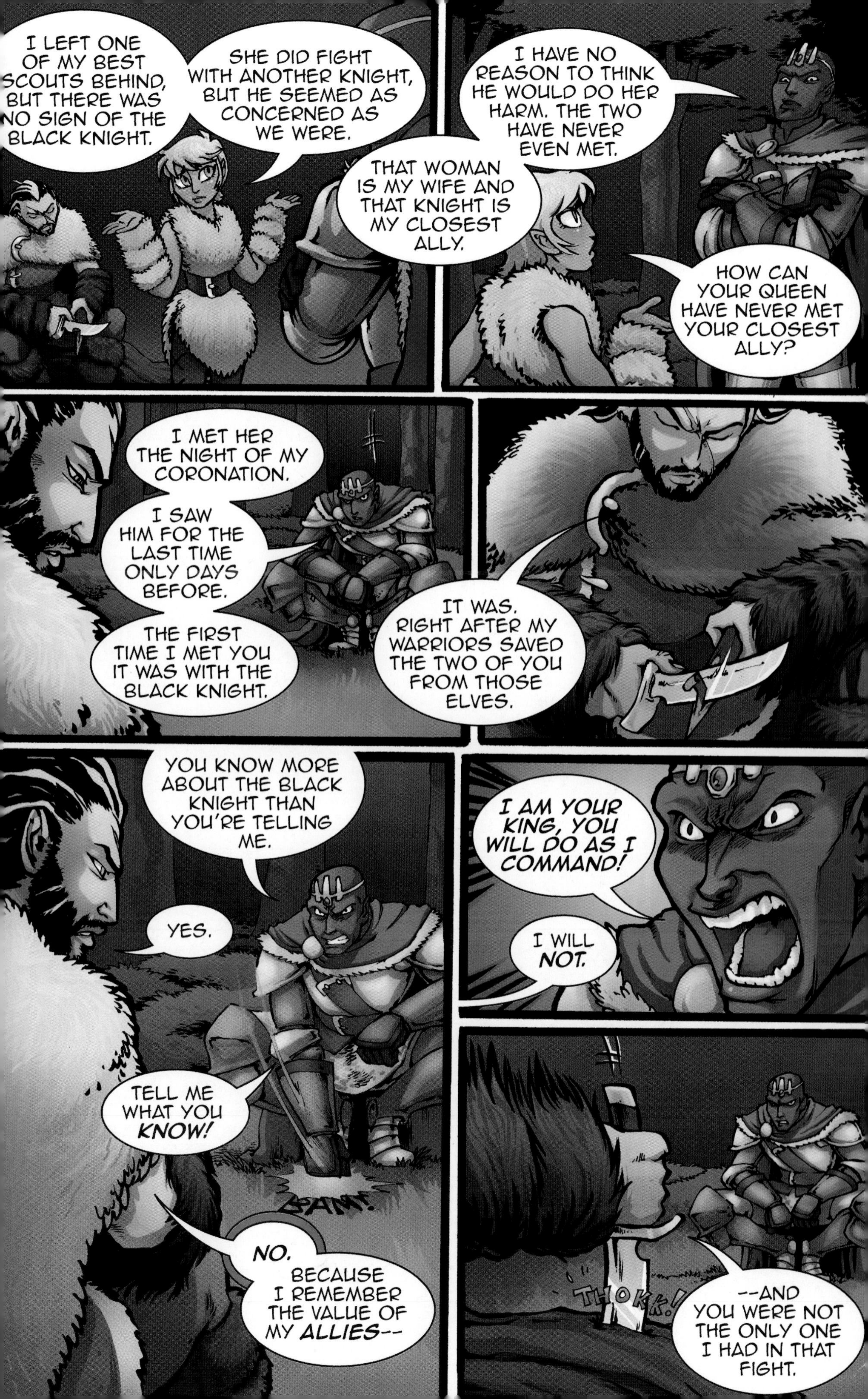
I LEFT ONE OF MY BEST SCOUTS BEHIND, BUT THERE WAS NO SIGN OF THE BLACK KNIGHT.
SHE DID FIGHT WITH ANOTHER KNIGHT, BUT HE SEEMED AS CONCERNED AS WE WERE.
I HAVE NO REASON TO THINK HE WOULD DO HER HARM. THE TWO HAVE NEVER EVEN MET.
THAT WOMAN IS MY WIFE AND THAT KNIGHT IS MY CLOSEST ALLY.
HOW CAN YOUR QUEEN HAVE NEVER MET YOUR CLOSEST ALLY?
I MET HER THE NIGHT OF MY CORONATION.
I SAW HIM FOR THE LAST TIME ONLY DAYS BEFORE.
THE FIRST TIME I MET YOU IT WAS WITH THE BLACK KNIGHT.
IT WAS. RIGHT AFTER MY WARRIORS SAVED THE TWO OF YOU FROM THOSE ELVES.
YOU KNOW MORE ABOUT THE BLACK KNIGHT THAN YOU'RE TELLING ME.
YES.
TELL ME WHAT YOU KNOW!
BAM!
NO. BECAUSE I REMEMBER THE VALUE OF MY ALLIES--
I AM YOUR KING, YOU WILL DO AS I COMMAND!
I WILL NOT.
THOKK!
--AND YOU WERE NOT THE ONLY ONE I HAD IN THAT FIGHT.

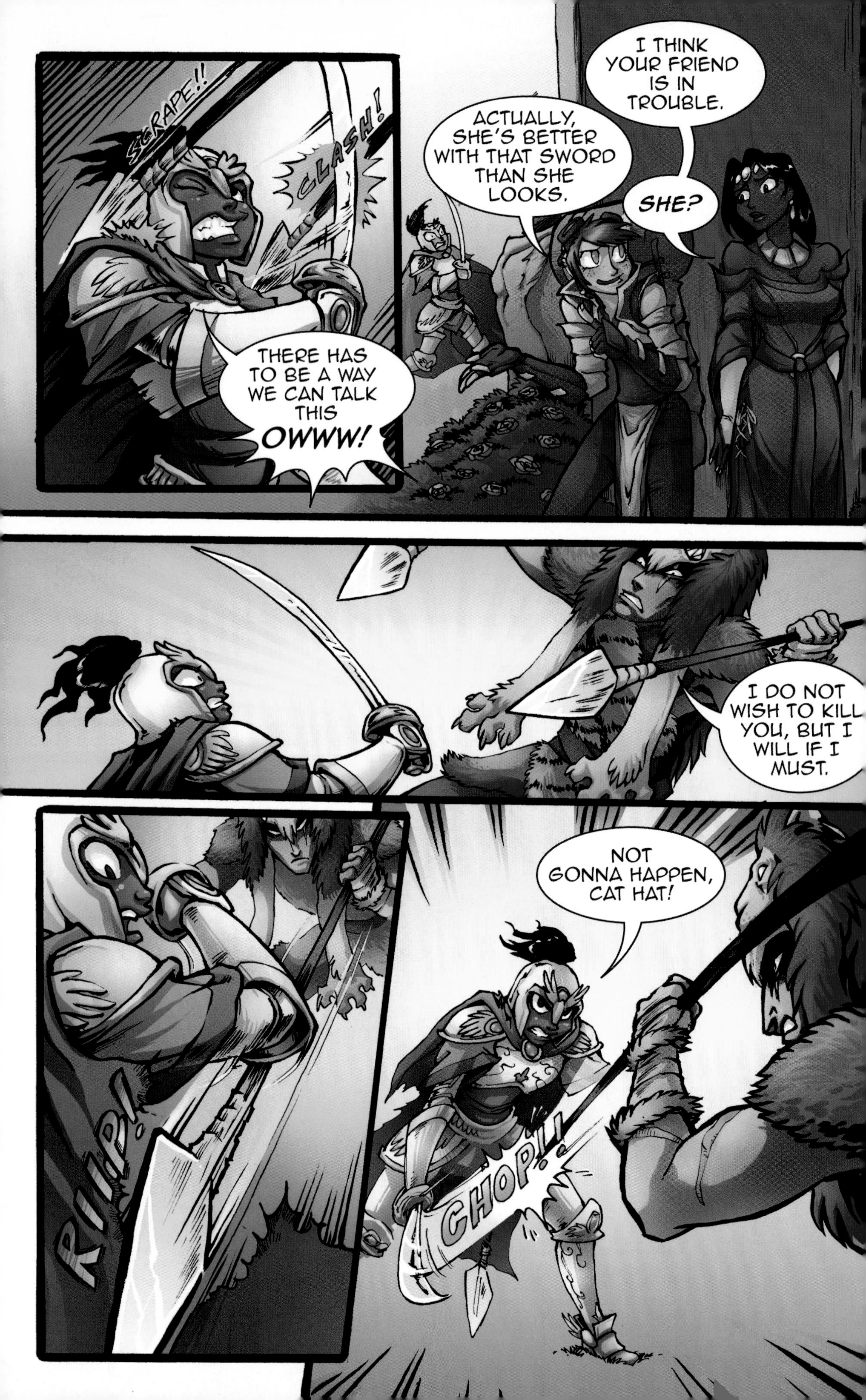
SCRAPE!!
CLASH!
THERE HAS TO BE A WAY WE CAN TALK THIS OWWW!
ACTUALLY, SHE'S BETTER WITH THAT SWORD THAN SHE LOOKS.
I THINK YOUR FRIEND IS IN TROUBLE.
SHE?
I DO NOT WISH TO KILL YOU, BUT I WILL IF I MUST.
RIIIP!
NOT GONNA HAPPEN, CAT HAT!
CHOP!!

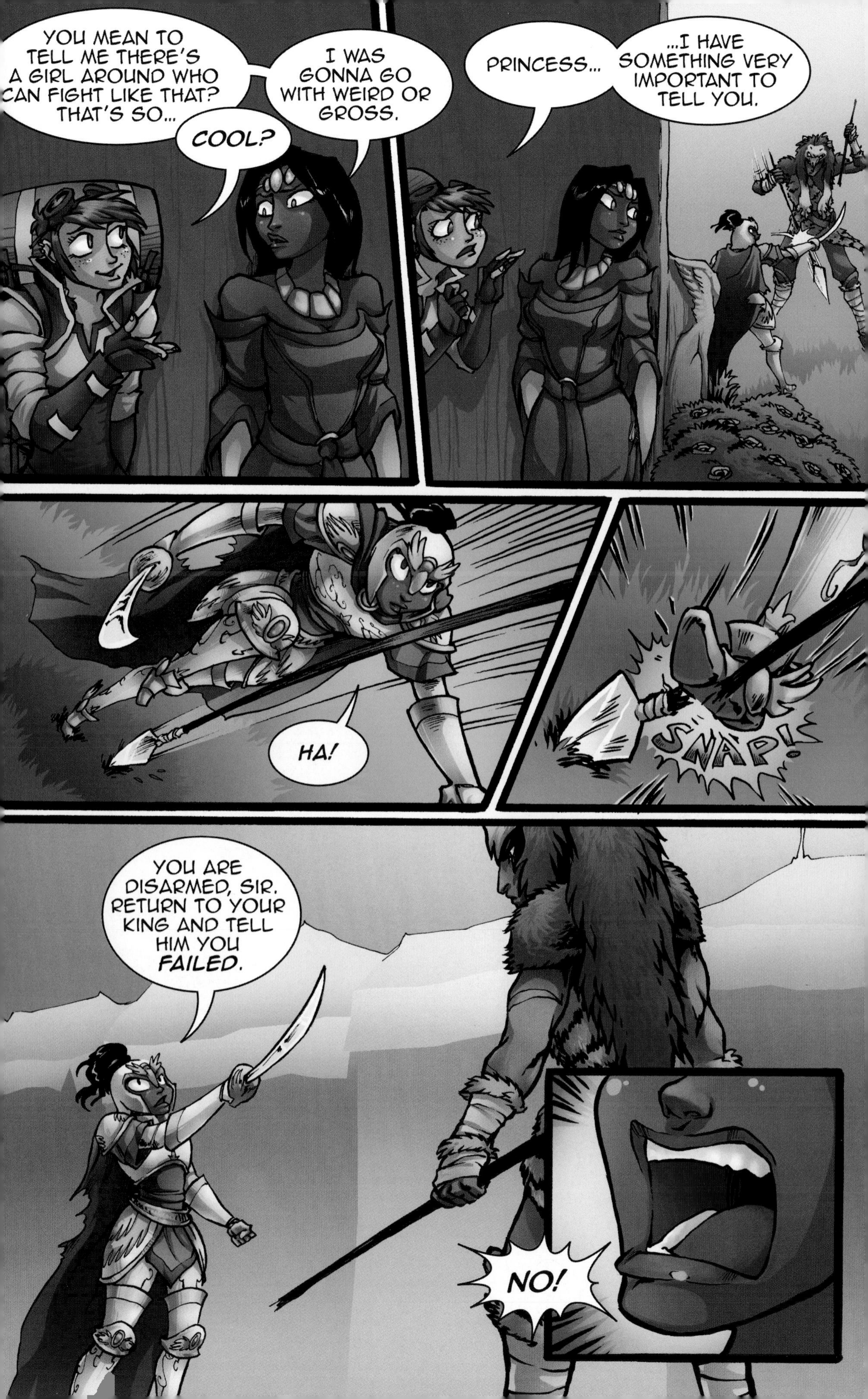
YOU MEAN TO TELL ME THERE'S A GIRL AROUND WHO CAN FIGHT LIKE THAT? THAT'S SO...
COOL?
I WAS GONNA GO WITH WEIRD OR GROSS.
PRINCESS...
...I HAVE SOMETHING VERY IMPORTANT TO TELL YOU.
HA!
SNAP!
YOU ARE DISARMED, SIR. RETURN TO YOUR KING AND TELL HIM YOU FAILED.
NO!

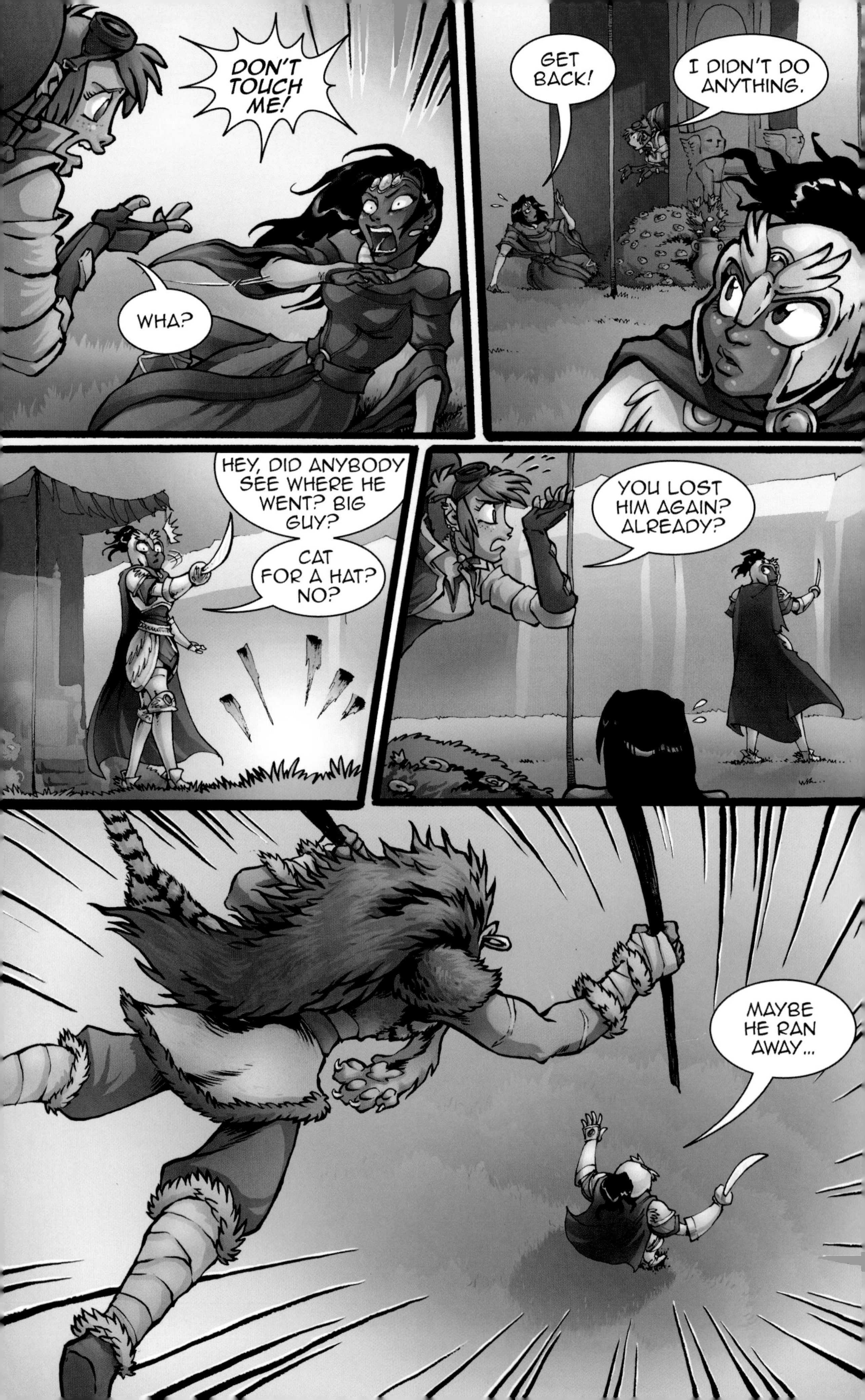
DON'T TOUCH ME!
WHA?
GET BACK!
I DIDN'T DO ANYTHING.
HEY, DID ANYBODY SEE WHERE HE WENT? BIG GUY?
CAT FOR A HAT? NO?
YOU LOST HIM AGAIN? ALREADY?
MAYBE HE RAN AWAY...

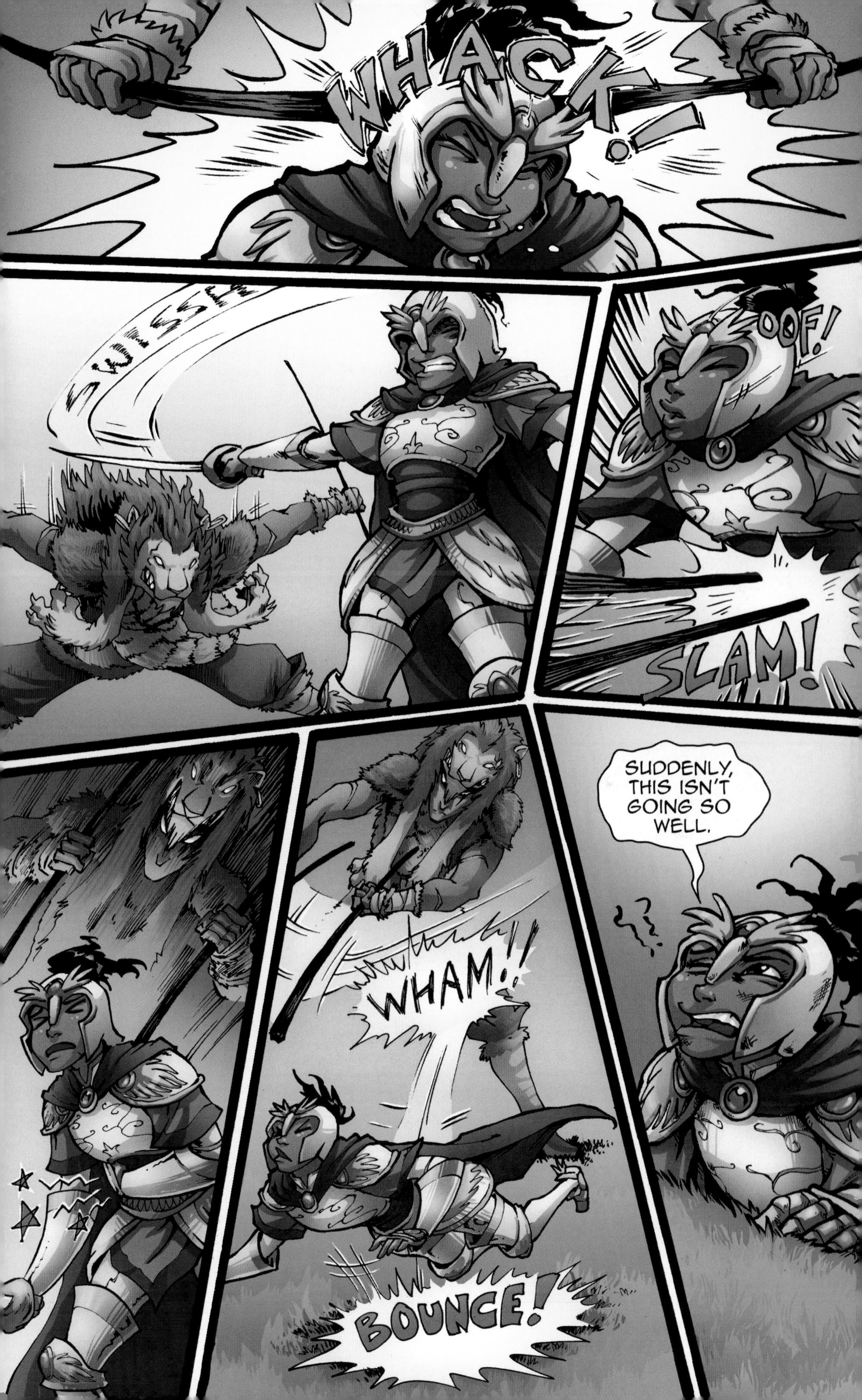
WHACK!
SWISH
OOF!
SLAM!
WHAM!!
BOUNCE!
SUDDENLY, THIS ISN'T GOING SO WELL.

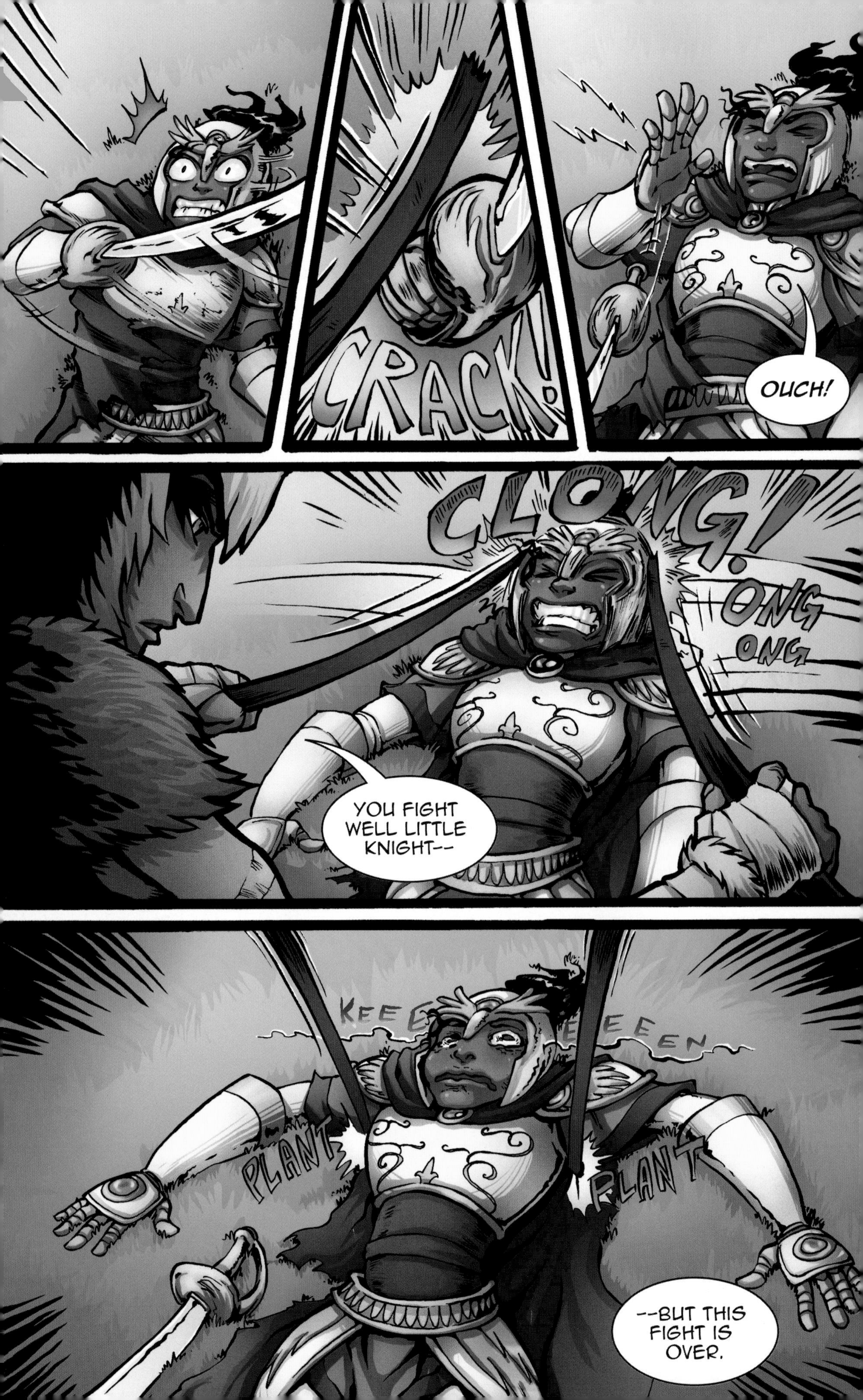
CRACK!
OUCH!
CLONG!
ONG
ONG
YOU FIGHT WELL LITTLE KNIGHT--
PLANT
PLANT
--BUT THIS FIGHT IS OVER.

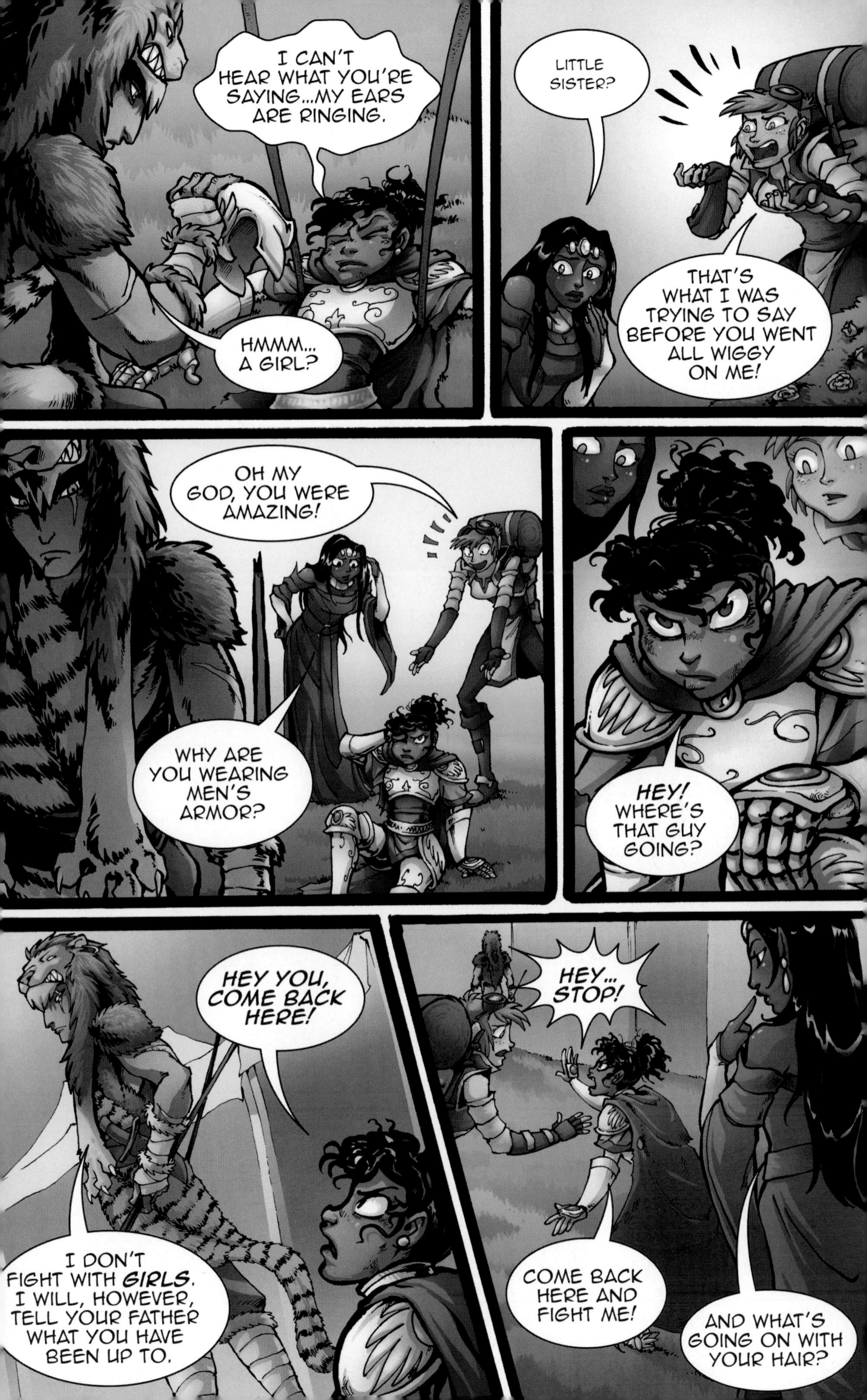
I CAN'T HEAR WHAT YOU'RE SAYING...MY EARS ARE RINGING.
HMMM... A GIRL?
LITTLE SISTER?
THAT'S WHAT I WAS TRYING TO SAY BEFORE YOU WENT ALL WIGGY ON ME!
OH MY GOD, YOU WERE AMAZING!
WHY ARE YOU WEARING MEN'S ARMOR?
HEY! WHERE'S THAT GUY GOING?
HEY YOU, COME BACK HERE!
I DON'T FIGHT WITH GIRLS. I WILL, HOWEVER, TELL YOUR FATHER WHAT YOU HAVE BEEN UP TO.
HEY... STOP!
COME BACK HERE AND FIGHT ME!
AND WHAT'S GOING ON WITH YOUR HAIR?

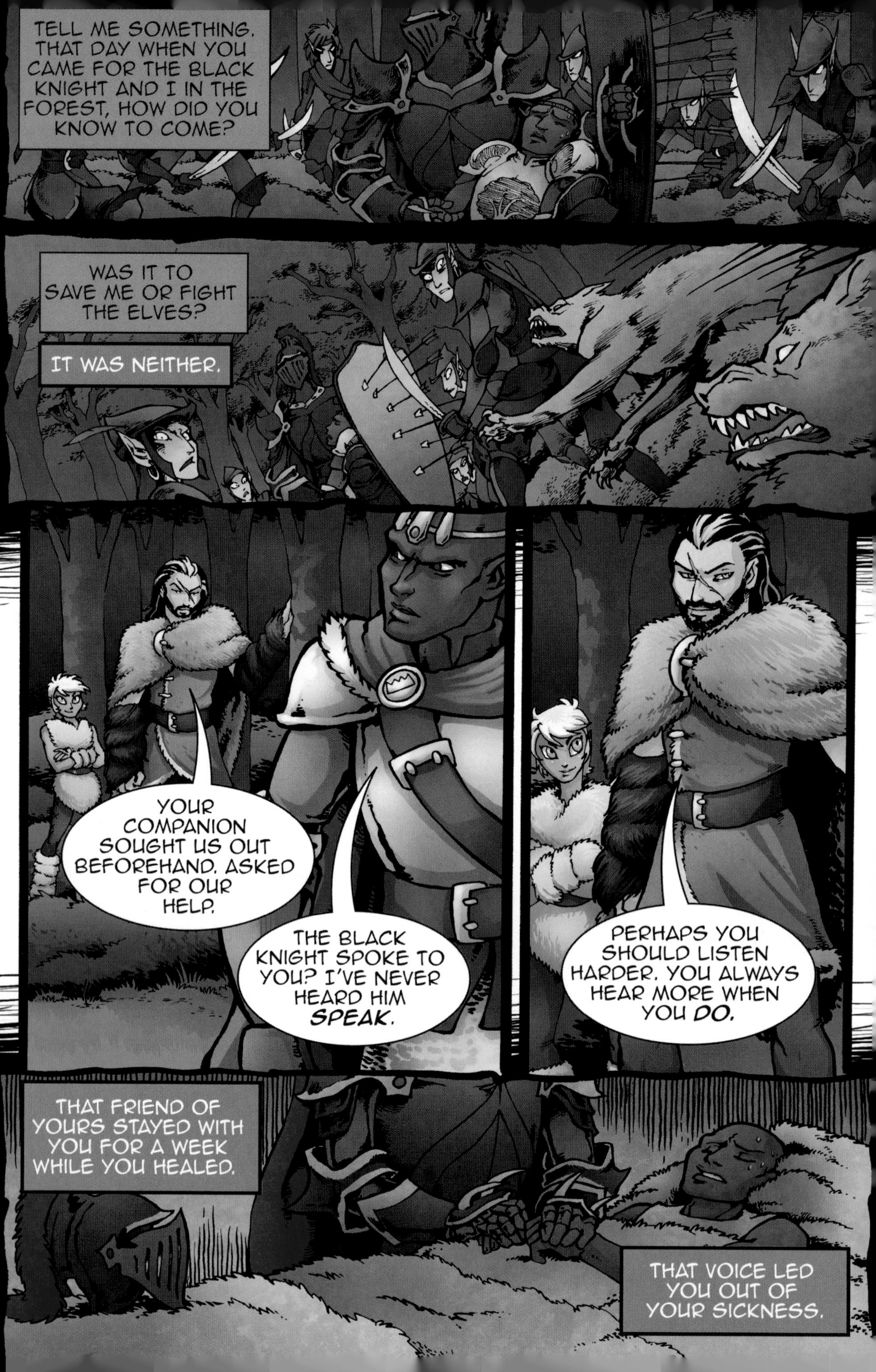
TELL ME SOMETHING. THAT DAY WHEN YOU CAME FOR THE BLACK KNIGHT AND I IN THE FOREST, HOW DID YOU KNOW TO COME?
WAS IT TO SAVE ME OR FIGHT THE ELVES?
IT WAS NEITHER.
YOUR COMPANION SOUGHT US OUT BEFOREHAND. ASKED FOR OUR HELP.
THE BLACK KNIGHT SPOKE TO YOU? I'VE NEVER HEARD HIM SPEAK.
PERHAPS YOU SHOULD LISTEN HARDER. YOU ALWAYS HEAR MORE WHEN YOU DO.
THAT FRIEND OF YOURS STAYED WITH YOU FOR A WEEK WHILE YOU HEALED.
THAT VOICE LED YOU OUT OF YOUR SICKNESS.

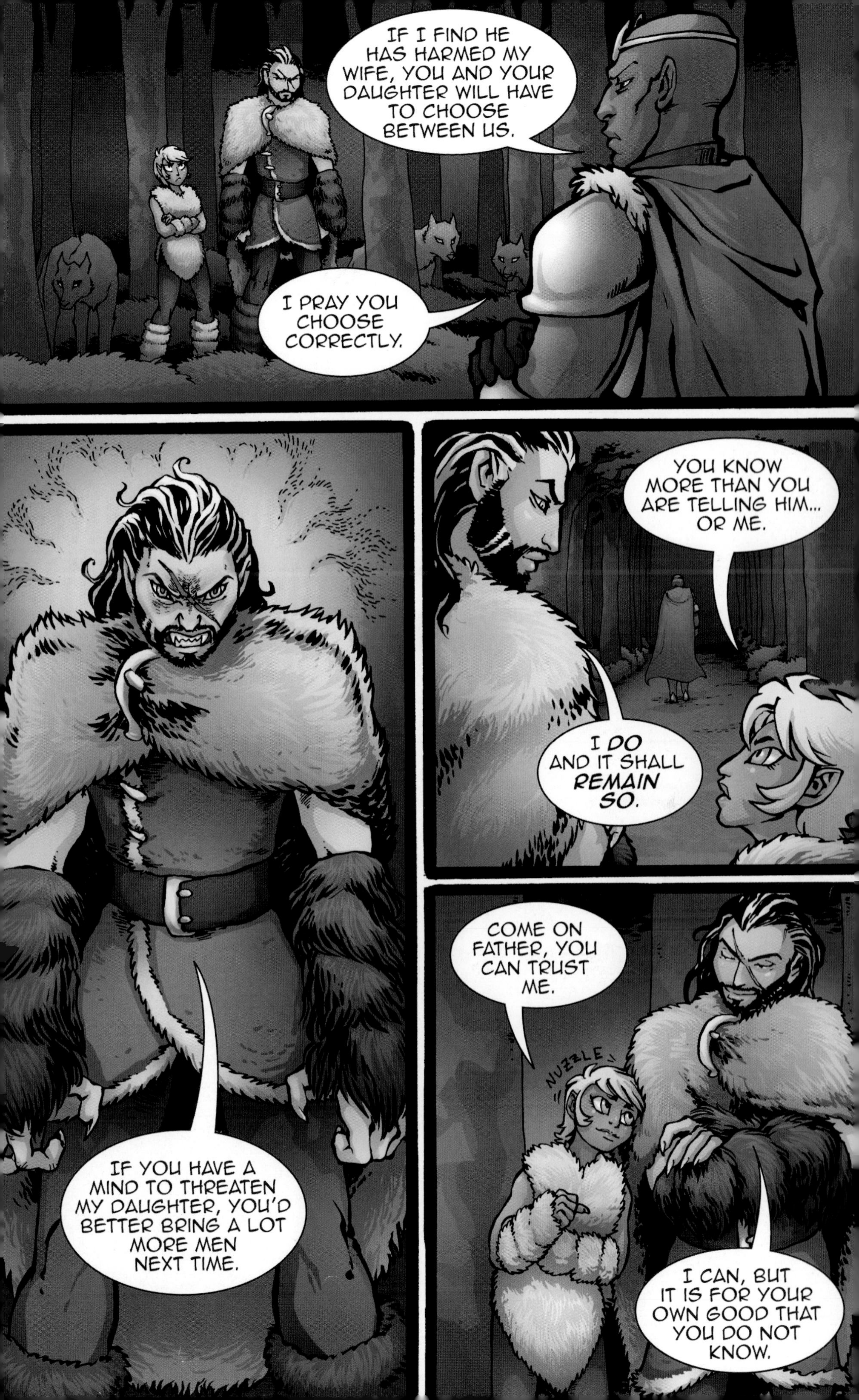
IF I FIND HE HAS HARMED MY WIFE, YOU AND YOUR DAUGHTER WILL HAVE TO CHOOSE BETWEEN US.
I PRAY YOU CHOOSE CORRECTLY.
IF YOU HAVE A MIND TO THREATEN MY DAUGHTER, YOU'D BETTER BRING A LOT MORE MEN NEXT TIME.
YOU KNOW MORE THAN YOU ARE TELLING HIM... OR ME.
I DO AND IT SHALL REMAIN SO.
COME ON FATHER, YOU CAN TRUST ME.
NUZZLE
I CAN, BUT IT IS FOR YOUR OWN GOOD THAT YOU DO NOT KNOW.

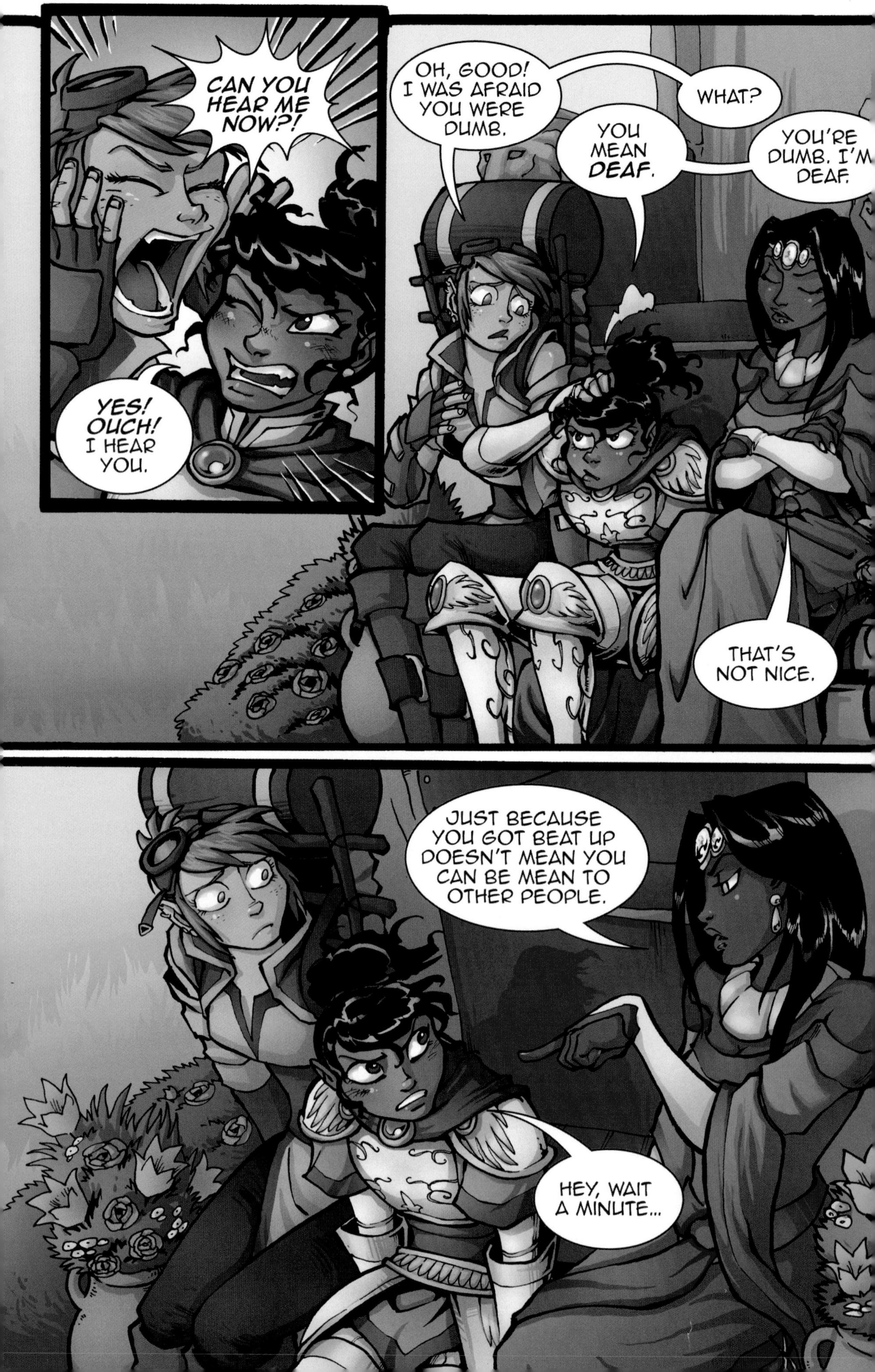
CAN YOU HEAR ME NOW?!
YES! OUCH! I HEAR YOU.
OH, GOOD! I WAS AFRAID YOU WERE DUMB.
WHAT?
YOU MEAN DEAF.
YOU'RE DUMB. I'M DEAF.
THAT'S NOT NICE.
JUST BECAUSE YOU GOT BEAT UP DOESN'T MEAN YOU CAN BE MEAN TO OTHER PEOPLE.
HEY, WAIT A MINUTE...

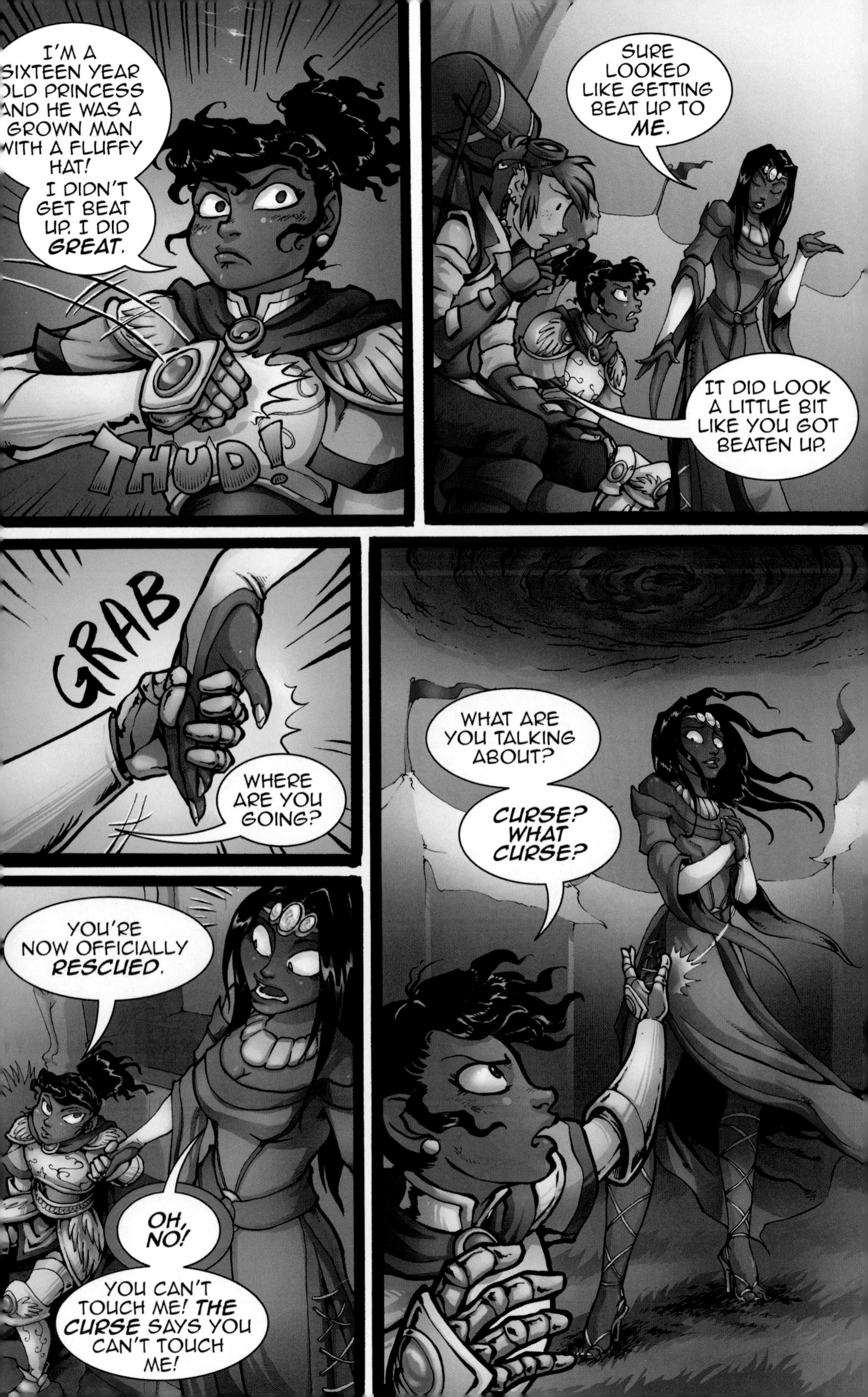
I'M A SIXTEEN YEAR OLD PRINCESS AND HE WAS A GROWN MAN WITH A FLUFFY HAT!
I DIDN'T GET BEAT UP. I DID GREAT.
THUD!
SURE LOOKED LIKE GETTING BEAT UP TO ME.
IT DID LOOK A LITTLE BIT LIKE YOU GOT BEATEN UP.
GRAB
WHERE ARE YOU GOING?
YOU'RE NOW OFFICIALLY RESCUED.
OH, NO!
YOU CAN'T TOUCH ME! THE CURSE SAYS YOU CAN'T TOUCH ME!
WHAT ARE YOU TALKING ABOUT?
CURSE? WHAT CURSE?

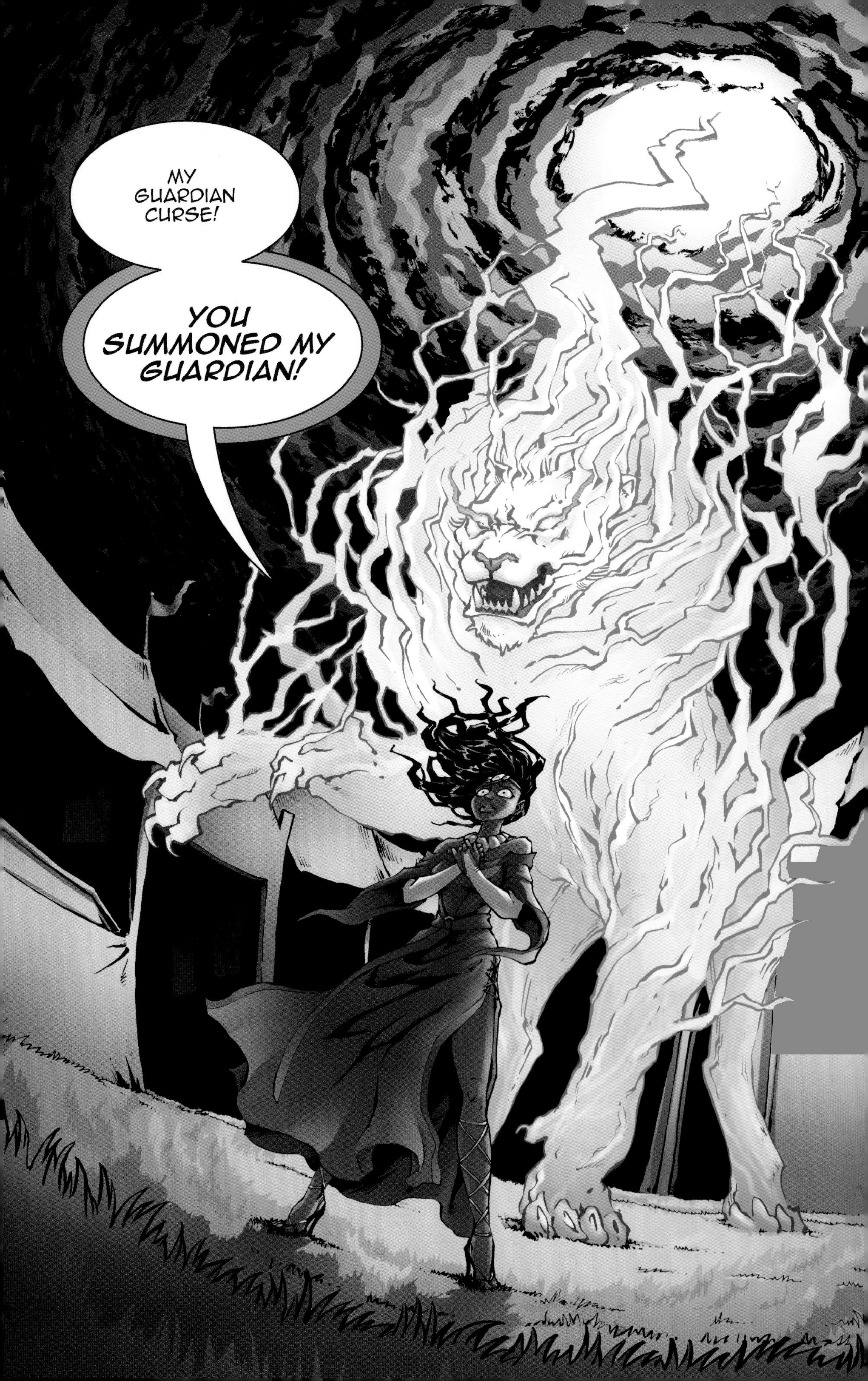
MY GUARDIAN CURSE!
YOU SUMMONED MY GUARDIAN!

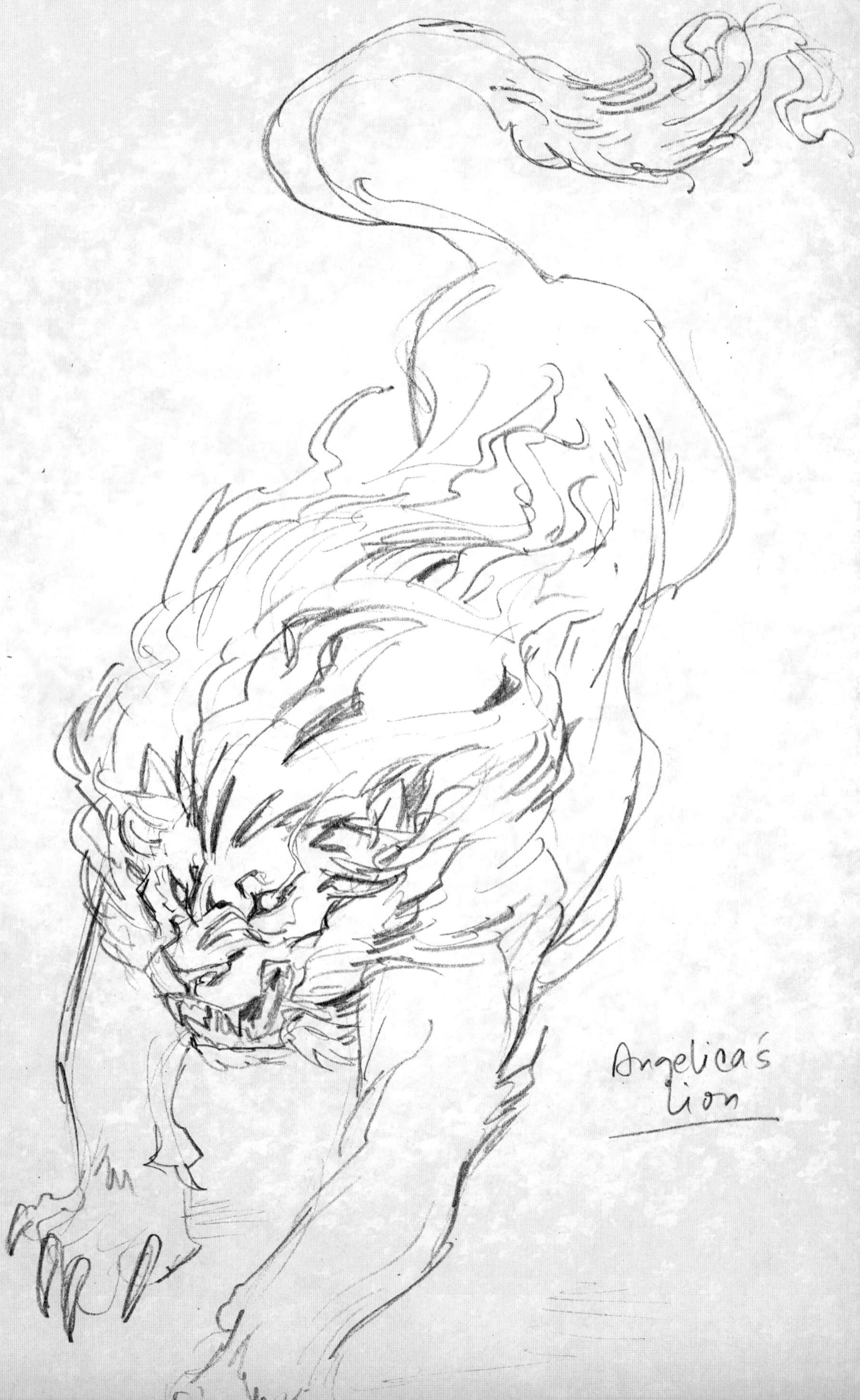
Angelica's Lion

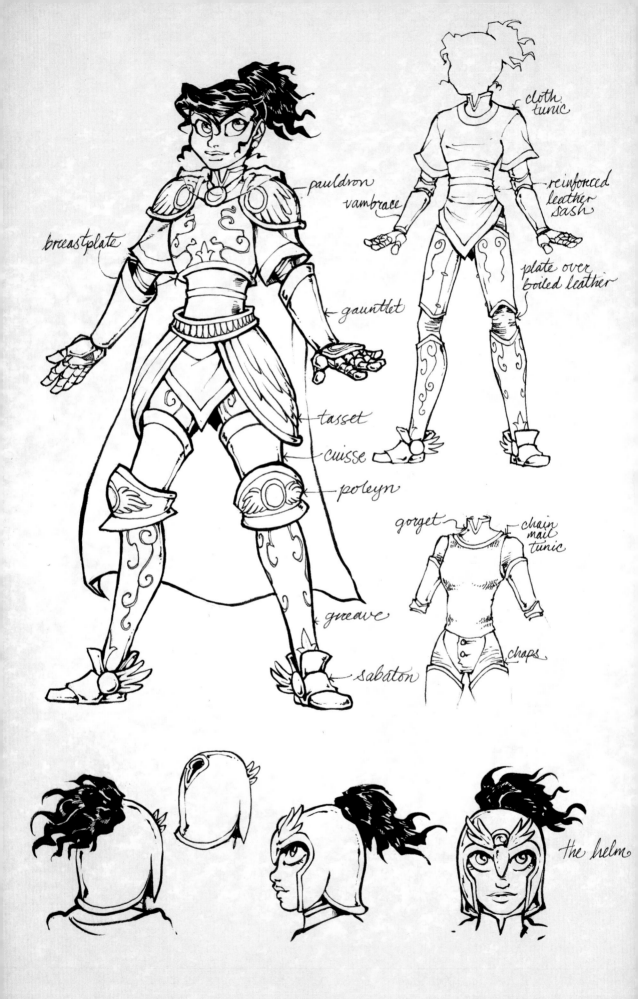

pauldron
vambrace
breastplate
gauntlet
tasset
cuisse
poleyn
greave
sabaton

cloth tunic
reinforced leather sash
plate over boiled leather

gorget
chain mail tunic
chaps

the helm

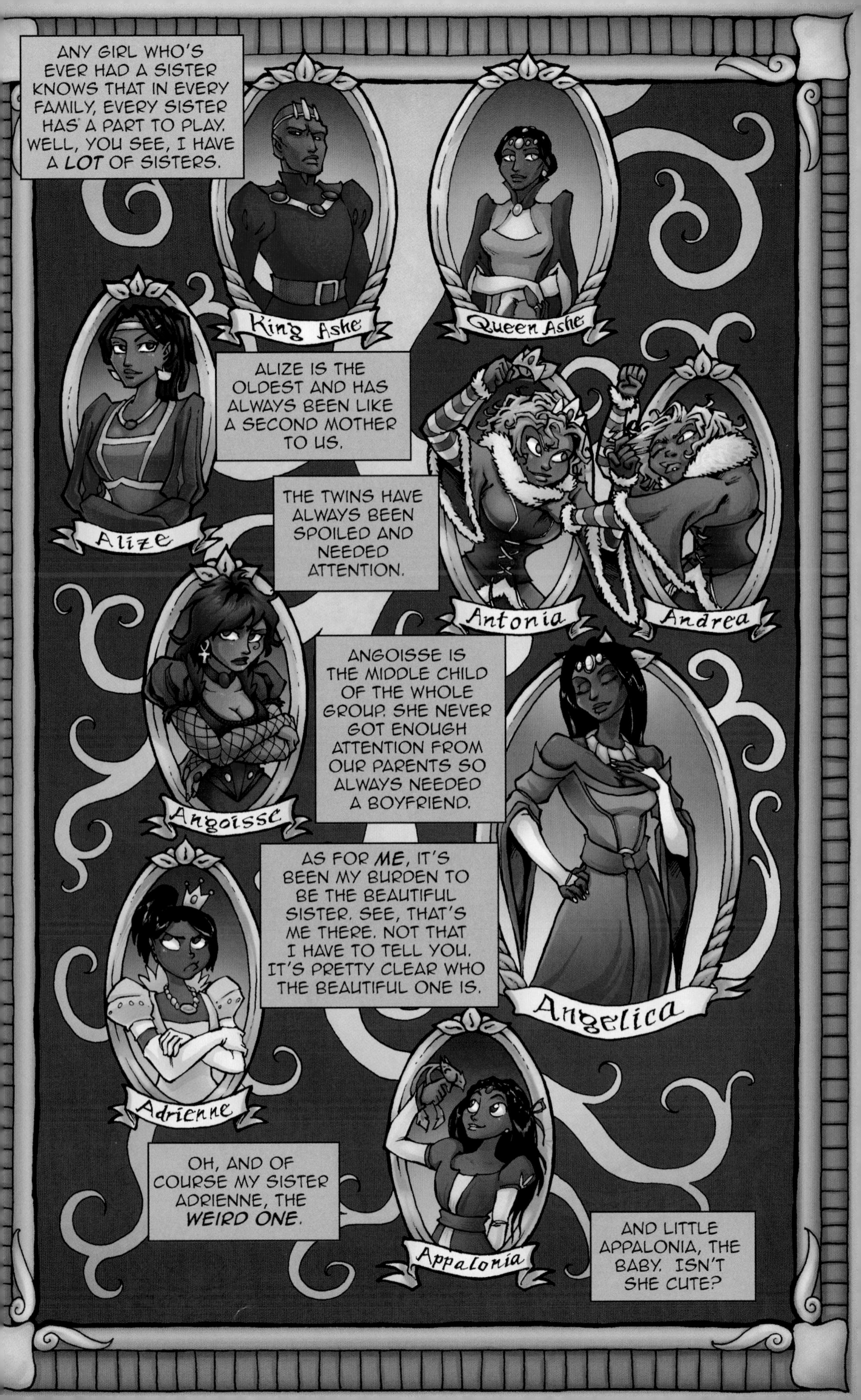
ANY GIRL WHO'S EVER HAD A SISTER KNOWS THAT IN EVERY FAMILY, EVERY SISTER HAS A PART TO PLAY. WELL, YOU SEE, I HAVE A LOT OF SISTERS.
King Ashe
Queen Ashe
Alize
ALIZE IS THE OLDEST AND HAS ALWAYS BEEN LIKE A SECOND MOTHER TO US.
THE TWINS HAVE ALWAYS BEEN SPOILED AND NEEDED ATTENTION.
Antonia
Andrea
Angoisse
ANGOISSE IS THE MIDDLE CHILD OF THE WHOLE GROUP. SHE NEVER GOT ENOUGH ATTENTION FROM OUR PARENTS SO ALWAYS NEEDED A BOYFRIEND.
AS FOR ME, IT'S BEEN MY BURDEN TO BE THE BEAUTIFUL SISTER. SEE, THAT'S ME THERE. NOT THAT I HAVE TO TELL YOU. IT'S PRETTY CLEAR WHO THE BEAUTIFUL ONE IS.
Angelica
Adrienne
OH, AND OF COURSE MY SISTER ADRIENNE, THE WEIRD ONE.
Appalonia
AND LITTLE APPALONIA, THE BABY. ISN'T SHE CUTE?

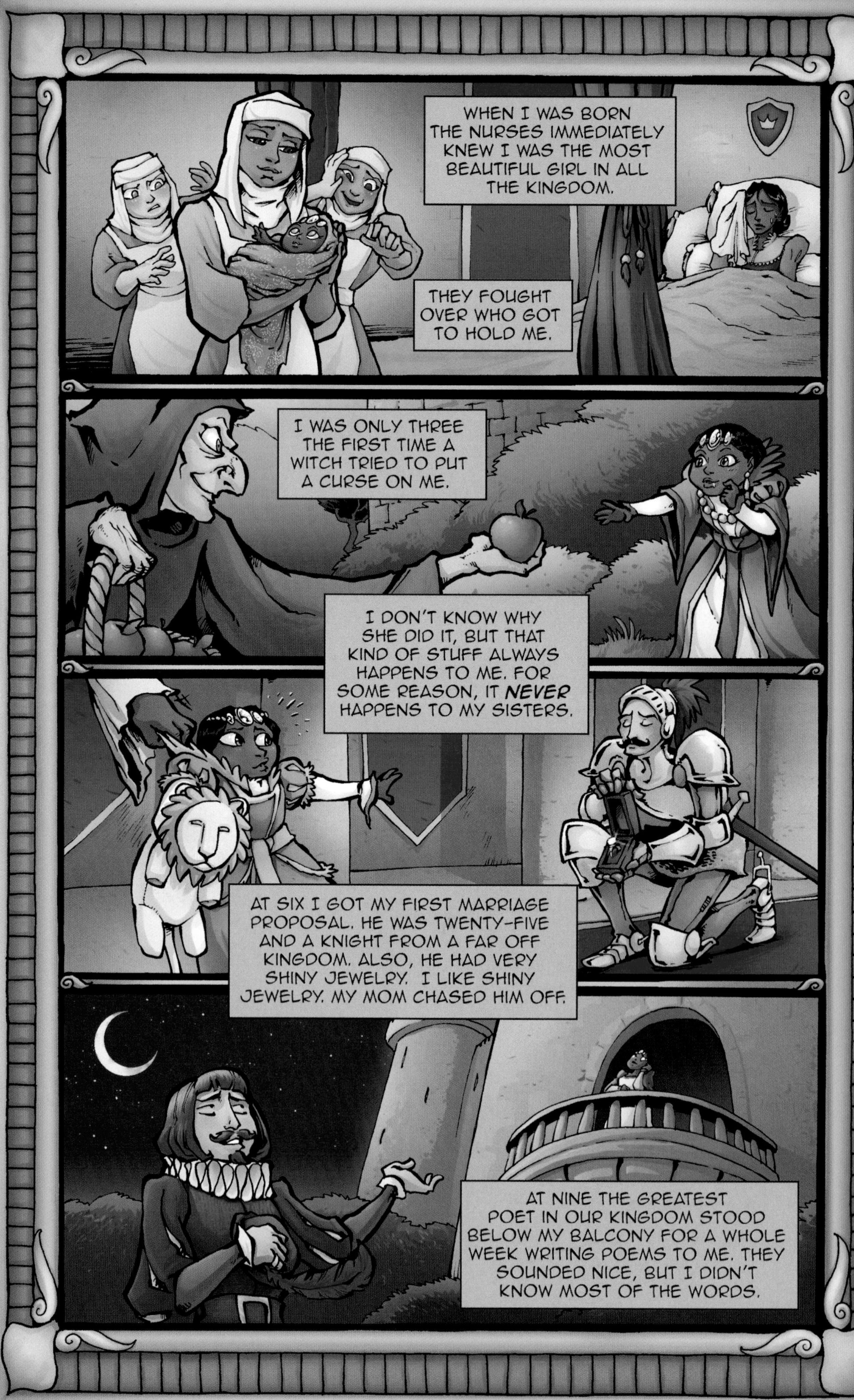
WHEN I WAS BORN THE NURSES IMMEDIATELY KNEW I WAS THE MOST BEAUTIFUL GIRL IN ALL THE KINGDOM.
THEY FOUGHT OVER WHO GOT TO HOLD ME.
I WAS ONLY THREE THE FIRST TIME A WITCH TRIED TO PUT A CURSE ON ME.
I DON'T KNOW WHY SHE DID IT, BUT THAT KIND OF STUFF ALWAYS HAPPENS TO ME. FOR SOME REASON, IT ***NEVER*** HAPPENS TO MY SISTERS.
AT SIX I GOT MY FIRST MARRIAGE PROPOSAL. HE WAS TWENTY-FIVE AND A KNIGHT FROM A FAR OFF KINGDOM. ALSO, HE HAD VERY SHINY JEWELRY. I LIKE SHINY JEWELRY. MY MOM CHASED HIM OFF.
AT NINE THE GREATEST POET IN OUR KINGDOM STOOD BELOW MY BALCONY FOR A WHOLE WEEK WRITING POEMS TO ME. THEY SOUNDED NICE, BUT I DIDN'T KNOW MOST OF THE WORDS.

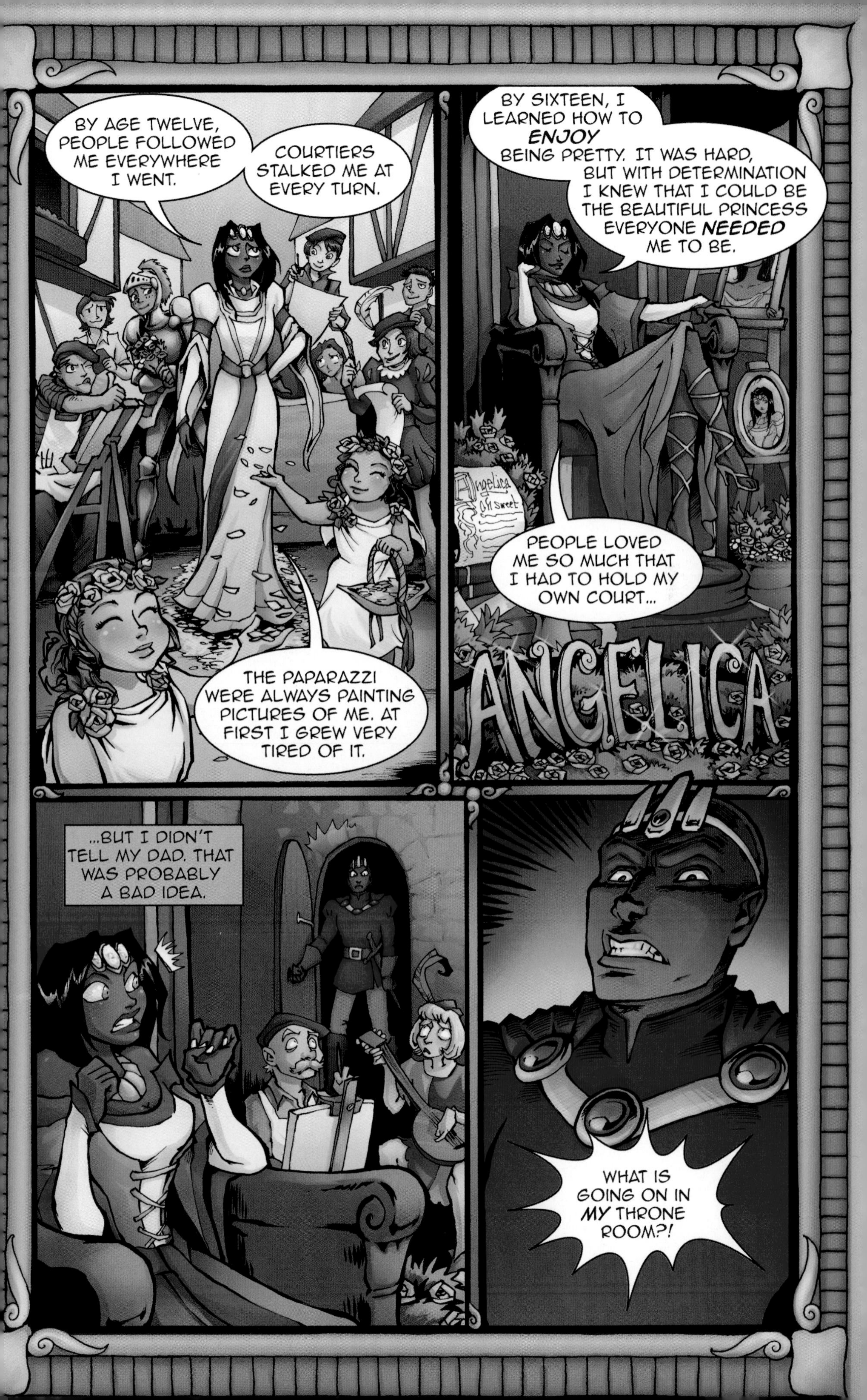
BY AGE TWELVE, PEOPLE FOLLOWED ME EVERYWHERE I WENT.
COURTIERS STALKED ME AT EVERY TURN.
THE PAPARAZZI WERE ALWAYS PAINTING PICTURES OF ME. AT FIRST I GREW VERY TIRED OF IT.
BY SIXTEEN, I LEARNED HOW TO ENJOY BEING PRETTY. IT WAS HARD, BUT WITH DETERMINATION I KNEW THAT I COULD BE THE BEAUTIFUL PRINCESS EVERYONE NEEDED ME TO BE.
PEOPLE LOVED ME SO MUCH THAT I HAD TO HOLD MY OWN COURT...
ANGELICA
...BUT I DIDN'T TELL MY DAD. THAT WAS PROBABLY A BAD IDEA.
WHAT IS GOING ON IN MY THRONE ROOM?!

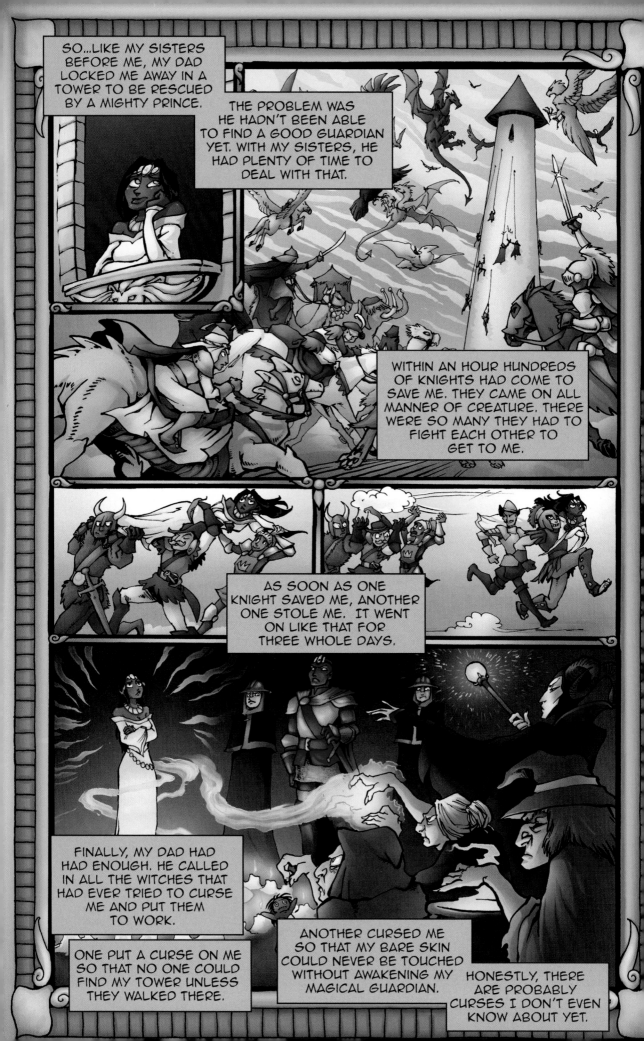

SO...LIKE MY SISTERS BEFORE ME, MY DAD LOCKED ME AWAY IN A TOWER TO BE RESCUED BY A MIGHTY PRINCE.

THE PROBLEM WAS HE HADN'T BEEN ABLE TO FIND A GOOD GUARDIAN YET. WITH MY SISTERS, HE HAD PLENTY OF TIME TO DEAL WITH THAT.

WITHIN AN HOUR HUNDREDS OF KNIGHTS HAD COME TO SAVE ME. THEY CAME ON ALL MANNER OF CREATURE. THERE WERE SO MANY THEY HAD TO FIGHT EACH OTHER TO GET TO ME.

AS SOON AS ONE KNIGHT SAVED ME, ANOTHER ONE STOLE ME. IT WENT ON LIKE THAT FOR THREE WHOLE DAYS.

FINALLY, MY DAD HAD HAD ENOUGH. HE CALLED IN ALL THE WITCHES THAT HAD EVER TRIED TO CURSE ME AND PUT THEM TO WORK.

ONE PUT A CURSE ON ME SO THAT NO ONE COULD FIND MY TOWER UNLESS THEY WALKED THERE.

ANOTHER CURSED ME SO THAT MY BARE SKIN COULD NEVER BE TOUCHED WITHOUT AWAKENING MY MAGICAL GUARDIAN.

HONESTLY, THERE ARE PROBABLY CURSES I DON'T EVEN KNOW ABOUT YET.

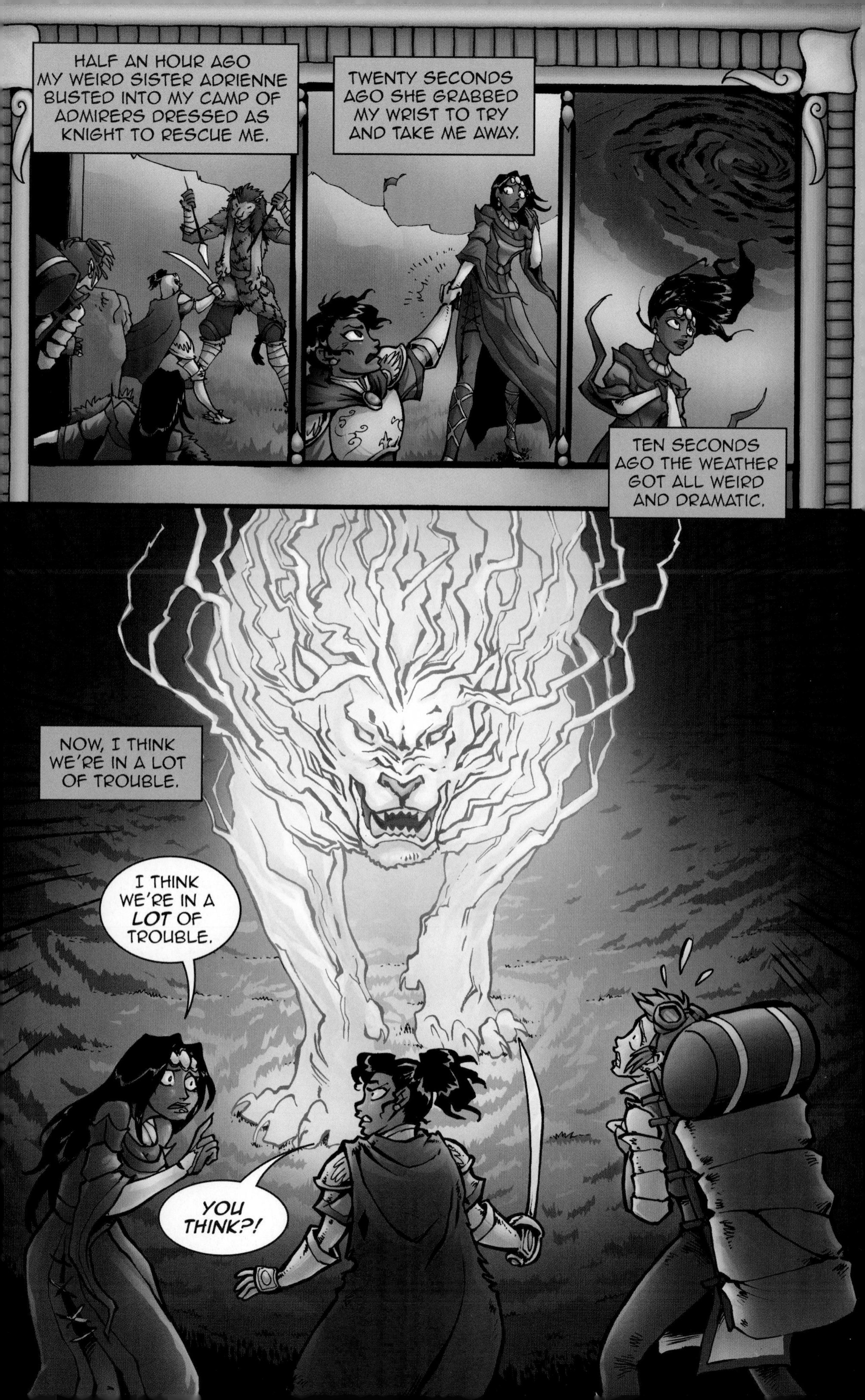
HALF AN HOUR AGO MY WEIRD SISTER ADRIENNE BUSTED INTO MY CAMP OF ADMIRERS DRESSED AS KNIGHT TO RESCUE ME.
TWENTY SECONDS AGO SHE GRABBED MY WRIST TO TRY AND TAKE ME AWAY.
TEN SECONDS AGO THE WEATHER GOT ALL WEIRD AND DRAMATIC.
NOW, I THINK WE'RE IN A LOT OF TROUBLE.
I THINK WE'RE IN A *LOT* OF TROUBLE.
YOU THINK?!

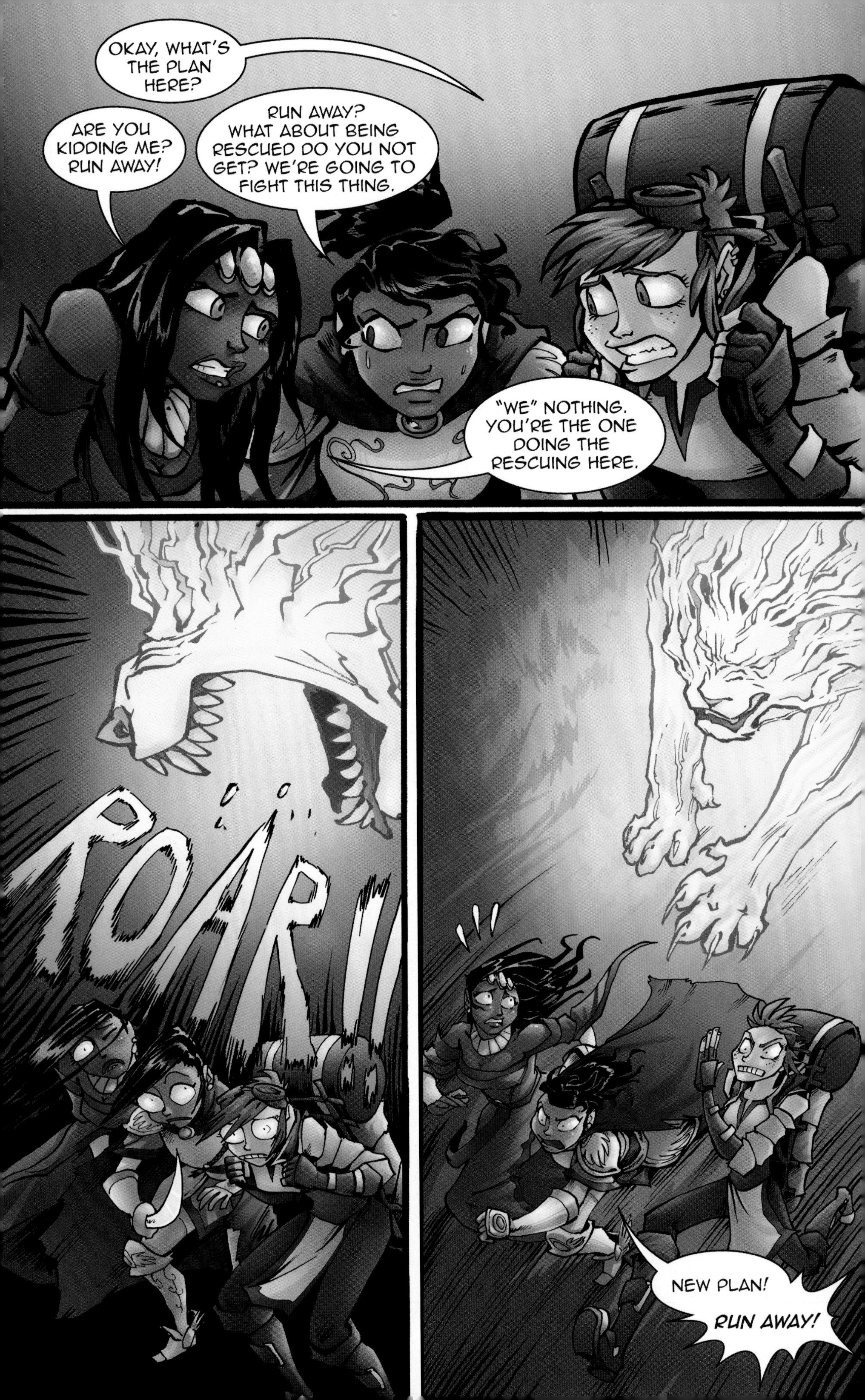
OKAY, WHAT'S THE PLAN HERE?
ARE YOU KIDDING ME? RUN AWAY!
RUN AWAY? WHAT ABOUT BEING RESCUED DO YOU NOT GET? WE'RE GOING TO FIGHT THIS THING.
"WE" NOTHING. YOU'RE THE ONE DOING THE RESCUING HERE.
ROAR!!
NEW PLAN!
RUN AWAY!

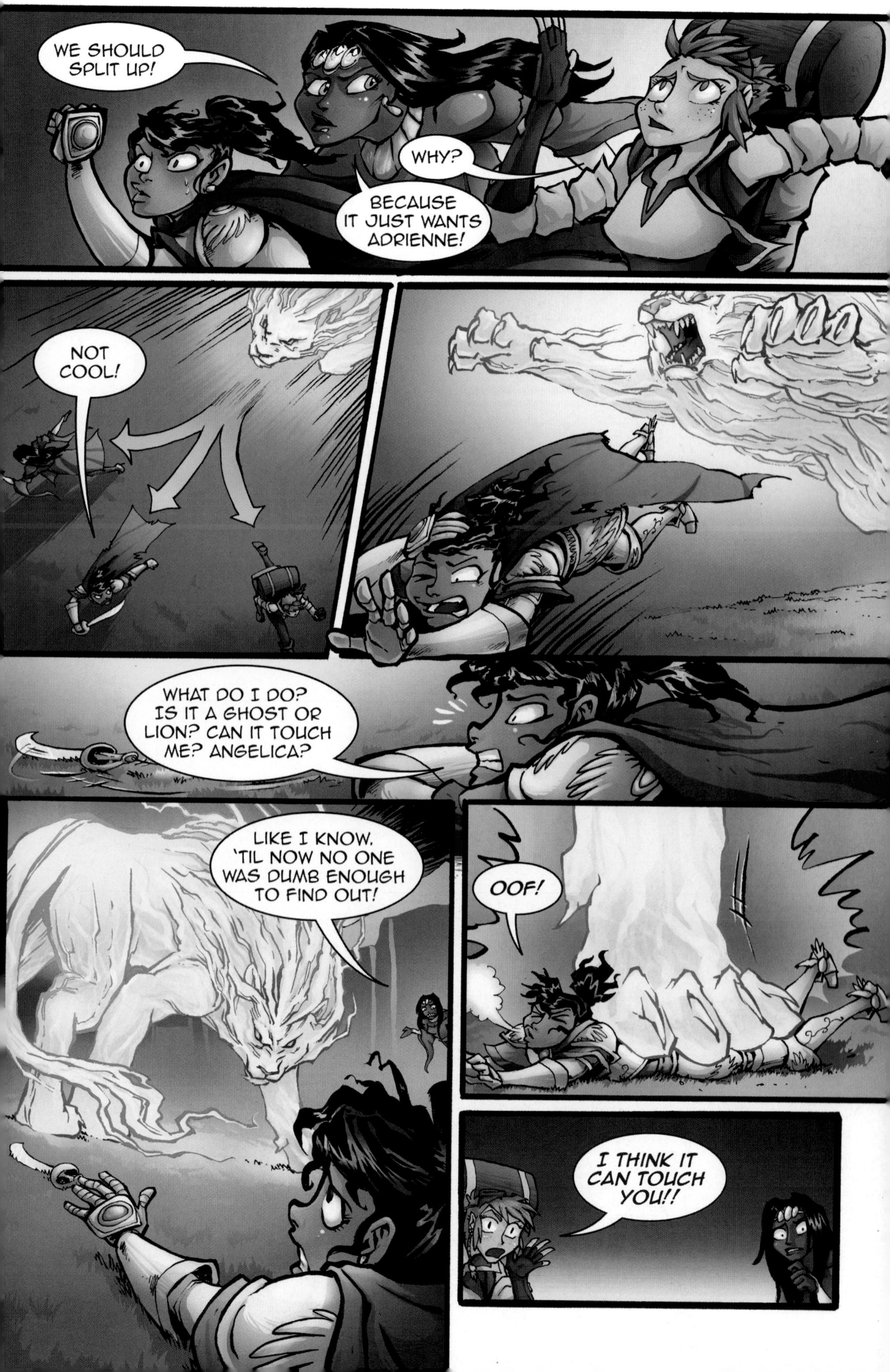
WE SHOULD SPLIT UP!
WHY?
BECAUSE IT JUST WANTS ADRIENNE!
NOT COOL!
WHAT DO I DO? IS IT A GHOST OR LION? CAN IT TOUCH ME? ANGELICA?
LIKE I KNOW. 'TIL NOW NO ONE WAS DUMB ENOUGH TO FIND OUT!
OOF!
I THINK IT CAN TOUCH YOU!!

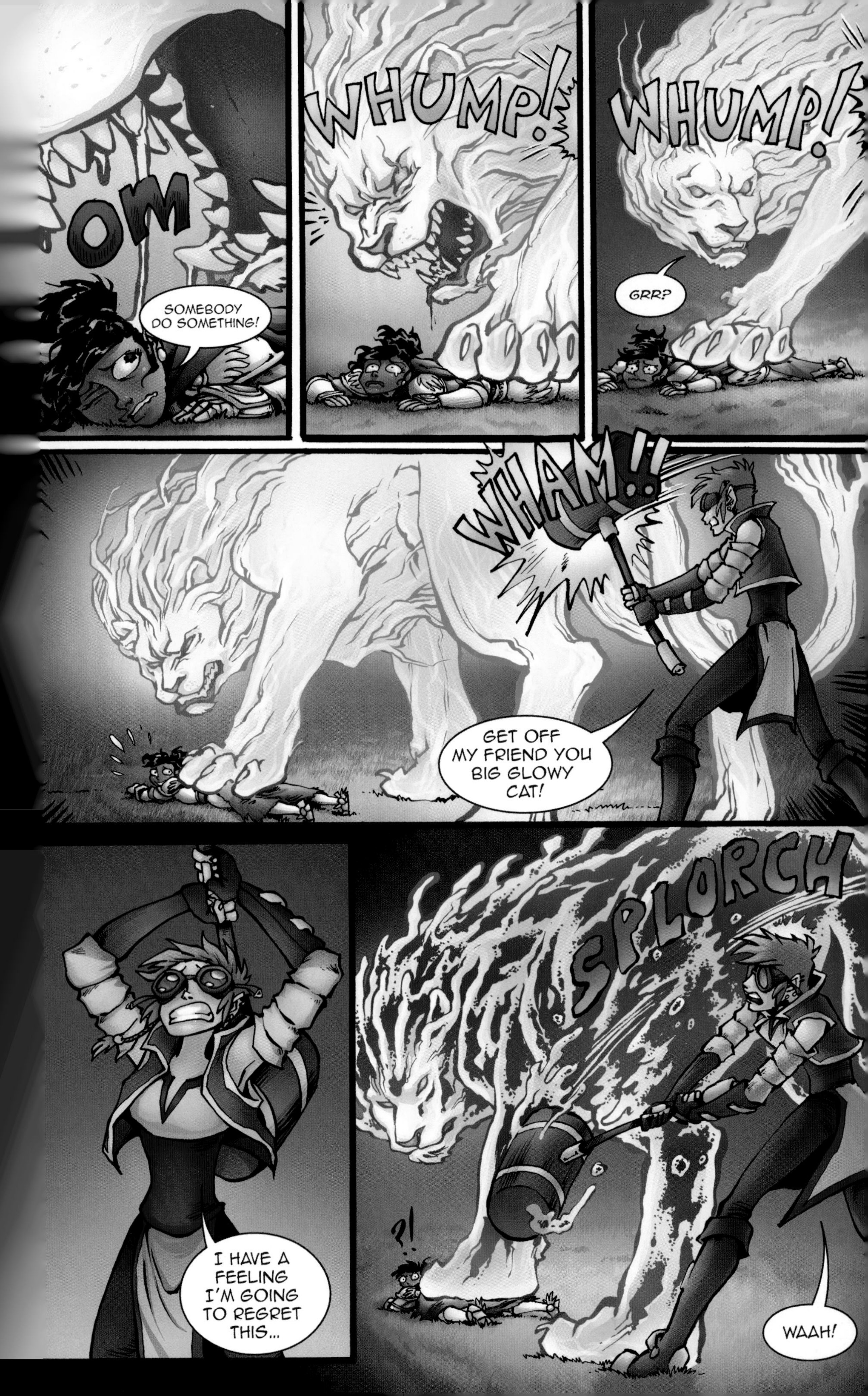
OM
SOMEBODY DO SOMETHING!
WHUMP!
WHUMP!
GRR?
WHAM!!
GET OFF MY FRIEND YOU BIG GLOWY CAT!
I HAVE A FEELING I'M GOING TO REGRET THIS...
SPLORCH
?!
WAAH!

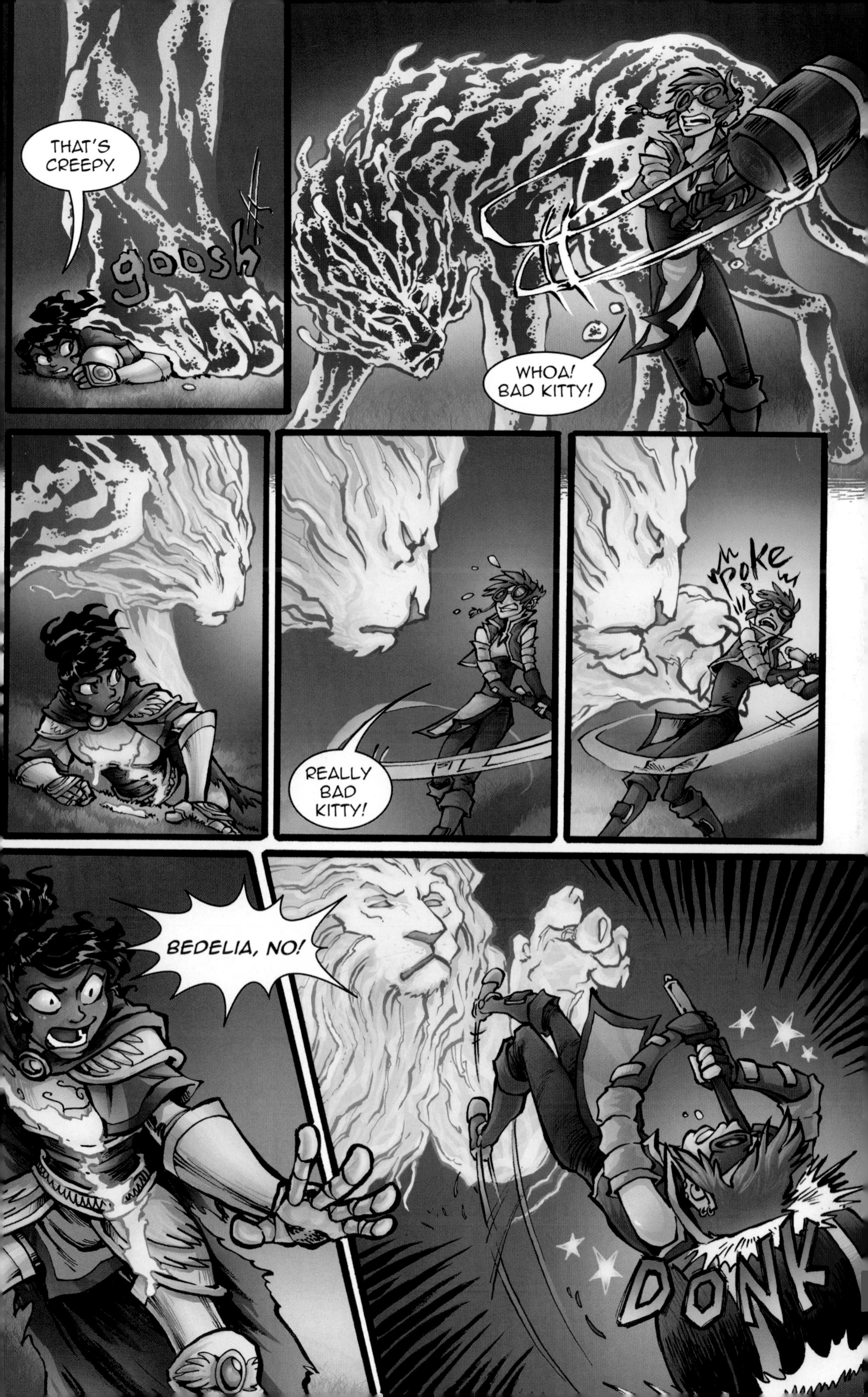
THAT'S CREEPY.
goosh
WHOA! BAD KITTY!
REALLY BAD KITTY!
poke
BEDELIA, NO!
DONK

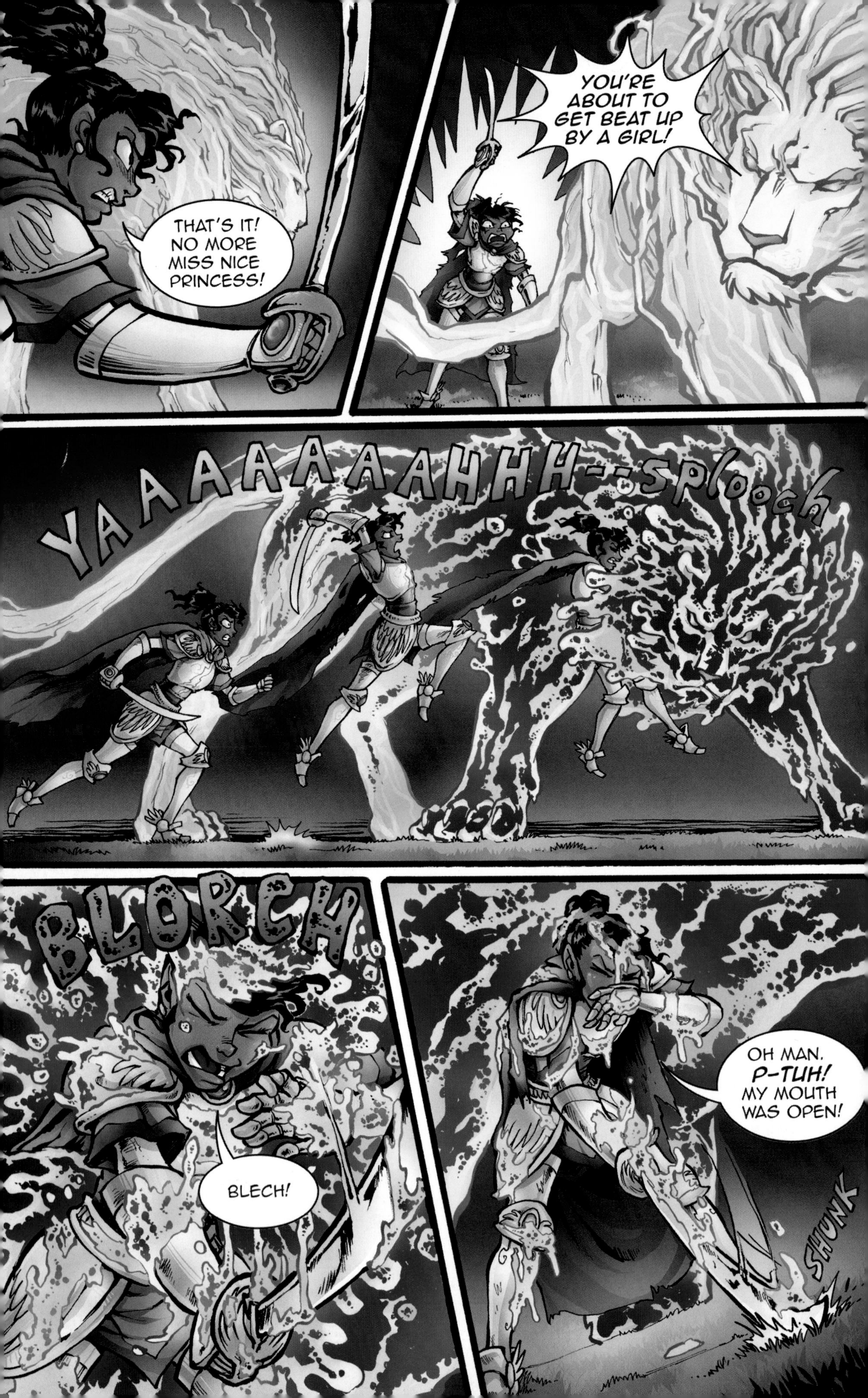
THAT'S IT! NO MORE MISS NICE PRINCESS!
YOU'RE ABOUT TO GET BEAT UP BY A GIRL!
YAAAAAAAHHH--sploooch
BLORCH
BLECH!
OH MAN. *P-TUH!* MY MOUTH WAS OPEN!
SHUNK

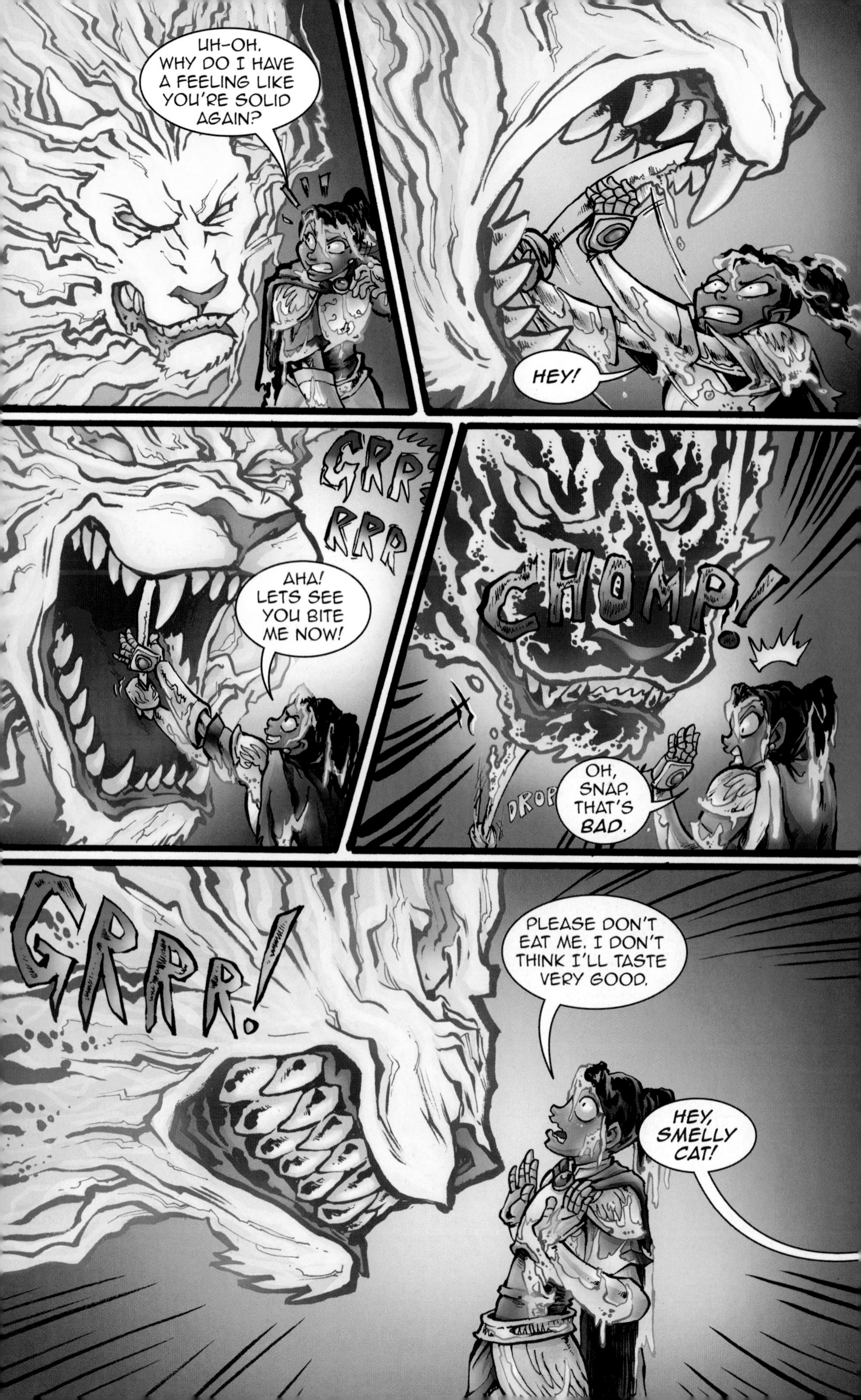

UH-OH. WHY DO I HAVE A FEELING LIKE YOU'RE SOLID AGAIN?
HEY!
GRRR RRR
AHA! LETS SEE YOU BITE ME NOW!
CHOMP!
DROP
OH, SNAP. THAT'S BAD.
GRRRR!
PLEASE DON'T EAT ME. I DON'T THINK I'LL TASTE VERY GOOD.
HEY, SMELLY CAT!

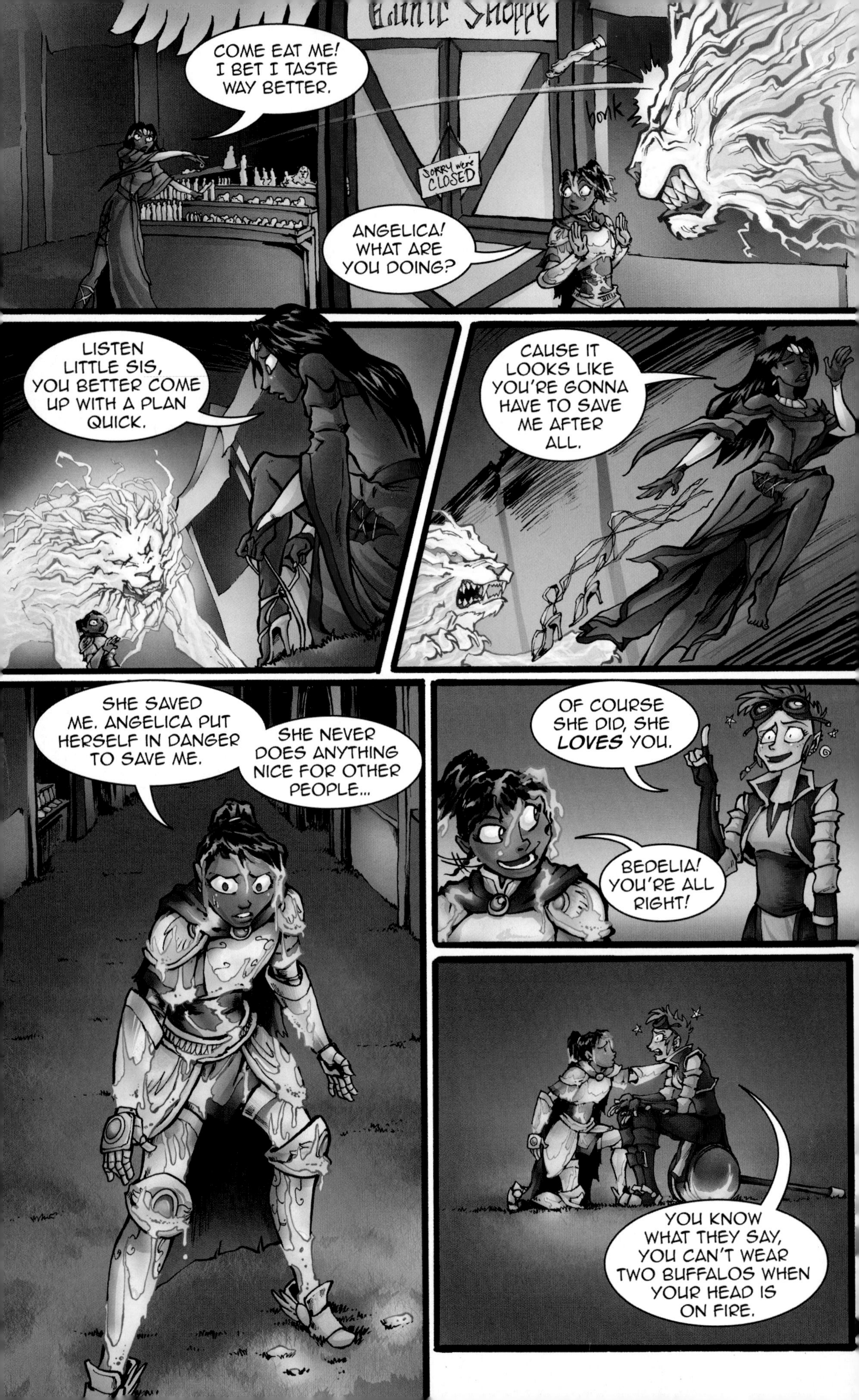

COME EAT ME! I BET I TASTE WAY BETTER.
bonk
SORRY we're CLOSED
ANGELICA! WHAT ARE YOU DOING?
LISTEN LITTLE SIS, YOU BETTER COME UP WITH A PLAN QUICK.
CAUSE IT LOOKS LIKE YOU'RE GONNA HAVE TO SAVE ME AFTER ALL.
SHE SAVED ME. ANGELICA PUT HERSELF IN DANGER TO SAVE ME.
SHE NEVER DOES ANYTHING NICE FOR OTHER PEOPLE...
OF COURSE SHE DID, SHE ***LOVES*** YOU.
BEDELIA! YOU'RE ALL RIGHT!
YOU KNOW WHAT THEY SAY, YOU CAN'T WEAR TWO BUFFALOS WHEN YOUR HEAD IS ON FIRE.

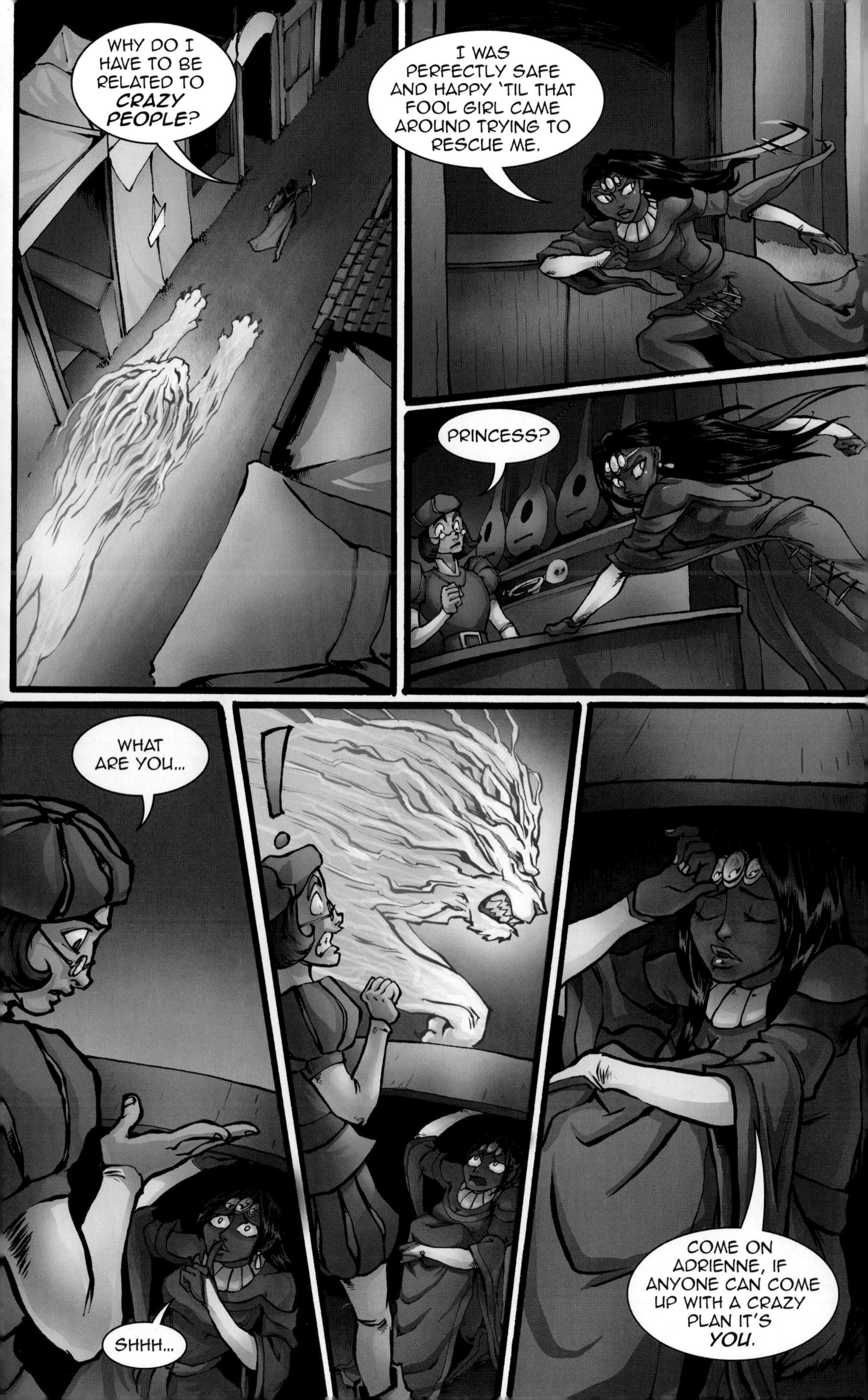
WHY DO I HAVE TO BE RELATED TO CRAZY PEOPLE?
I WAS PERFECTLY SAFE AND HAPPY 'TIL THAT FOOL GIRL CAME AROUND TRYING TO RESCUE ME.
PRINCESS?
WHAT ARE YOU...
SHHH...
!
COME ON ADRIENNE, IF ANYONE CAN COME UP WITH A CRAZY PLAN IT'S YOU.

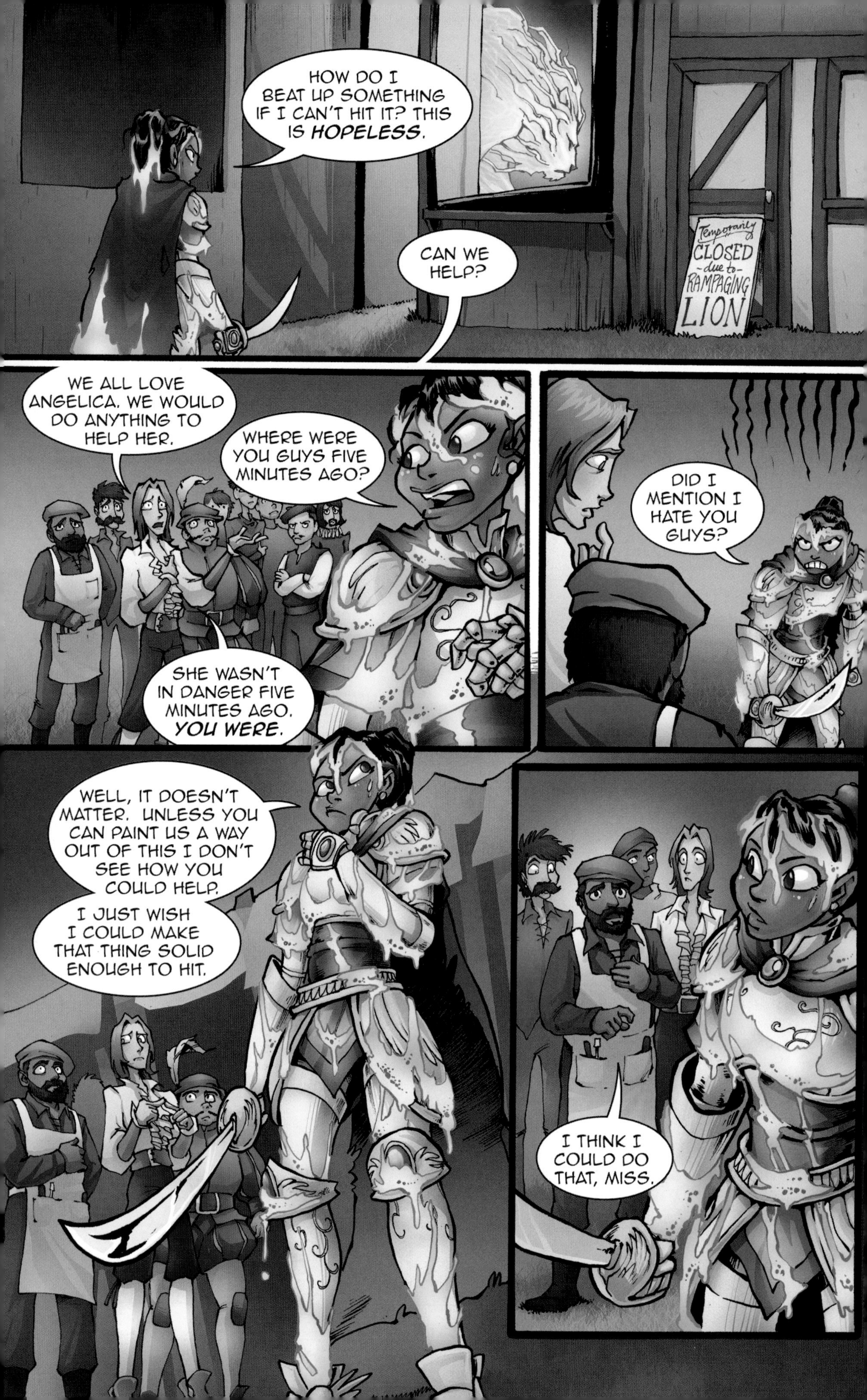
HOW DO I BEAT UP SOMETHING IF I CAN'T HIT IT? THIS IS HOPELESS.
Temporarily CLOSED -due to- RAMPAGING LION
CAN WE HELP?
WE ALL LOVE ANGELICA. WE WOULD DO ANYTHING TO HELP HER.
WHERE WERE YOU GUYS FIVE MINUTES AGO?
SHE WASN'T IN DANGER FIVE MINUTES AGO. YOU WERE.
DID I MENTION I HATE YOU GUYS?
WELL, IT DOESN'T MATTER. UNLESS YOU CAN PAINT US A WAY OUT OF THIS I DON'T SEE HOW YOU COULD HELP.
I JUST WISH I COULD MAKE THAT THING SOLID ENOUGH TO HIT.
I THINK I COULD DO THAT, MISS.

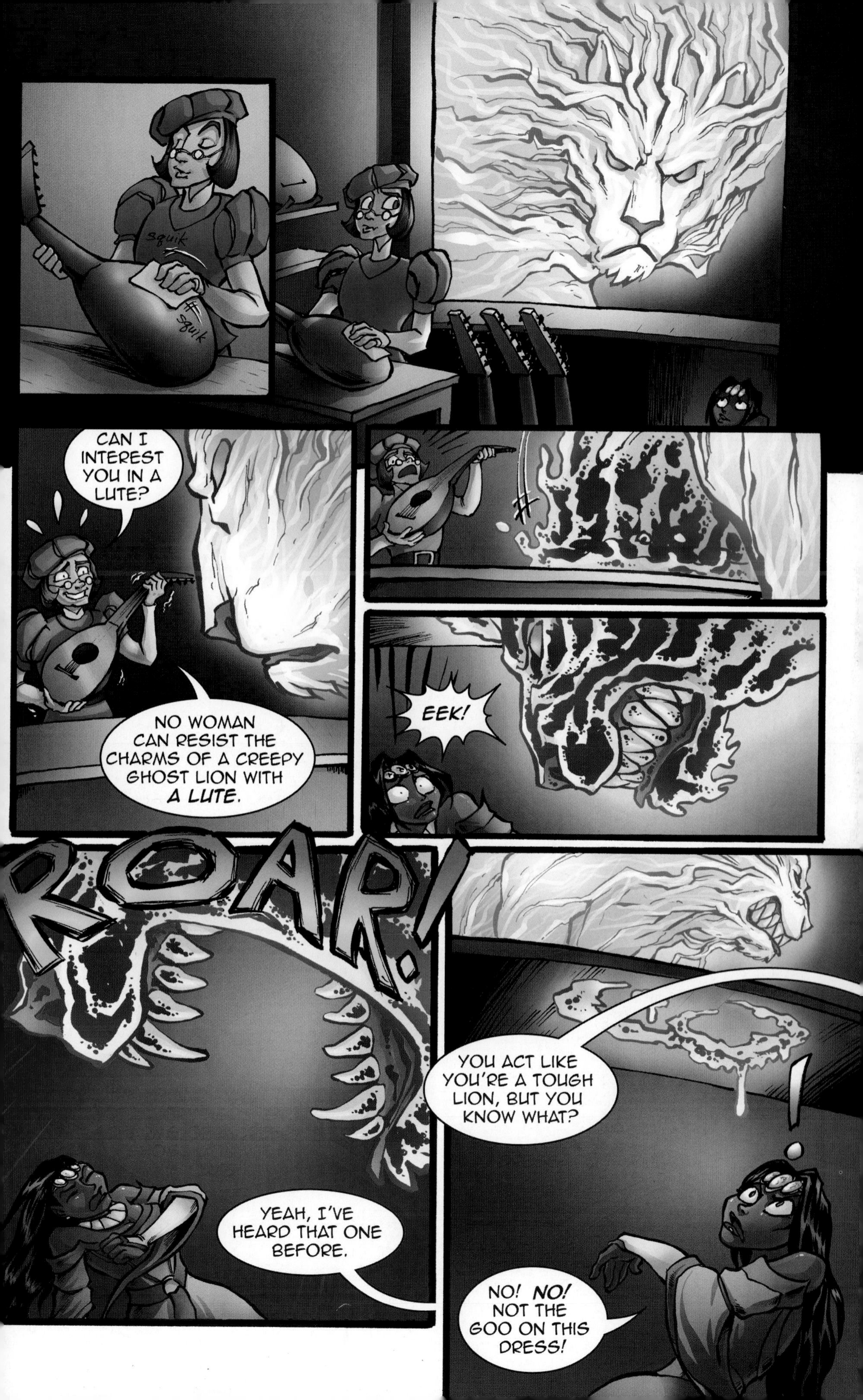
squik
squik
CAN I INTEREST YOU IN A LUTE?
NO WOMAN CAN RESIST THE CHARMS OF A CREEPY GHOST LION WITH *A LUTE*.
EEK!
ROAR!
YEAH, I'VE HEARD THAT ONE BEFORE.
YOU ACT LIKE YOU'RE A TOUGH LION, BUT YOU KNOW WHAT?
!
NO! ***NO!*** NOT THE GOO ON THIS DRESS!

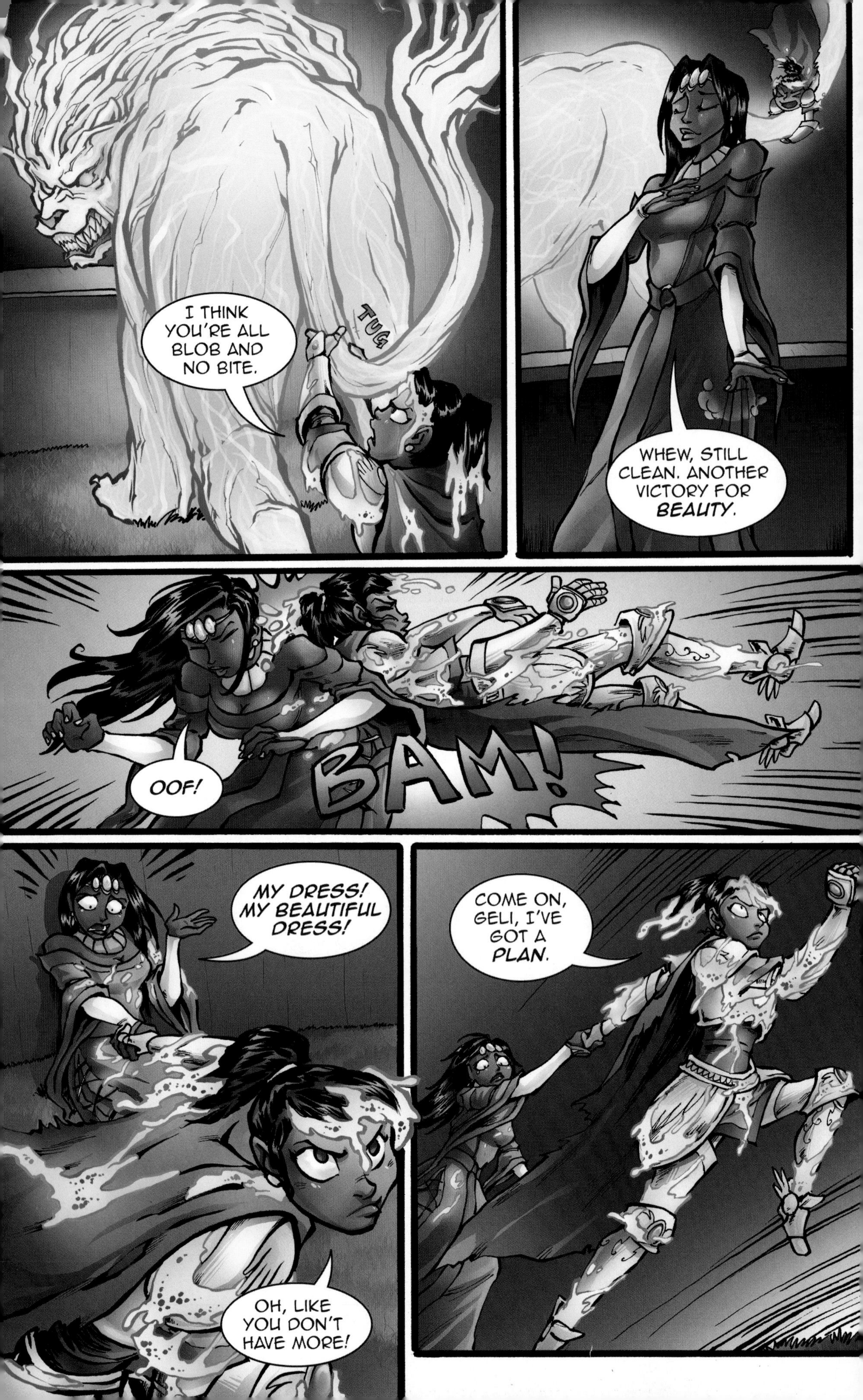
I THINK YOU'RE ALL BLOB AND NO BITE.
TUG
WHEW, STILL CLEAN. ANOTHER VICTORY FOR BEAUTY.
OOF!
BAM!
MY DRESS! MY BEAUTIFUL DRESS!
OH, LIKE YOU DON'T HAVE MORE!
COME ON, GELI, I'VE GOT A PLAN.

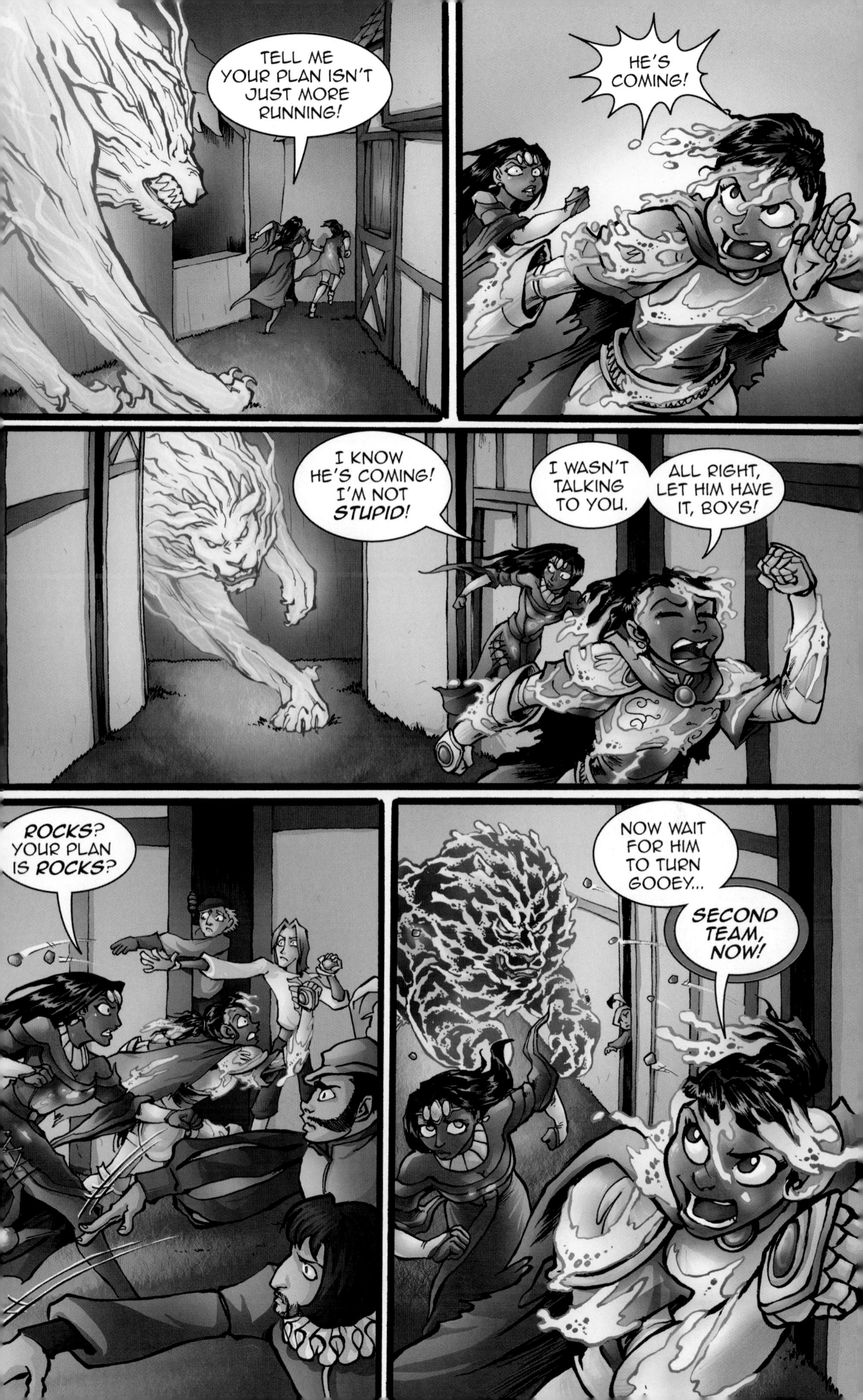
TELL ME YOUR PLAN ISN'T JUST MORE RUNNING!
HE'S COMING!
I KNOW HE'S COMING! I'M NOT *STUPID*!
I WASN'T TALKING TO YOU.
ALL RIGHT, LET HIM HAVE IT, BOYS!
ROCKS? YOUR PLAN IS *ROCKS*?
NOW WAIT FOR HIM TO TURN GOOEY...
SECOND TEAM, NOW!

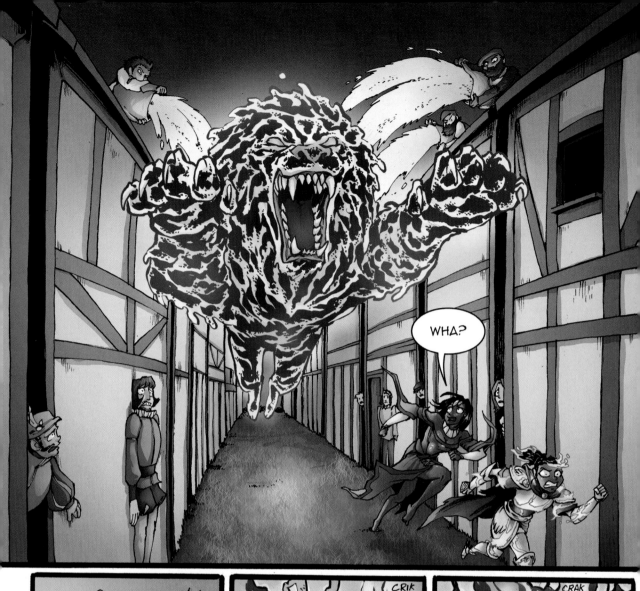

WHA?

OUCH!

ANGELICA! GET UP!

CRIK CRIK

CRIK

CRAK

NO!

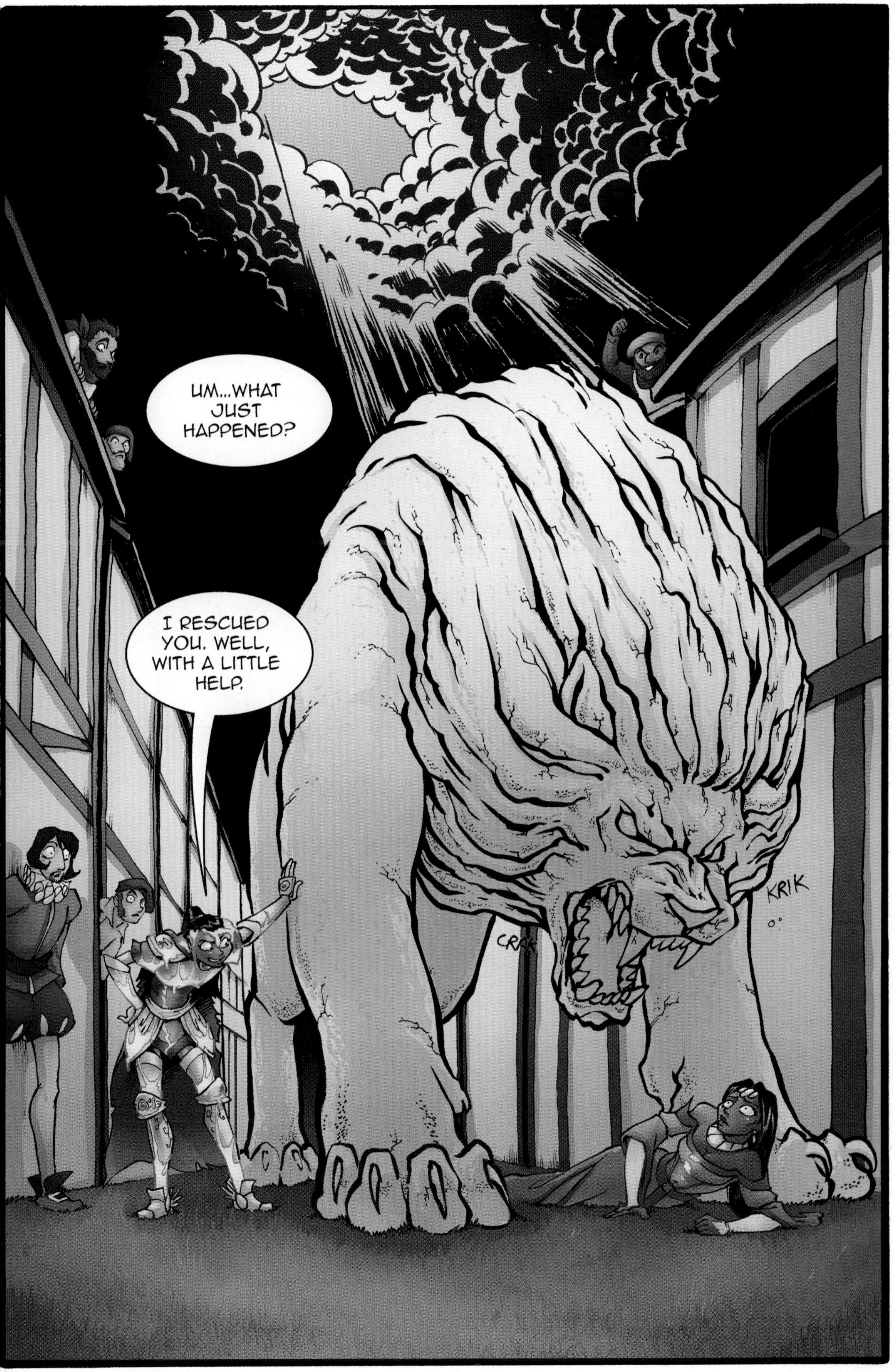
UM...WHAT JUST HAPPENED?
I RESCUED YOU. WELL, WITH A LITTLE HELP.
KRIK
CRAK

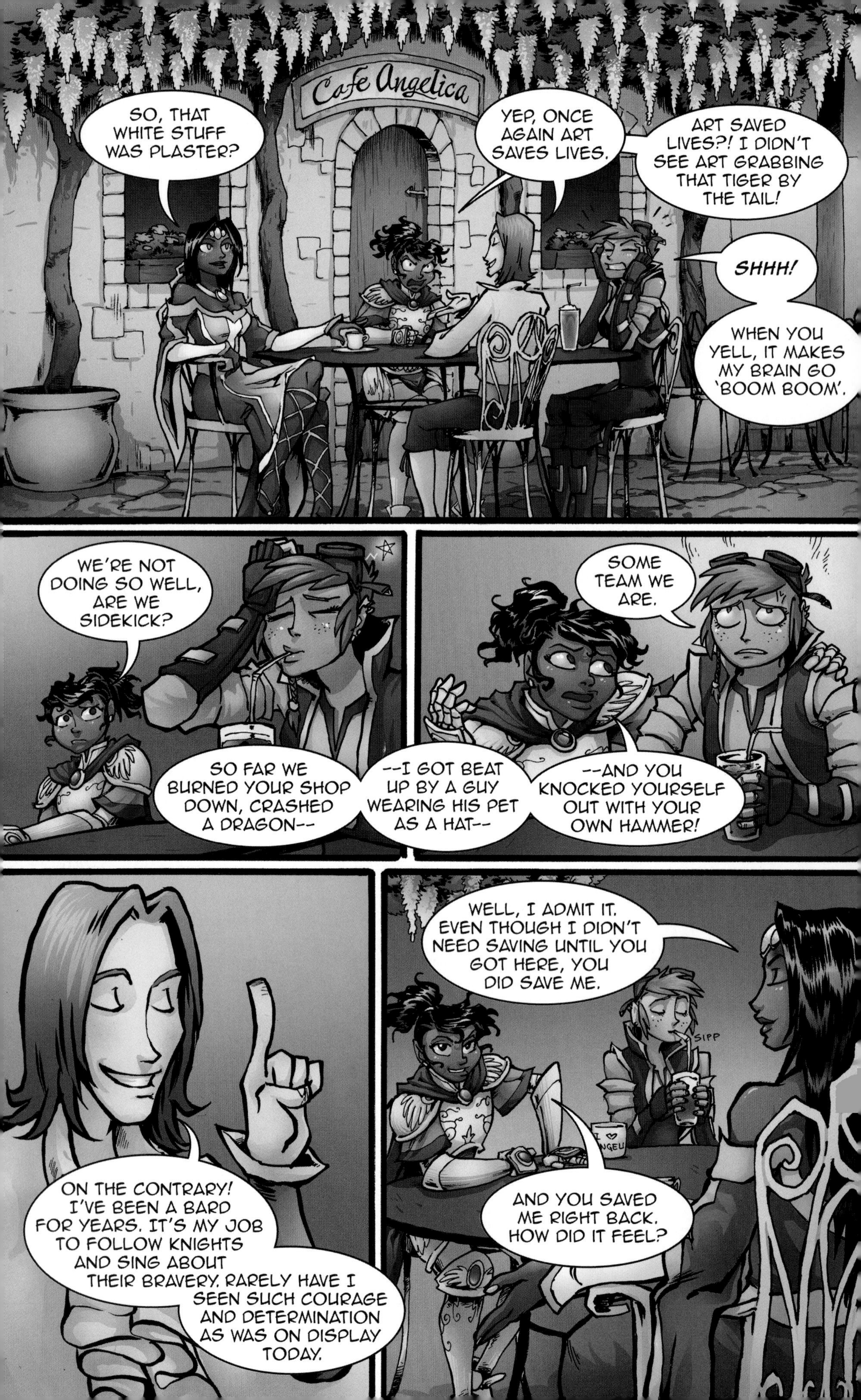
Cafe Angelica
SO, THAT WHITE STUFF WAS PLASTER?
YEP, ONCE AGAIN ART SAVES LIVES.
ART SAVED LIVES?! I DIDN'T SEE ART GRABBING THAT TIGER BY THE TAIL!
SHHH!
WHEN YOU YELL, IT MAKES MY BRAIN GO 'BOOM BOOM'.
WE'RE NOT DOING SO WELL, ARE WE SIDEKICK?
SO FAR WE BURNED YOUR SHOP DOWN, CRASHED A DRAGON--
SOME TEAM WE ARE.
--I GOT BEAT UP BY A GUY WEARING HIS PET AS A HAT--
--AND YOU KNOCKED YOURSELF OUT WITH YOUR OWN HAMMER!
ON THE CONTRARY! I'VE BEEN A BARD FOR YEARS. IT'S MY JOB TO FOLLOW KNIGHTS AND SING ABOUT THEIR BRAVERY. RARELY HAVE I SEEN SUCH COURAGE AND DETERMINATION AS WAS ON DISPLAY TODAY.
WELL, I ADMIT IT. EVEN THOUGH I DIDN'T NEED SAVING UNTIL YOU GOT HERE, YOU DID SAVE ME.
SIPP
AND YOU SAVED ME RIGHT BACK. HOW DID IT FEEL?

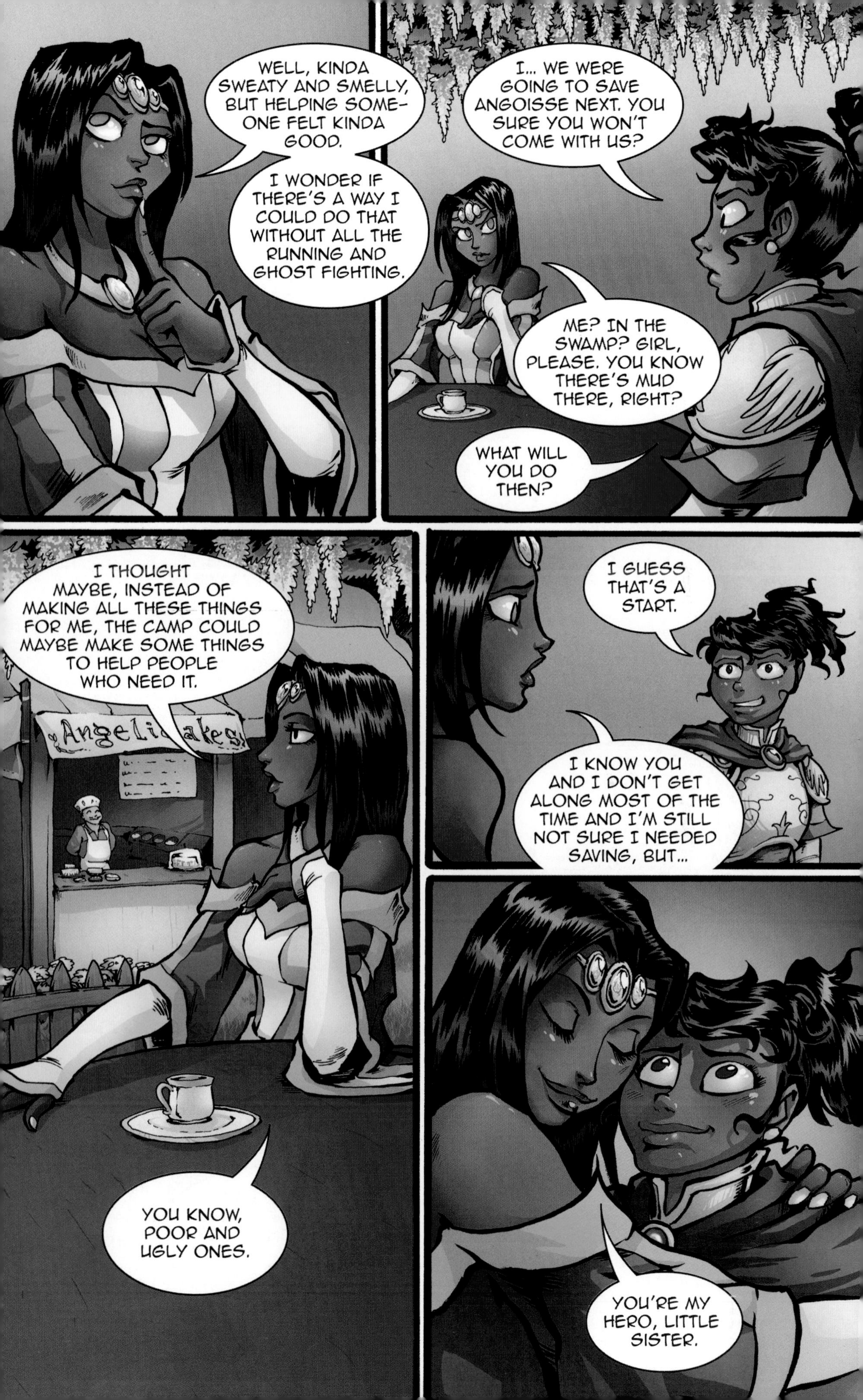

WELL, KINDA SWEATY AND SMELLY, BUT HELPING SOME-ONE FELT KINDA GOOD.
I WONDER IF THERE'S A WAY I COULD DO THAT WITHOUT ALL THE RUNNING AND GHOST FIGHTING.
I... WE WERE GOING TO SAVE ANGOISSE NEXT. YOU SURE YOU WON'T COME WITH US?
ME? IN THE SWAMP? GIRL, PLEASE. YOU KNOW THERE'S MUD THERE, RIGHT?
WHAT WILL YOU DO THEN?
I THOUGHT MAYBE, INSTEAD OF MAKING ALL THESE THINGS FOR ME, THE CAMP COULD MAYBE MAKE SOME THINGS TO HELP PEOPLE WHO NEED IT.
YOU KNOW, POOR AND UGLY ONES.
I GUESS THAT'S A START.
I KNOW YOU AND I DON'T GET ALONG MOST OF THE TIME AND I'M STILL NOT SURE I NEEDED SAVING, BUT...
YOU'RE MY HERO, LITTLE SISTER.

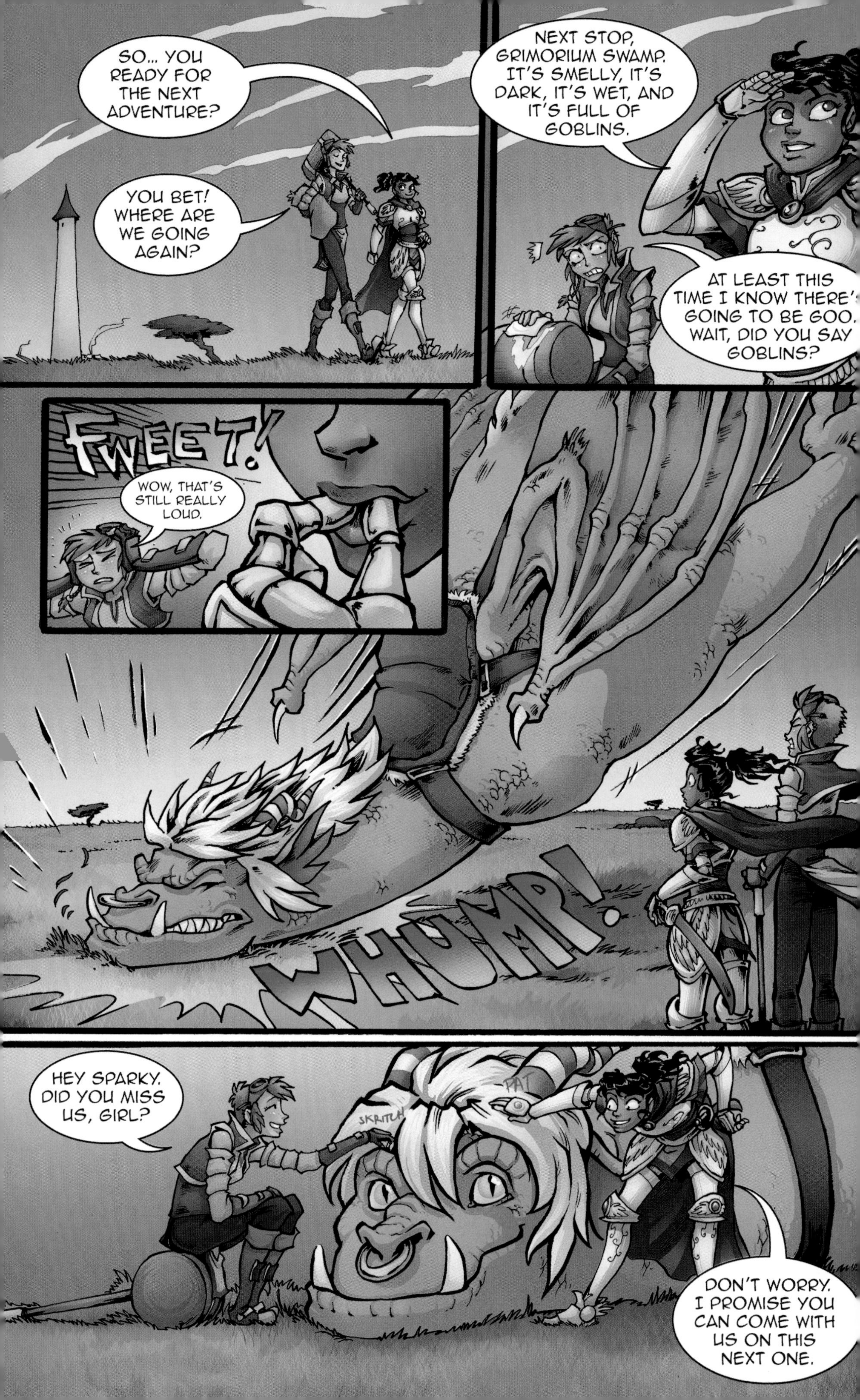
SO... YOU READY FOR THE NEXT ADVENTURE?
YOU BET! WHERE ARE WE GOING AGAIN?
NEXT STOP, GRIMORIUM SWAMP. IT'S SMELLY, IT'S DARK, IT'S WET, AND IT'S FULL OF GOBLINS.
AT LEAST THIS TIME I KNOW THERE'S GOING TO BE GOO. WAIT, DID YOU SAY GOBLINS?
FWEET!
WOW, THAT'S STILL REALLY LOUD.
WHUMP!
HEY SPARKY. DID YOU MISS US, GIRL?
SKRITCH
PAT
DON'T WORRY. I PROMISE YOU CAN COME WITH US ON THIS NEXT ONE.

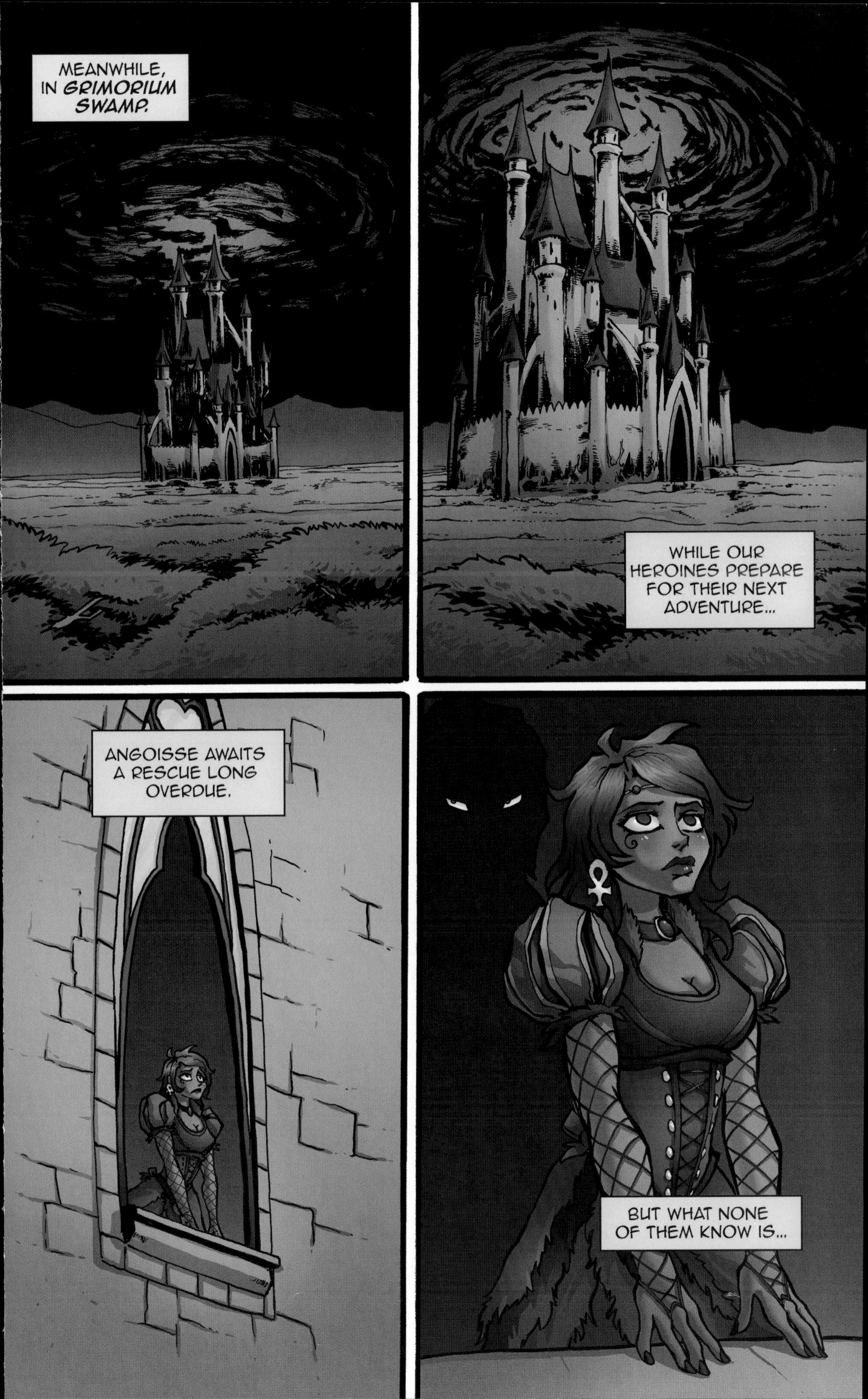
MEANWHILE, IN GRIMORIUM SWAMP.
WHILE OUR HEROINES PREPARE FOR THEIR NEXT ADVENTURE...
ANGOISSE AWAITS A RESCUE LONG OVERDUE.
BUT WHAT NONE OF THEM KNOW IS...

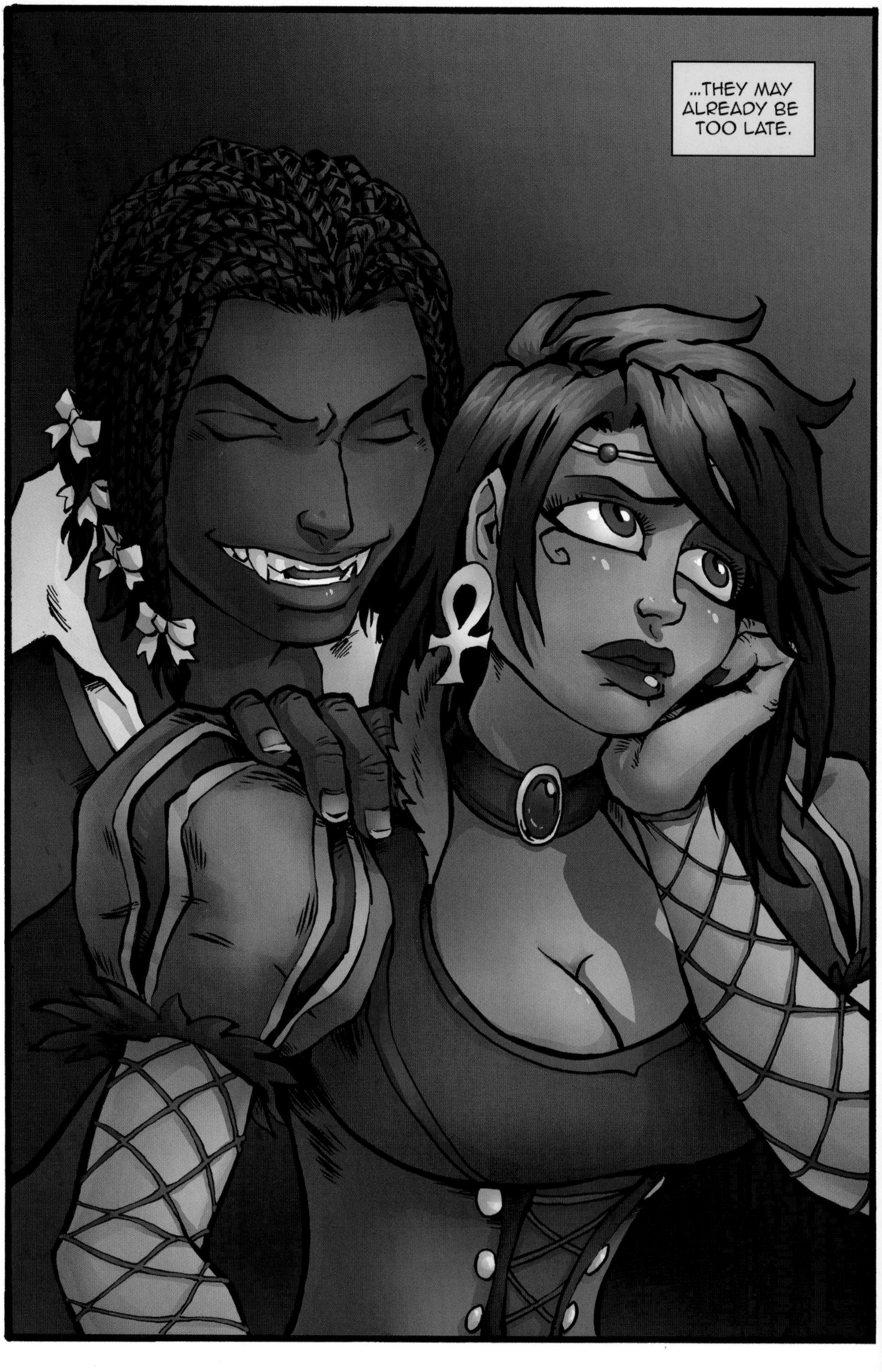
...THEY MAY ALREADY BE TOO LATE.

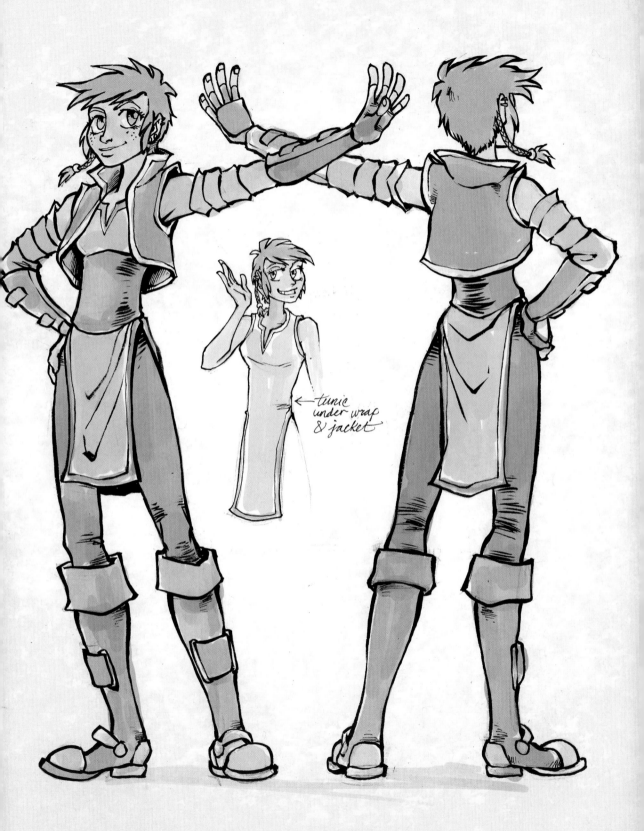

tunic
under wrap
& jacket

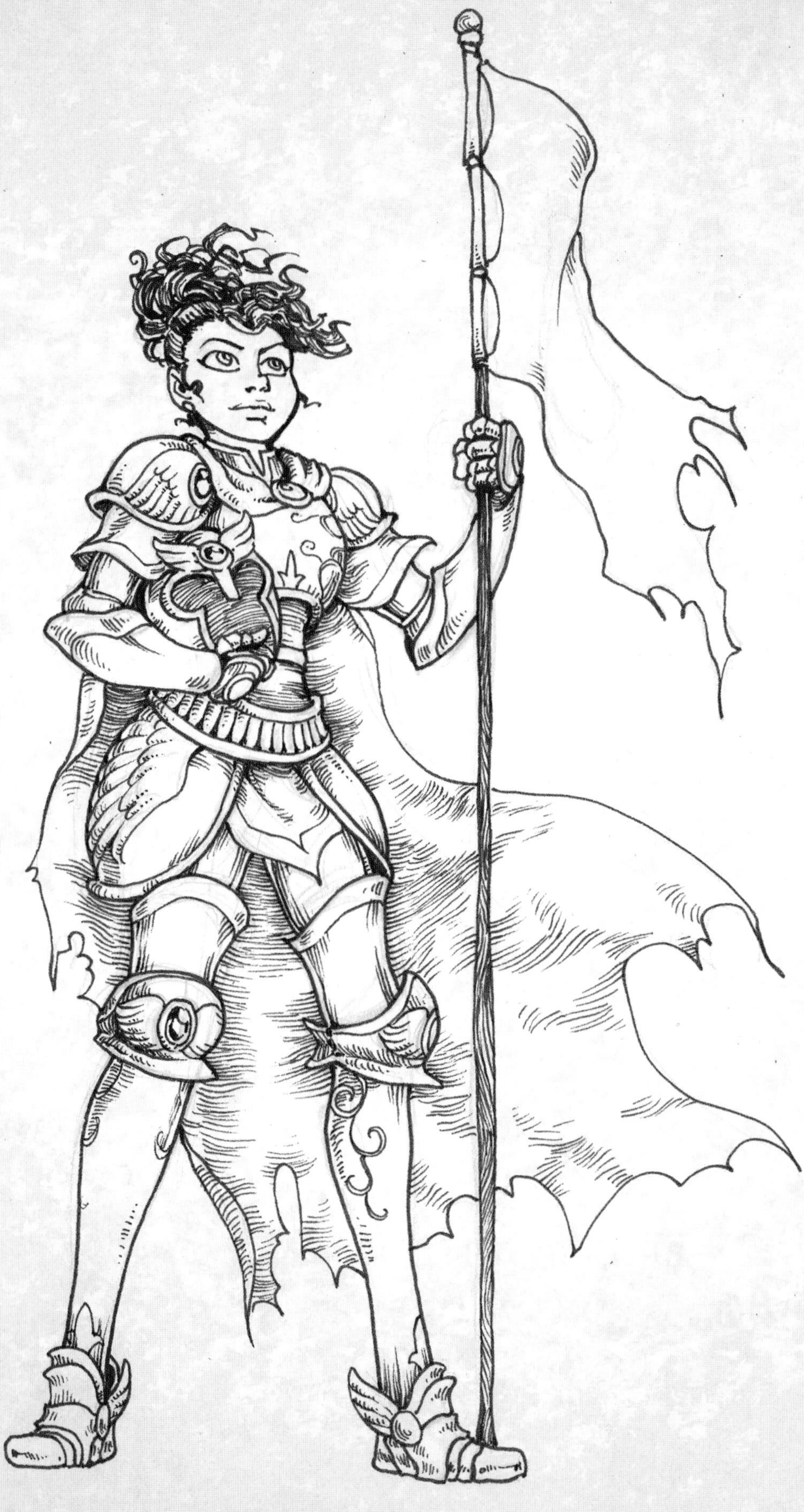

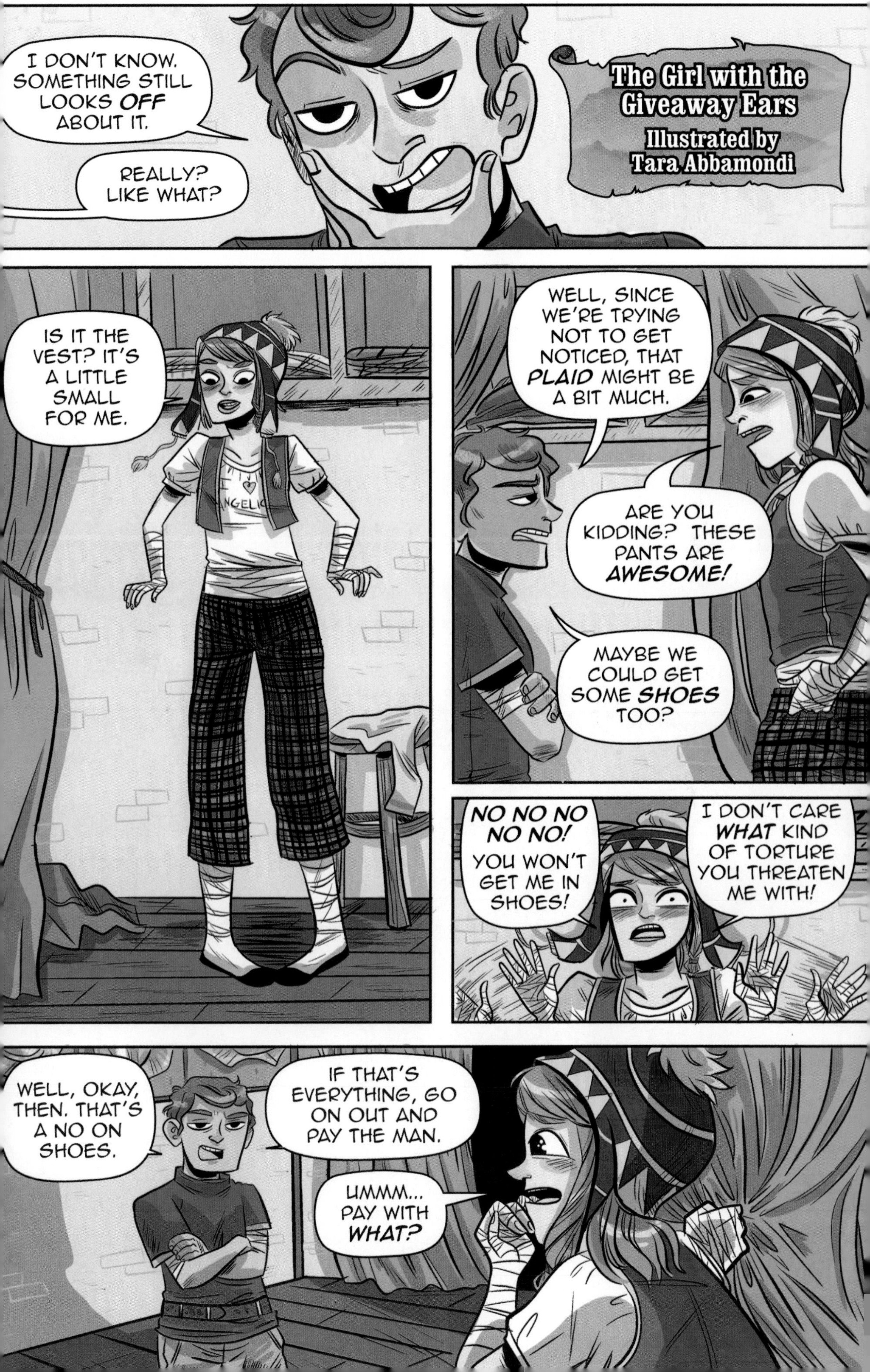
I DON'T KNOW. SOMETHING STILL LOOKS *OFF* ABOUT IT.
REALLY? LIKE WHAT?
The Girl with the Giveaway Ears
Illustrated by Tara Abbamondi
IS IT THE VEST? IT'S A LITTLE SMALL FOR ME.
WELL, SINCE WE'RE TRYING NOT TO GET NOTICED, THAT *PLAID* MIGHT BE A BIT MUCH.
ARE YOU KIDDING? THESE PANTS ARE *AWESOME!*
MAYBE WE COULD GET SOME *SHOES* TOO?
NO NO NO NO NO! YOU WON'T GET ME IN SHOES!
I DON'T CARE *WHAT* KIND OF TORTURE YOU THREATEN ME WITH!
WELL, OKAY, THEN. THAT'S A NO ON SHOES.
IF THAT'S EVERYTHING, GO ON OUT AND PAY THE MAN.
UMMM... PAY WITH *WHAT?*

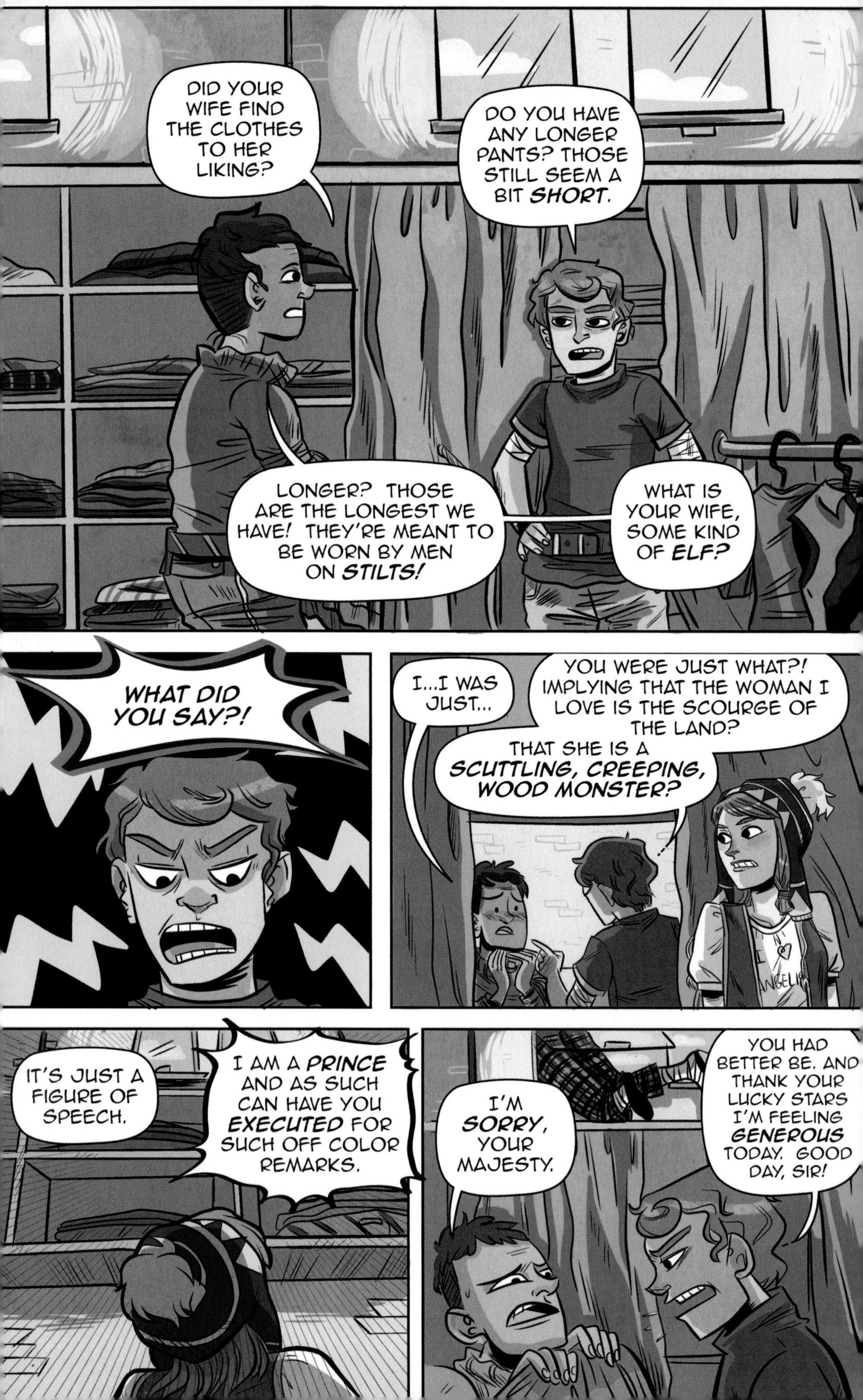
DID YOUR WIFE FIND THE CLOTHES TO HER LIKING?
DO YOU HAVE ANY LONGER PANTS? THOSE STILL SEEM A BIT SHORT.
LONGER? THOSE ARE THE LONGEST WE HAVE! THEY'RE MEANT TO BE WORN BY MEN ON STILTS!
WHAT IS YOUR WIFE, SOME KIND OF ELF?
WHAT DID YOU SAY?!
I...I WAS JUST...
YOU WERE JUST WHAT?! IMPLYING THAT THE WOMAN I LOVE IS THE SCOURGE OF THE LAND?
THAT SHE IS A SCUTTLING, CREEPING, WOOD MONSTER?
IT'S JUST A FIGURE OF SPEECH.
I AM A PRINCE AND AS SUCH CAN HAVE YOU EXECUTED FOR SUCH OFF COLOR REMARKS.
I'M SORRY, YOUR MAJESTY.
YOU HAD BETTER BE. AND THANK YOUR LUCKY STARS I'M FEELING GENEROUS TODAY. GOOD DAY, SIR!

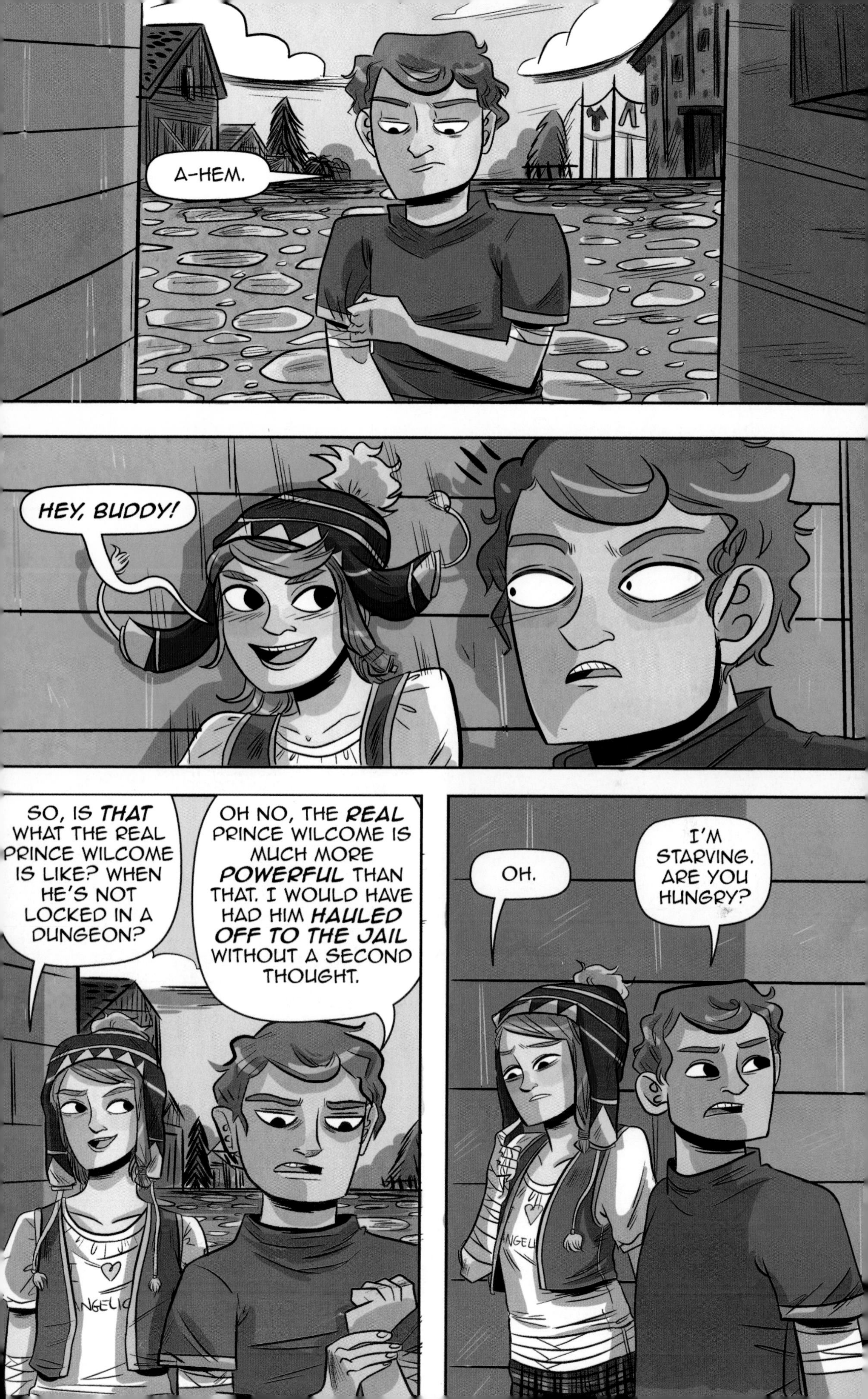
A-HEM.
HEY, BUDDY!
SO, IS THAT WHAT THE REAL PRINCE WILCOME IS LIKE? WHEN HE'S NOT LOCKED IN A DUNGEON?
OH NO, THE REAL PRINCE WILCOME IS MUCH MORE POWERFUL THAN THAT. I WOULD HAVE HAD HIM HAULED OFF TO THE JAIL WITHOUT A SECOND THOUGHT.
OH.
I'M STARVING. ARE YOU HUNGRY?

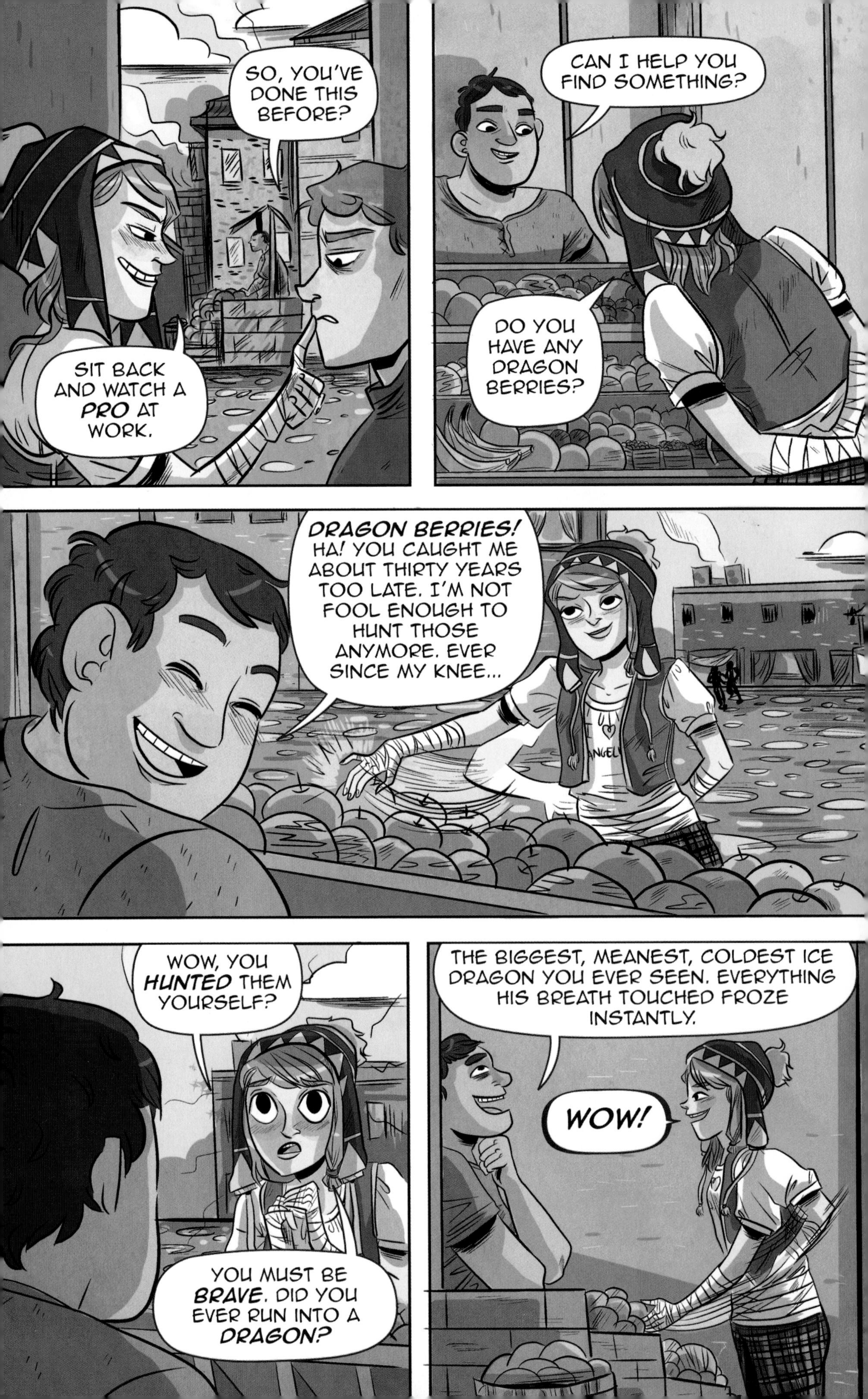
SO, YOU'VE DONE THIS BEFORE?
SIT BACK AND WATCH A *PRO* AT WORK.
CAN I HELP YOU FIND SOMETHING?
DO YOU HAVE ANY DRAGON BERRIES?
DRAGON BERRIES! HA! YOU CAUGHT ME ABOUT THIRTY YEARS TOO LATE. I'M NOT FOOL ENOUGH TO HUNT THOSE ANYMORE. EVER SINCE MY KNEE...
ANGEL
WOW, YOU *HUNTED* THEM YOURSELF?
YOU MUST BE *BRAVE*. DID YOU EVER RUN INTO A *DRAGON?*
THE BIGGEST, MEANEST, COLDEST ICE DRAGON YOU EVER SEEN. EVERYTHING HIS BREATH TOUCHED FROZE INSTANTLY.
WOW!

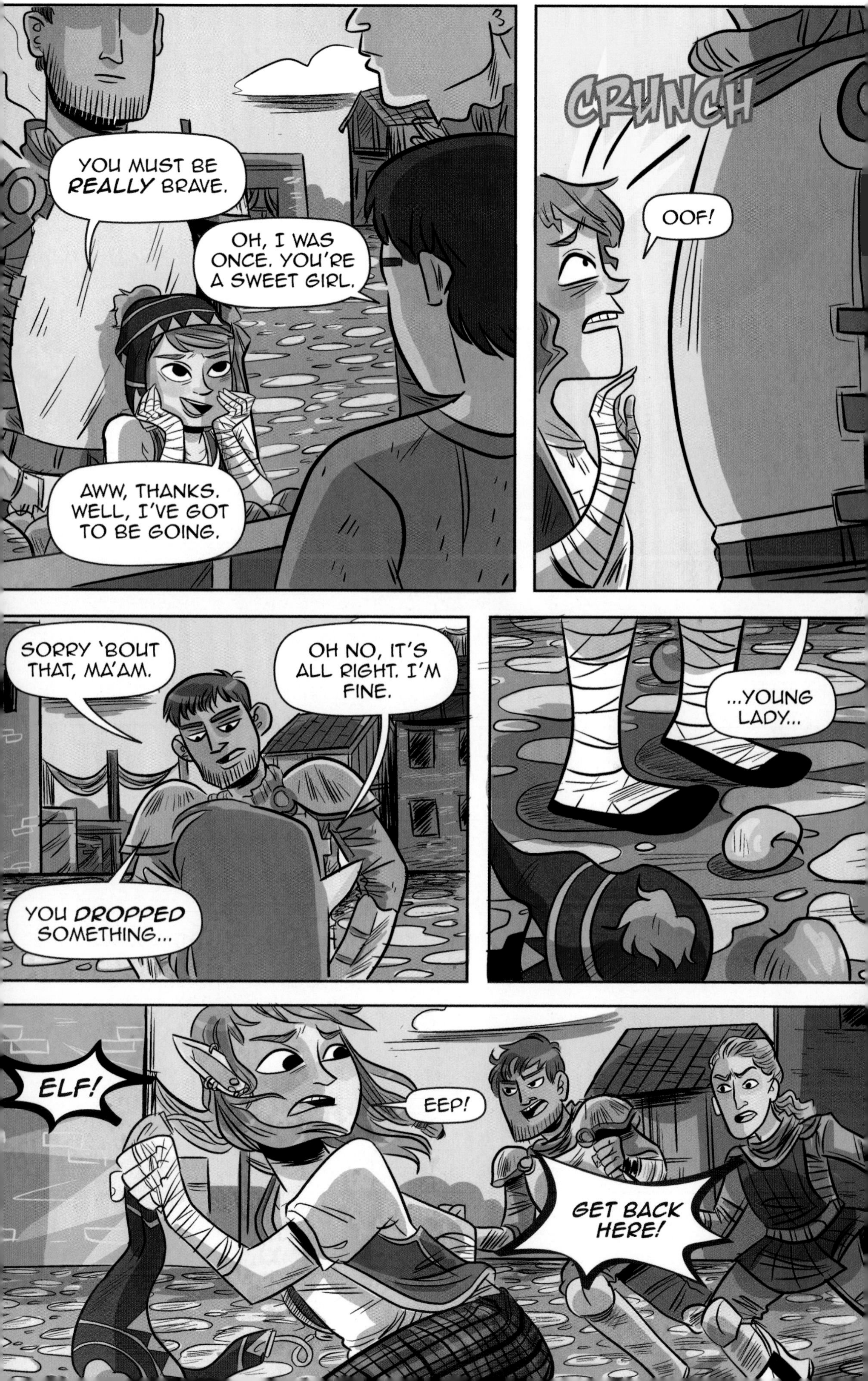
YOU MUST BE *REALLY* BRAVE.
OH, I WAS ONCE. YOU'RE A SWEET GIRL.
AWW, THANKS. WELL, I'VE GOT TO BE GOING.
CRUNCH
OOF!
SORRY 'BOUT THAT, MA'AM.
OH NO, IT'S ALL RIGHT. I'M FINE.
YOU *DROPPED* SOMETHING...
...YOUNG LADY...
ELF!
EEP!
GET BACK HERE!

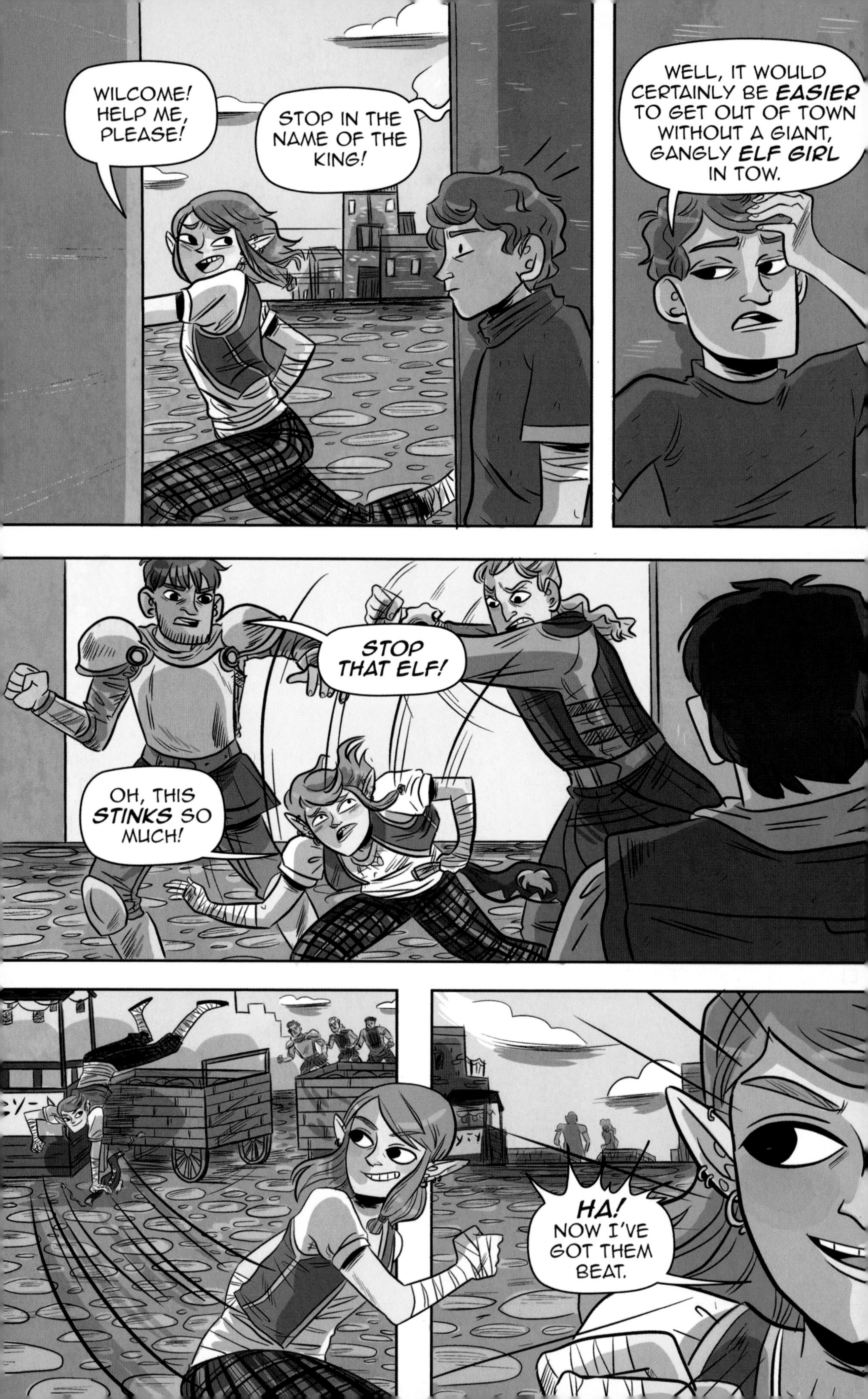
WILCOME! HELP ME, PLEASE!
STOP IN THE NAME OF THE KING!
WELL, IT WOULD CERTAINLY BE EASIER TO GET OUT OF TOWN WITHOUT A GIANT, GANGLY ELF GIRL IN TOW.
STOP THAT ELF!
OH, THIS STINKS SO MUCH!
HA! NOW I'VE GOT THEM BEAT.

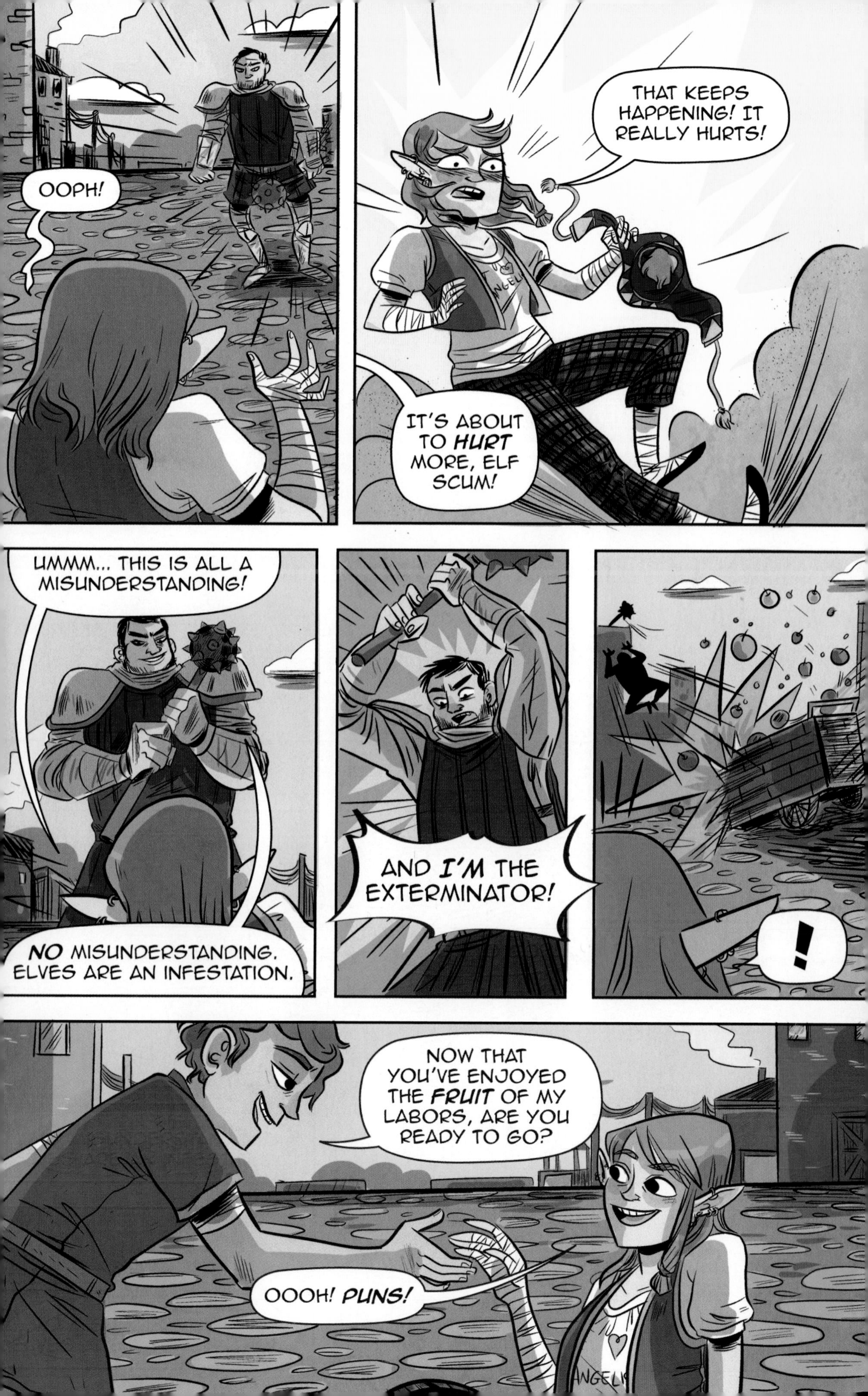
OOPH!
THAT KEEPS HAPPENING! IT REALLY HURTS!
IT'S ABOUT TO HURT MORE, ELF SCUM!
UMMM... THIS IS ALL A MISUNDERSTANDING!
NO MISUNDERSTANDING. ELVES ARE AN INFESTATION.
AND I'M THE EXTERMINATOR!
!
NOW THAT YOU'VE ENJOYED THE FRUIT OF MY LABORS, ARE YOU READY TO GO?
OOOH! PUNS!

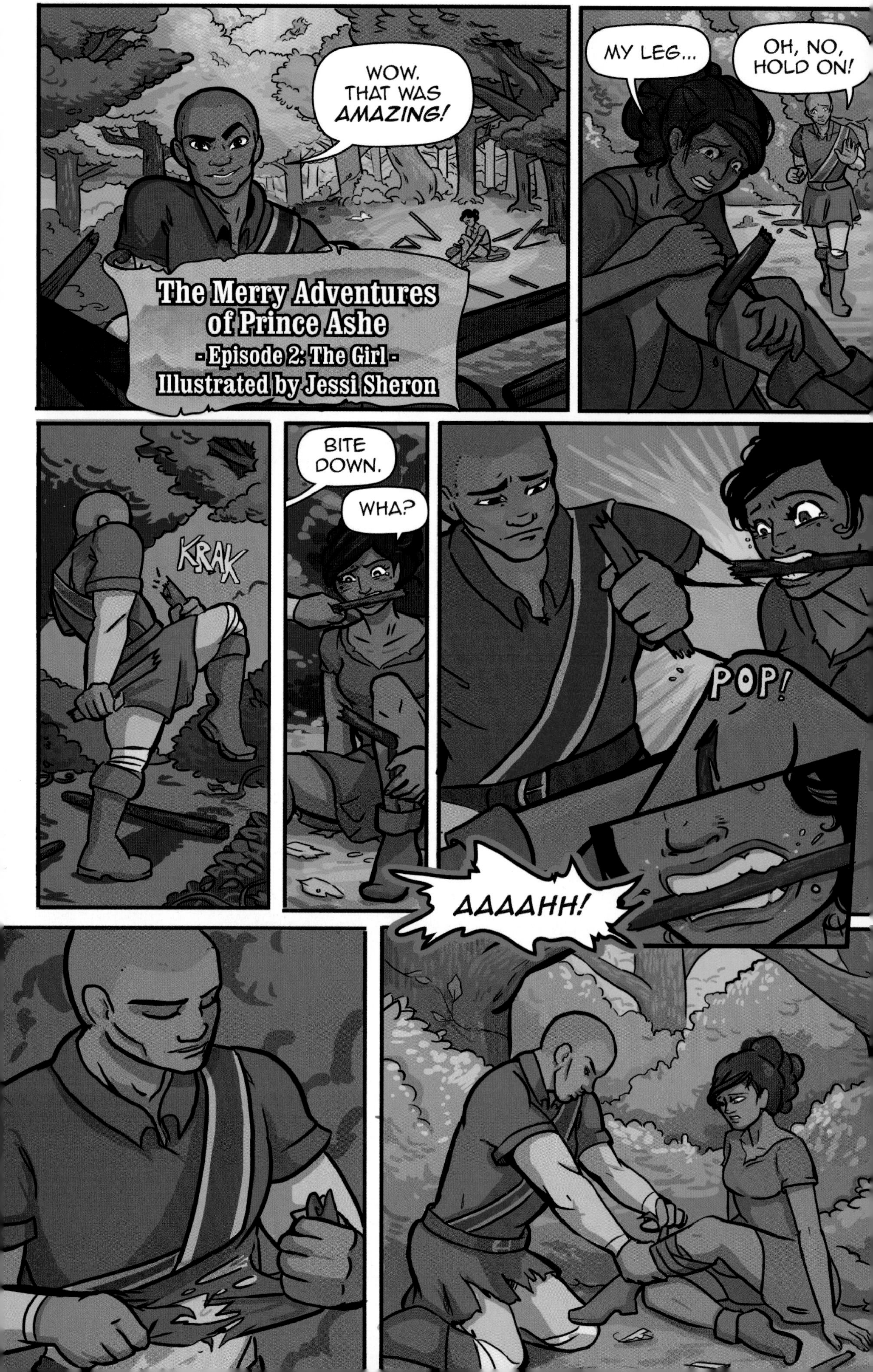
WOW. THAT WAS AMAZING!
The Merry Adventures of Prince Ashe
- Episode 2: The Girl -
Illustrated by Jessi Sheron
MY LEG...
OH, NO, HOLD ON!
KRAK
BITE DOWN.
WHA?
POP!
AAAAHH!

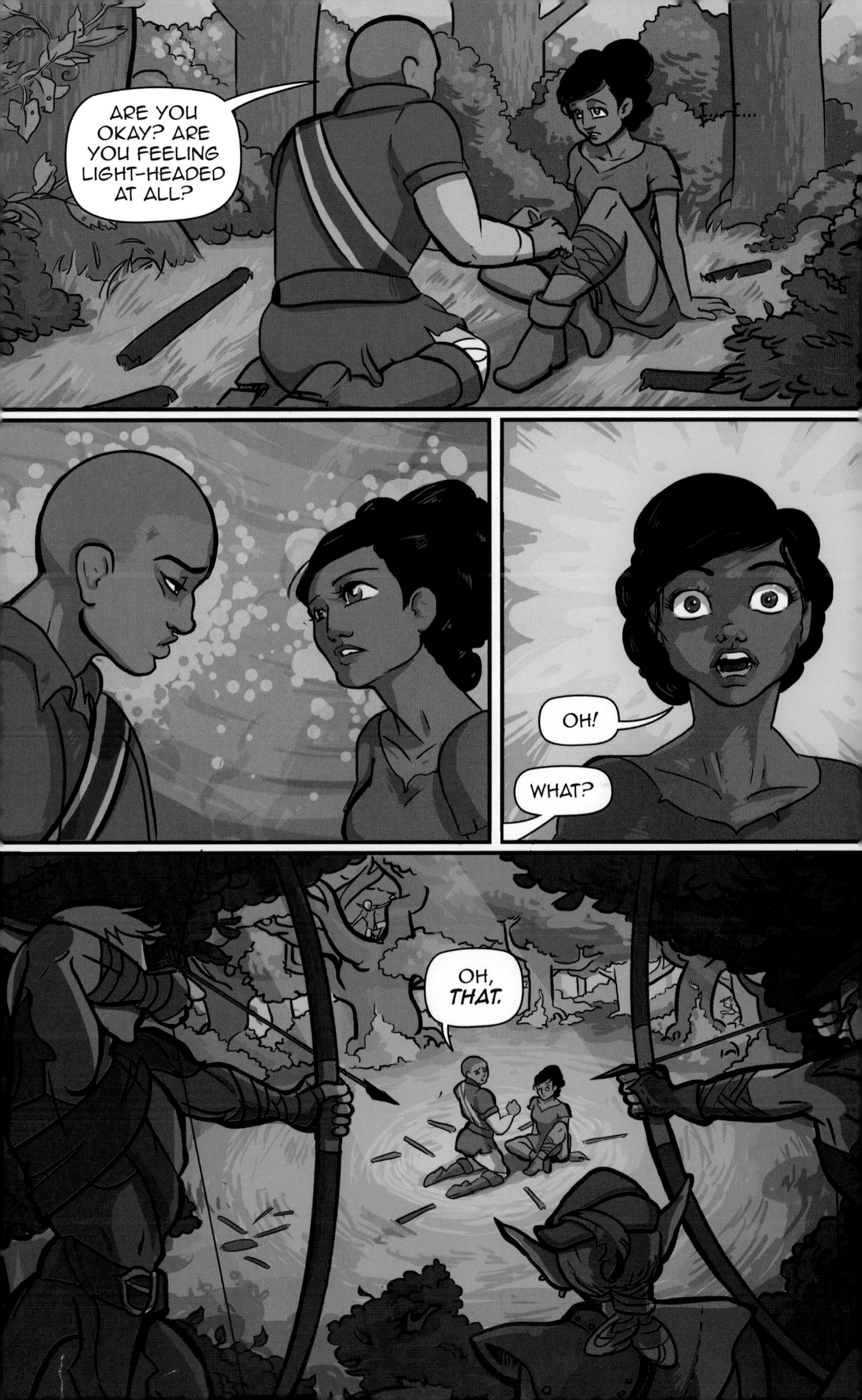
ARE YOU OKAY? ARE YOU FEELING LIGHT-HEADED AT ALL?
I... I...
OH!
WHAT?
OH, *THAT.*

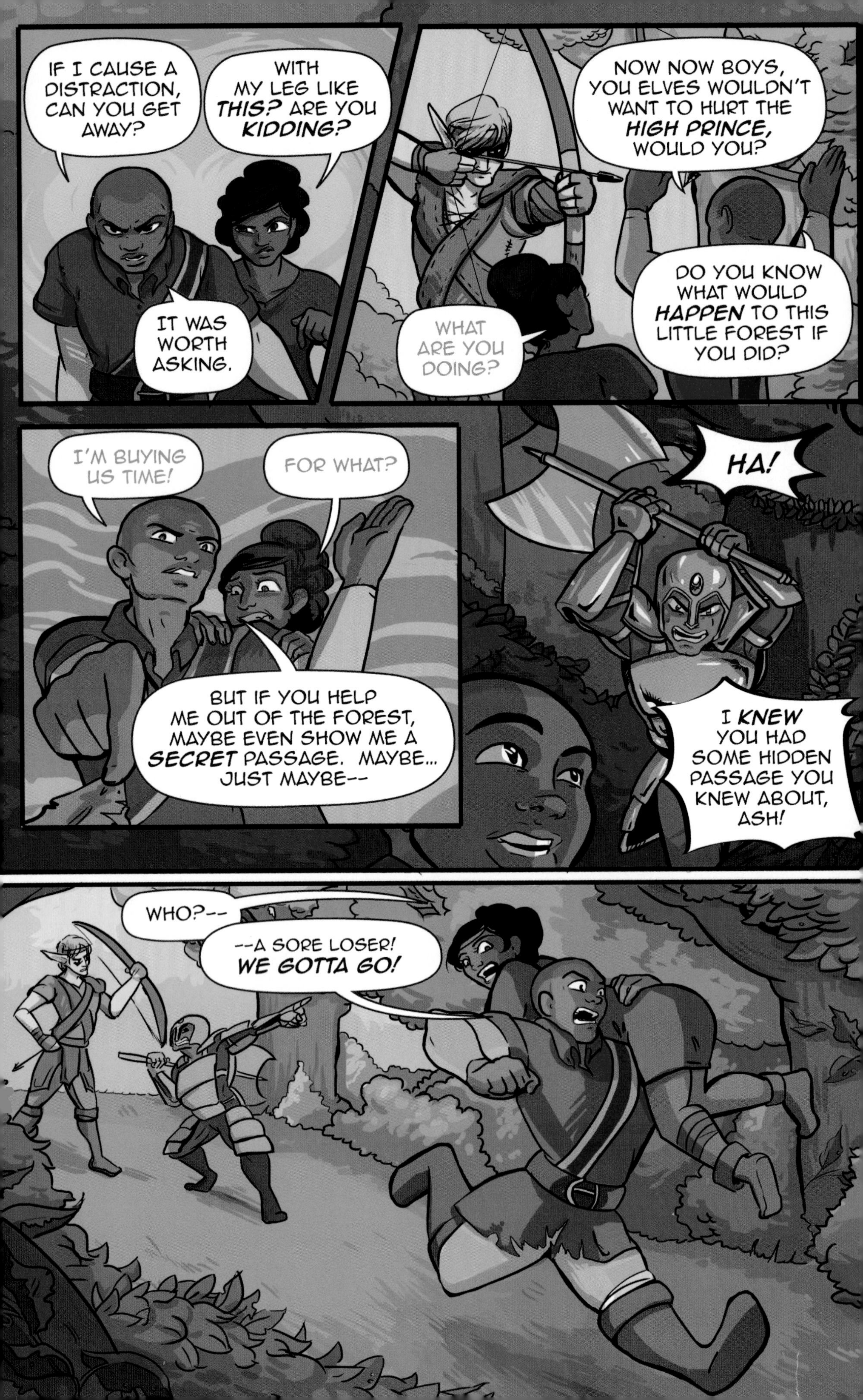
IF I CAUSE A DISTRACTION, CAN YOU GET AWAY?
WITH MY LEG LIKE *THIS?* ARE YOU *KIDDING?*
IT WAS WORTH ASKING.
NOW NOW BOYS, YOU ELVES WOULDN'T WANT TO HURT THE *HIGH PRINCE,* WOULD YOU?
WHAT ARE YOU DOING?
DO YOU KNOW WHAT WOULD *HAPPEN* TO THIS LITTLE FOREST IF YOU DID?
I'M BUYING US TIME!
FOR WHAT?
BUT IF YOU HELP ME OUT OF THE FOREST, MAYBE EVEN SHOW ME A *SECRET* PASSAGE. MAYBE... JUST MAYBE--
HA!
I *KNEW* YOU HAD SOME HIDDEN PASSAGE YOU KNEW ABOUT, ASH!
WHO?--
--A SORE LOSER! *WE GOTTA GO!*

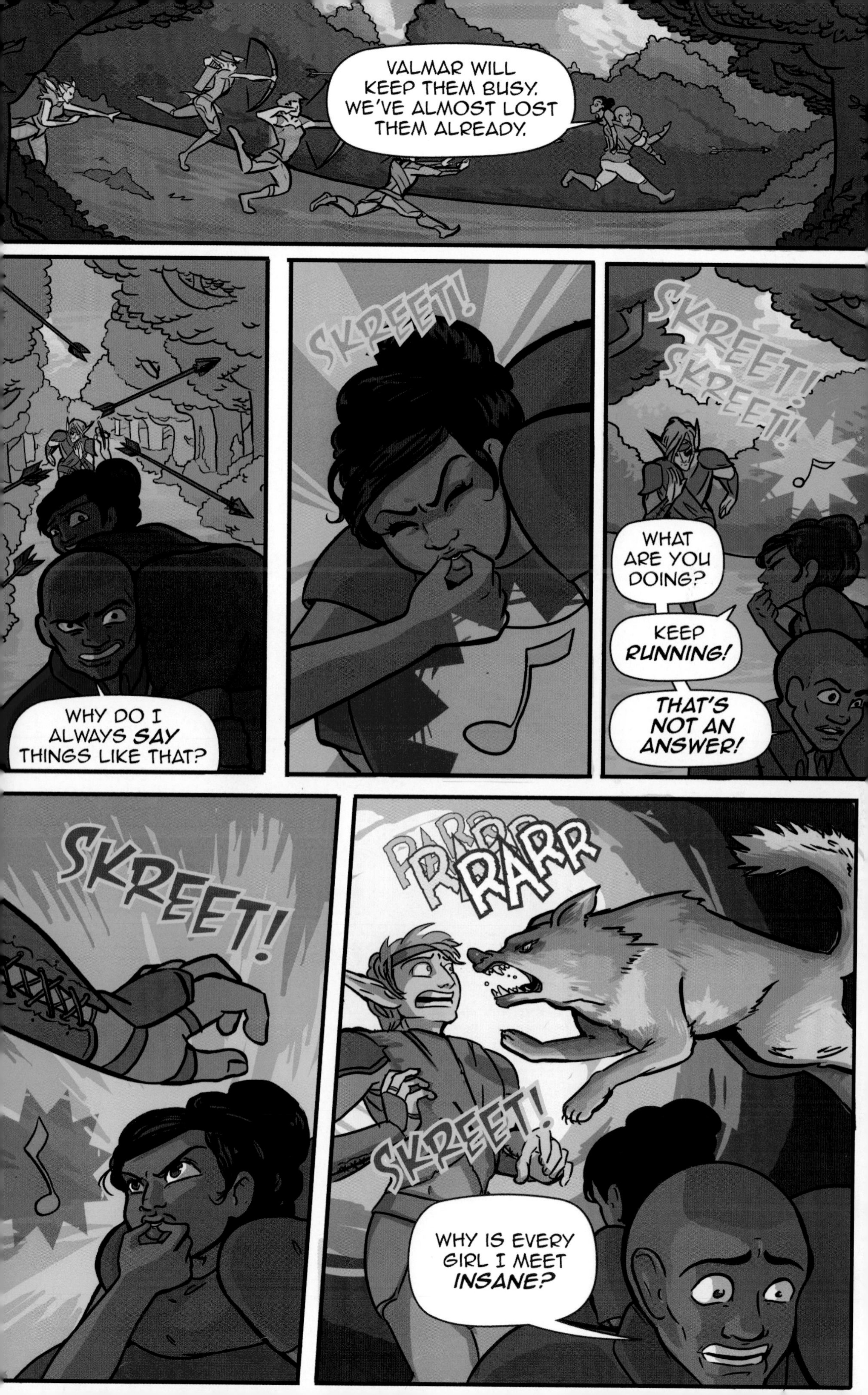
VALMAR WILL KEEP THEM BUSY. WE'VE ALMOST LOST THEM ALREADY.
WHY DO I ALWAYS SAY THINGS LIKE THAT?
SKREEET!
SKREEET! SKREEET!
WHAT ARE YOU DOING?
KEEP RUNNING!
THAT'S NOT AN ANSWER!
SKREEET!
RARR
SKREEET!
WHY IS EVERY GIRL I MEET INSANE?

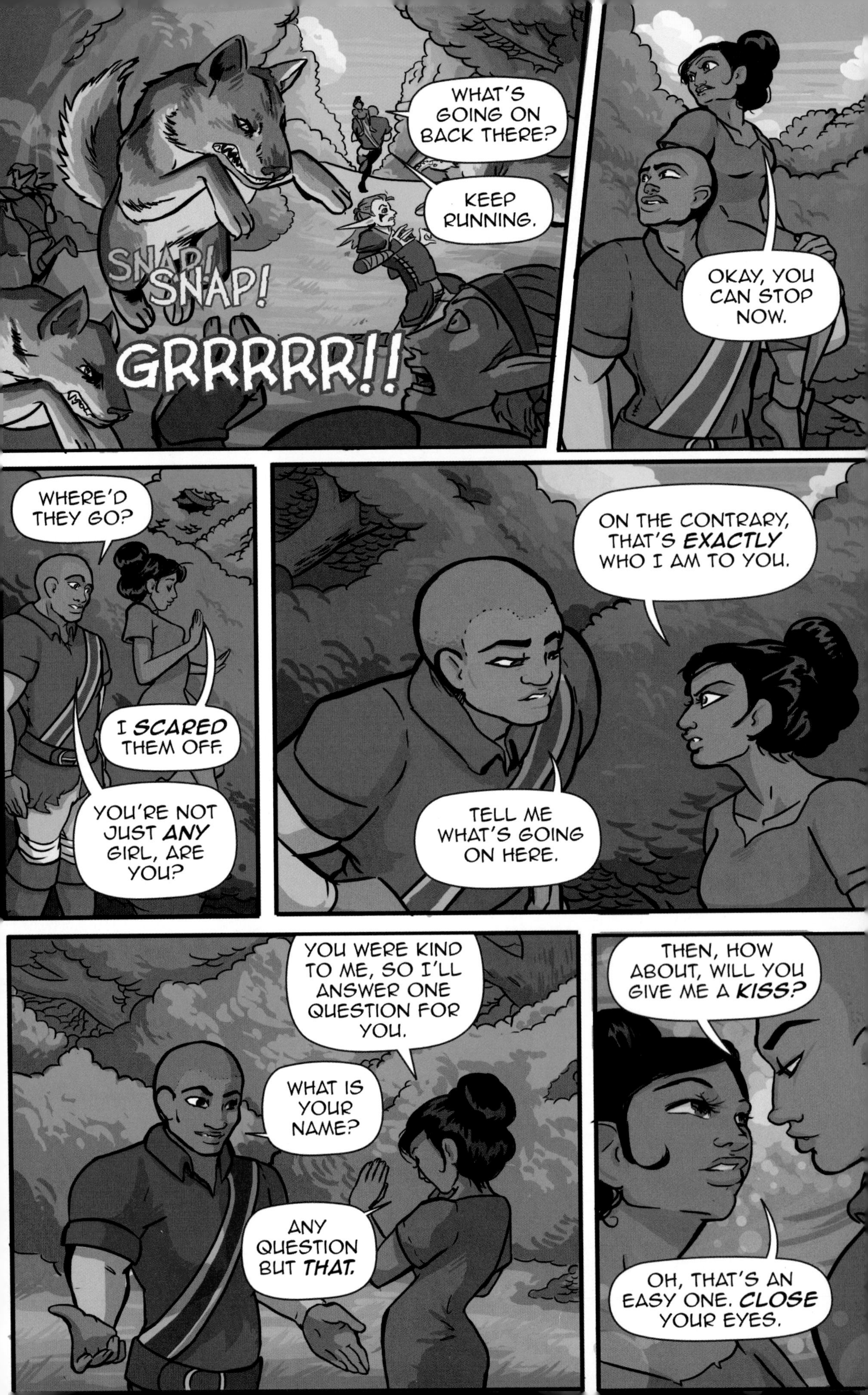
WHAT'S GOING ON BACK THERE?
KEEP RUNNING.
SNAP! SNAP!
GRRRRRR!!
OKAY, YOU CAN STOP NOW.
WHERE'D THEY GO?
I *SCARED* THEM OFF.
YOU'RE NOT JUST *ANY* GIRL, ARE YOU?
ON THE CONTRARY, THAT'S *EXACTLY* WHO I AM TO YOU.
TELL ME WHAT'S GOING ON HERE.
YOU WERE KIND TO ME, SO I'LL ANSWER ONE QUESTION FOR YOU.
WHAT IS YOUR NAME?
ANY QUESTION BUT *THAT.*
THEN, HOW ABOUT, WILL YOU GIVE ME A *KISS?*
OH, THAT'S AN EASY ONE. *CLOSE* YOUR EYES.

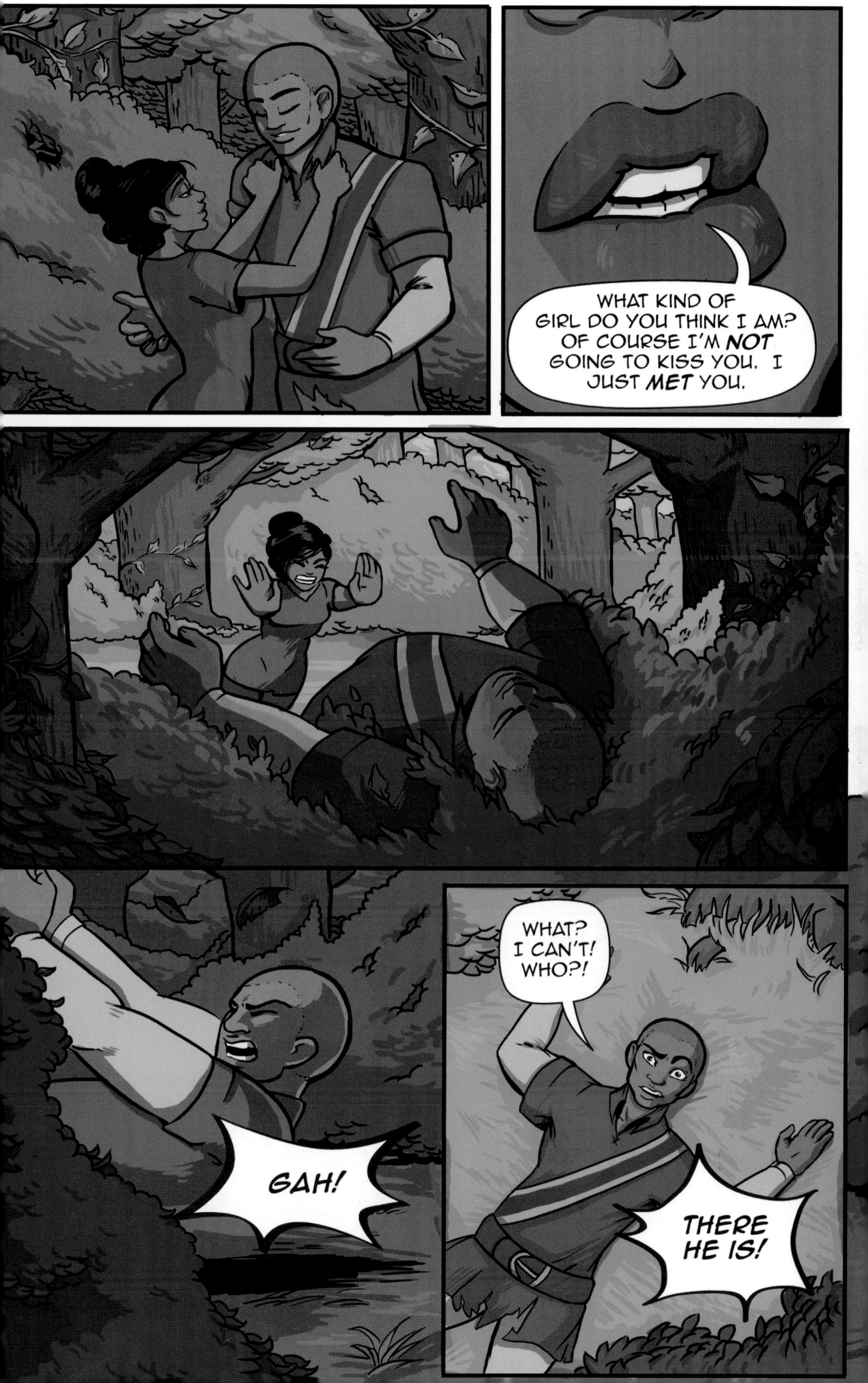
WHAT KIND OF GIRL DO YOU THINK I AM? OF COURSE I'M **NOT** GOING TO KISS YOU. I JUST **MET** YOU.
GAH!
WHAT? I CAN'T! WHO?!
THERE HE IS!

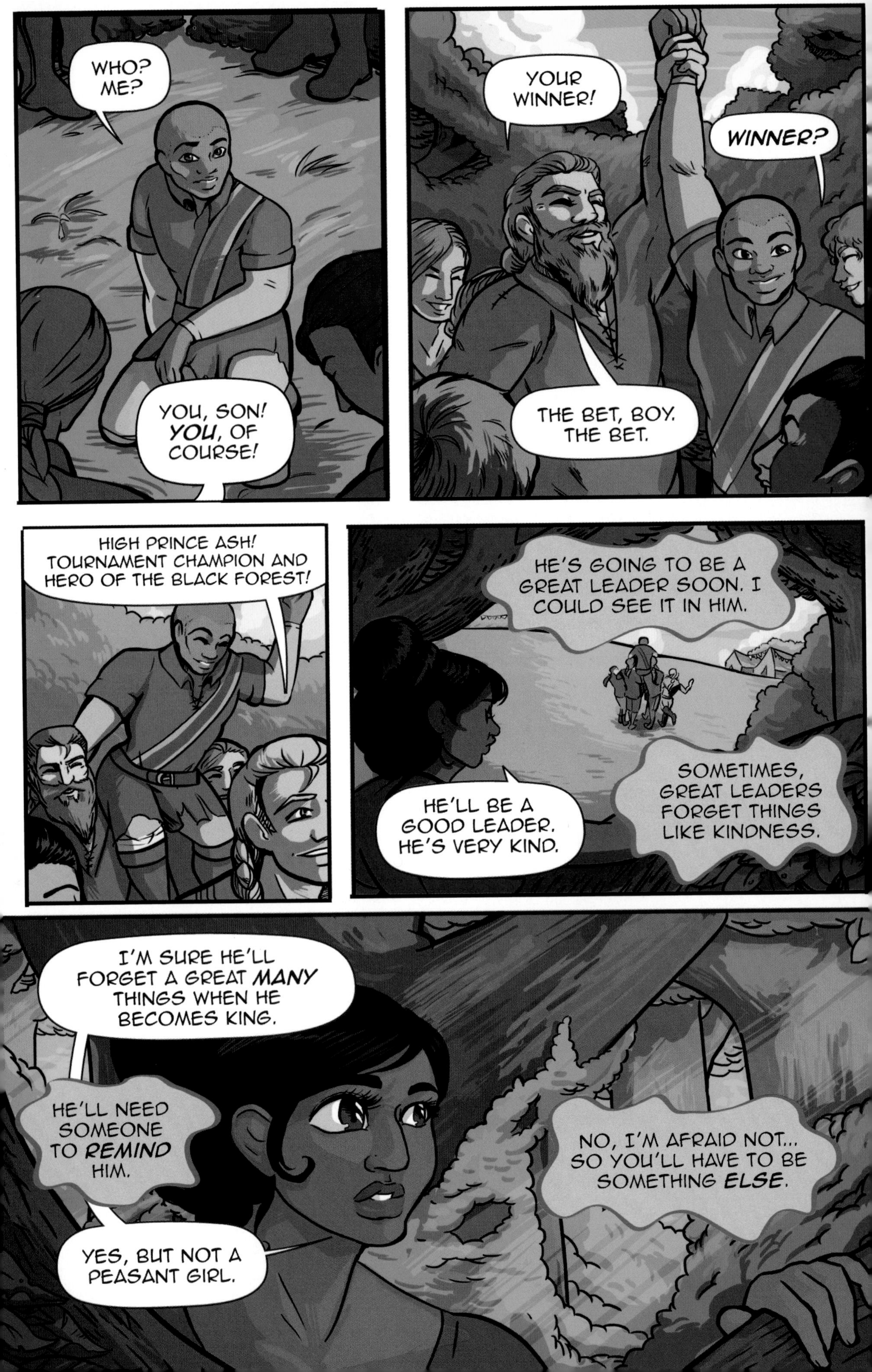
WHO? ME?
YOU, SON! YOU, OF COURSE!
YOUR WINNER!
WINNER?
THE BET, BOY. THE BET.
HIGH PRINCE ASH! TOURNAMENT CHAMPION AND HERO OF THE BLACK FOREST!
HE'S GOING TO BE A GREAT LEADER SOON. I COULD SEE IT IN HIM.
HE'LL BE A GOOD LEADER. HE'S VERY KIND.
SOMETIMES, GREAT LEADERS FORGET THINGS LIKE KINDNESS.
I'M SURE HE'LL FORGET A GREAT MANY THINGS WHEN HE BECOMES KING.
HE'LL NEED SOMEONE TO REMIND HIM.
YES, BUT NOT A PEASANT GIRL.
NO, I'M AFRAID NOT... SO YOU'LL HAVE TO BE SOMETHING ELSE.

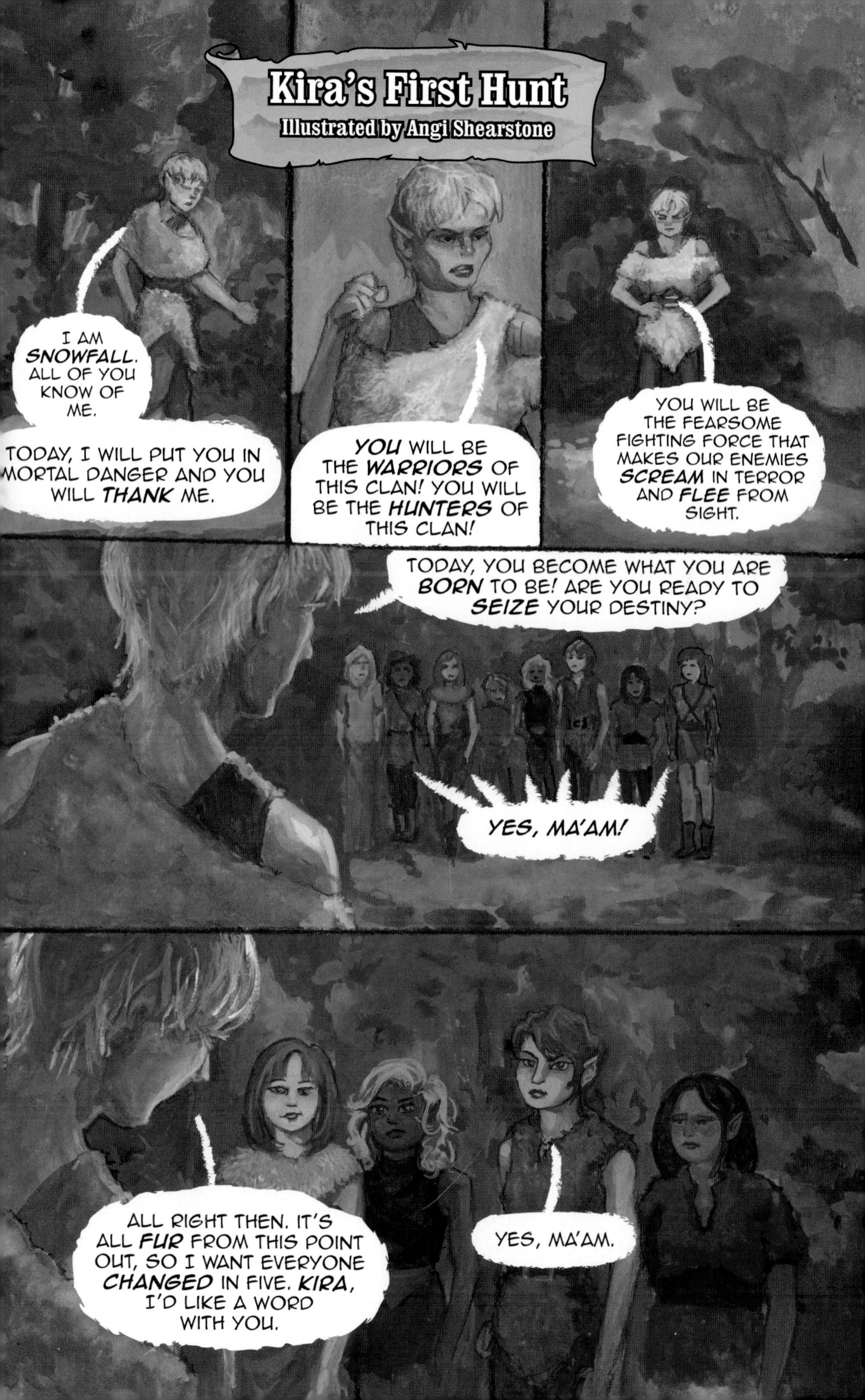
Kira's First Hunt
Illustrated by Angi Shearstone
I AM SNOWFALL. ALL OF YOU KNOW OF ME.
TODAY, I WILL PUT YOU IN MORTAL DANGER AND YOU WILL THANK ME.
YOU WILL BE THE WARRIORS OF THIS CLAN! YOU WILL BE THE HUNTERS OF THIS CLAN!
YOU WILL BE THE FEARSOME FIGHTING FORCE THAT MAKES OUR ENEMIES SCREAM IN TERROR AND FLEE FROM SIGHT.
TODAY, YOU BECOME WHAT YOU ARE BORN TO BE! ARE YOU READY TO SEIZE YOUR DESTINY?
YES, MA'AM!
ALL RIGHT THEN. IT'S ALL FUR FROM THIS POINT OUT, SO I WANT EVERYONE CHANGED IN FIVE. KIRA, I'D LIKE A WORD WITH YOU.
YES, MA'AM.

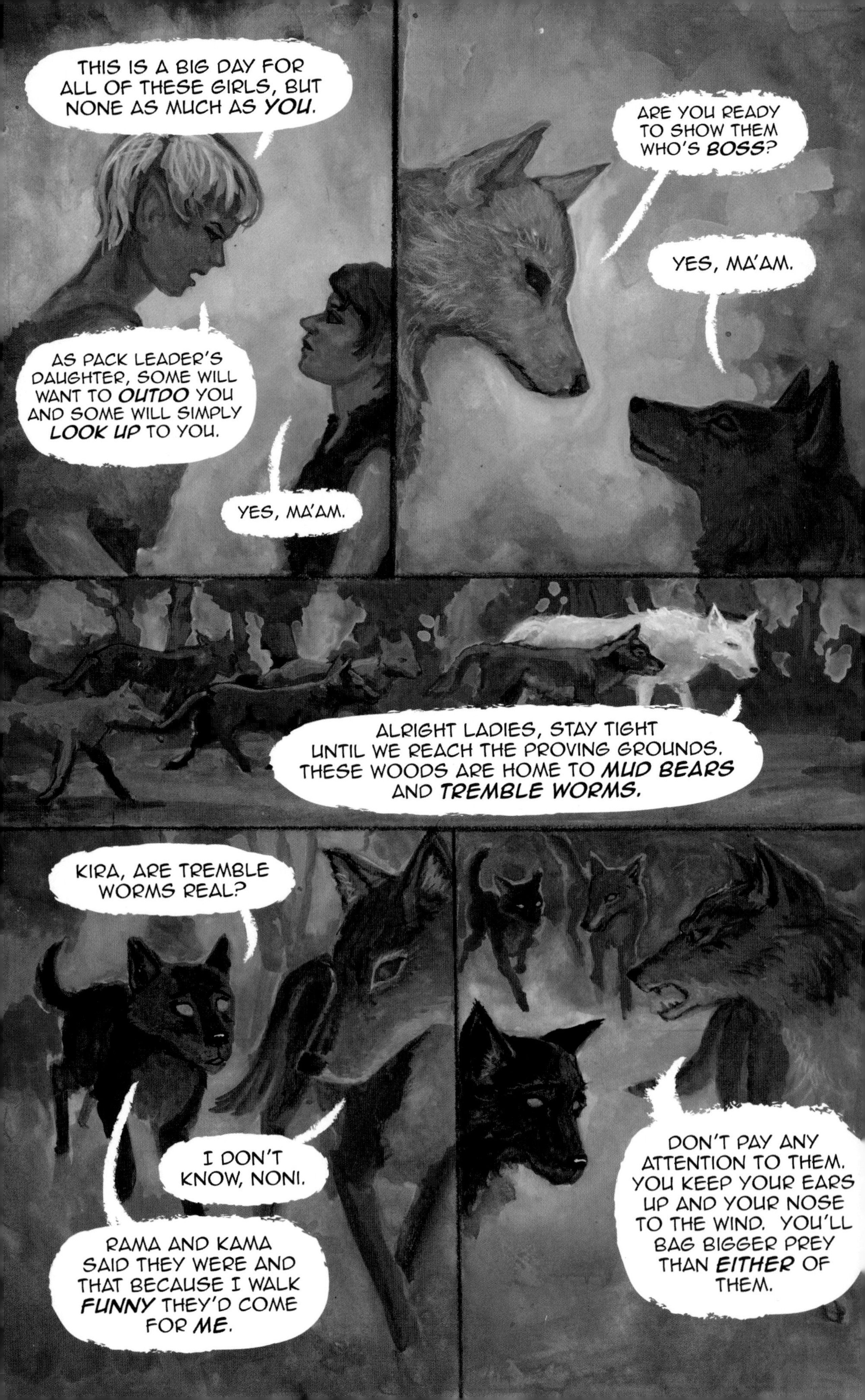
THIS IS A BIG DAY FOR ALL OF THESE GIRLS, BUT NONE AS MUCH AS *YOU*.
AS PACK LEADER'S DAUGHTER, SOME WILL WANT TO *OUTDO* YOU AND SOME WILL SIMPLY *LOOK UP* TO YOU.
YES, MA'AM.
ARE YOU READY TO SHOW THEM WHO'S *BOSS*?
YES, MA'AM.
ALRIGHT LADIES, STAY TIGHT UNTIL WE REACH THE PROVING GROUNDS. THESE WOODS ARE HOME TO *MUD BEARS* AND *TREMBLE WORMS.*
KIRA, ARE TREMBLE WORMS REAL?
I DON'T KNOW, NONI.
RAMA AND KAMA SAID THEY WERE AND THAT BECAUSE I WALK *FUNNY* THEY'D COME FOR *ME*.
DON'T PAY ANY ATTENTION TO THEM. YOU KEEP YOUR EARS UP AND YOUR NOSE TO THE WIND. YOU'LL BAG BIGGER PREY THAN *EITHER* OF THEM.

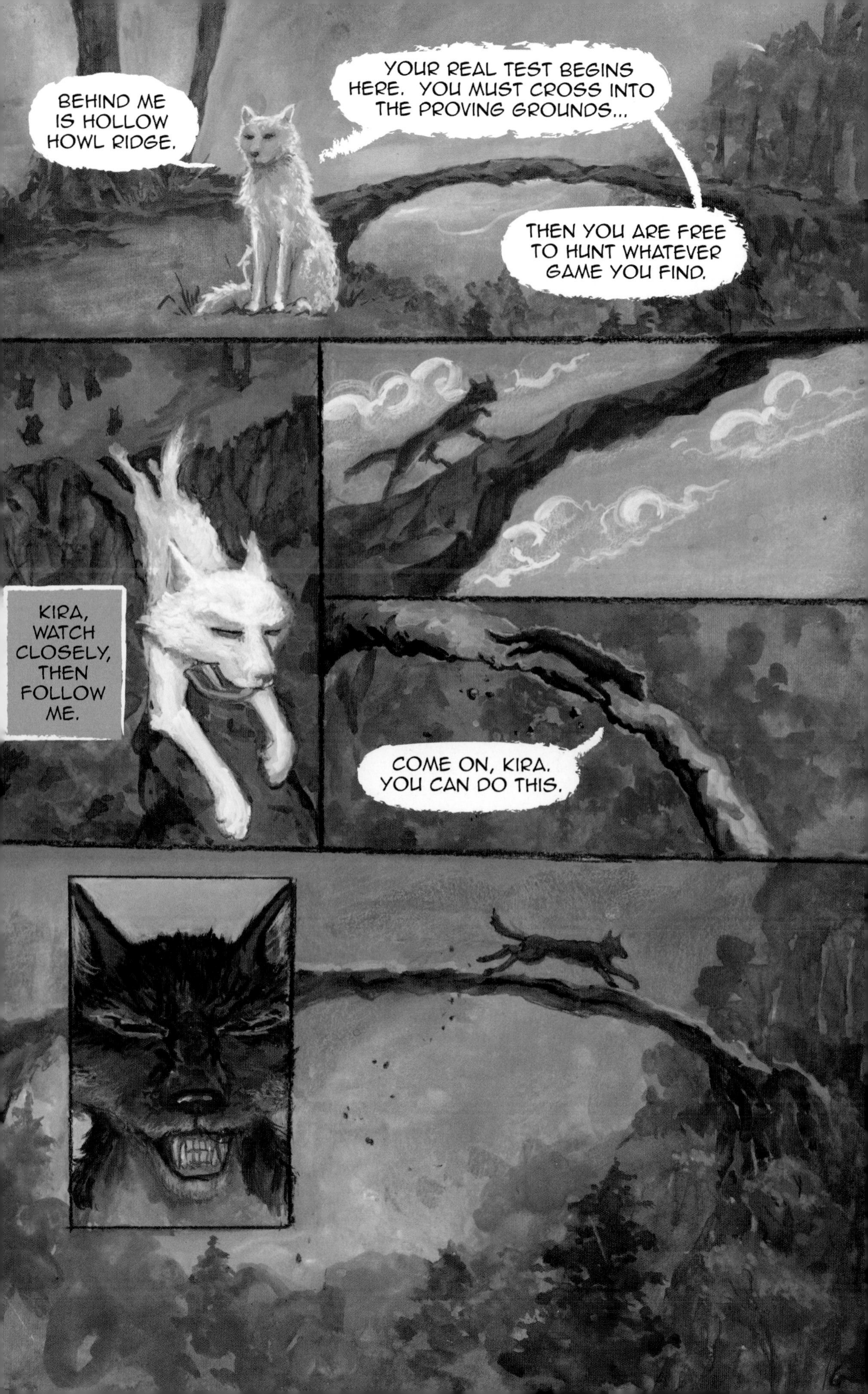
BEHIND ME IS HOLLOW HOWL RIDGE.
YOUR REAL TEST BEGINS HERE. YOU MUST CROSS INTO THE PROVING GROUNDS...
THEN YOU ARE FREE TO HUNT WHATEVER GAME YOU FIND.
KIRA, WATCH CLOSELY, THEN FOLLOW ME.
COME ON, KIRA. YOU CAN DO THIS.

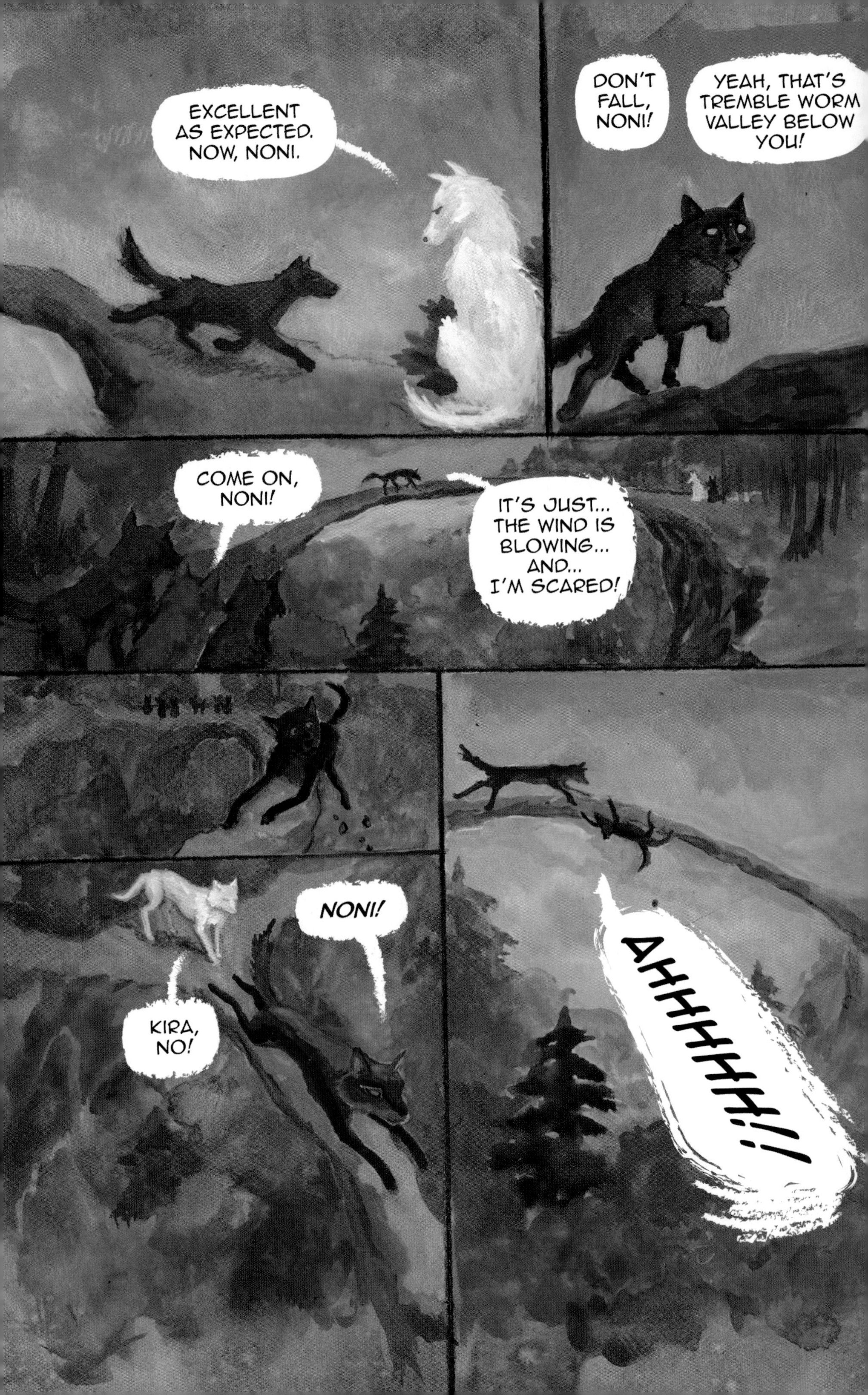
EXCELLENT AS EXPECTED. NOW, NONI.
DON'T FALL, NONI!
YEAH, THAT'S TREMBLE WORM VALLEY BELOW YOU!
COME ON, NONI!
IT'S JUST... THE WIND IS BLOWING... AND... I'M SCARED!
NONI!
KIRA, NO!
AHHHHH!!

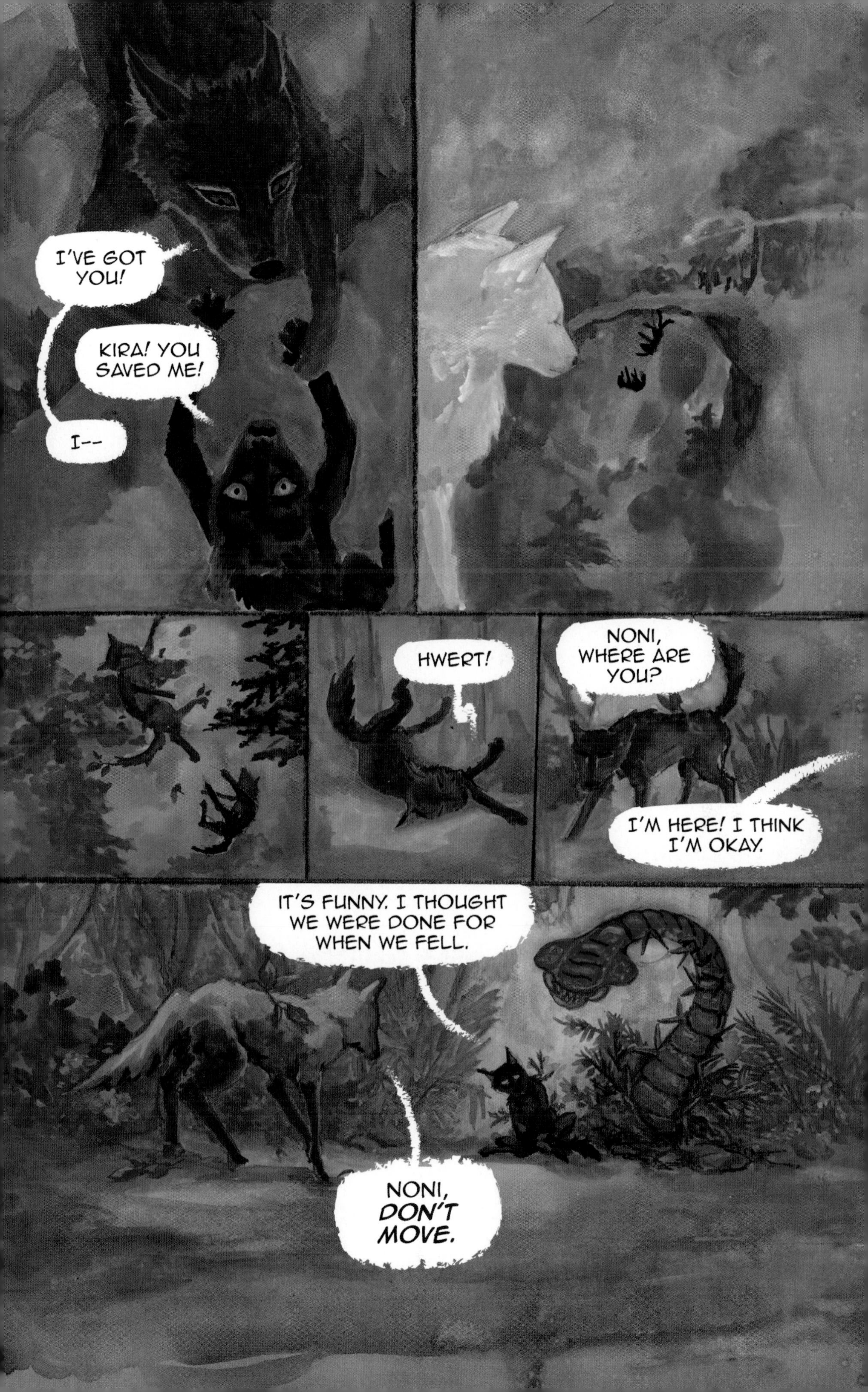
I'VE GOT YOU!
KIRA! YOU SAVED ME!
I--
HWERT!
NONI, WHERE ARE YOU?
I'M HERE! I THINK I'M OKAY.
IT'S FUNNY. I THOUGHT WE WERE DONE FOR WHEN WE FELL.
NONI, *DON'T MOVE.*

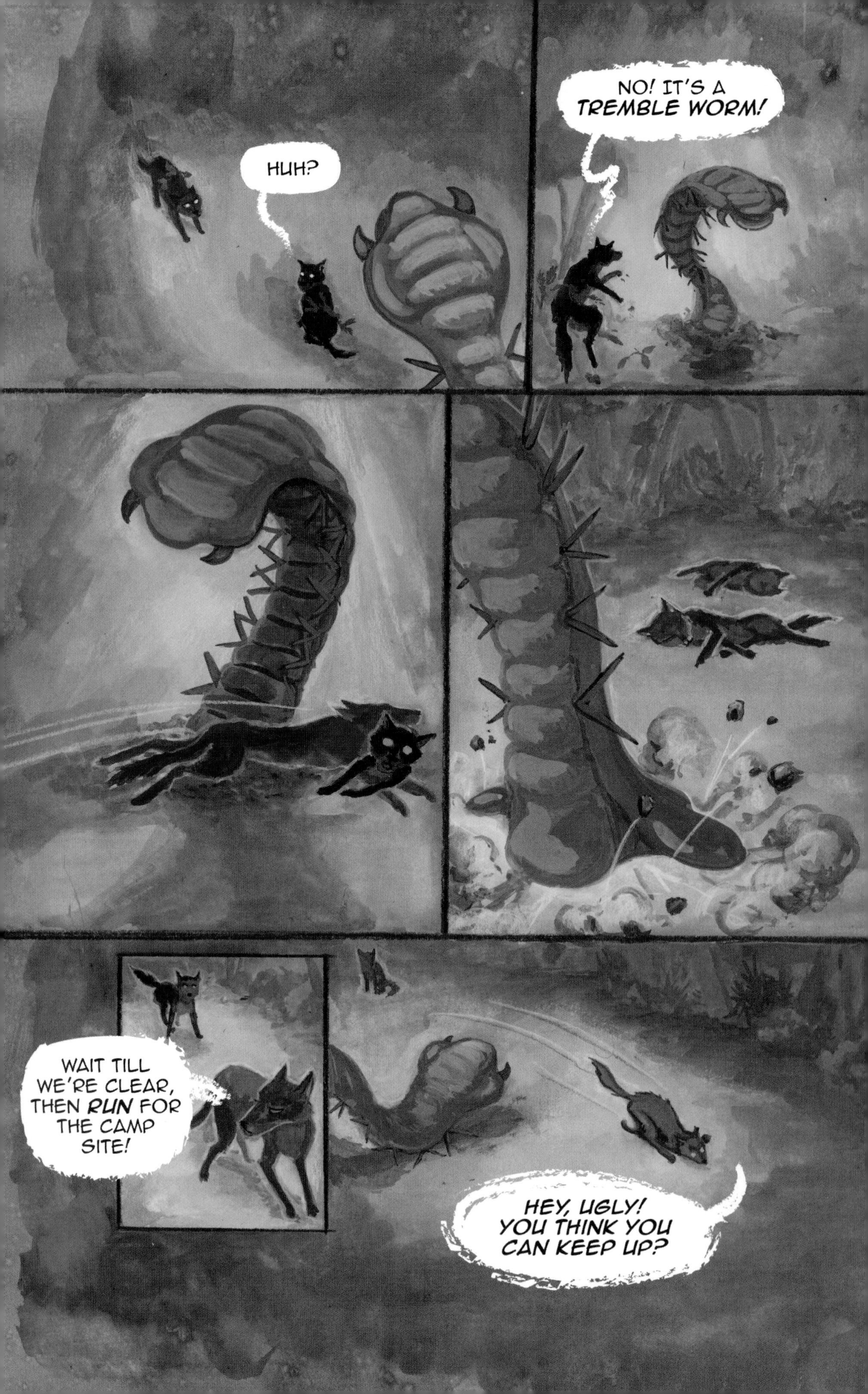
HUH?
NO! IT'S A TREMBLE WORM!
WAIT TILL WE'RE CLEAR, THEN RUN FOR THE CAMP SITE!
HEY, UGLY! YOU THINK YOU CAN KEEP UP?

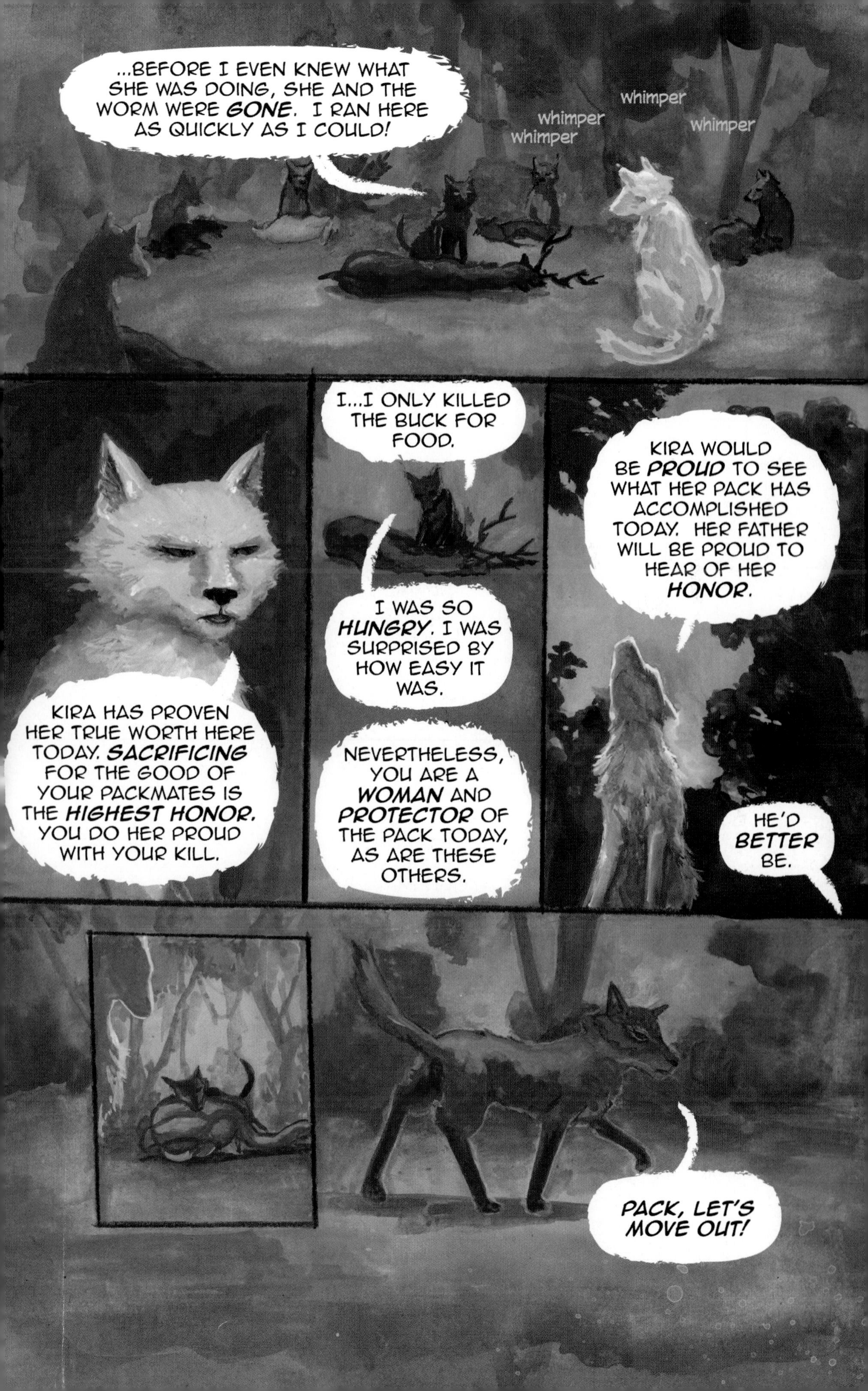
...BEFORE I EVEN KNEW WHAT SHE WAS DOING, SHE AND THE WORM WERE GONE. I RAN HERE AS QUICKLY AS I COULD!
whimper
whimper
whimper
whimper
KIRA HAS PROVEN HER TRUE WORTH HERE TODAY. SACRIFICING FOR THE GOOD OF YOUR PACKMATES IS THE HIGHEST HONOR. YOU DO HER PROUD WITH YOUR KILL.
I...I ONLY KILLED THE BUCK FOR FOOD.
I WAS SO HUNGRY. I WAS SURPRISED BY HOW EASY IT WAS.
NEVERTHELESS, YOU ARE A WOMAN AND PROTECTOR OF THE PACK TODAY, AS ARE THESE OTHERS.
KIRA WOULD BE PROUD TO SEE WHAT HER PACK HAS ACCOMPLISHED TODAY. HER FATHER WILL BE PROUD TO HEAR OF HER HONOR.
HE'D BETTER BE.
PACK, LET'S MOVE OUT!

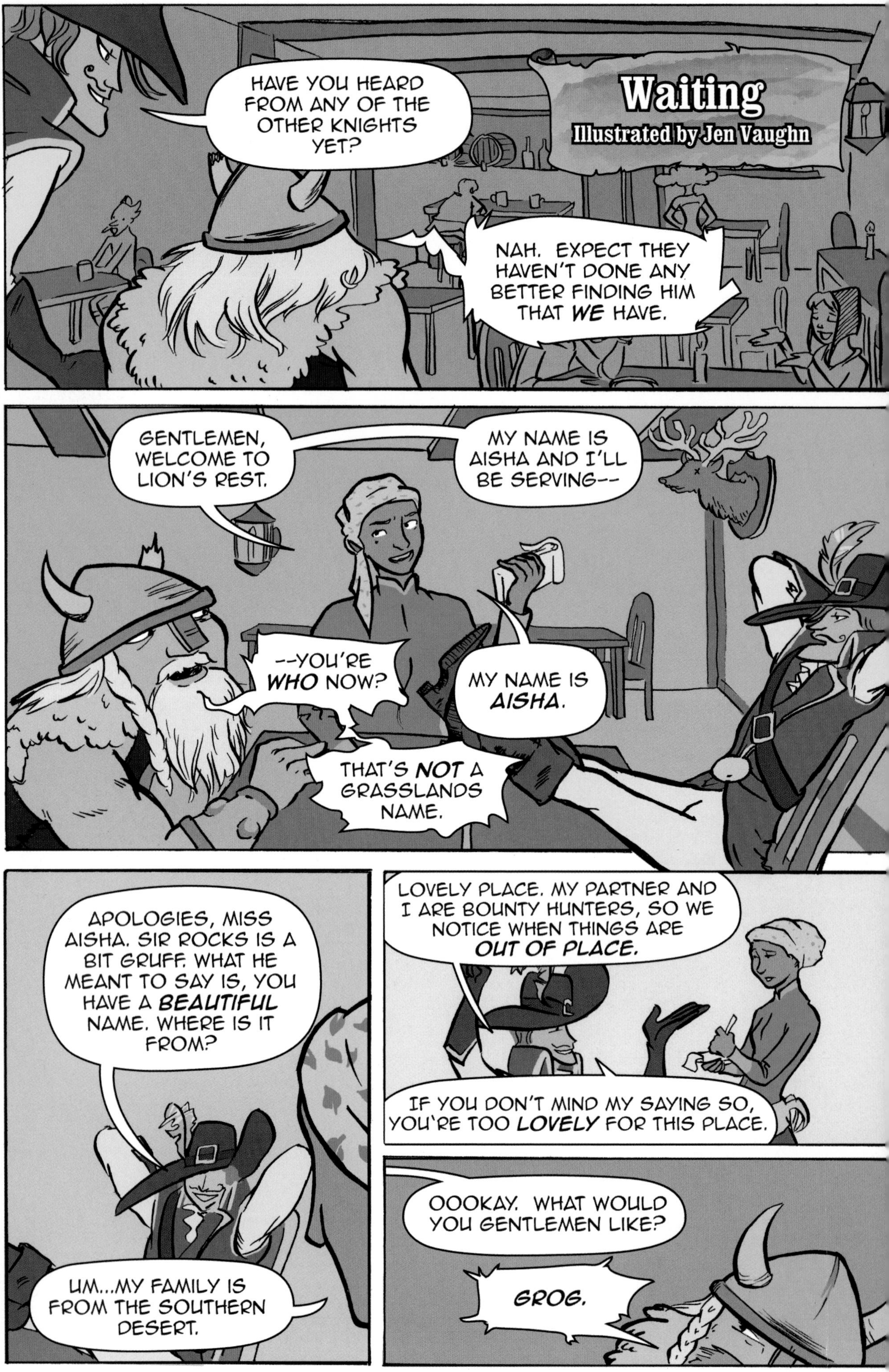
Waiting
Illustrated by Jen Vaughn
HAVE YOU HEARD FROM ANY OF THE OTHER KNIGHTS YET?
NAH. EXPECT THEY HAVEN'T DONE ANY BETTER FINDING HIM THAT WE HAVE.
GENTLEMEN, WELCOME TO LION'S REST.
MY NAME IS AISHA AND I'LL BE SERVING--
--YOU'RE WHO NOW?
MY NAME IS AISHA.
THAT'S NOT A GRASSLANDS NAME.
APOLOGIES, MISS AISHA. SIR ROCKS IS A BIT GRUFF. WHAT HE MEANT TO SAY IS, YOU HAVE A BEAUTIFUL NAME. WHERE IS IT FROM?
UM...MY FAMILY IS FROM THE SOUTHERN DESERT.
LOVELY PLACE. MY PARTNER AND I ARE BOUNTY HUNTERS, SO WE NOTICE WHEN THINGS ARE OUT OF PLACE.
IF YOU DON'T MIND MY SAYING SO, YOU'RE TOO LOVELY FOR THIS PLACE.
OOOKAY. WHAT WOULD YOU GENTLEMEN LIKE?
GROG.

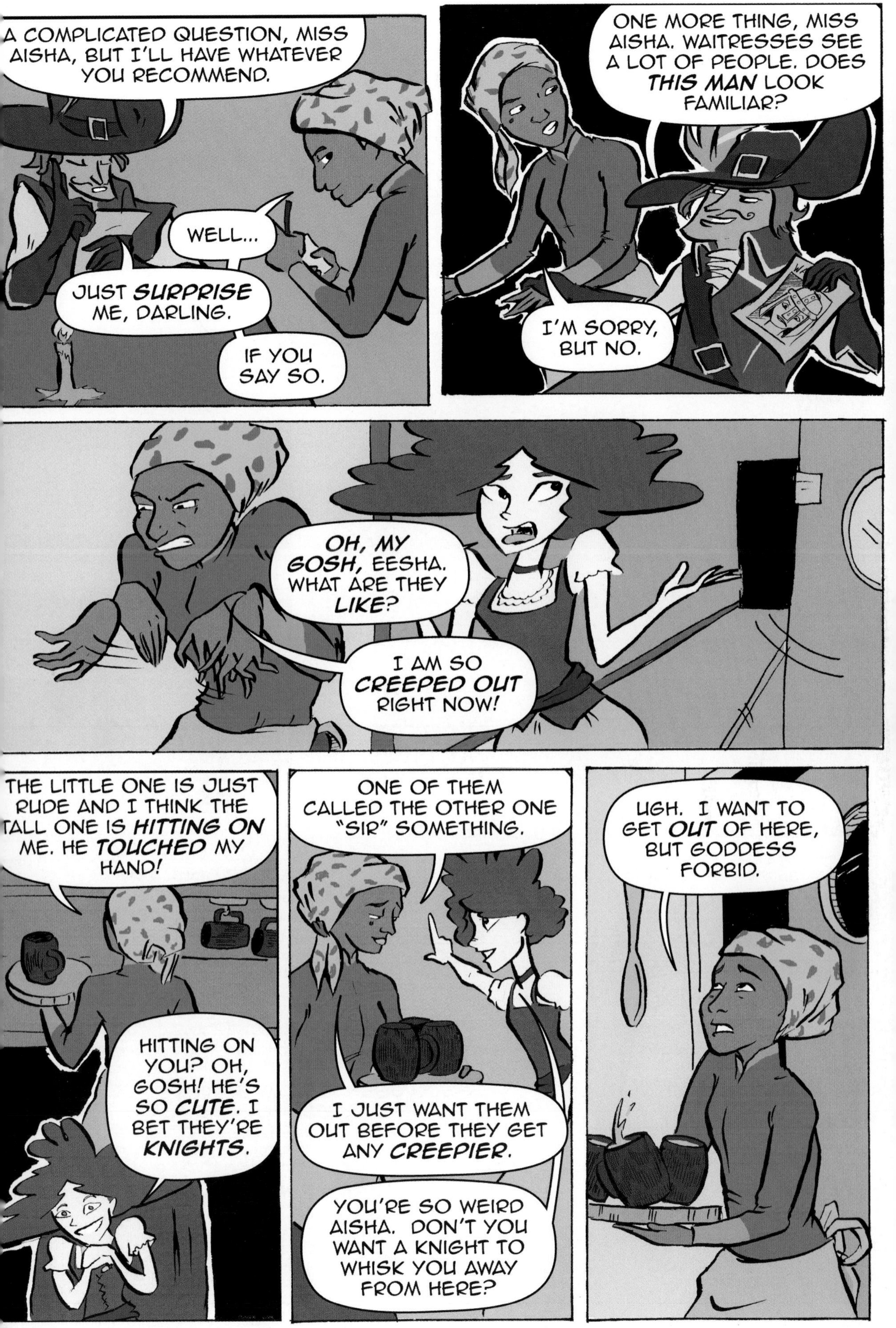
A COMPLICATED QUESTION, MISS AISHA, BUT I'LL HAVE WHATEVER YOU RECOMMEND.
WELL...
JUST SURPRISE ME, DARLING.
IF YOU SAY SO.
ONE MORE THING, MISS AISHA. WAITRESSES SEE A LOT OF PEOPLE. DOES THIS MAN LOOK FAMILIAR?
I'M SORRY, BUT NO.
OH, MY GOSH, EESHA. WHAT ARE THEY LIKE?
I AM SO CREEPED OUT RIGHT NOW!
THE LITTLE ONE IS JUST RUDE AND I THINK THE TALL ONE IS HITTING ON ME. HE TOUCHED MY HAND!
HITTING ON YOU? OH, GOSH! HE'S SO CUTE. I BET THEY'RE KNIGHTS.
ONE OF THEM CALLED THE OTHER ONE "SIR" SOMETHING.
I JUST WANT THEM OUT BEFORE THEY GET ANY CREEPIER.
YOU'RE SO WEIRD AISHA. DON'T YOU WANT A KNIGHT TO WHISK YOU AWAY FROM HERE?
UGH. I WANT TO GET OUT OF HERE, BUT GODDESS FORBID.

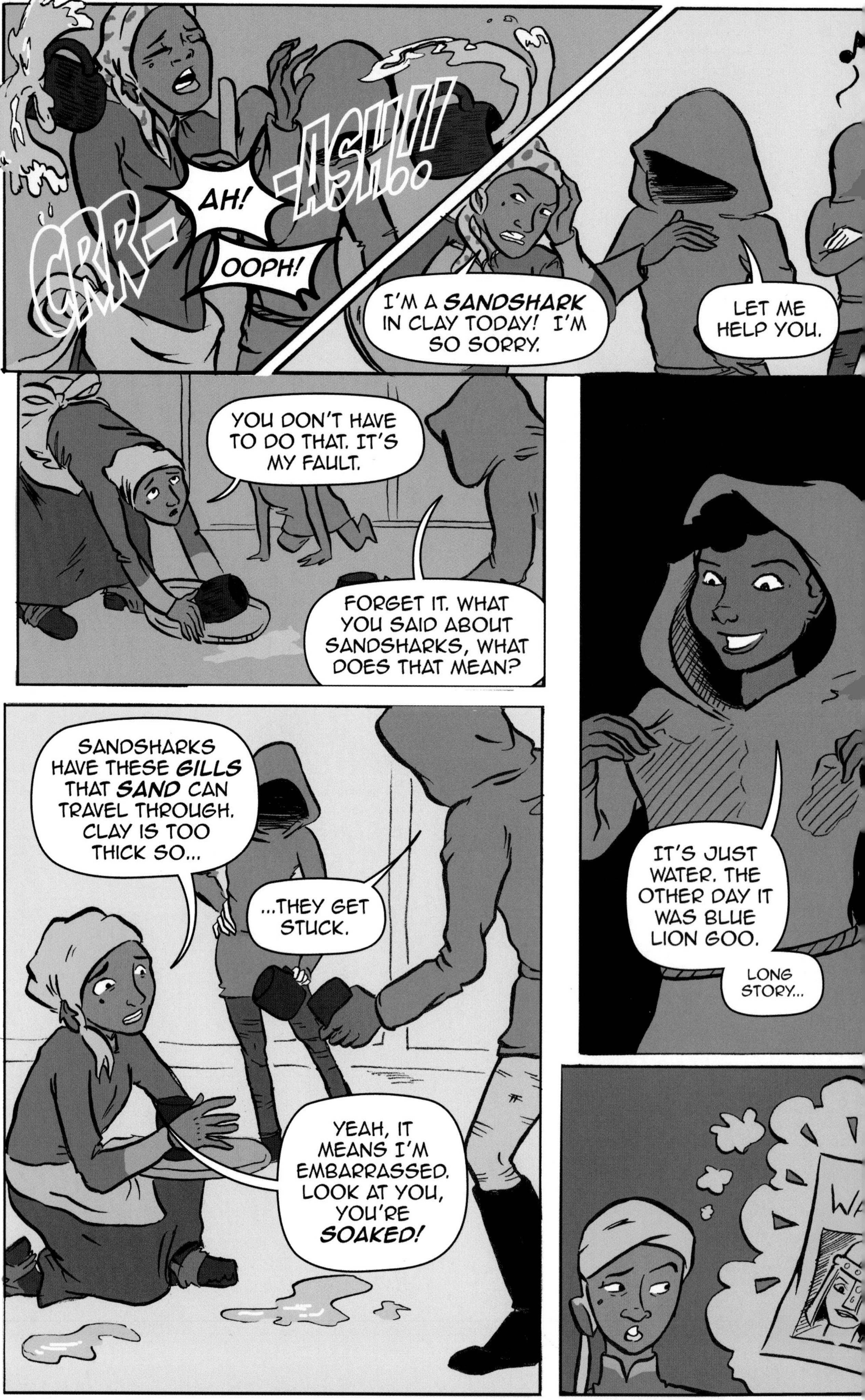

CRR-
AH!
OOPH!
-ASH!!
I'M A SANDSHARK IN CLAY TODAY! I'M SO SORRY.
LET ME HELP YOU.
YOU DON'T HAVE TO DO THAT. IT'S MY FAULT.
FORGET IT. WHAT YOU SAID ABOUT SANDSHARKS, WHAT DOES THAT MEAN?
SANDSHARKS HAVE THESE GILLS THAT SAND CAN TRAVEL THROUGH. CLAY IS TOO THICK SO...
...THEY GET STUCK.
YEAH, IT MEANS I'M EMBARRASSED. LOOK AT YOU, YOU'RE SOAKED!
IT'S JUST WATER. THE OTHER DAY IT WAS BLUE LION GOO.
LONG STORY...

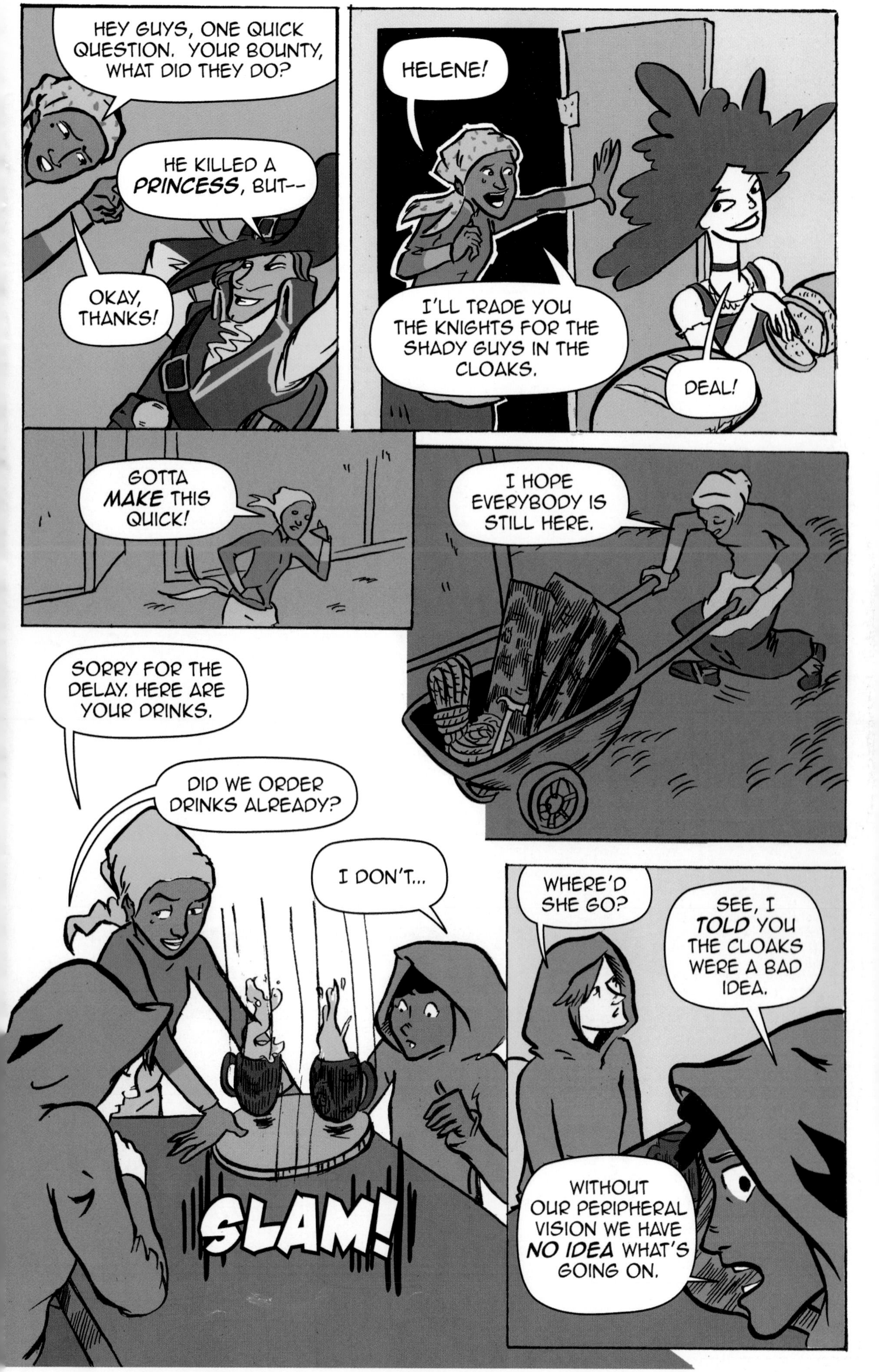
HEY GUYS, ONE QUICK QUESTION. YOUR BOUNTY, WHAT DID THEY DO?
HE KILLED A *PRINCESS*, BUT--
OKAY, THANKS!
HELENE!
I'LL TRADE YOU THE KNIGHTS FOR THE SHADY GUYS IN THE CLOAKS.
DEAL!
GOTTA *MAKE* THIS QUICK!
I HOPE EVERYBODY IS STILL HERE.
SORRY FOR THE DELAY. HERE ARE YOUR DRINKS.
DID WE ORDER DRINKS ALREADY?
I DON'T...
SLAM!
WHERE'D SHE GO?
SEE, I *TOLD* YOU THE CLOAKS WERE A BAD IDEA.
WITHOUT OUR PERIPHERAL VISION WE HAVE *NO IDEA* WHAT'S GOING ON.

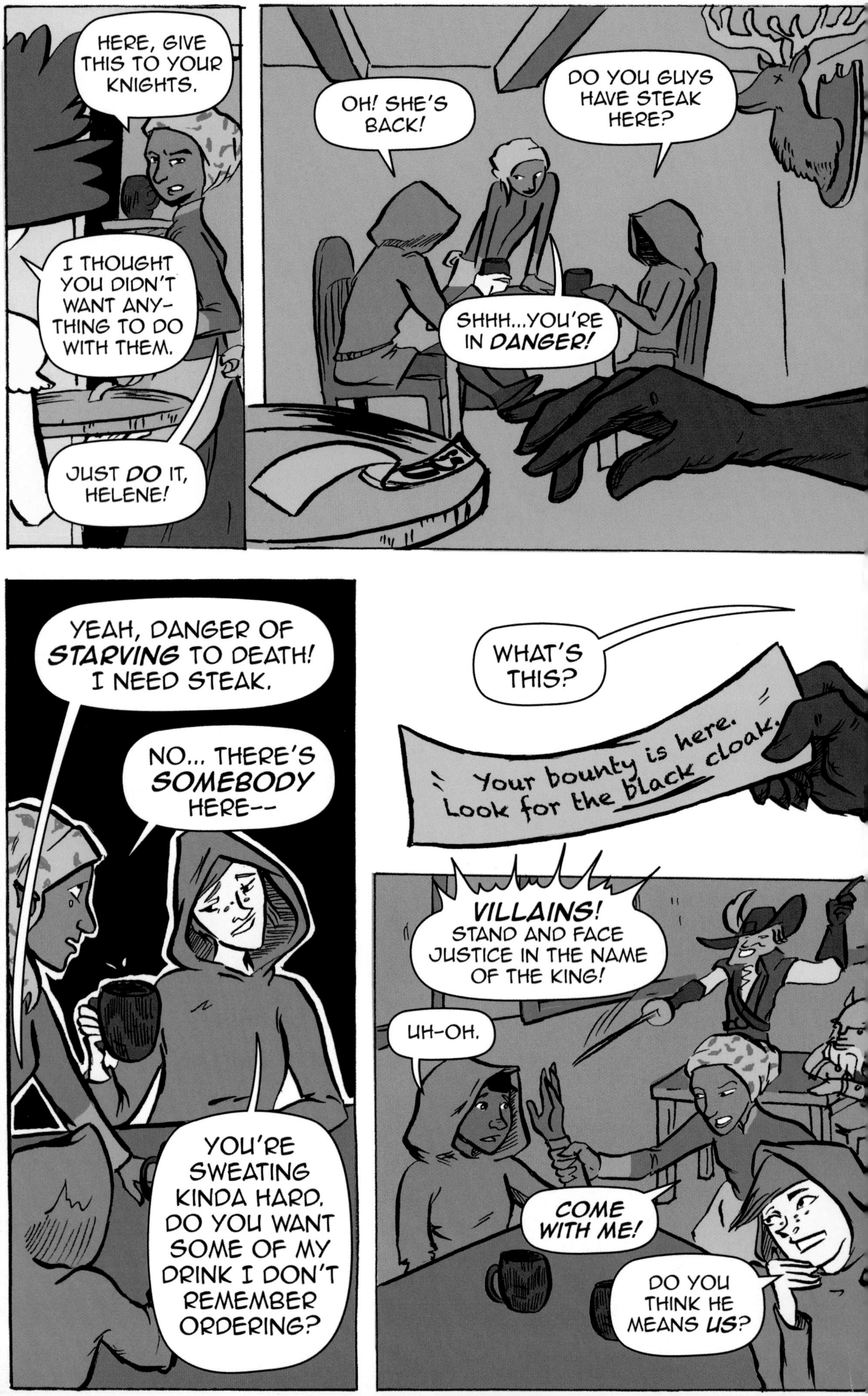
HERE, GIVE THIS TO YOUR KNIGHTS.
I THOUGHT YOU DIDN'T WANT ANY-THING TO DO WITH THEM.
JUST DO IT, HELENE!
OH! SHE'S BACK!
DO YOU GUYS HAVE STEAK HERE?
SHHH...YOU'RE IN DANGER!
YEAH, DANGER OF STARVING TO DEATH! I NEED STEAK.
NO... THERE'S SOMEBODY HERE--
YOU'RE SWEATING KINDA HARD. DO YOU WANT SOME OF MY DRINK I DON'T REMEMBER ORDERING?
WHAT'S THIS?
Your bounty is here. Look for the black cloak.
VILLAINS! STAND AND FACE JUSTICE IN THE NAME OF THE KING!
UH-OH.
COME WITH ME!
DO YOU THINK HE MEANS US?

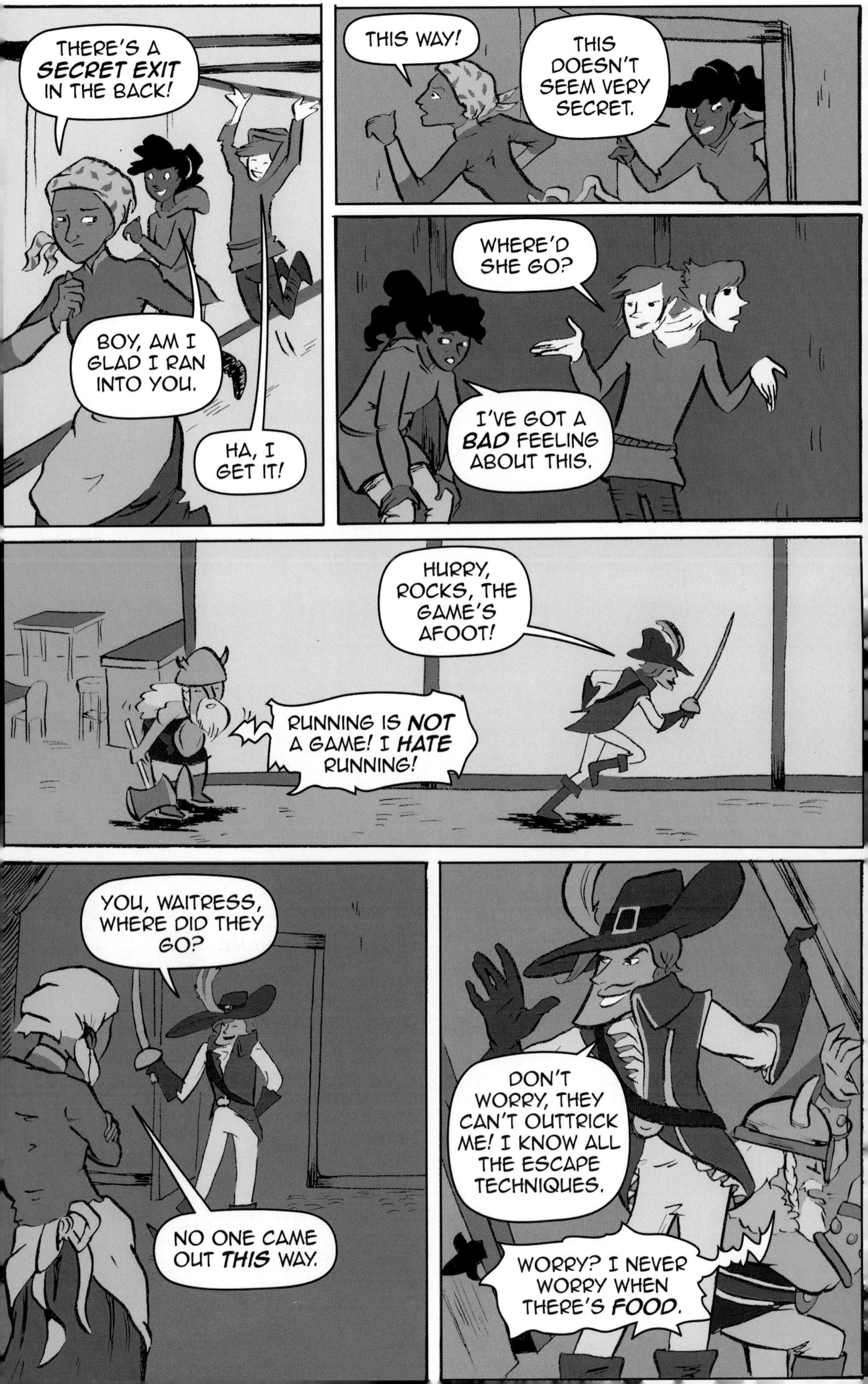
THERE'S A SECRET EXIT IN THE BACK!
BOY, AM I GLAD I RAN INTO YOU.
HA, I GET IT!
THIS WAY!
THIS DOESN'T SEEM VERY SECRET.
WHERE'D SHE GO?
I'VE GOT A BAD FEELING ABOUT THIS.
HURRY, ROCKS, THE GAME'S AFOOT!
RUNNING IS NOT A GAME! I HATE RUNNING!
YOU, WAITRESS, WHERE DID THEY GO?
NO ONE CAME OUT THIS WAY.
DON'T WORRY, THEY CAN'T OUTTRICK ME! I KNOW ALL THE ESCAPE TECHNIQUES.
WORRY? I NEVER WORRY WHEN THERE'S FOOD.

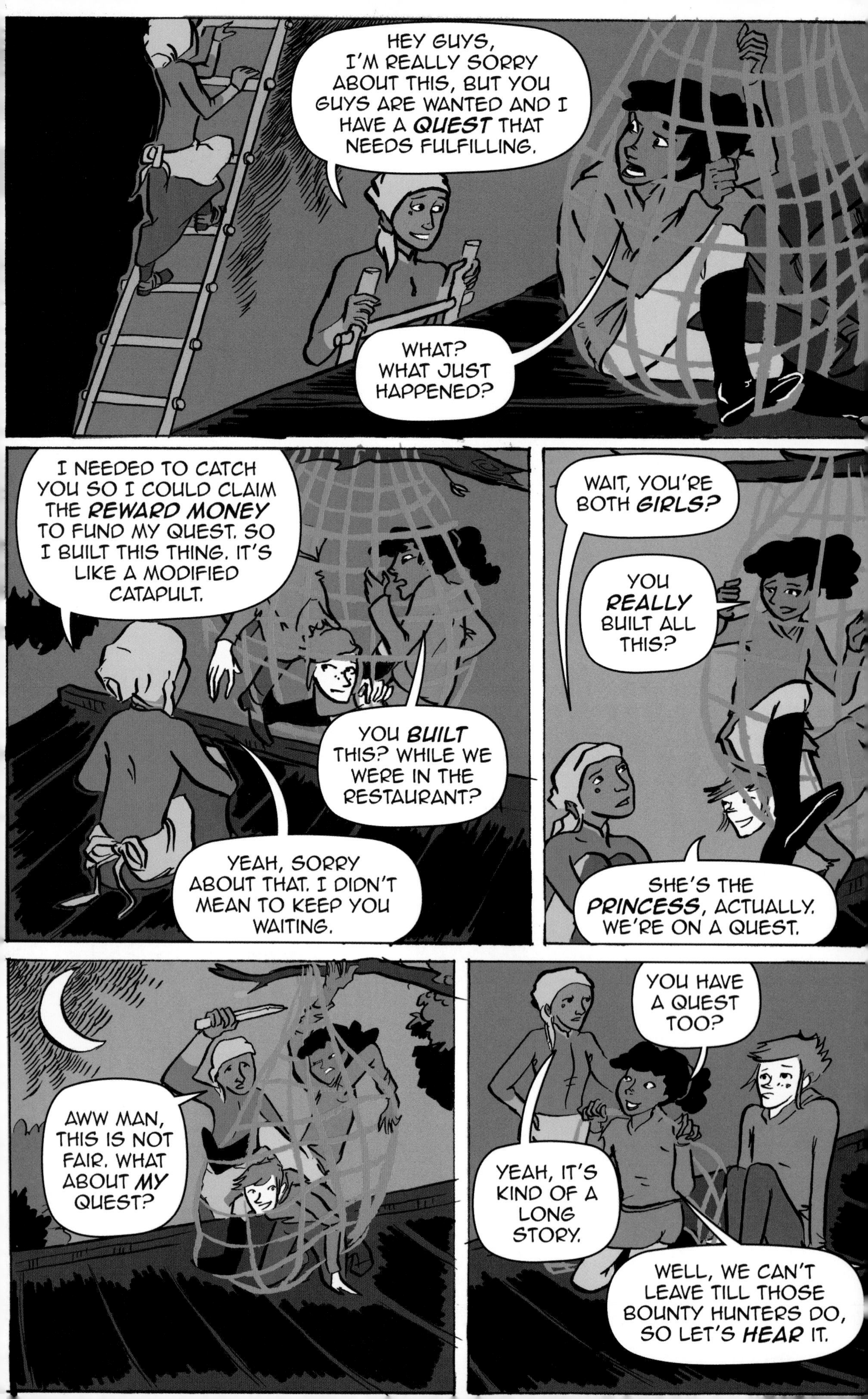
HEY GUYS, I'M REALLY SORRY ABOUT THIS, BUT YOU GUYS ARE WANTED AND I HAVE A *QUEST* THAT NEEDS FULFILLING.
WHAT? WHAT JUST HAPPENED?
I NEEDED TO CATCH YOU SO I COULD CLAIM THE *REWARD MONEY* TO FUND MY QUEST. SO I BUILT THIS THING. IT'S LIKE A MODIFIED CATAPULT.
YOU *BUILT* THIS? WHILE WE WERE IN THE RESTAURANT?
YEAH, SORRY ABOUT THAT. I DIDN'T MEAN TO KEEP YOU WAITING.
WAIT, YOU'RE BOTH *GIRLS?*
YOU *REALLY* BUILT ALL THIS?
SHE'S THE *PRINCESS*, ACTUALLY. WE'RE ON A QUEST.
AWW MAN, THIS IS NOT FAIR. WHAT ABOUT *MY* QUEST?
YOU HAVE A QUEST TOO?
YEAH, IT'S KIND OF A LONG STORY.
WELL, WE CAN'T LEAVE TILL THOSE BOUNTY HUNTERS DO, SO LET'S *HEAR* IT.

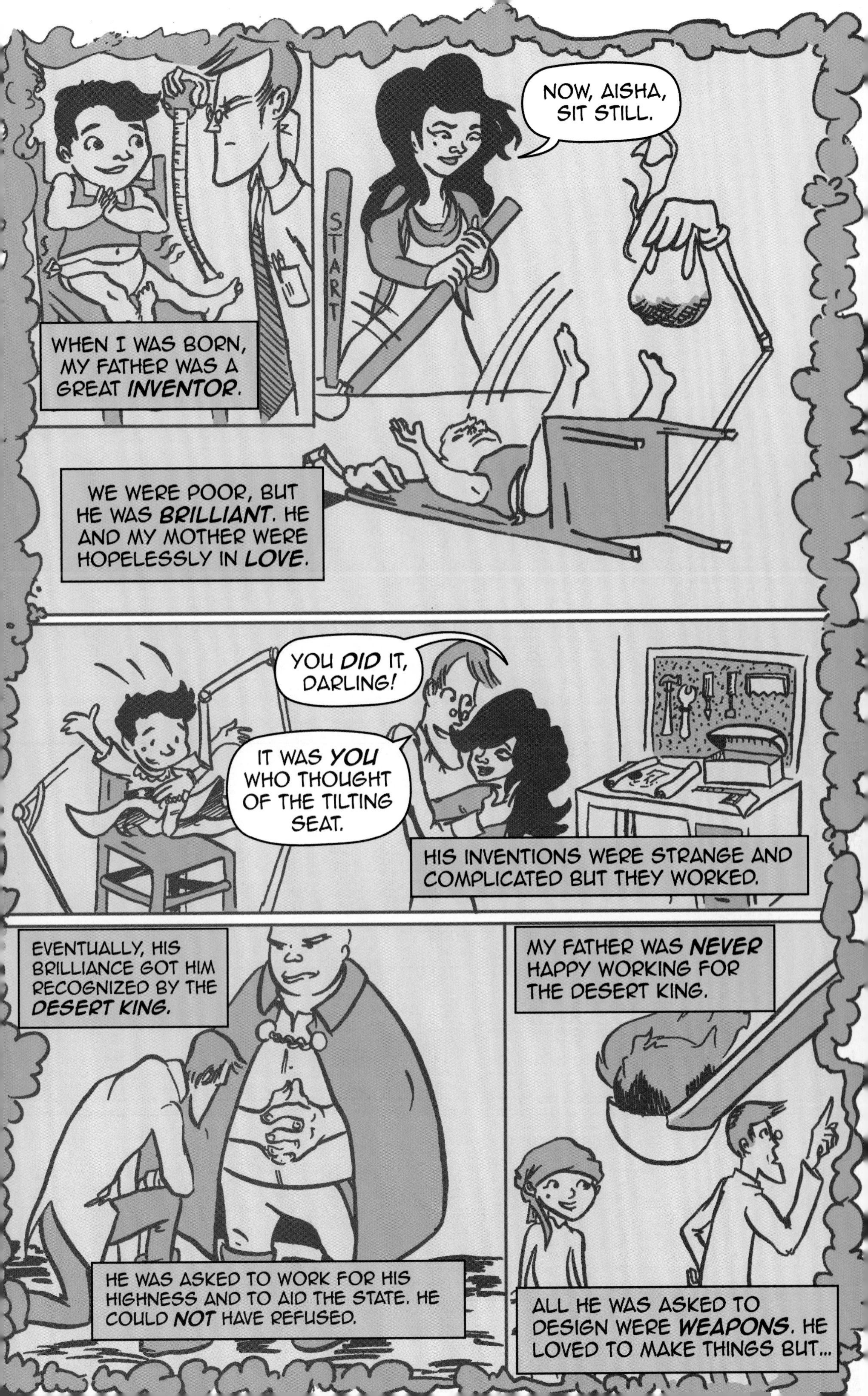

WHEN I WAS BORN, MY FATHER WAS A GREAT *INVENTOR*.
NOW, AISHA, SIT STILL.
START
WE WERE POOR, BUT HE WAS *BRILLIANT*. HE AND MY MOTHER WERE HOPELESSLY IN *LOVE*.
YOU *DID* IT, DARLING!
IT WAS *YOU* WHO THOUGHT OF THE TILTING SEAT.
HIS INVENTIONS WERE STRANGE AND COMPLICATED BUT THEY WORKED.
EVENTUALLY, HIS BRILLIANCE GOT HIM RECOGNIZED BY THE *DESERT KING*.
HE WAS ASKED TO WORK FOR HIS HIGHNESS AND TO AID THE STATE. HE COULD *NOT* HAVE REFUSED.
MY FATHER WAS *NEVER* HAPPY WORKING FOR THE DESERT KING.
ALL HE WAS ASKED TO DESIGN WERE *WEAPONS*. HE LOVED TO MAKE THINGS BUT...

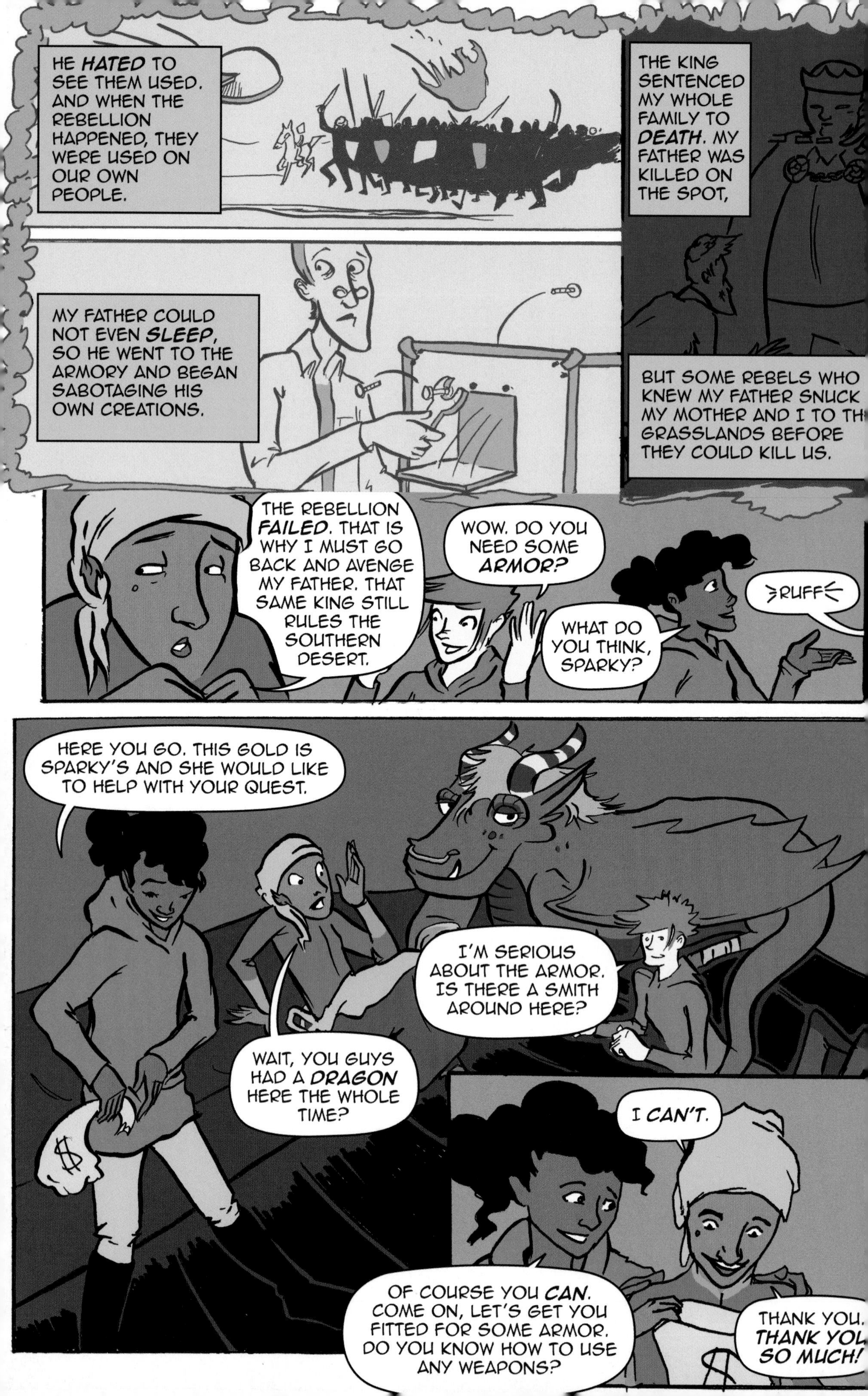
HE HATED TO SEE THEM USED. AND WHEN THE REBELLION HAPPENED, THEY WERE USED ON OUR OWN PEOPLE.
THE KING SENTENCED MY WHOLE FAMILY TO DEATH. MY FATHER WAS KILLED ON THE SPOT,
MY FATHER COULD NOT EVEN SLEEP, SO HE WENT TO THE ARMORY AND BEGAN SABOTAGING HIS OWN CREATIONS.
BUT SOME REBELS WHO KNEW MY FATHER SNUCK MY MOTHER AND I TO TH GRASSLANDS BEFORE THEY COULD KILL US.
THE REBELLION FAILED. THAT IS WHY I MUST GO BACK AND AVENGE MY FATHER. THAT SAME KING STILL RULES THE SOUTHERN DESERT.
WOW. DO YOU NEED SOME ARMOR?
WHAT DO YOU THINK, SPARKY?
RUFF
HERE YOU GO. THIS GOLD IS SPARKY'S AND SHE WOULD LIKE TO HELP WITH YOUR QUEST.
I'M SERIOUS ABOUT THE ARMOR. IS THERE A SMITH AROUND HERE?
WAIT, YOU GUYS HAD A DRAGON HERE THE WHOLE TIME?
I CAN'T.
OF COURSE YOU CAN. COME ON, LET'S GET YOU FITTED FOR SOME ARMOR. DO YOU KNOW HOW TO USE ANY WEAPONS?
THANK YOU. THANK YOU SO MUCH!

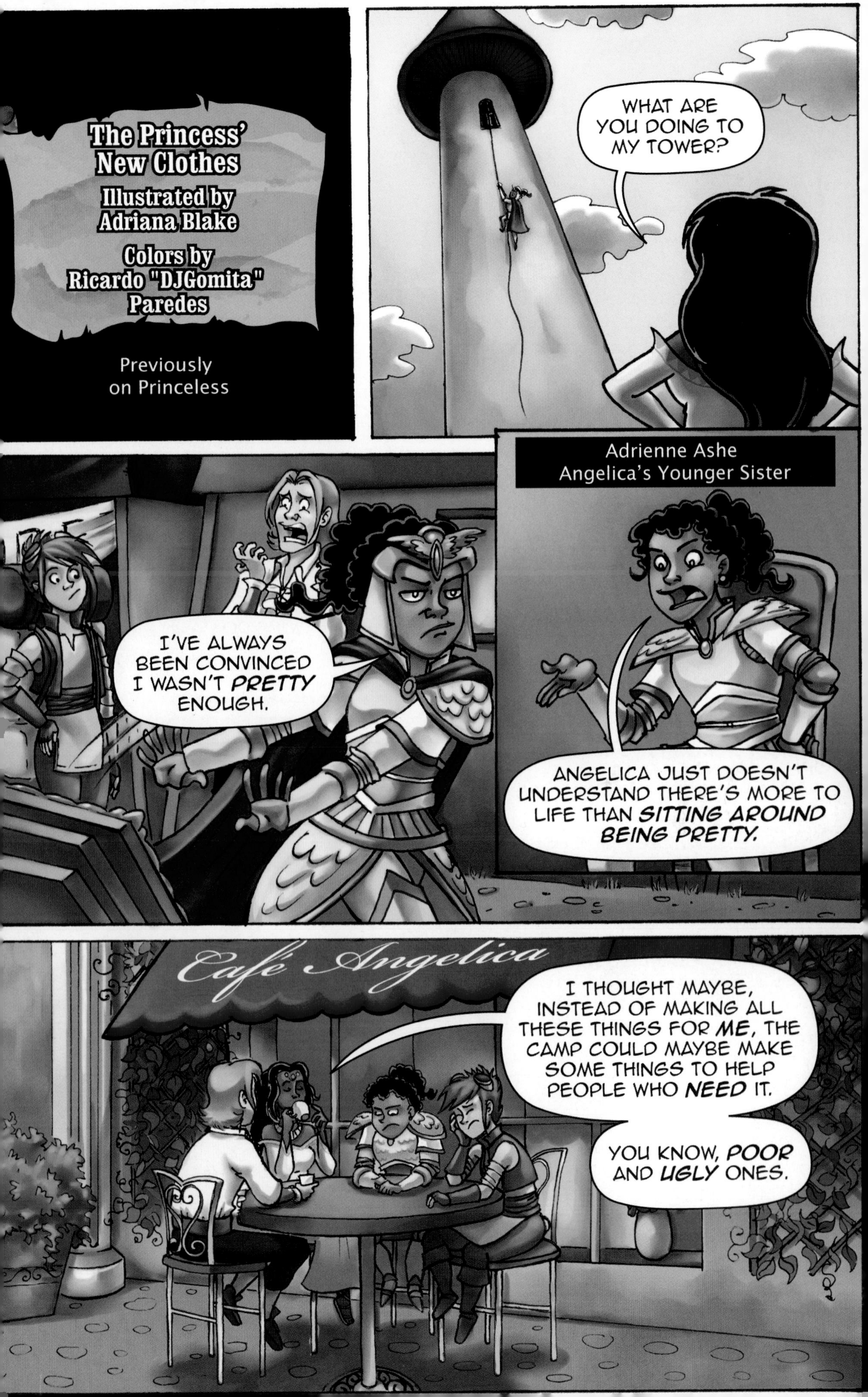
The Princess' New Clothes
Illustrated by Adriana Blake
Colors by Ricardo "DJGomita" Paredes
Previously on Princeless
WHAT ARE YOU DOING TO MY TOWER?
Adrienne Ashe
Angelica's Younger Sister
I'VE ALWAYS BEEN CONVINCED I WASN'T PRETTY ENOUGH.
ANGELICA JUST DOESN'T UNDERSTAND THERE'S MORE TO LIFE THAN SITTING AROUND BEING PRETTY.
Café Angelica
I THOUGHT MAYBE, INSTEAD OF MAKING ALL THESE THINGS FOR ME, THE CAMP COULD MAYBE MAKE SOME THINGS TO HELP PEOPLE WHO NEED IT.
YOU KNOW, POOR AND UGLY ONES.

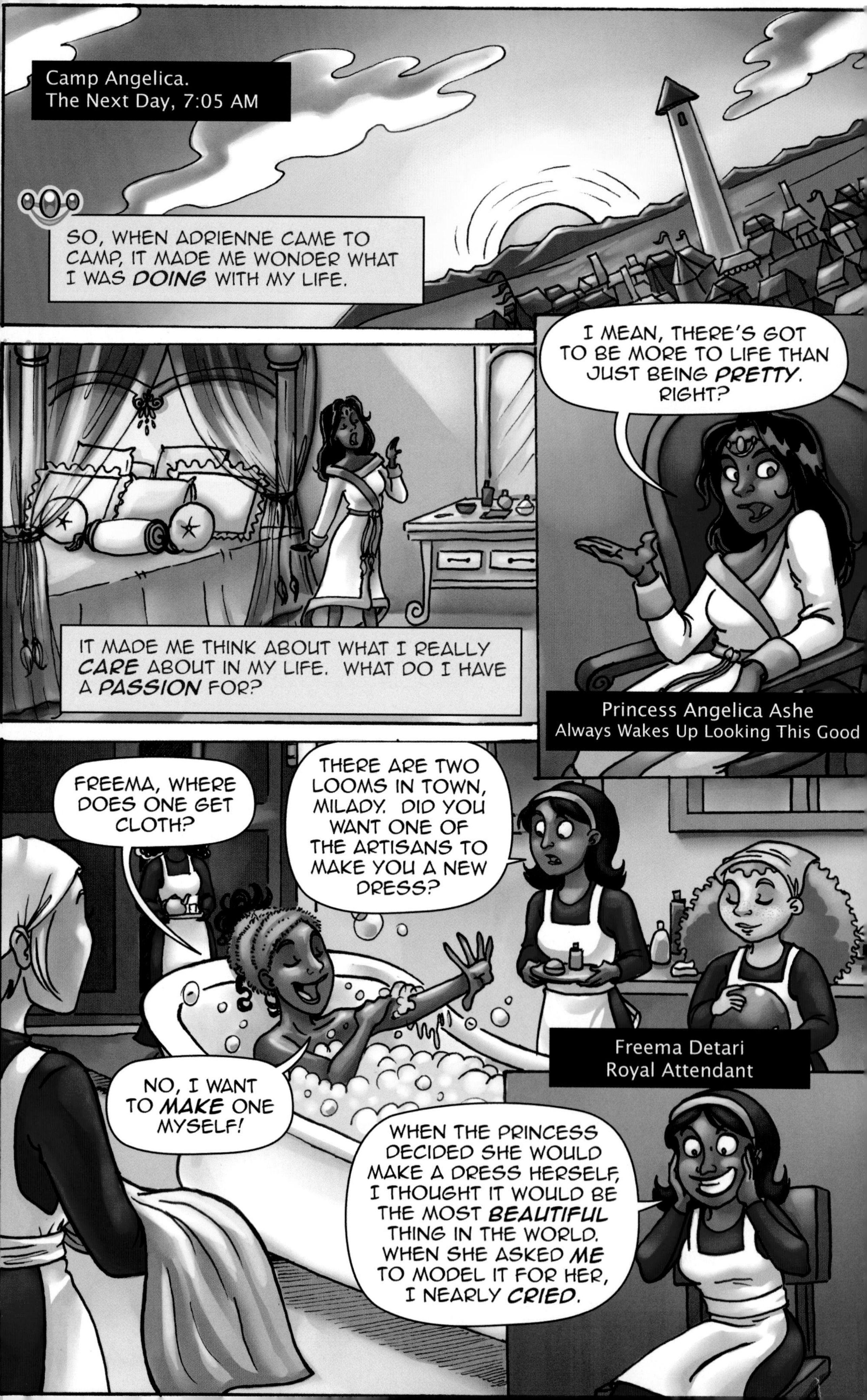
Camp Angelica.
The Next Day, 7:05 AM
SO, WHEN ADRIENNE CAME TO CAMP, IT MADE ME WONDER WHAT I WAS *DOING* WITH MY LIFE.
IT MADE ME THINK ABOUT WHAT I REALLY *CARE* ABOUT IN MY LIFE. WHAT DO I HAVE A *PASSION* FOR?
I MEAN, THERE'S GOT TO BE MORE TO LIFE THAN JUST BEING *PRETTY*. RIGHT?
Princess Angelica Ashe
Always Wakes Up Looking This Good
FREEMA, WHERE DOES ONE GET CLOTH?
THERE ARE TWO LOOMS IN TOWN, MILADY. DID YOU WANT ONE OF THE ARTISANS TO MAKE YOU A NEW DRESS?
NO, I WANT TO *MAKE* ONE MYSELF!
Freema Detari
Royal Attendant
WHEN THE PRINCESS DECIDED SHE WOULD MAKE A DRESS HERSELF, I THOUGHT IT WOULD BE THE MOST *BEAUTIFUL* THING IN THE WORLD. WHEN SHE ASKED *ME* TO MODEL IT FOR HER, I NEARLY *CRIED*.

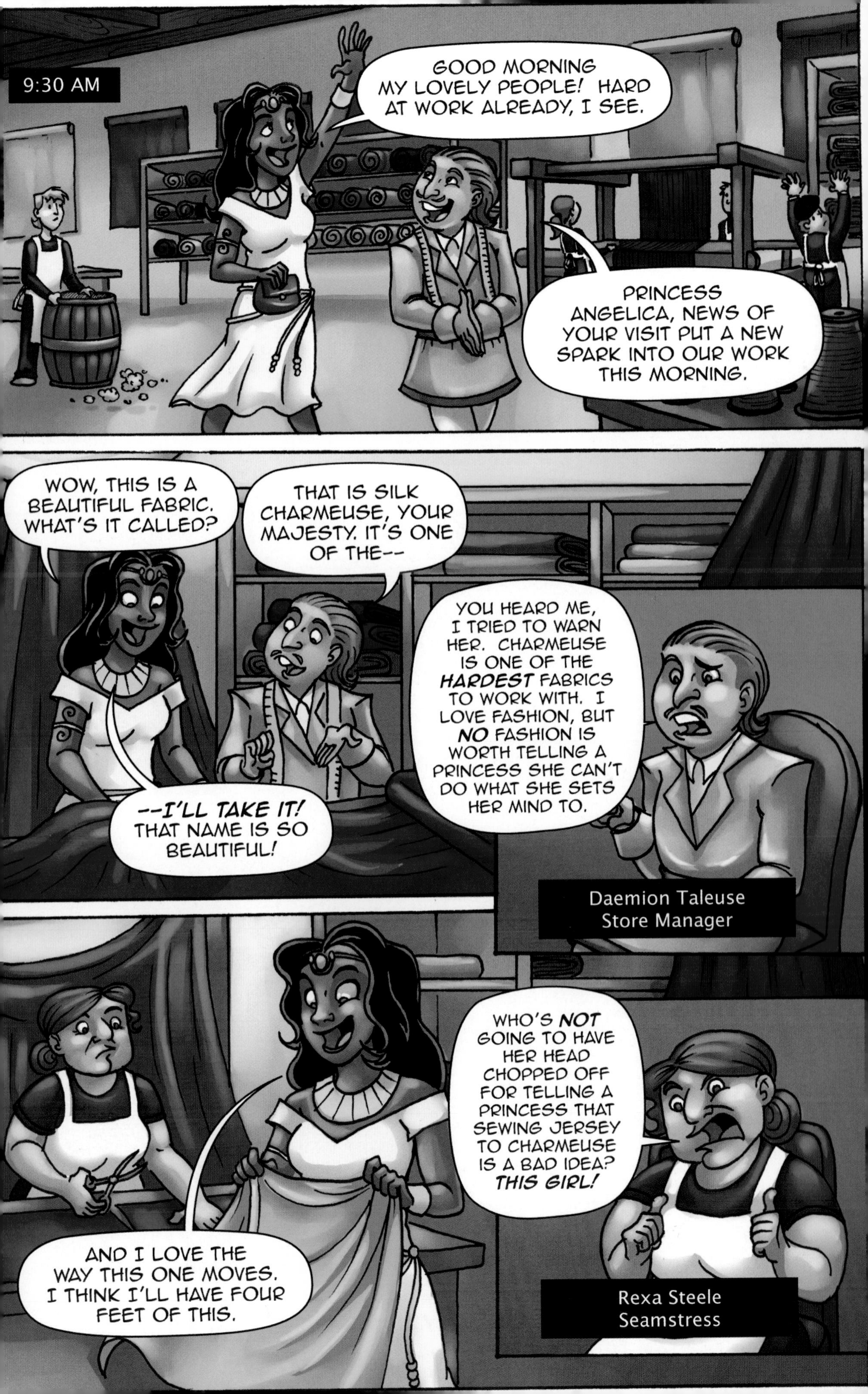
9:30 AM
GOOD MORNING MY LOVELY PEOPLE! HARD AT WORK ALREADY, I SEE.
PRINCESS ANGELICA, NEWS OF YOUR VISIT PUT A NEW SPARK INTO OUR WORK THIS MORNING.
WOW, THIS IS A BEAUTIFUL FABRIC. WHAT'S IT CALLED?
THAT IS SILK CHARMEUSE, YOUR MAJESTY. IT'S ONE OF THE--
--I'LL TAKE IT! THAT NAME IS SO BEAUTIFUL!
YOU HEARD ME, I TRIED TO WARN HER. CHARMEUSE IS ONE OF THE HARDEST FABRICS TO WORK WITH. I LOVE FASHION, BUT NO FASHION IS WORTH TELLING A PRINCESS SHE CAN'T DO WHAT SHE SETS HER MIND TO.
Daemion Taleuse
Store Manager
AND I LOVE THE WAY THIS ONE MOVES. I THINK I'LL HAVE FOUR FEET OF THIS.
WHO'S NOT GOING TO HAVE HER HEAD CHOPPED OFF FOR TELLING A PRINCESS THAT SEWING JERSEY TO CHARMEUSE IS A BAD IDEA? THIS GIRL!
Rexa Steele
Seamstress

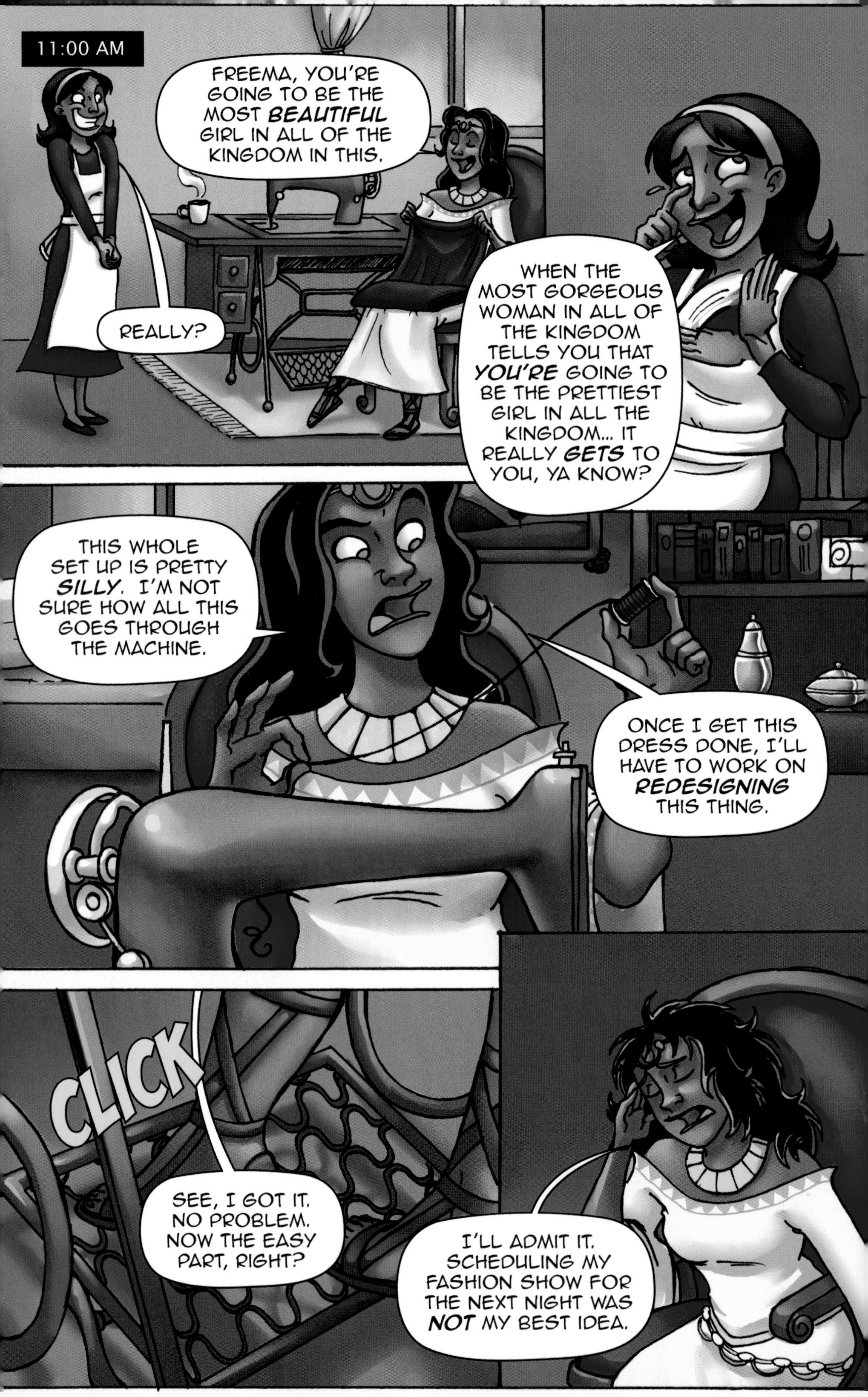
11:00 AM
FREEMA, YOU'RE GOING TO BE THE MOST BEAUTIFUL GIRL IN ALL OF THE KINGDOM IN THIS.
REALLY?
WHEN THE MOST GORGEOUS WOMAN IN ALL OF THE KINGDOM TELLS YOU THAT YOU'RE GOING TO BE THE PRETTIEST GIRL IN ALL THE KINGDOM... IT REALLY GETS TO YOU, YA KNOW?
THIS WHOLE SET UP IS PRETTY SILLY. I'M NOT SURE HOW ALL THIS GOES THROUGH THE MACHINE.
ONCE I GET THIS DRESS DONE, I'LL HAVE TO WORK ON REDESIGNING THIS THING.
CLICK
SEE, I GOT IT. NO PROBLEM. NOW THE EASY PART, RIGHT?
I'LL ADMIT IT. SCHEDULING MY FASHION SHOW FOR THE NEXT NIGHT WAS NOT MY BEST IDEA.

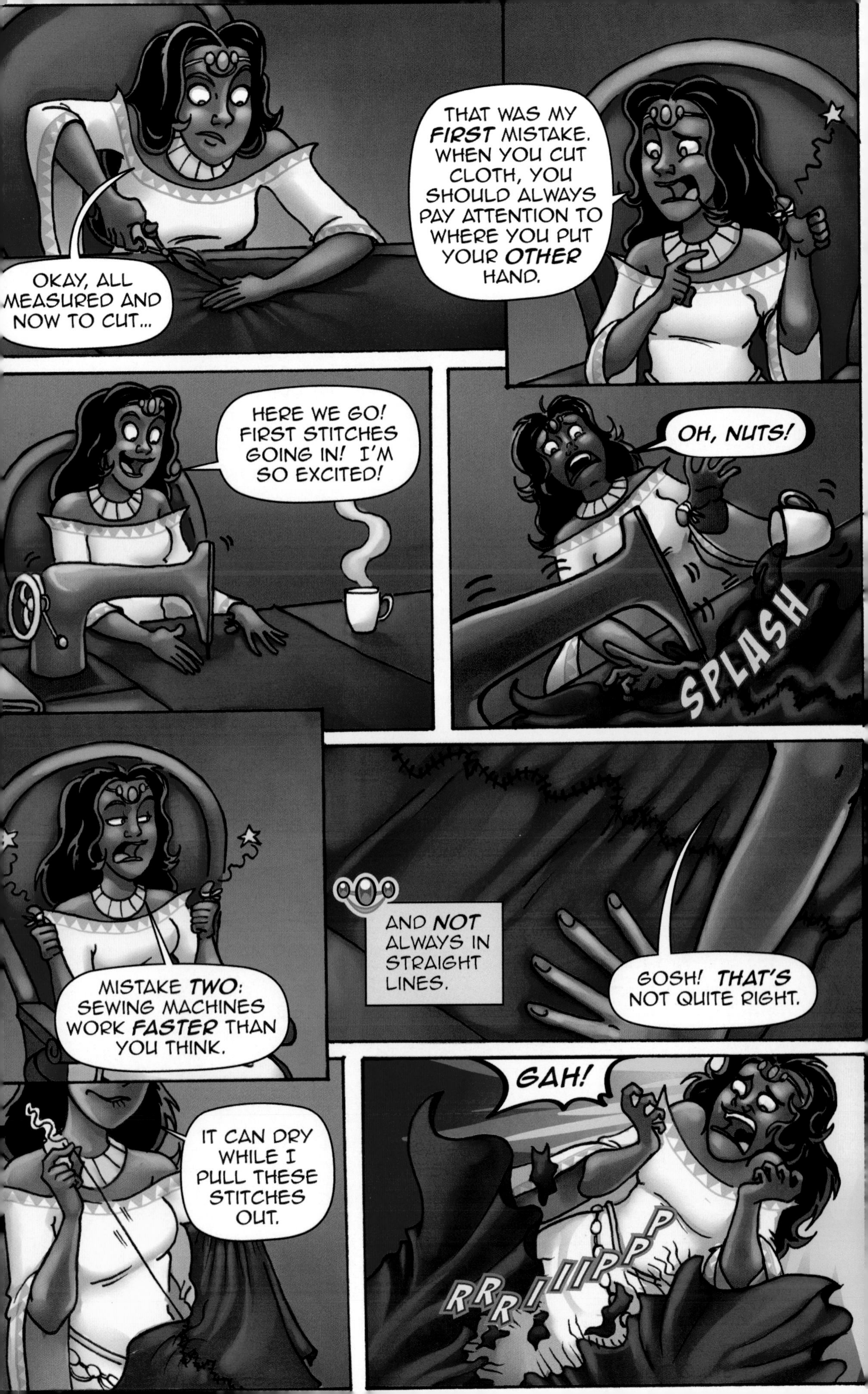
OKAY, ALL MEASURED AND NOW TO CUT...
THAT WAS MY FIRST MISTAKE. WHEN YOU CUT CLOTH, YOU SHOULD ALWAYS PAY ATTENTION TO WHERE YOU PUT YOUR OTHER HAND.
HERE WE GO! FIRST STITCHES GOING IN! I'M SO EXCITED!
OH, NUTS!
SPLASH
MISTAKE TWO: SEWING MACHINES WORK FASTER THAN YOU THINK.
AND NOT ALWAYS IN STRAIGHT LINES.
GOSH! THAT'S NOT QUITE RIGHT.
IT CAN DRY WHILE I PULL THESE STITCHES OUT.
GAH!
RRRIIIIPPP

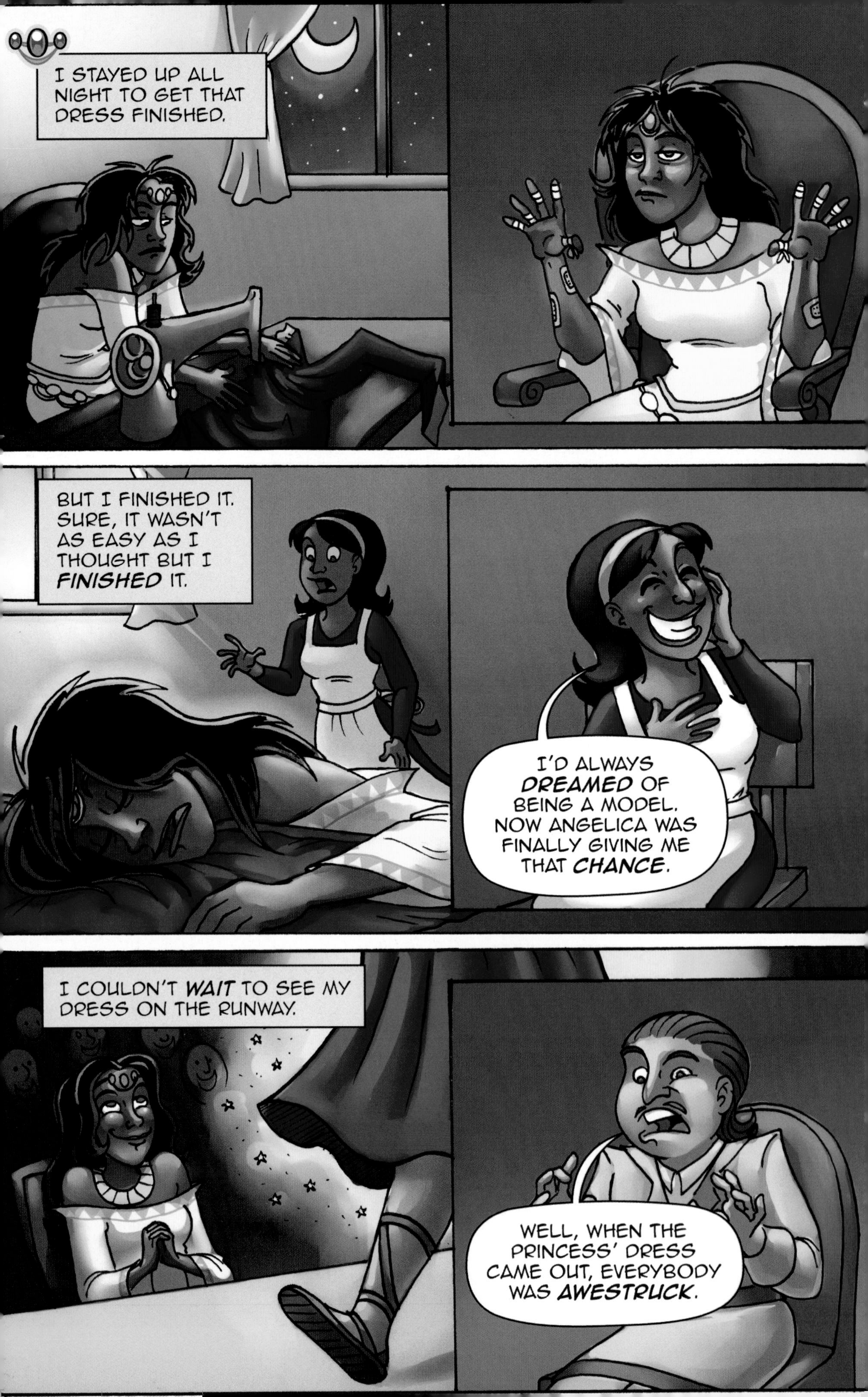
I STAYED UP ALL NIGHT TO GET THAT DRESS FINISHED.
BUT I FINISHED IT. SURE, IT WASN'T AS EASY AS I THOUGHT BUT I FINISHED IT.
I'D ALWAYS DREAMED OF BEING A MODEL. NOW ANGELICA WAS FINALLY GIVING ME THAT CHANCE.
I COULDN'T WAIT TO SEE MY DRESS ON THE RUNWAY.
WELL, WHEN THE PRINCESS' DRESS CAME OUT, EVERYBODY WAS AWESTRUCK.

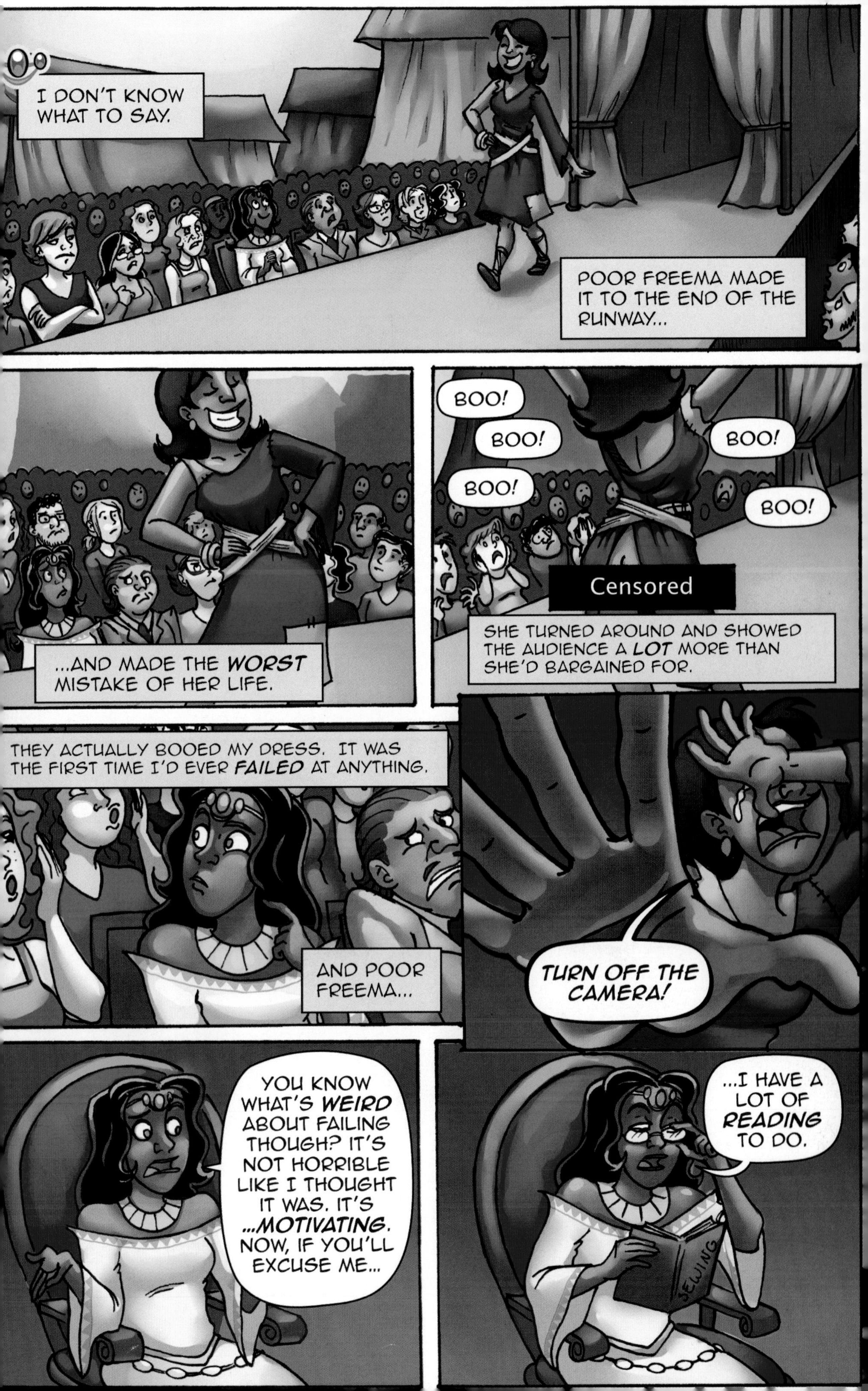

I DON'T KNOW WHAT TO SAY.
POOR FREEMA MADE IT TO THE END OF THE RUNWAY...
...AND MADE THE WORST MISTAKE OF HER LIFE.
BOO!
BOO!
BOO!
BOO!
BOO!
Censored
SHE TURNED AROUND AND SHOWED THE AUDIENCE A LOT MORE THAN SHE'D BARGAINED FOR.
THEY ACTUALLY BOOED MY DRESS. IT WAS THE FIRST TIME I'D EVER FAILED AT ANYTHING.
AND POOR FREEMA...
TURN OFF THE CAMERA!
YOU KNOW WHAT'S WEIRD ABOUT FAILING THOUGH? IT'S NOT HORRIBLE LIKE I THOUGHT IT WAS. IT'S ...MOTIVATING. NOW, IF YOU'LL EXCUSE ME...
...I HAVE A LOT OF READING TO DO.
SEWING

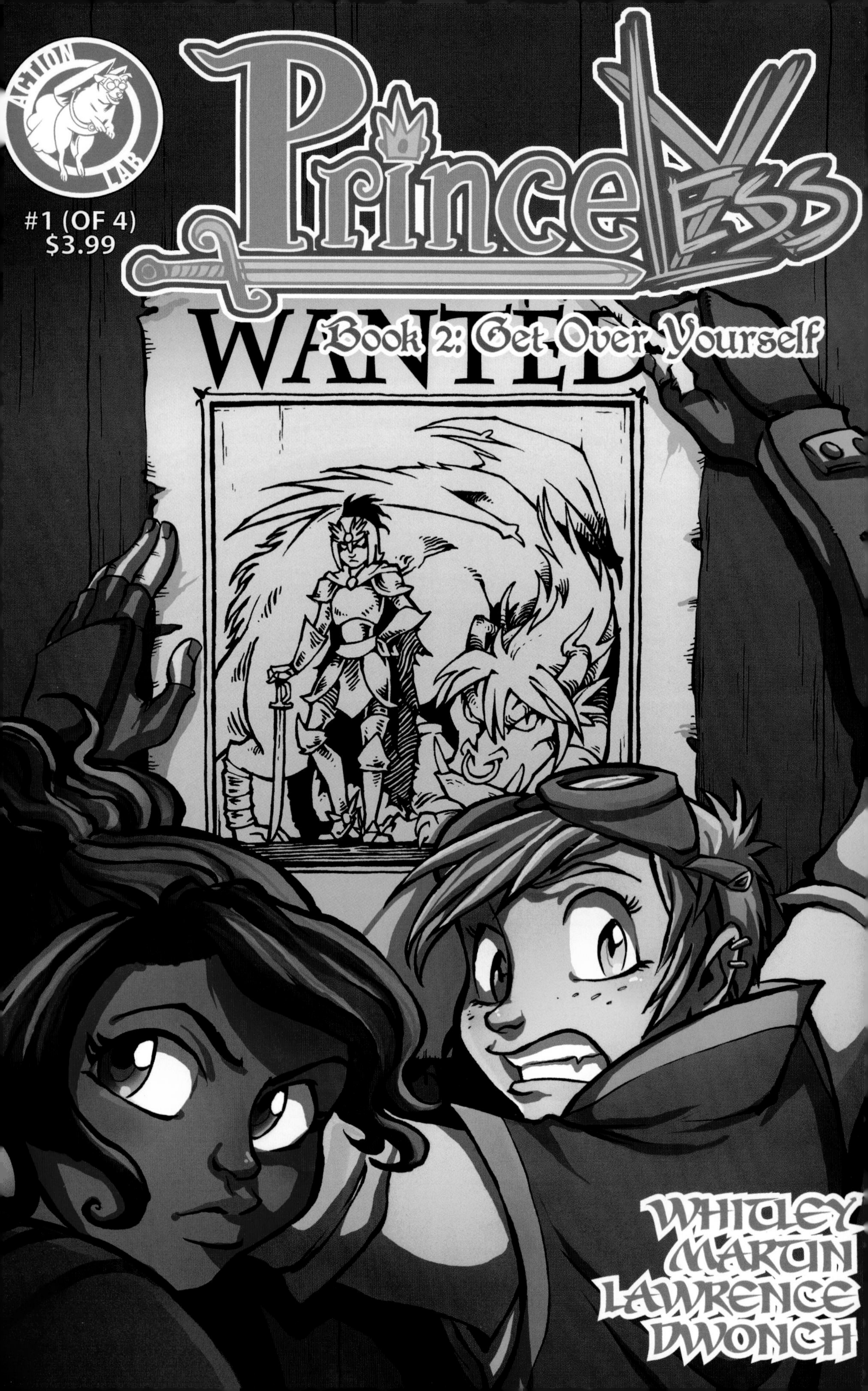
ACTION LAB
Princeless
#1 (OF 4)
$3.99
WANTED
Book 2: Get Over Yourself
WHITLEY
MARTIN
LAWRENCE
DWONCH

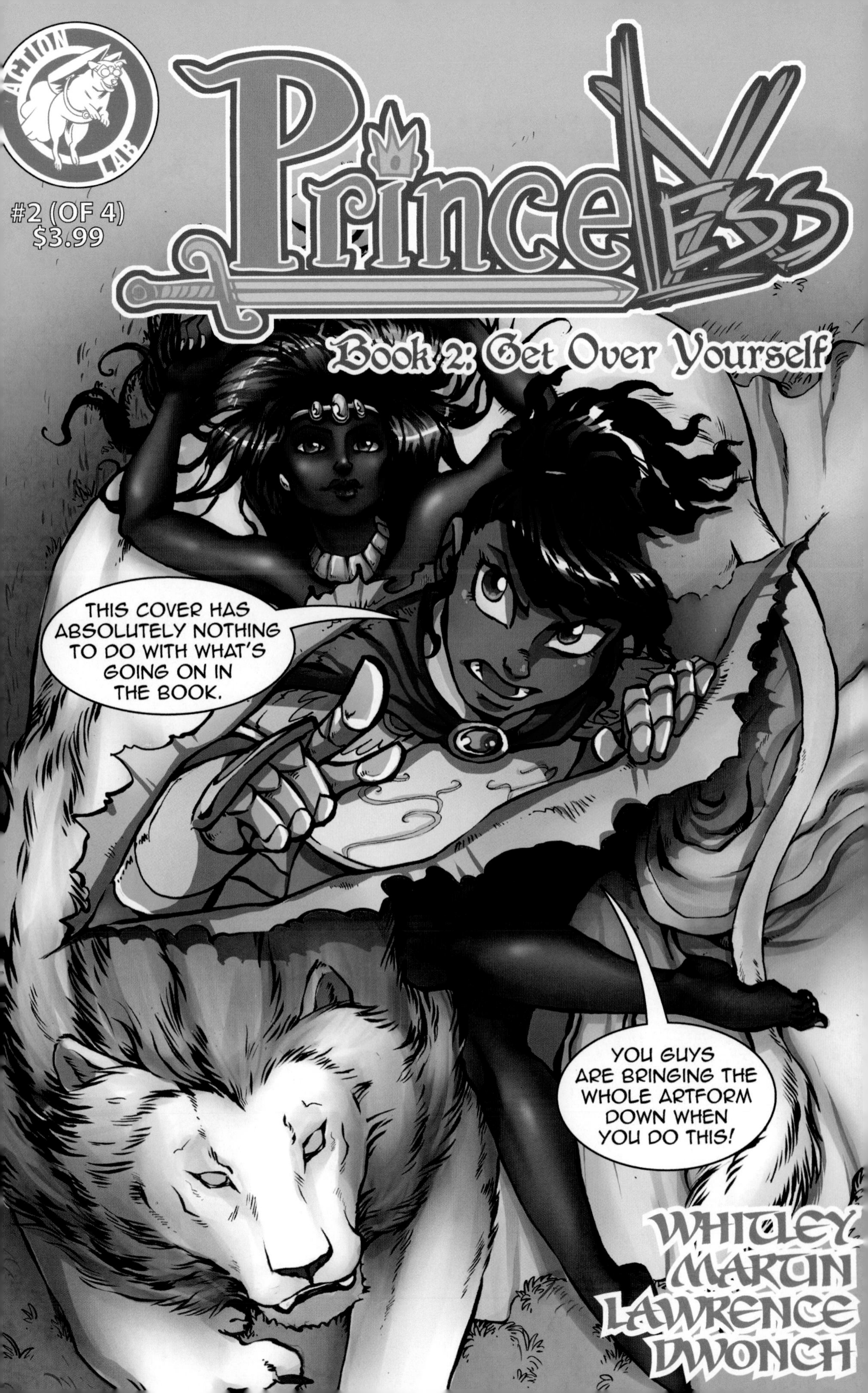
ACTION LAB
#2 (OF 4)
$3.99
Princeless
Book 2: Get Over Yourself
THIS COVER HAS ABSOLUTELY NOTHING TO DO WITH WHAT'S GOING ON IN THE BOOK.
YOU GUYS ARE BRINGING THE WHOLE ARTFORM DOWN WHEN YOU DO THIS!
WHITLEY
MARTIN
LAWRENCE
DWONCH

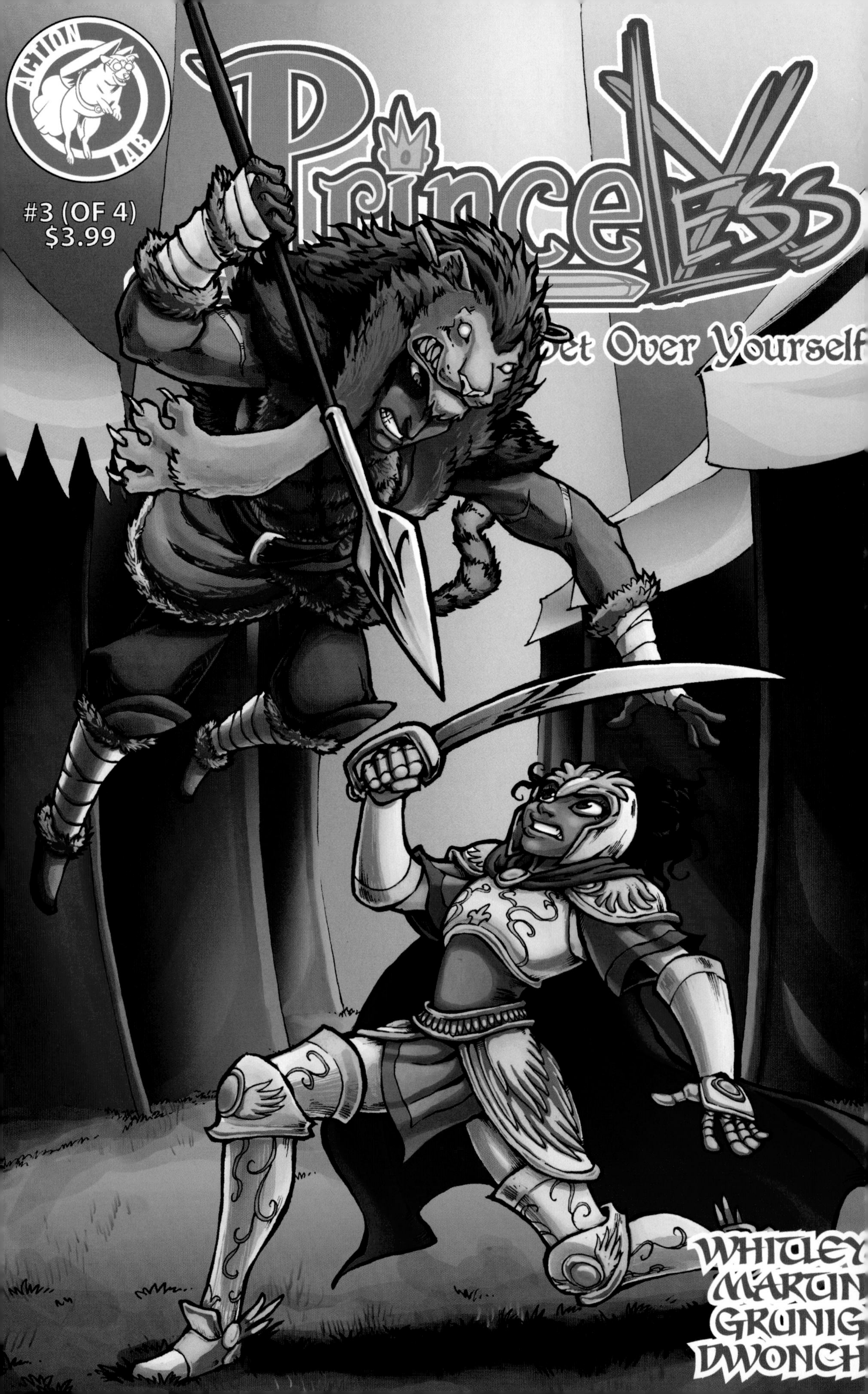

ACTION LAB
Princeless
Get Over Yourself
#3 (OF 4)
$3.99
WHITLEY
MARTIN
GRUNIG
DWONCH

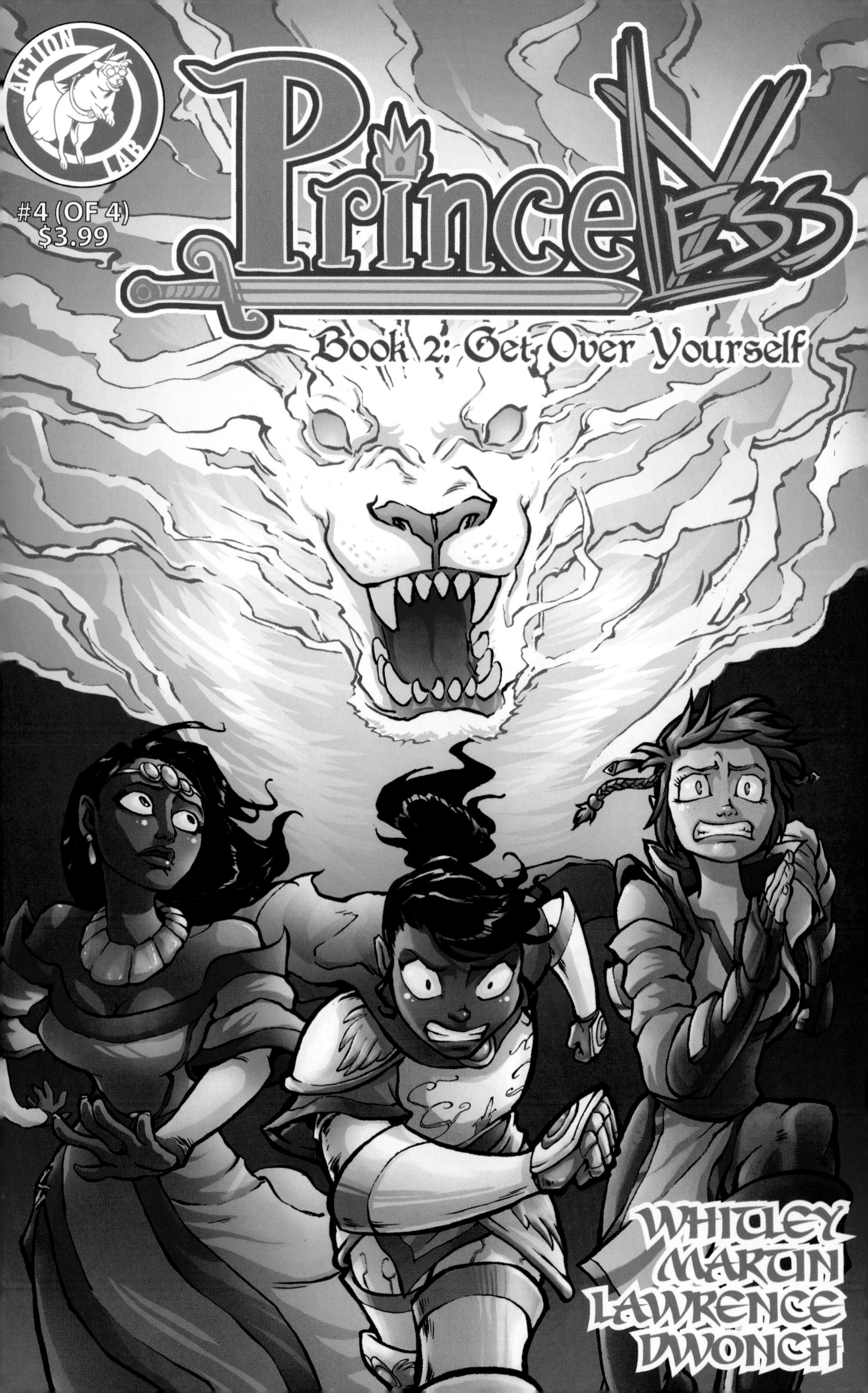

ACTION LAB
#4 (OF 4)
$3.99
Princeless
Book 2: Get Over Yourself
WHITLEY
MARTIN
LAWRENCE
DWONCH

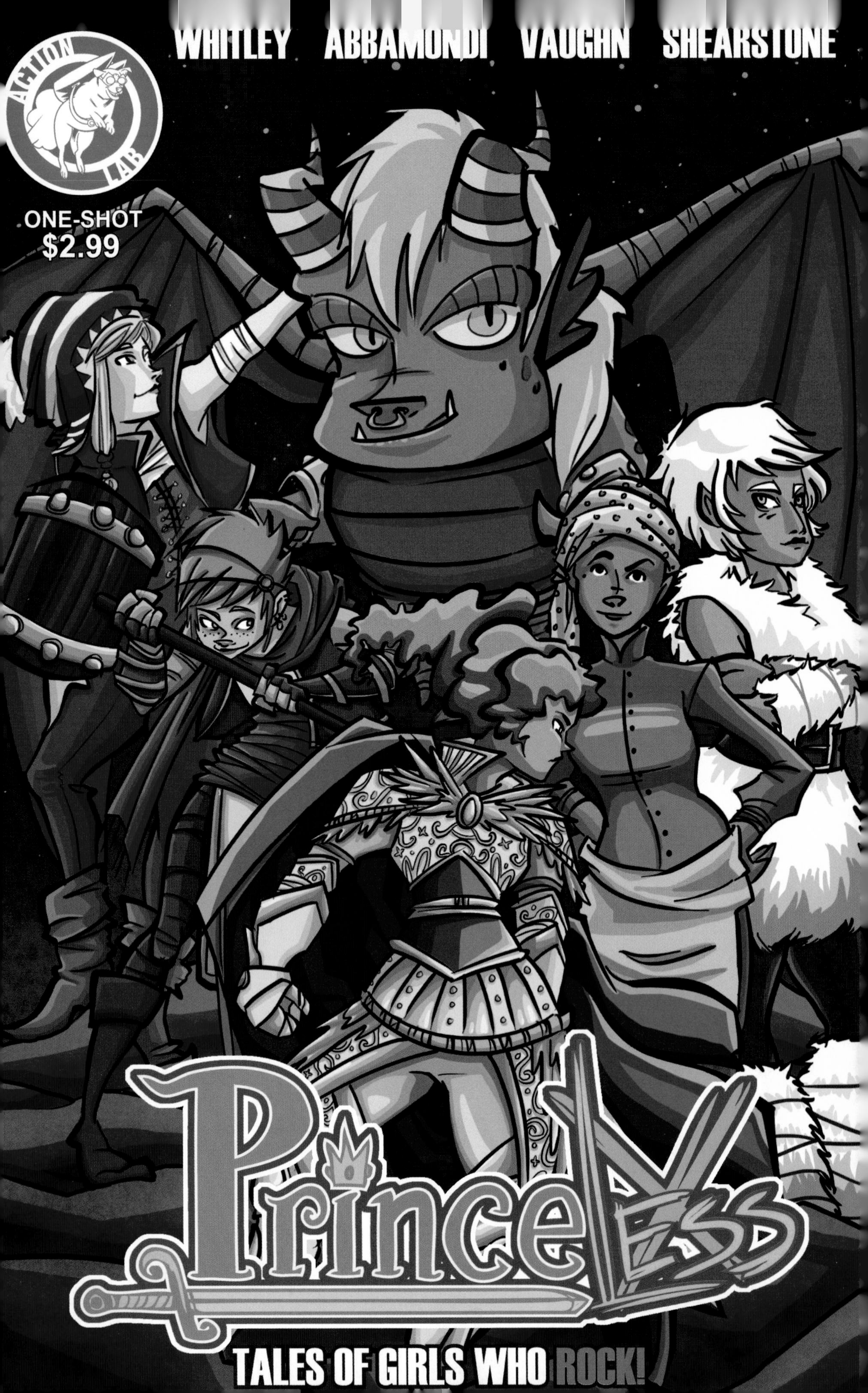
WHITLEY ABBAMONDI VAUGHN SHEARSTONE
ACTION LAB
ONE-SHOT
$2.99
Princeless
TALES OF GIRLS WHO ROCK!

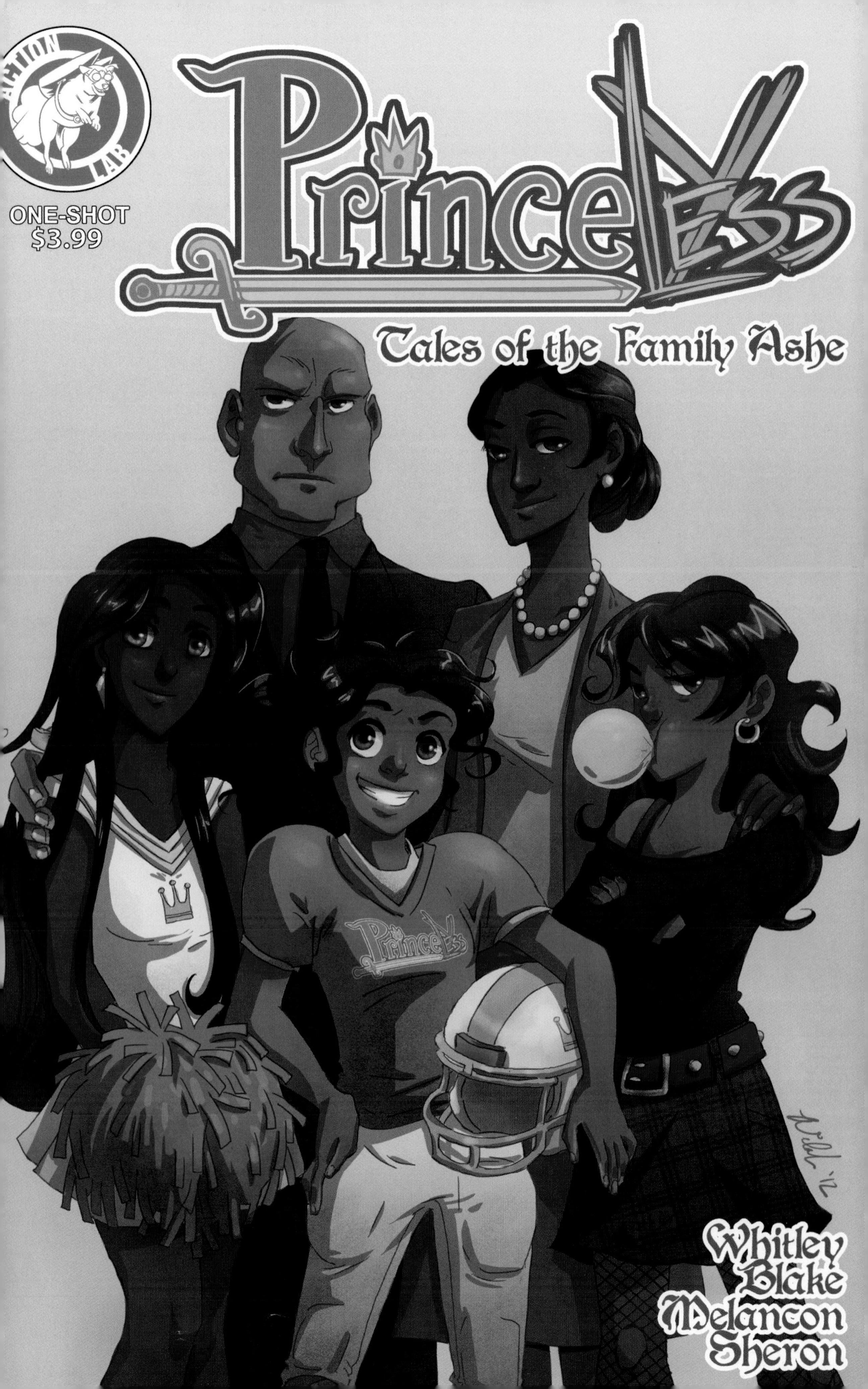
ACTION LAB
ONE-SHOT
$3.99
Princeless
Tales of the Family Ashe
Whitley
Blake
Melancon
Sheron

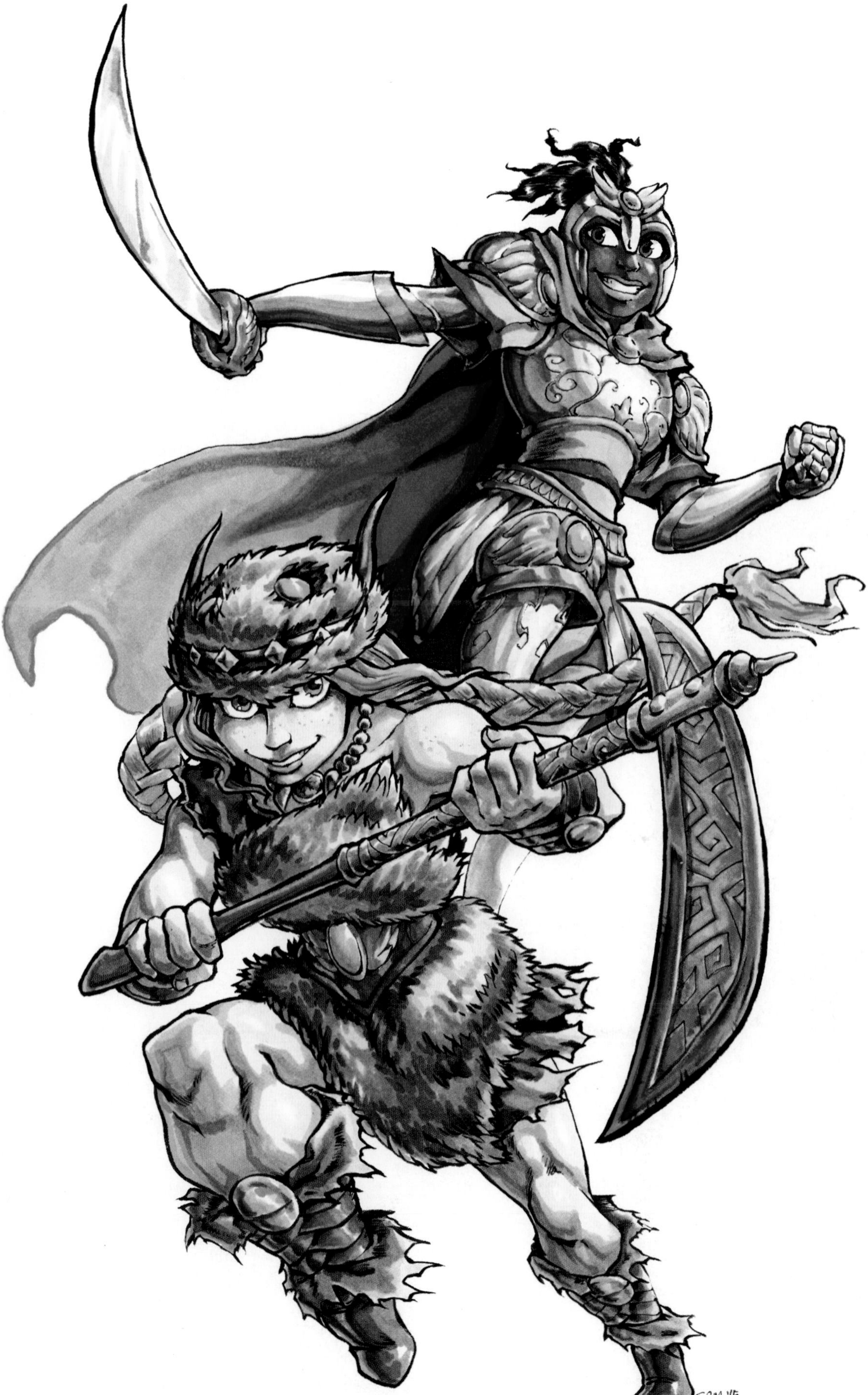
ECM '15

Ülga is property of Princess Ugg and belongs to Ted Naifeh

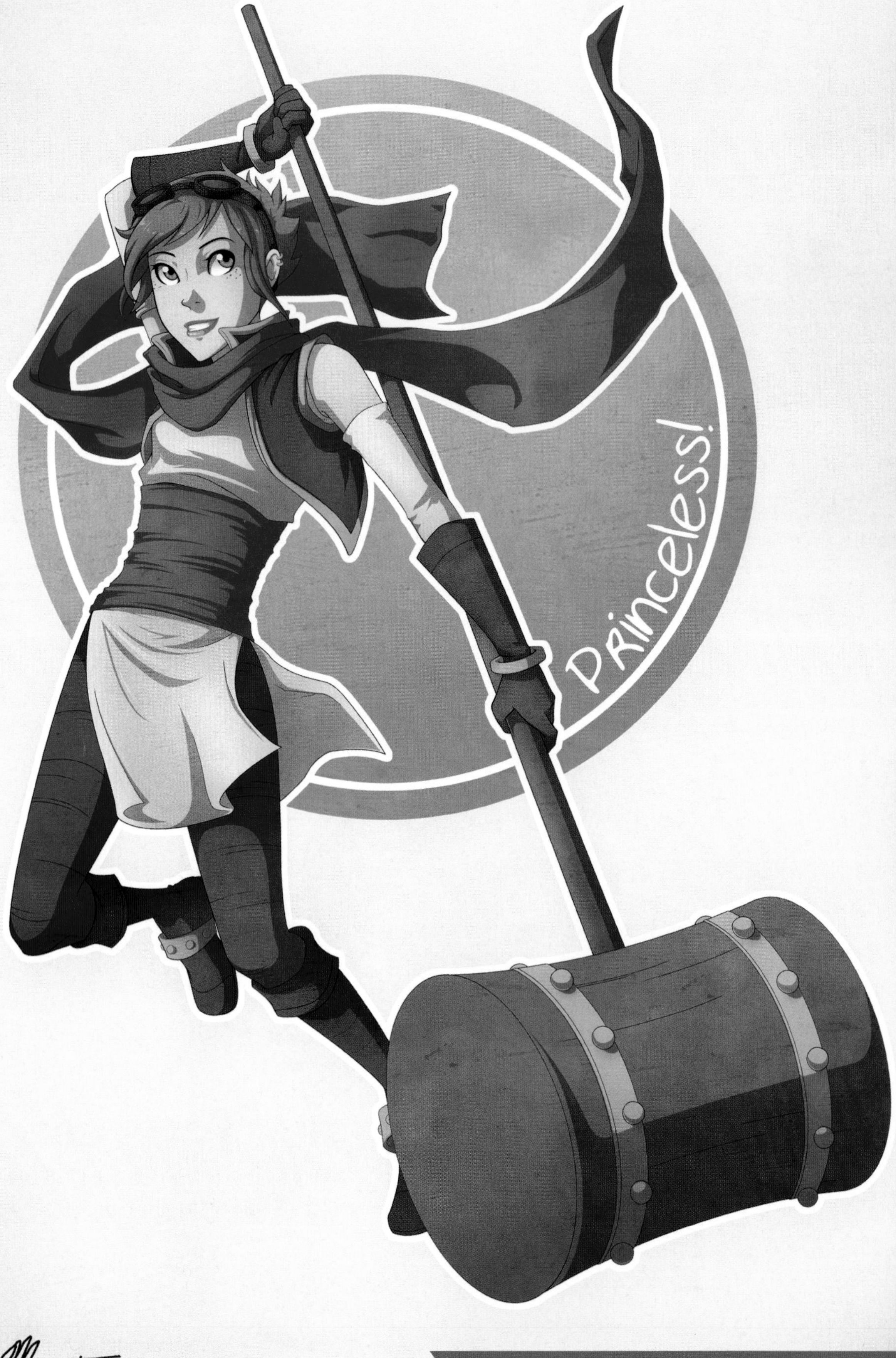
Princeless!
M Moriarty 2012

PIN-UP BY MERIDITH MORIARTY

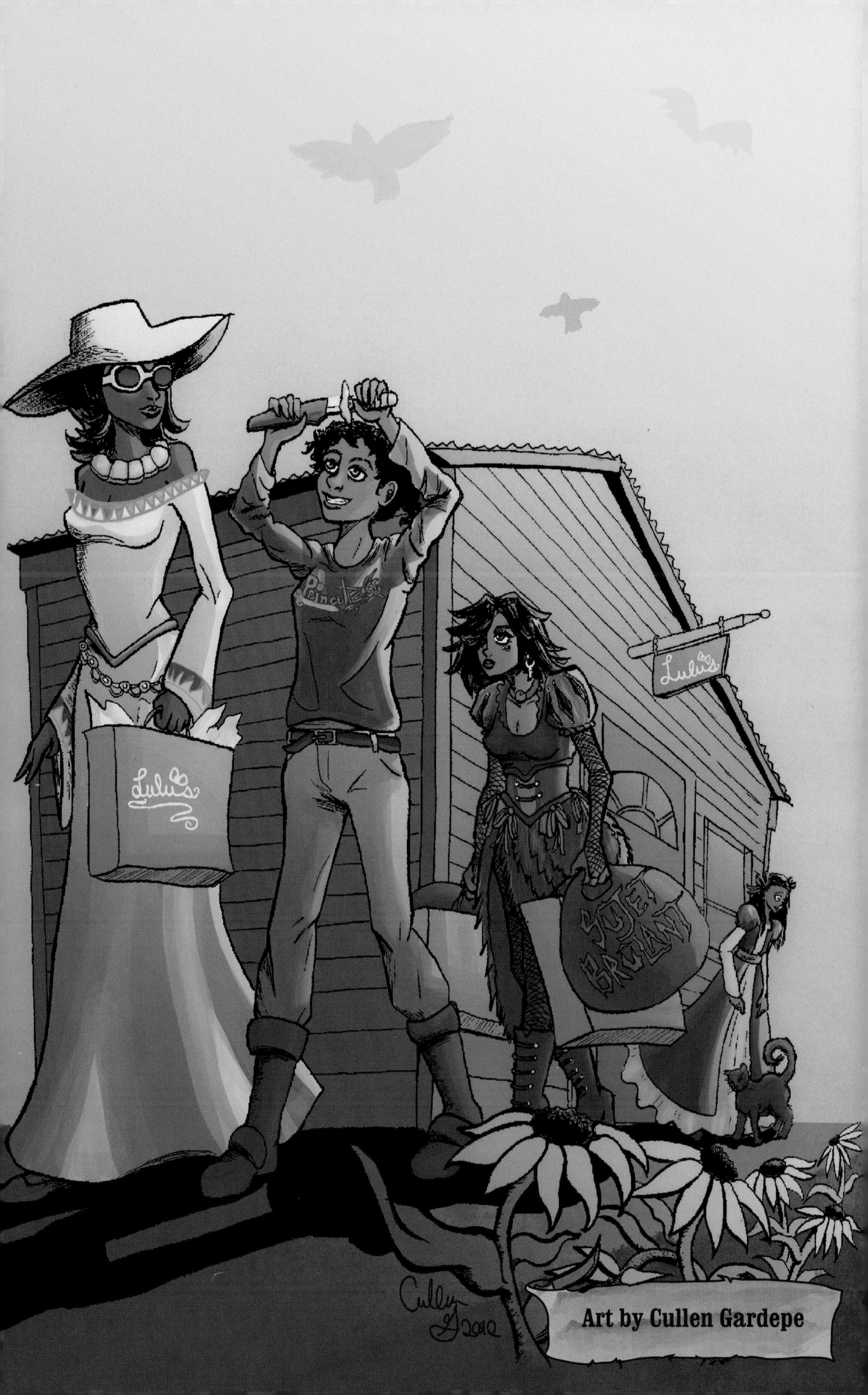
Lulu's
Lulu's
Cullen G 2012
Art by Cullen Gardepe

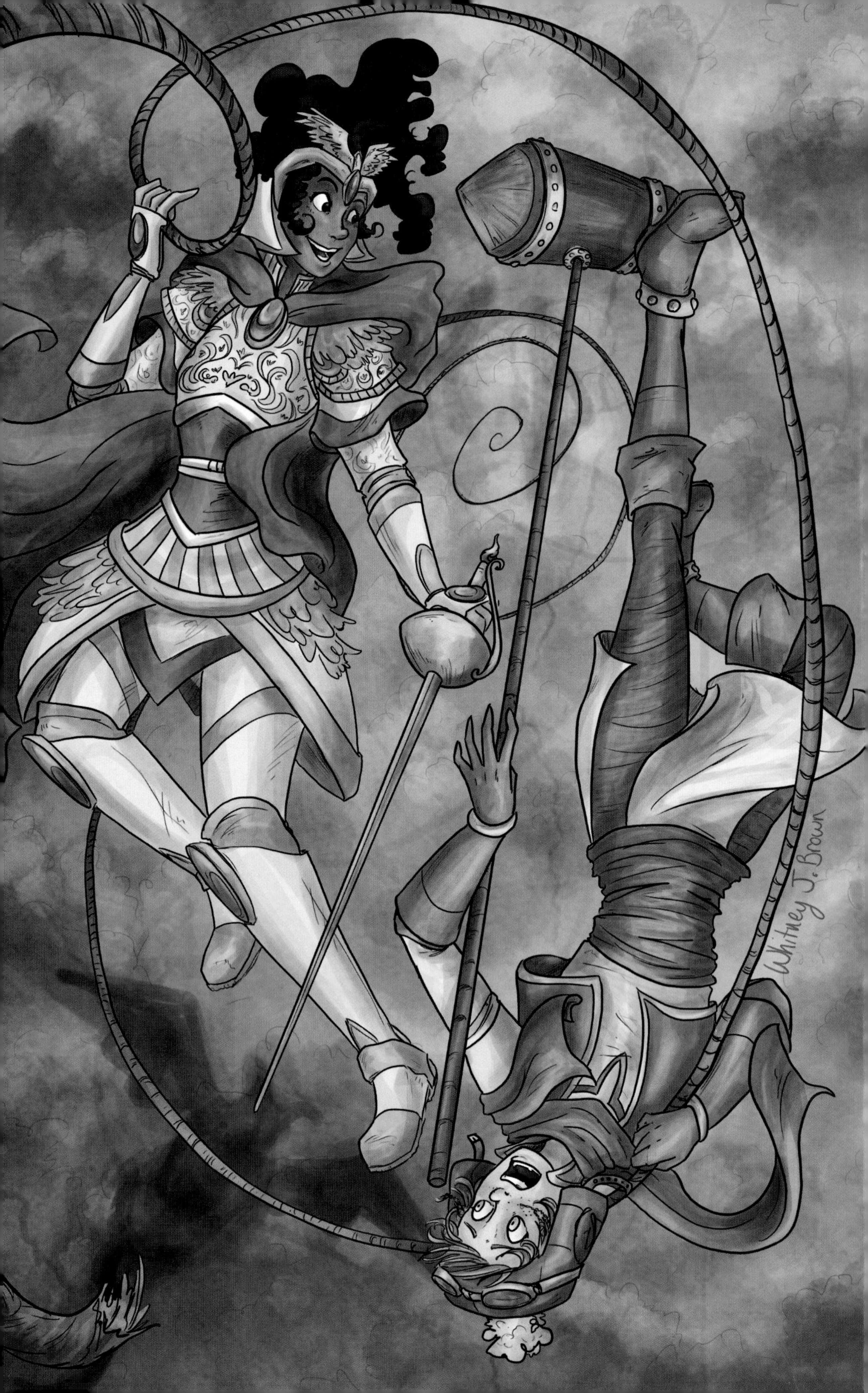
Whitney J. Brown

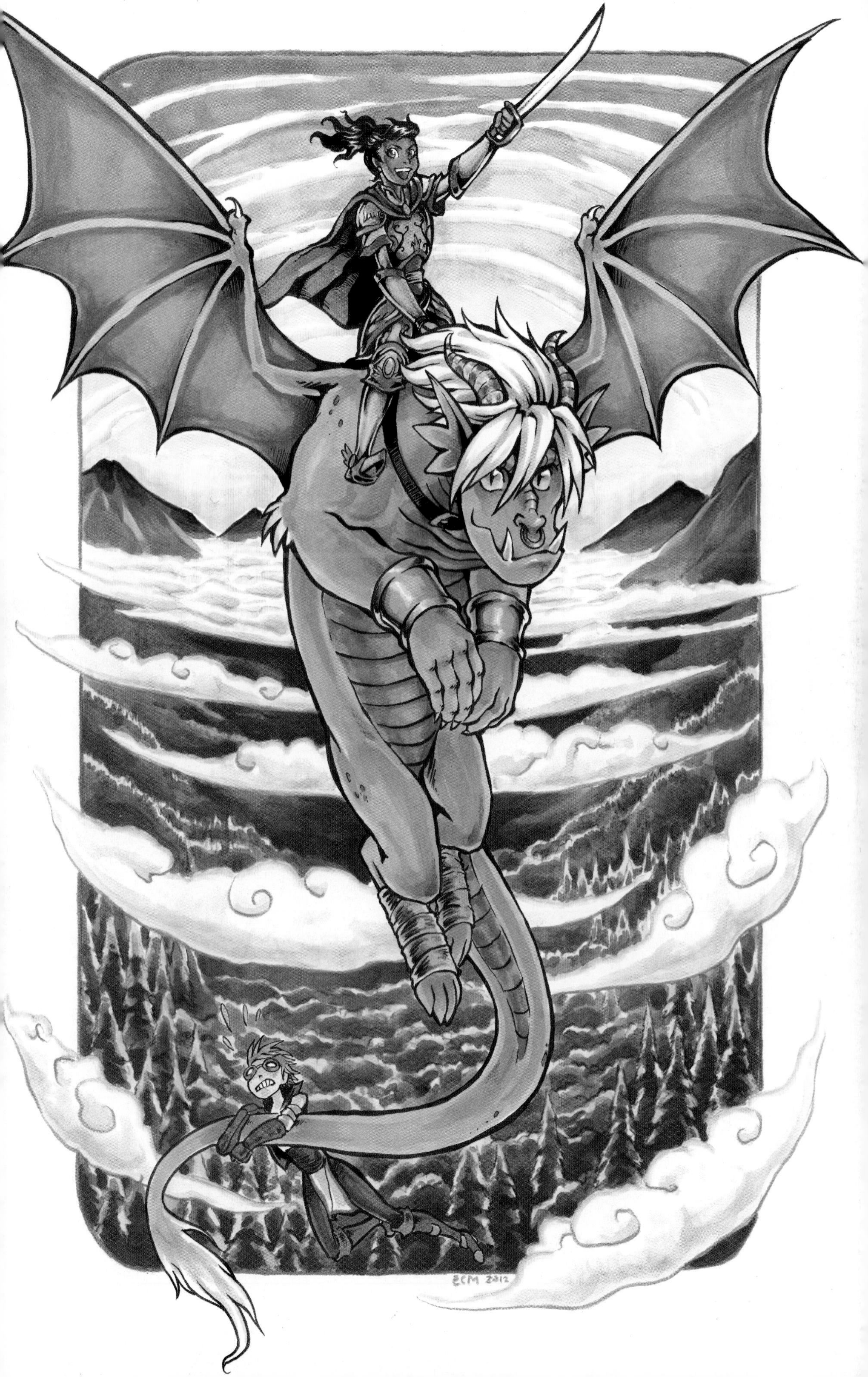
ECM 2012